Vengeance OF THE Demons

USA TODAY BESTSELLING AUTHOR

REBEKAH R. GANIERE

FALLEN ANGEL PRESS

ISBN: 978-1-63300-049-0
ISBN: 978-1-63300-055-1

Cover art by Rebekah R. Ganiere
vwzdesigns.com

DEDICATION

For all the Creatures who own the Night

NEWSLETTER

To claim your Two FREE Books and find out more about
Rebekah R. Ganiere and her other Upcoming Releases
You can Go Here:
www.RebekahGaniere.com/Newsletter

GLOSSARY

Coven Lord – The ruling governor over a given area.

Human – Anyone person born of two human parents who wasn't mutated by the V2000 virus. Those of pure human blood who were born human and have not been turned into vampyr.

Minion – A Vampire servant, assistant or companion, who has both rights and a salary.

Rogue Syndrome – A degrading disease similar to syphilis that causes vamps to go insane with bloodlust.

Slave – A human in the service of a Vampire or vampyr who is not paid and is bought and sold like property.

Slavers – Vampires and vampyr who hunt down humans and sell them to the highest bidder.

The High Council – The Society governing body. Made up of the Salvatori family, the High Council is the law. Members of the High Council are over 1000 years of age and rule from their place of power in Romania. Lucian Salvatori is the Venerable King and head of the High Council.

Three Kings – The Three Kings of America govern all of the Coven Lords and answer only to The High Council.

Tracking Squad – The police of the Vampire World. The Trackers are the highest trained Vampires and vampyr available for hire.

Vamp – Once human, now mutated by the V2000 virus, they are a vampire subspecies and the grunt workers of the Vampire Society. Gray of skin and black blooded they eat human food and can walk during the daylight.

Vampire (vamp—ire) – A pureblooded Vampire who is born a Vampire. They are the royalty of The Society that now run the world.

Vampyr (vamp—eer) – A lesser member of the Vampire Society. Vampyr are not born Vampires. They were once humans that have been bitten, or are the offspring of one human parent and one Vampire parent.

CHAPTER ONE

William took another deep draw from Sue's neck as his body shook with the strain of holding back. The soft throaty moans she uttered along with how deep her nails scored his skin told him that she was almost there herself.

Her thick, rich blood slid down his throat and tingled his limbs with energy.

"William." She panted his name the same way she had every time she climaxed. Over the last year of using Sue for a blood servant, he'd explored every last fantasy he'd spent his life dreaming of but never fulfilling.

Her breathing quickened and her nails dug deeper into his skin as she sucked in a sharp breath. He rocked himself through his climax then licked her neck wound shut and rolled away.

She laughed. "Wow, that was a quick one."

"Sorry. It's been a while." In truth he'd been envisioning her as someone else and that had gotten him excited in ways he'd not expected

She lifted his hand, kissing it. "I'm not complaining."

He sat up and wrapped his watch around his wrist. A nice watch was something he'd always wanted but never would have been able to afford before becoming a vampyr. His father had had a nice watch. No where near as nice as William's, but he'd always told William that an expensive watch was the true testament of a man's status.

"*Nice watch. Nice Shoes. Nice Car,*" his father always used to say... It was one of the only things he still remembered about his father.

Behind him, Sue slipped out of bed and pulled on her clothes. "Have you given any thought to what I said before?"

A gnawing sledge-hammer pounded his gut. "I've told you. I'm a fledgling. I'm not old enough to have a human of my own yet."

"William, you practically run this coven next to Danika and Mason. You could do whatever the hell you want."

Her words may be sound, but that didn't change the fact that she would never be the one he wanted.

"We have fun. That's all it can be." He turned to her. "If that isn't what you want, I completely understand and respect that. You are welcome to find a different member of the society to spend time with."

She stared at him for a moment and then sighed and shook her head. She climbed back onto the bed and leaned over to him. Her mousy brown hair hung haphazardly around her face, a testament to their recent intimacies.

"You know what your problem is?"

He shook his head. "Tell me."

"You're too nice. I've never met a guy who as nice as you before. Not pureblooded Vampire, or a bitten vampyr. Not even those mutated vamps or stupid human men are as nice as you.

You'd think that with the vamps and humans being lowest on the totem pole that they'd be the nicest people ever. But nope. It's you."

"I hope that whomever you end up with, they are much nicer than I," he replied.

If she even had a clue that every time for the past two months they had been together, he'd been envisioning her as someone else... No. He wasn't as nice as she thought.

He pulled on his slacks and sweater, ran his fingers through his hair, and stepped into his loafers.

"Come on. I'll walk you to the barracks."

She nodded and moved to the door. He held it for her, and they both headed into the hallway. They proceeded onto the landing and down the stairs to the grand foyer.

Selene and Neeman stood talking to Sinya and Lance. Selene cooed over Sinya's new baby. Seeing Lance wearing a baby carrier, and Neeman with a smile on his face were only the newest of strange sights changing his world. Most were for the better.

Selene caught William's eye and walked over. "Hey."

William motioned for Sue to continue into the kitchen area. "Evening, Selene."

She lowered her voice. "We still haven't found the rift, but we're getting closer."

"Good." If they didn't find the rift soon, all hell was going to break loose on Chicago- literally. The Demon attacks were taking their toll, and it was only a matter of time before a vamp saw something and the news spread. They'd quarantined the area surrounding a park they suspected was the location of the rift. For now.

"Have there been any Vampire sightings tonight?" he asked.

She shook her head.

"Let me get Sue back to the barracks, and then we can all sit down and debrief before sun up."

Selene nodded and walked back to Neeman, slipping her hand in his back pocket.

William joined Sue in the kitchen and ushered her to the back door. They'd just stepped out into the fresh night air when his ribcage squeezed.

A strong, blonde-haired beauty with peachy skin and eyes like aquamarines strolled out of the barracks. She spotted William and Sue.

"Well, well, what have we here?" asked Evan.

"Good evening, Evan." Just looking at her made his throat dry like instant paint. His skin prickled and he tried to keep his hands steady as his desire spiked.

"Midnight snack at the local concession stand?" asked Evan.

"Shut up. You're just jealous." Sue walked past Evan.

"Jealous? That you let a bloodsucker drain you and have his way with you? I think not, bloodwhore."

"Stuck-up redneck. If you hate it here so much, do us all a favor and leave. Nothing's keeping you. Lord Danika said any of us that wanted to leave could." Sue pointed to the gate.

"That's enough." William strode forward. "Sue, please go inside. I need to have a word with Evan."

Sue rolled her eyes and stormed into the barracks.

Evan put on a falsely jovial smile. "Oh yippee, is it time for my 'be a good girl' speech again from the big powerful Vampire? I swear, William, you're like a broken record."

"How many times do I have to tell you I'm not a pure-blooded Vampire? I was bitten. That makes me a vampyr. Meaning I used to be human." He grabbed her by the arm. "Come on."

"Dude, let go of me." She ripped from his grasp. "What? Did you mix me up with Sue? See, I'm the pretty blonde and she's the plain brunette."

William clenched his jaw several times. "You shouldn't talk about her that way."

"Why, because she's your Lovermuffin? Vampyr."

"No, because she's a nice person."

"Oooooh, right. The world's just full of nice people now, isn't it?"

This wasn't going the way he had planned. He'd rehearsed this. He only wanted to have a civil conversation with her about helping them out. But he'd have better luck talking a tornado out of spinning than he would talking to her. Evan reminded him of a hurricane. All bluster and noise, leaving destruction in her wake. Why had he told everyone that her helping would be a good idea?

He blew out a heavy breath. Her blue eyes raked him up and down.

"I need to speak to you. Can we please go up to your room?"

"Are you joking? No way. I'm not like your blood buddy, Sue."

"Fine, then we can go to my room."

"Are you out of your gourd? Dude, I wouldn't be caught dead being seen walking into your bedroom."

Her contagious anger had William taking a deep breath to keep from exploding on her. "What's wrong with you? Why are you so mean all the time?"

Her jaw dropped. "Me? I'm not the one holding people here against their will."

"No one is a prisoner here. You know that. But if we let you go, you'd be picked up by slavers for sure."

She shrugged. "I can handle myself. I got places I can go."

He chuckled. "You think you can, but you have no idea."

"And I bet you're so tough. How many slavers have you killed in your fine silk sweater and shiny, expensive loafers?"

The memory of plunging a knife deep into the neck of a slaver who'd injured Mason raced through his mind. It had been a recurring nightmare of his over the last year.

"One," he said quietly. "Just one."

She snorted and crossed her arms over her chest. "Yeah, I bet."

"The night that we were captured. I killed him because he tried to to kill my friends."

She laughed again and then stared at him for a minute. "You're serious."

"It's not something I'm proud of, and it's harder than you think. So that's why you're better here. Even if you don't want to be."

"You're damn right I don't want to be here. You bloodsuckers think you know everything and that you're so much better than us humans."

"No, they don't."

"They?" Her eyebrows knit together. "You're one of them. Or haven't you noticed?"

Yes, technically he was a member of the Vampire Society, but he still saw himself as human in some ways. It wasn't easy to identify as something for over twenty years and then overnight be told you were no longer that person.

"Please, Evan. I need to speak to you. And we need to go somewhere that no one will overhear. The bedrooms in the barracks are cement blocks. They're practically soundproof."

She stared at him for a moment and then her posture relaxed. "Fine. But you better not try anything."

"I would never think of it." Well, he'd surely think of it, but he wouldn't act on it.

He followed Evan toward the front of the barracks. When he'd been human, she was the kind of girl who wouldn't have given him a second glance. The hot ones never wanted the geeks, no matter what the movies used to portray. Even so, he knew that deep down she put up a big show because inwardly she was scared. He couldn't blame her. They all were.

She threw open the door while looking straight ahead. A group of guys were in the kitchen making popcorn. They stopped when she walked in, but she ignored them and headed up the stairs. The humans stared at William and nodded but didn't speak.

One of the things William actually appreciated about being a vampyr was the respect. As a human, he'd never been respected, not even very well liked. No matter how hard he'd tried. At least if people didn't like him now, they still had to respect him and that was good enough for the time being.

He'd headed for the stairs when he heard whispers from the kitchen.

"Lord Danika really turned that guy?" asked one.

"Do you think he wanted to be turned?" asked another.

"I heard he saved her life and in return she made him a vampyr as some sort of honor," said another.

"What a traitor to humankind. To want to sell out and be one of them."

"Shut up. You'd do it too if someone offered, Matthew."

He continued up the stairs, and clenched his fists. A traitor? Was that how humans saw him? As a traitor to his kind? Little did they know that his turning had been an accident. All he'd done was try to save Danika's life by taking a bullet for her. In return, she'd tried to heal him with her blood.

He shook his head and sighed. He'd been wrong. Humans still didn't respect him.

He reached the upstairs hallway and walked down to the open door. Evan sat back on her bed, picked up a pencil, and flipped it through her fingers.

He closed the door quietly.

"I need your help," he said without pretense.

"What?" Suspicion clouded her voice. "What kind of help?"

"Can I trust you to keep something quiet?"

She put on a pageant queen smile. "Of course you can, because we're BFFs."

"I'm serious."

"So am I. Can we braid each other's hair and paint nails too while we—"

"Will you shut up?" William hated losing his temper.

Her mouth snapped closed and she stared at him for a moment. William pinched the bridge of his nose and blew out a breath. Why did he think this would be easy? In all the time he'd known her, she'd not made one single thing easy.

"Okay, what?" Her voice no longer held the mocking tone it had a moment before.

Their gazes met. After he told her, there was no going back. If he brought her into the circle of trust...

"Seriously, either tell me or let me get something to eat."

"You know Mason, Lord Danika's mate?"

She sat forward. "Dude, is it me or is that guy enormous?"

"He seriously is the biggest guy I've ever met." They laughed together for a moment, and in that instant William really saw Evan. But in a flash the girl vanished.

She began flipping the pencil again. "Okay, what about him?"

"You know he's not human, right?"

8

"He's a Vampire?" Her eyes widened. "That explains a lot."

"No, no. He's not a Vampire or a vampyr. He's something else."

Her eyebrows drew together. "Something else?"

"He's a Demon."

She snorted. "A Demon. Like, angels and demons and heaven and hell?"

"I'm not joking."

Her smile fell and she leapt to her feet, dropping the pencil to the ground. "You're serious?"

"Yes. And Selene is his half-sister."

"So, she's a Demon as well?"

"Half Demon, half Fae."

She grabbed her hair with both hands and pulled on it. "There are fairy people as well?"

The tension in the air thickened. He wasn't doing it right. The worry and horror that now etched her features threatened to explode.

"Okay, why don't you sit down?" he offered.

"I'm fine. I can handle it. Just tell me. Are there tortoise ninjas too? Because if a talking tortoise sporting nunchucks walks in here—"

"A month or so back, before you returned to us, there was an explosion." William shoved his hands in his pockets.

"At the tracker compound, I heard."

"A group of demons caused it."

She closed her eyes and rubbed at them for a moment. He observed her quietly, waiting to gauge her reaction.

"Where did they come from?" she asked. "Have they always been here?"

At least she didn't explode. "No. The point is—and this is the point that I need you to promise to keep to yourself—there are more coming, and we can't fend them off alone. We need help. We want you to take us to the humans."

"Are you out of your friggin' mind? No. No way." She stared at him as if he'd sprouted a set of horns.

"We're out of options. We're sending emissaries out to all the covens to try and get them to side with us, but who knows if they will. And I overheard you saying to Selene that you knew of an enclave that had weapons—"

"Nope." She shook her head. "For all I know you're trying to get in there so you can get more slaves."

"Humans aren't slaves here anymore. You know that."

"Come on, William, I'm not an idiot. You bloodsuckers are going to run out of blood some time. You're going to run out of humans unless you allow us to have families. But if you do that, then you won't have a free-for-all blood-buffet at your beck and call. Do you really think Sue would come running back to you every time you snapped your fingers after she drives carpool and picks up her husband's dry cleaning?"

"This isn't about blood."

"You say that, but how do I know?"

"I'm not lying to you."

"All bloodsuckers lie. It's what you're good at."

He moved to her in a blur of speed. "I don't." Anger and frustration gripped him tight making it hard to breathe. "You can accuse me of many things—and you'd probably be right—but being disingenuous isn't one of them."

She blinked rapidly, and, in their close proximity, her eyes changed. Heat wafted off her skin as did the scent of lust. For as much as she professed to hate him, her body chemistry said something else entirely.

She laid her hand on his chest and the warmth of her

fingers spread through his sweater. His gut tightened and for a moment he thought she might kiss him.

He'd dreamt of the taste of her lush petal lips more times than he cared to remember.

"You say you don't lie, but you told me outside that you wouldn't try anything. Yet here you are inches from me." She pushed him away and stepped back herself. "I see the way you look at me. Watch me. You think I'm naïve? I know what you really want and you'll never get it. And that, William, is not a lie."

He should have known better than to think she'd want to help— even if it meant helping herself.

"You know what? Forget it. But believe me when I say if you utter a word of this to anyone, Danika will kill you." He left without another word.

She couldn't be trusted. As much as he wanted to believe there was good in her, she wasn't the one.

He jogged down to the first floor. The human men had gathered around a television to watch a movie. They eyed him as he passed.

His entire life he'd wanted to be included in a group the way they were. Sitting around watching a movie. Throwing jabs at each other. He'd never known that kind of camaraderie as a human. But now, because of Danika, he'd found a place he belonged. In the Vampire society.

"Did you get her to put out?" asked one of them. "That one's a ball buster."

William stopped. He turned to the group. Matthew stared at him with a smirk on his face.

"If I were you, Matthew, I'd keep my comments to myself. I know for a fact that there are two males in Coven House who'd like any excuse to rip you limb from limb because of what you've done with their mates. Do you really want to add a third to the list?"

Matthew's smirk fell as his eyes did. The other guys snickered. As William pushed out into the yard, the men burst into laughter, jibing Matthew.

William stormed into the garden. For the first time it struck him just how much he'd changed. How much he'd grown. How much he'd advanced.

He was no longer human. And he was fine with that.

CHAPTER TWO

Evan watched William's firm backside as he walked out. She tried not to, but she couldn't help it. For as much as she hated what he was, she couldn't deny the way his expensive sweater fit his trim, athletic physique.

She shook her head. *No.* She refused to be taken in by him. His kind only took, and killed, and threw away. She'd experienced it firsthand.

A handsome face floated into view, and Evan swallowed hard, pushing the memory away.

He'd said he needed help. She threw her hands over her face. What if it wasn't a lie? What if they really were in trouble, facing an army of demons? Her stomach growled. It didn't matter. It wasn't her problem.

She headed to the door. Pulling it open, she peeked into the hall to make sure William had really left. The sounds of laughter taunted her from the downstairs common room. How could humans be so stupid? So complacent?

She walked to the kitchen dreading having to interact

with them. All she wanted was to get back to her home and family. And just because the people she shared the barracks with were the same species, it didn't mean they were family. She'd tried to tell them there were places they could go. Enclaves that would take them in and protect them. But none of them seemed to care. In all the households of all the Vampires that had bought and returned her, she'd only ever found a handful of humans who were interested in what she had to say.

Sue's question struck her once more. Why didn't she leave? If they weren't slaves anymore and they were all allowed to choose, why didn't she go?

Because with no vehicle, no money, no supplies, how far would she get outside Chicago before a slaver picked her up and took her to a different area and sold her? No, she had to be smart. Bide her time and stir the pot as long as she could. Then when she'd gotten things in order, then she would run... Problem was, she'd already been there six months and she had gotten no closer to getting a car or supplies than when she'd first arrived.

A group of guys lounged on the sofa watching some sci-fi movie and eating popcorn. Several females chatted in the kitchen. Soft, they'd all become so soft. They'd forgotten the struggles of those who still tried to remain free from the Vampire slave markets.

"Hey, Evan, why don't you come sit with us?" asked Matthew.

His friendship and flirtation had never once been reciprocated... that didn't stop him from trying though. But even more than Vampires, she couldn't abide humans who actually liked being bitten.

"Not on your life."

The men burst into laughter and one held his hand out to the others. "Pay up! I told you she wouldn't do it."

"Dicks." She shook her head and strode into the kitchen. The females scattered around her. She didn't care that no one liked her. She'd be gone as soon as the situation presented itself.

She opened the fridge, and pulled out a plate of food and a bottle of water.

She laughed to herself. Bottled water. Something so simple yet elusive to those humans still out there in most enclaves. The one she'd come from, though large, had scraped to provide fresh water until their last move. The new setup had all the water they could handle. If the others would listen to her, they'd see how happy they could be in the enclave she'd come from.

She walked up to the second floor past the pasty white walls void of decoration to the last room on the right. She pushed open the door and then stepped out of her sneakers. Setting the plate on her large white bed, she plopped down and then pulled her hair from its band and stripped down to her underwear.

Her mission, if she'd ever gotten captured, was to get as many humans as she could out of the slave houses and back with their own kind. To that end, she'd failed miserably. Perhaps if she was nicer to people, they'd listen.

She sighed. Being raised by her uncle and two male cousins hadn't taught her much in the way of manners.

She turned on the stereo while she ate, listening to music that she didn't care for, but at least it broke the silence. Back in her enclave, she'd collected CDs over the years. She sure wished she had some with her now.

As a love song came on the radio, her mind drifted to places she normally didn't allow. *A handsome man in a tailored suit. A cold night huddled with other survivors in a cave. Staring into the eyes of her little sister as she took her last breath.* Memories. So many memories. And lastly, a tiny pink hand, clutching her thumb.

She shoved the plate onto her nightstand, no longer hungry, and turned off the light. She had to get out. She had to get back to her people. If what William had said was true, it wasn't optional.

WILLIAM KNOCKED ON THE DOOR TO DANIKA'S DEN AND THEN entered. Roth, Neeman, Selene, Sinya, Danika, and Mason were already present.

"Well?" asked Danika.

William shook his head. "I don't trust her."

"But you're the one who vouched for her in the first place," said Neeman.

"I was wrong. She won't help us. We'll have to figure something else out," said William. The fact that he'd been wrong about her twisted like a knife to the shoulder blades.

"Do you think she'll talk?" asked Mason.

"Sooner or later she's bound to tell the others, or worse, bolt." William slid into a seat and rubbed his temples. Why did she have to be so damned rebellious?

"What do we do now?" asked Roth. "We've recruited all the trackers we can. Even now, we only have about sixty of us. The demons are going to strike again. It's been weeks since their last real attack."

"And those weren't even real attacks," said Mason. "We need more bodies if we're going to survive."

"Maybe we should tell the humans and vamps," Sinya suggested.

Mason shook his head. "That would be chaos."

"You're going to have that soon enough with the demons coming. You know father isn't going to need much more time to gather his army." Selene stared at Mason.

"Why don't we give Evan what she wants?" asked Roth.

All gazes traveled to him.

"She wants to leave," said William.

"Let her go?" asked Danika.

Roth shrugged. "Yes. Let her go and monitor her. Follow her."

"Why?"

"What does she want more than anything?" he asked.

"To go home." Though William couldn't understand why.

"We plant a car with a tracking device and follow where she leads. She is going to make a run for it sooner or later, why not have it be on our terms?"

"I don't think that's exactly the best way to gain the humans' friendship." Sinya chuckled. "If what we want is to form a relationship with the humans and convince them to join in the fight, subterfuge doesn't seem like a good way to start."

"We have no idea where any of the enclaves are, and if all of her bragging to the other humans is correct, hers is the largest one out there, and has ties to all the others. We need to form a relationship with them. She won't take us there willingly," said William. "I'll go. I'll follow her and track her whereabouts. If she meets up with her enclave, I'll send word." He really wasn't sure if he'd offered to go because he wanted to help out Danika and their family, or because he feared losing Evan all together.

"No, William, you're too valuable," said Danika.

"Actually, I'm the most expendable," he countered. "Roth and Neeman are needed to lead the trackers. You're the Coven Lord. Mason and Selene are needed for their strength and knowledge, but I'm nothing."

"You underestimate how we rely on you."

William chuckled. "I'm not trying to get you to flatter me. I'm telling you something you already know. Roth said himself you need every body here. Which means that no tracker can go. And there isn't anyone else outside this room that knows of the threat besides King Sherman and those that sided with them a month ago. Let me go. I'll make contact with the humans and try to reason with them."

"And if you fail?" asked Roth.

He shrugged, trying to fake his way past the fear that taunted him like a circus clown. "Well then I hope they kill me before the demons show up because I have a feeling the demons won't be so kind."

The group fell silent. They had to see it was the right decision.

"Okay," Danika whispered. The emotion on her face struck him to the core. "Roth, you set up the fake escape for Evan. Make sure William has everything he needs not only to follow her, but also to keep himself safe. This has to work. We only get one shot."

"I'll do it myself," Roth replied.

Mason stepped forward and his large palm fell on Danika's shoulder. She met William's gaze. "You'll take two phones with you."

"Of course."

"And you check in every six hours."

"Yes."

"And if you don't..." Her eyes misted.

"I'll come for you myself," said Mason.

"I appreciate that." This absolutely was his family. A pang of apprehension hit him. He'd lived in a small enclave until a year ago when he'd been captured by slavers and sold to Danika. In all that time, he'd never gone anywhere by himself. If he got stuck out there in the daytime with nowhere to go...

"Come on." Neeman slapped him on the shoulder. "Let's plan this out."

William nodded and stood. Finally, he would be useful. There was no backing out now.

CHAPTER THREE

William removed a crisp blue dress shirt from its hanger and folded it. He could only take one suitcase, so he had to choose wisely the things he might need. That shirt would be the only nice one he would bring. Everything else needed to be comfortable and practical. He realized, looking over his wardrobe, that since working for Danika his wardrobe had become less practical and more for show. A thousand dollar suit wouldn't go over well when meeting humans for the first time... or even the second... or third... or—

Shouts caught his attention. Heavy footsteps pounded down the landing to the floor below. He dropped the shirt into his suitcase, rushed into the hallway and then to the balcony. Men shouted from below. Roth and Mason organized trackers into cars.

"Demons?" he called.

Roth nodded and continued barking orders. William ran

down the stairs to the front door. Mason caught him by the arm.

"No. You have a different mission. We'll handle this."

"I can help."

"You can, but this isn't your fight. Finish packing. You leave as soon as we return."

Mason took off outside and jumped into the last SUV in the driveway. William closed the front door as they pulled out of sight. He wasn't a fighter, though he could fight, but he wanted to be out there protecting his friends. His family.

"William." Danika's voice made him turn. The look of trepidation on her face struck him.

"How many are there?" he asked.

She shook her head. "I didn't get a chance to find out before Mason ran out. I was on the phone with Sherman."

William squeezed her arm. "They'll be fine. They know what they're doing."

She nodded and gave him her stoic Coven Lord expression. "Are you ready to go?"

"Not yet. I need to finish packing."

She linked her arm in his. "Come. I'll help you."

"You don't have to do that."

"I am well aware of that, but it will help me keep my mind off the fact that just about everyone in my family is out fighting demons."

William inclined his head and led Danika up to his room.

THE SOUNDS OF CARS APPROACHING HAD BOTH DANIKA AND WILLIAM rushing to the front door two hours later.

The door burst inward and Mason entered carrying

Neeman. William's stomach turned at the sight of Selene, whose red-rimmed eyes tracked Mason's movements.

"Take him right to Doc," she said.

Mason spoke something to Selene in draconic, his voice soft and soothing.

She rushed beside Neeman and whispered into his ear. Danika put her arm around Selene's shoulder and the group moved swiftly to the elevator. As they passed William, he spotted a huge gash down the side of Neeman's face that continued down his throat and flayed open his shoulder to his chest. The deep wound revealed not only muscle but bone.

He turned away and cursed under his breath. This was why they needed the humans' cooperation and the weapons they possibly possessed. If he didn't get them soon, there would be no one left to defend against the demons. No one had a choice in it, the entire country needed to come together on this one. Even the complacent vamps would be forced to fight if things got worse.

The rest of the trackers as well as Roth piled in the house.

"What happened?" he asked.

"There were more than ever. They fanned out and surrounded us. Neeman and Selene got pinned down by the edge of the park. We got there too late. If not for Selene going full Demon, he'd be dead."

He didn't look too far off from that now. "How many did we lose?" William asked.

"Three. Three good men. We'll bury them tomorrow evening with the rest."

William searched Roth's hard and rugged face. A gash in his dark hairline caught William's attention. "You should see Doc for that gash."

"I'll feed and be fine. I've had worse. Much worse." Roth's

bright blue eyes glanced at his watch. "Damn. We're supposed to be at the airport in thirty minutes. Are you ready to go?"

"Almost. I just need to get Evan."

Roth nodded. "Do that, and then we'll head out. The sooner you find those weapons the sooner we'll stop burying friends."

William swallowed. "Do you think Neeman will make it?"

Roth blinked several times and licked his lips. "I honestly don't know. If he does though, I don't know how much fighting he'll do in the future. That arm..." He coughed and clapped William on the shoulder with a heavy hand. "Let's get you on your way."

William stood outside Evan's room and took a deep breath. He clutched a dry-cleaner's bag full of clothing. It had been days since he'd had his fateful conversation with her.

He knocked.

A moment later the door opened and Evan peered at him through her aquamarine eyes. She cocked an eyebrow when he didn't say anything.

"Here." He shoved the dry-cleaning bag at her.

Her brow furrowed and she snickered. "Okay." She held up the bag inspecting it. "And this is?"

"Put it on." He rubbed his slick palms on his slacks. "Gather your things. You're leaving."

A fearful expression crossed her face, and then she snorted and shoved the clothes back at him. "Ha-ha. Very funny."

He handed them back. "Lord Danika has decided you can no longer stay here. You're being transferred."

"Transferred or sold?" Her gaze hardened like steel.

"You leave in fifteen minutes. Be downstairs or I'll send the house guard up to get you." He turned and headed down the hallway.

"Wait. William."

He swallowed hard and refused to turn. He couldn't blow this.

WILLIAM WAITED BY THE FRONT DOOR WHEN MASON EMERGED FROM the elevator that led to the underground bunker and Doc's office. Covered in blood and dirt he crossed to William when he spotted him.

"Hey."

"How's Neeman?"

Mason shook his head. "He'll make it but it isn't good. We have no idea yet if he'll ever regain use of his arm."

"Doc's as good as they come. If anyone can sew Neeman up, it'll be him."

Mason nodded, but his expression said he wasn't convinced. "You getting ready to head out?"

"Just waiting on Evan. She should be down any minute."

"I have something for you." He pulled a small leather pouch attached to a leather strap from his pocket and handed it to William.

William turned the soft leather over in his hands and then pulled on the drawstring. A small, warm vial rolled into William's palm.

"It's my blood," said Mason. "Doc drew it for me downstairs. It's in case... In case you get in trouble. If you need a boost, that should get you through."

William had witnessed firsthand the effect Mason's blood could have on a Vampire. It strengthened at best and enraged at worst.

"Thank you." William put the vial back into the pouch and shoved it in the pocket of his leather jacket.

The back door opened and Evan walked in.

Mason laid his warm hand on William's shoulder. "I meant what I said. If you're in any trouble, you tell us, and I'll come at once."

"Thank you."

Mason's amber eyes searched William's face for a moment. "You're the closest thing I've ever had to a little brother. I would hate to lose you."

William gave him a tight smile. "And I you."

Evan approached and Mason dropped his hand and stepped away. A mask of anger rooted on her face. She'd put on the black pants and white shirt of a slave that he'd given her, but her expression remained one of utter defiance.

"Well," she said. "Are we leaving or not?"

William opened the door and motioned toward the car. "After you."

She marched out to the car, slid in and slammed the door closed.

Mason squeezed his shoulder. "Good luck."

"I'm gonna need it, going to an enclave who knows how big."

Mason snorted. "No. I meant with her."

EVAN TILTED HER CHIN HIGHER AND REFUSED TO LET THE FEAR SHOW. Her dress slacks were the nicest thing she'd worn in a while, but the uniform of a slave wasn't something she appreciated. They may control her clothes, her food and where she went, but they didn't control her.

William got in the driver's side and started the car. He glanced over. "Put on your seatbelt, please."

"Why? Afraid of hurting someone else's merchandise?"

"Suit yourself."

The car rolled forward, and she silently snapped her seatbelt on. William looked both directions as he pulled onto the road. His wavy brown hair covered one eye, and he pushed it back.

They drove past other expensive homes with every second of silence hanging between them like a solid wall.

Evan wrapped herself in a hug and chewed her lip. The neighborhood flew by as they picked up speed and headed to a less residential area.

Her curiosity finally got the better of her. "So where am I going?" She hated being so weak as to ask, but she couldn't help it.

"I don't know for sure."

"You can tell me. I'm a big girl."

"No, really. I have no idea where you're going. I think it's to one of the European covens. Maybe her family in Russia."

Her stomach lurched and her head lightened. "Europe?"

"Lord Danika felt it would be a better fit for someone of your... high spirit."

Evan's heart beat so fast she feared it might actually give out. She'd never heard of anyone coming back to the US once they were sold over there. No one knew what it was like, but rumor had it that outside the US, Vampires were not kind to slaves in any way.

She couldn't go there. She needed to get back to her enclave. To her family. "Okay. Say I was willing to help you," she said. "Take you to my enclave."

William glanced at her but then shook his head. "I'm sorry but it's too late. Lord Danika has made arrangements."

"Please don't do this." The weak, breathy sound of her own

voice made her despise herself. "I'm sorry." The pleading words that clung to the roof of her mouth and stuck there with her pride.

"William."

He turned on the radio and stared at the road.

Tears welled in her eyes, and she breathed slowly through her mouth to hide her shame while she turned to stare out the window.

This was the price she paid for trying to fulfill her mission. She'd betrayed her people once before. She refused to do it again, no matter the cost to her personally.

WILLIAM PULLED THE CAR ONTO THE TARMAC OF THE AIRPORT AND parked several yards from a small personal jet. A silver ramp descended to the ground, flanked by two guards. Wherever she was going awaited her on the other side of the open door.

William parked the car but left it running and stepped out. "Get out."

Evan's heart pounded with the slam of his door. He walked to the guards and shook hands with them. She couldn't let this happen.

William spotted her still in the car and walked back. As his hand touched the handle, she locked the doors. A confused expression crossed his features as he tried the handle.

"Very funny, Evan. Open up."

This was it. Her chance. Yes, they might drag her back, but what if they didn't? She could get pretty far on a full tank of gas.

William rapped on the window. "Open the door."

She stared at him, unable to move. She'd waited over six

months to gain access to a vehicle or supplies and now she had both.

William's expression hardened. His sharp knock mimicked his angered tone. "Open it now."

Evan hopped into the driver's side, and William slammed his hand on the roof and swore.

She'd never driven a car before. She'd never been given the chance, but she'd seen her uncle and cousins do it hundreds of times. William's fist hit the driver's side door window making her jump.

"Don't do this!"

She scanned the buttons and knobs and looked to the stick on the dashboard. She pressed a pedal with her foot and the engine roared, matching the smash of William's hand onto the glass again.

Evan's head whipped to his. He yelled through the closed window, but she couldn't hear the words over the pumping of blood in her ears.

The two guards jogged forward and William spoke to them. It was now or never. She pressed her foot onto the pedal that wasn't the gas and moved the stick to the letter D like she'd seen her cousin Peter do. Slowly she released the brake and put her other foot on the gas, and the car lurched forward with William hanging on.

One of the guards shot at the glass, and she screamed. Slamming her foot on the pedal, she sped forward and the car squealed to life. She checked her rearview mirror. William and the guards chased after her. One of the guards shot at the back windshield. She turned her eyes on the pavement just in time to spin the car around to avoid hitting the airport hangar. She smiled at her quick reflexes. William and one of the guards ran at the car. She locked eyes on him and for a split second and a shred of hesitation pricked her heart.

For as much as she wanted to get back to her family, a part of her would miss William. *No! Not again.*

She punched the gas and took off again as more gunshots rang out. Her heart pounded and adrenaline pumped as William dove out of the way at the last second. She looked in the rearview mirror to see him already hopping to his feet.

She smiled as she flew out onto the road. She glanced in the rear view for several miles as she turned off the highway and down side streets and then back onto the highway several minutes later.

She drove out of Chicago as fast as the car would go and then pulled off the highway and hid the vehicle in an abandoned convenience store. Heart pounding, limbs shaking she waited for any sound of an engine, or sight of a moving vehicle from her vantage point overlooking the long stretch of blacktop.

She laughing, while watching the highway, until everything caught up with her and her laughter turned to tears.

She sucked in a deep breath and wiped her eyes. She'd done it. She'd really done it. She'd gotten free.

She was going home.

CHAPTER FOUR

"She took the bait," said William.

"Good," replied Roth. "The SUV is in the hangar. Tell the other two to close up my plane and get back here."

"Will do. How's Neeman?"

"Alive."

William walked toward the airplane hangar that Evan had barely missed running into.

"You call in six hours," said Roth.

"Talk to you then." William clicked his phone off and continued to the building. Two trackers waited outside. "Roth said to close up his plane and get back to Coven House."

One of them tossed William a set of keys before heading to the plane. He pressed the unlock button and the SUV beeped in the corner of the giant room. He jogged to it and hopped in. On the front seat lay a laptop and in the back sat bags upon bags of supplies.

He flipped open the laptop and it booted up right to the

GPS page. She'd already gotten out of the city, heading south. But where was she going? He'd find out soon enough.

He put the SUV in gear and pulled to the entrance of the hangar. The trackers had Roth's plane lined up and ready to put away.

William waved as he passed them and drove toward the freeway.

Thirty minutes later Danika called to check on him. If she kept that up, it would be a very long trek. He loved her like a sister, but he'd had an overprotective mother before. It had gotten her killed. He didn't want to see the same thing happen to Danika because she freaked out if he didn't answer his phone for half an hour.

He KEPT HIS DISTANCE FROM EVAN. HER SEEING HIM FOLLOWING would spoil everything.

He turned on the radio and let the music flow through him as he drove down the darkened, deserted highway. Vamps didn't travel between cities and Vampires usually had no reason to by car. Only slavers moved from city to city, but with Danika's new edict freeing slaves, none of them would be close to Chicago. They wouldn't want to risk being caught with slaves in her territory. She'd made it a punishable offense. So far only one other Coven Lord in the US had joined her in the banning of slaves, but they continued talks with the other Lords.

He remembered what it was like before the Outbreak as he continued down the highway. Cars everywhere. People moving from place to place. Trucks crowding the highways as they moved goods from one coast to the other. Now those things were kept to a minimum. The trucks still moved, but not as many.

He tried to formulate what he would say to the humans. How he would get them on his side. The hardest part would be winning Evan over. She'd already told him no, and, after her little jailbreak stunt, she was going to be mad as bees getting their honey stolen when she found out it had all been a rouse. He smiled, thinking of her. That feistiness had most likely kept her alive and out of the breeding slave market for as long as it had.

Thinking of what it would be like to take her as his breeding slave and making love to her heated his blood. He could never do it. Force her to have sex with him. He could never force anyone. He'd never had sex will anyone who wasn't willing. And Evan wasn't.

EVAN CHECKED HER GAS GAUGE. *DAMN.* SHE'D MADE IT TEN MILES from Bloomington, Illinois and only had a quarter tank left, but she hated having to get gas at night.

Vampires could be anywhere. She had no idea if they'd put out an announcement or something looking for her. There weren't police anymore, only the Tracking Squad. And if they were following her, they'd have to come from Chicago and she'd have maybe a thirty-minute head start. Not much time to waste. Not that they even knew where she'd gone. After taking off from the airport she could have gone in any direction.

She'd have to risk it. She wouldn't be able to push the car all the way to where she was headed. If she knew how to break into and steal a car, she would have done that instead. Unfortunately, her male family members had never thought to teach her that secret. Stupid, sexist lugheads. She smiled, thinking of them. For as much as she hated their overbearing ways, she loved and missed them fiercely. They were the ones who had taught her to fight and hunt and survive. They were the ones who had protected her and kept her safe for all those years. They were her family and all she had left.

Evan pulled off the exit and looked up and down the road before turning right. There weren't any cars so far outside of Chicago, but she could never be too careful—she'd learned that the hard way. She rolled up to a gas station next to the highway. The dark store's sign had been broken, so it only read - even e-ven.

She pulled next to a pump, jumped out, and then opened the gas hatch on the car. Twisting the cap off, she glanced around but there still wasn't another person in sight. The scent of burned rubber filled her nostrils and caused her head to throb as she removed the nozzle, and put it in the tank. The tires on the vehicle looked okay, but she'd obviously given them a workout. She lifted the handle of the gas pump and nothing happened.

Her heart dropped to her toes.

She jerked on it over and over and still nothing. She cursed and kicked the curb. A pain shot up her foot and she grabbed at it. *Great.*

Letting out a huge breath, she hobbled to the store and tried the door. Locked. Scanning the ground, she found a fallen brick. She picked it up and threw it at the door. The glass cracked but held. Again she threw the brick and the cracked glass spider-webbed out. She took a step back and threw it one more time. The glass shattered and the brick clattered across the floor inside.

She let out a whoop, high fived herself and ducked under the door handle. Inside the dusty and stuffy store she picked up two baskets and headed around the store pulling things off the shelves. No raiding parties came this close to Chicago, and apparently no vamps or Vampires liked everlasting Twinkies and stale corn chips. All humans knew the more reckless you were, the more likely you were to be caught.

Though most of the items had passed their expiration dates, she knew from experience that some things could be eaten for years afterward. She grabbed as many cans of food as she could manage, flipped on the pumps behind the counter, and carried everything out to the car. She ran back inside while the car filled with gas and grabbed every container of jerky, bottle of water, and candy bar she could find.

The whole thing took less than ten minutes. If the Vampires were coming for her, she still had a twenty-minute head start. She glanced at the clock. Three hours till sun up. If she could make it until then, they'd have to stop to rest. She peeled out of the gas station and back onto the highway. Pulling a piece of jerky from its pack, she stuck it in her mouth and sucked on it to soften it up. She just had to drive for three hours without getting caught. Three more and she'd have the whole day to drive unseen.

WILLIAM YAWNED AS TANGERINE AND PLUM COLORED STRANDS blended into the horizon. Dawn loomed close. Two hours into the trip, Evan had stopped for about ten minutes and he had as well, to stretch his legs. He wasn't used to being in a car for so long anymore. He hadn't been on raids for supplies since he'd been captured a year ago.

He needed somewhere to stop for the day. He checked his GPS and found an old Yogi Bear's Jellystone Park about thirty minutes outside St. Louis. Cutting it that close made him nervous, but he didn't want to sleep in the SUV, and he didn't want to get too far behind Evan.

BY THE TIME HE PULLED INTO THE SMALL, DESERTED MOTEL, WILLIAM had to shield his eyes and the skin on his hands blistered from the sun's rays.

He grabbed his bags and jumped from his vehicle. Kicking open the first faded brown door he came to he ran inside and slammed it shut. Dropping the bags to the floor, he flopped onto the bed. Fatigued laced its way through his muscles and weighed him down like he'd run a marathon. He lifted his hand and depressed the button, locking the car.

Light filtered through the large window. It took every ounce of his strength to trudge to it and pull the blackout curtain closed. His hands burned and shot pain up his arms with every movement. He stumbled to the nightstand light and flipped it on, revealing a faded pink bedspread and two flat pillows. Stripping off his shirt, he sighed, and shucked off his pants before heading to the bathroom. He turned the faucet but nothing happened. *Damn.* He banged on the pipes and still nothing happened.

Steadying himself on the sink, he cursed. Of course, there was no water. There were few amenities in most parts of the country anymore unless they were in a big city.

He trudged out to the bed and pulled over the medical bag. He searched for some kind of burn gel before noticing that the blisters had already disappeared. He sighed in relief. Sometimes being a vampyr was awesome.

WILLIAM AWOKE TO A PAIR OF STRONG HANDS PINNING HIM TO THE bed. He tried to react but his body mostly still slept.

"Get his arms," came a crackly voice.

Panic scratched up his spine, and his mind snapped into action. He struggled against his assailants.

"Damn, this one's strong. Hurry up." The man pinning him pressed a knee into William's back. "Get the flex cuffs!"

"I thought you had that stupid needle ready," said the crackly voice.

"Get the hell off me." William struck out with his legs and connected with someone, sending them flying across the room. They collided with the wall and something heavy crashed to the floor.

William bucked underneath his assailant and then turned his head and bit into flesh. The man cried out as William bit through skin and muscle; his incisors hit bone and latched on. The man let go of William's arms, trying to pull his wrist free. Blood seeped into William's mouth, and the bitter taste made William release. He spit and jumped from the bed, tripping over something and sending it spinning across the floor.

In the dark he took in a deep breath and located the two vamps easily. They reeked of urine, and sweat wafted off them as if they relished it. He headed for the injured one and jumped on him in a flash. The man swung wildly, but William caught the punch and spun him around to face the wall. He slammed the vamp's head into the crumbling plaster twice, and dropped him to the floor in a heap.

The second attacked from behind and leapt on his back.

William flipped the guy off. The air whooshed out of his lungs as the vamp hit the hard, threadbare floor. A long, rubbery rope caught William's foot and he grabbed it, wrapped it around the vamp's neck, and yanked it tight.

"Stop, stop!" the vamp gasped.

Anger rippled through William. "What the hell are you doing out here?" William demanded.

"We're scavengers. Just scavengers."

William squeezed the rubbery tube harder. "What do you want with my kind?"

"We... we sell blood." Air barely sucked in the man's windpipe.

William pulled the vamp's face close. "What?"

"Blood. Vampire blood. We sell it."

"To who?"

"Vamps," he croaked.

A chill raced down his spine, and his throat slammed shut like a vault door. Vamps couldn't drink human blood without it driving them crazy, but he'd never heard of vamps drinking Vampire blood.

"Why? What does it do?" he demanded.

"Stronger... Makes us like you."

William smashed the vamp in the face again spraying black blood on the floor. *Damn.* Vamps becoming vampyr. That was a new one. Rancid vamp blood permeated the room. The coughing and wheezing of the injured vamps pounded in his head. He punched the man in the face one final time, cracking his nose and knocking him out.

He needed to inform Danika, but first he had to get on the road. He had a mission. The fact that there were vamps selling vampyr and Vampire blood could wait until he'd gotten out of that hell hole.

William stood and shook his hand, flexing his fingers to make sure nothing had been broken. He turned on the lamp and surveyed the room. The two ratty vamps lay crumpled on the floor. The rubber rope was actually a rubber tube with a needle on one end and a large glass jar on the other. His stomach soured as though he'd drunk bad blood. He'd been stupid, careless. Why had he thought that just because he'd become a vampyr that he'd be safe? That there weren't people out there who would want to hurt him. He could possibly be in as much danger traveling alone as Evan was.

He walked to the window and inched back the curtains. The sun hung low in the sky. Time to go.

He pulled a towel from the bathroom and rubbed the black blood from his hands and chest. He stared at the two unconscious vamps and wished more than ever he had some running water, but that would have to wait.

THIRTY MINUTES LATER WILLIAM HEADED OUT ON THE ROAD, following Evan's GPS signal. He pulled out his phone and dialed Danika.

"William?"

"I'm all right. Just leaving for Kansas."

"Have you had any problems?"

"A bit. Some vamps jumped me in my motel room."

"Vamps?" Her voice held concern.

"Scavengers. They said they round up our kind to sell our blood. To turn them into vampyr."

Silence stretched out across the line. "Did they say who they sold it to?"

"Uh... Sorry. I didn't really get that far before I lost my temper."

"Understandable. That's something we'll need to look into further. We still have no idea how they are doing it. And if it has gone beyond just Chase turning Xenock and now the vamps are doing it as well..." She sighed. "The last thing we need is an army of renegade vamps turned vampyr overrunning the cities and causing problems."

"How are things there? How's Neeman?"

"We're regrouping. Neeman is... tough. Selene has him in bed recouping."

"Give them both my best. I'll call when I stop again."

"Be safe."

He flipped off the phone. Vamps outnumbered Society members almost three to one. If they started hunting Vampires, along with the Demon attacks going on, or worse yet, if they joined with the humans... It would be the Outbreak wars all over again.

And this time, there was no telling who would win.

CHAPTER FIVE

Evan pulled to the side of the road, barely able to keep her eyes from sealing shut. She'd already fallen asleep three times, only to be woken by the bumps on the edge of the highway. Fatigue beckoned her down into a comfortable cocoon. She had to sleep.

She'd just passed Amarillo, Texas and still had a good fourteen hours to go, but with the sun setting, her eyelids grew droopy like she'd attached lead weights to them. She'd been driving for almost sixteen hours straight. Surely, she could take a nap for a few minutes.

She veered the car into the ditch on the side of the road in an effort to disguise it as one of the millions of other abandoned vehicles. The big cities had more of them than the open road, but even out here, it hadn't been uncommon to see an abandoned car every few miles.

She rummaged around in the backseat and pushed all the food to the floor. Her last stop had been a treasure trove. A gas station with an attached sporting goods store. She'd grabbed two sleeping bags, food, water, medical supplies, fishing gear, two tents, anything she could get her hands on that could be useful to her enclave.

Her heart squeezed for the first time thinking about her enclave. It had been almost three years since she'd been there. They'd only just begun to automate their new home when she'd gone out with a raiding group and had been captured. She sent up a silent prayer that they were still there. Especially her uncle and cousins.

Her throat swelled closed thinking about her time in the slave market. The degradation, the terror, the bidders, and finally a tall, handsome, dark-haired Vampire. His smile kind, his eyes the perfect shade of blue.

She crawled into the backseat, pulled out one of the sleeping bags, and laid it over the floor, covering the food. Then she pulled out the second one and slid into it up to the top of her head. She pulled it shut and closed her eyes. Her heart pounded as memories and nightmares assaulted her.

She swallowed hard against the boulder blocking her throat and once more saw a perfect little pink hand. Fingers curled around her own in a tight grip.

That had been the night that she'd stopped sleeping. That terrible night a year and a half ago. She took a deep breath, relaxing her muscles and clearing her thoughts. Just a couple hours sleep. She'd get a couple hours and then she'd start out again. She peeked out of her sleeping bag and looked around. If anyone came upon the car, they'd think it was abandoned like all the others. At least, she hoped so.

It had been almost six hours when William looked over at the dormant GPS signal. He was only four hours from where Evan's signal still sat and he feared she'd ditched the car for a different one. Abandoned vehicles lay like grave markers on the road. If she'd ditched the car, he was screwed.

Something flashed in his rearview mirror. He hit the brakes in the middle of the road and turned around in his seat, staring as hard and far as his expert sight would let him, scanning the area for danger. Nothing moved on the barren road. No car rolled forward. No tree rustled in the breeze. Nothing lived.

A good ten minutes passed before he faced forward again. He cracked his neck and blew out a heavy breath trying to release the paranoia that had hitchhiked along for a ride. He hit the gas and continued.

He hadn't experienced anything like the attack in the motel since the Outbreak wars had started. One moment he'd been asleep in his bed, the next he'd been awakened by a scream. There'd been a tremendous blast, and then his mom had run into his room and snatched him out of bed. She wore her pink flannel nightgown dotted with red specks and a large bag over her shoulder.

Without a word, she'd grabbed his emergency bag packed with several pairs of underwear and changes of clothes, a few toys and books. They'd raced out the rickety fire escape of their apartment building. Her tears had flowed over his still half-asleep face until she'd hit the street. Barefoot and with the wind whipping through her dark brown hair, she'd run down the road and never looked back.

He remembered the smell of blood and gunpowder. The feel of strong hands pulling him from his mom's arms and into a large white van. Then crouching in the corner of the van with her and a dozen other people. That had been his last night sleeping in an actual house until going to live with Danika.

He remembered his small room in the apartment with his parents. The faded blue walls covered in robot posters. His five Matchbox cars lined up on his dresser. The black, outer-space blanket with the multicolored planets on it. His tiny bookshelf full of easy-reader books and the rocket ship mobile hanging in his window. Small things, child things. And his mother and father.

His gut clenched. Good people. Working people who did everything they could to keep him fed, warm, and safe. All the way to the end.

William found out later that his father had sacrificed himself against a vampyr to save them. After three years in the enclave, his mother had succumbed to septicemia after a run-in with a rusty nail. From then on, William had been alone.

And he still was. He had Danika and Mason and all the other coven members, but for all of their love and support, he remained alone. He blew out a harsh breath and laughed. He'd been given so much and still he wanted more.

"Selfish, William Scott," he could hear his mother say. *"Selfishness is an ugly trait."*

He still missed her.

AN HOUR LATER THE GPS SIGNAL MOVED AND HE BLEW OUT A BREATH of relief. The clock read almost two AM, and he still had a good three hours before he caught up to her. She had the advantage with not having to stop for the day. So far in the last thirty-six hours, she'd only had six hours of sleep that he could count. How did she do it?

The one flaw of being a vampyr. Lack of sleep could get you killed as easily as not feeding. Even going a day or two without sleeping could have major effects on the vampyr or Vampire body. As if being up at the same time as the sun was somehow poisonous.

He pulled a bottle of Savor from his cooler and popped the top. Sadly he'd become more accustomed to synthetic than actual blood. Human blood tasted great and did amazing things for his body, but he still had a hard time getting over the fact that he'd once been one of them.

William never really thought of himself as no longer being one of them as much as he felt somehow evolved. Apparently, humans didn't see it that way. At least not the house slaves. He wondered what his mother would think of him.

He gulped down the Savor, put the top back on, and threw the empty bottle on the floor. It bothered him do it, cleanliness was another thing he'd learned from being a vampyr in Danika's care, but he liked the thought of throwing it out the window even less.

THE HOURS ROLLED ON AS DID THE MILES THAT STRETCHED BEFORE him. The pitch-black night gave way to the birth of dawn and he checked his map for somewhere to stop.

The quiet deafened him and his skin itched to get out of the car and stretch. For as much as he liked his privacy, he'd never gotten used to silence. First in the enclave and then the coven house, even the raiding party vans he used to go out on were rarely silent. There had always been people around. Whispers, songs, laughing. Being out on the road alone made him wish for companionship more than ever.

He remembered the small shacks and the field of tents that held every human he knew. The enclave had been little better than existing day to day, but it had been his home for almost a decade. He wondered if it was still there or if someone else from their group had given up the location. It wouldn't matter if they did. With more than one raiding van going missing, the enclave was sure to have packed up and moved on. They'd leave clues for the raiding parties as to which way they'd headed, but nothing that the slavers could decipher.

He looked at the GPS. He'd made good time but he had to pull off the road. Unable to bring himself to go into a motel again, he found a stretch of road where half a dozen cars had been pushed to the side, and he rode down into the ditch to where they clustered together.

He drove his SUV in between two of them and killed the engine. Glancing in the backseat, he groaned. This day's sleep might actually be worse than the previous.

He climbed back, retrieved his solar reflective blanket, locked the car, and pulled the blanket around himself. It was small, but not as uncomfortable as he'd imagined. He reached into the back pocket of the passenger seat and pulled out a gun, cradled it to his chest, and closed his eyes. He wasn't taking any chances again.

THE GAS LIGHT CAME ON AND EVAN SWORE LOUDLY. SHE HADN'T SEEN a deserted gas station for over fifty miles. She should've stopped earlier. Now, smack dab in the middle of Albuquerque, she had no option but to gas up in a populated area.

She wasn't an idiot. Going into a city, even the outskirts of a city, was a bad idea. And stealing gas—even worse. Which meant she'd have to go inside and give them cash.

A sign popped up on the road. No more gas for one hundred miles. She slammed her hand on the steering wheel. She wouldn't make it that far.

Blowing out a harsh breath, she turned the wheel to the right and headed for the off ramp.

A large red and yellow gas station sign gleamed like a light-house in the burgeoning dawn. She pulled into the station, and parked at the pump- not another car in sight. Digging in a bag, she found the forty bucks she'd snatched from a cash register the day before and shoved it in her pocket. She grabbed a coat and put it on, zipping it and pulling up the puffy hood.

She crossed to the front of the convenience store and kept her eyes on her shoes as she opened the door. She glanced toward the vamp cashier who sat with his feet up on the counter, reading a smut magazine. She marched over quickly, slapped down the forty bucks, and turned to go.

Her heart pounded as she headed back for the door. "Forty on pump two."

"Sure," the vamp replied. The stool creaked and his boots hit the floor. She hurried out and tried to calm her shaking body. She went to the pump and shoved the nozzle into the gas tank. Out of the corner of her eye, lights flashed as a vehicle rolled into the station. A large black van pulled to the pump beside hers and stopped.

She glanced over her shoulder at the horizon. The sky light-ened by the minute. Dawn would be upon them quickly, and she needed to be well on her way by then. The gas pump ticked upward at an excruciatingly slow pace. Twenty four... twenty four and a half... twenty five... twenty five and a half...

The van opened up and voices and laughter trailed out of it. She resisted the urge to turn and willed the gas to pump faster.

Behind her, several bodies passed her car and headed into the convenience store. The thundering in her chest grew louder. "Come on, dammit!" she said through clenched teeth.

"I'm sorry, did you say something?" asked a male voice from behind her.

Evan froze. "Uh... nope."

He chuckled. "Those things never do seem to go fast enough, do they?"

She swallowed the bile that scorched a trail up her throat. "Nope, they don't."

She glanced at the pump. Five dollars to go.

"You from around here?"

Screw it. She yanked the nozzle from the car, and set it back in the cradle. Calm. She needed to stay calm.

The man stood at the hood of her car. She kept her head down and walked to the driver's side.

She gave a small wave, being sure to keep her eyes on her feet. "Have a good day."

"Yeah, you too," he said slowly. He took a step closer and she reached for the handle.

Quick as a flash he stood at her side. Her head snapped up and her hood fell back. A cruel smile rolled across his handsome face revealing his shorter vampyr fangs.

"Well, well, well, what have we here?"

She reached for the door, but he slammed his hand on it, holding it closed.

"I'm getting my master's car fueled for him for tonight," she said. "Please move."

47

He glanced inside the car and chuckled. "I think not. Now if you want a real master, I'm happy to help you out with that."

Anger and fear mixed in an explosive cocktail inside her. "Remove your hand."

He thought for a second. "No."

She glanced at the convenience store where his buddies messed with the cashier inside, but they wouldn't be gone forever.

"What do you want?" she asked.

"Oh precious, a beautiful human like you should be able to figure that out easily." He leapt at her and Evan backed away. He laughed and chased her around the car. They circled twice before she ended up on the wrong side. "You know I can keep this up all day, right?" he taunted.

"I doubt that. In less than five minutes the sun'll be up." She circled the car once more and pulled the driver's side door open. She dove inside and he seized her legs. She reached out, trying to grab onto something. Anything.

"Come on, baby, don't be that way. Let's have some fun."

Evan kicked her attacker in the chest. He flew backward into the pump and growled. She scrambled farther into the car and felt around on the floor for a weapon.

The vampyr climbed in the driver's side and gripped her by the hair, dragging her out. Everything she'd been taught by her uncle and cousins flooded back to her. Every muscle in her body tensed and her vision intensified. Blood rushed through her limbs and she twisted in his grip and punched him in the groin. He doubled over and she headbutted him in the nose. He cried out and let go of her.

"You bitch!" The vampyr reached behind his back.

She dove back in the car and reached under the passenger seat. Her fingers closed around a warm piece of metal, and she raised her hand and pointed. The sound of the gun firing resounded in the car, making her head buzz and her sensitive ears ring.

The vampyr lunged at Evan and planted a long hunting knife into her thigh. She kicked him with her right leg before firing the rest of the clip. The vampyr dropped in a heap, and she hauled herself back into the car. Blood rushed through her, pumping in her head and making it pound. Tears streamed from her eyes as she ripped the knife from her leg and threw it into the seat next to her.

His buddies tore out of the store, and she put the car into drive. Her stomach roiled as she peeled out of the gas station, and she had to force herself to keep from throwing up. Taking off down the road, and back to the highway she skidded onto the ramp, heart pounding.

Pain shot up her leg and she slapped her palm onto it, her only thought to getting as far down the road as possible. She took a dozen deep breaths, topping one hundred in the car and trying to keep herself from shattering into a million pieces. Blood seeped through her fingers and pooled in the seat by her rear. She pressed her left hand into the wound harder, trying to staunch the flow.

Ten minutes later the adrenaline shakes tapered off and the throbbing in her leg increased painful. She pulled to the shoulder, ripped off the overly warm coat, and looked down. A wide, six-inch gash split her black pants as well as her skin. Blood poured from a wound deep enough that she didn't have the stomach to inspect fully. She pressed her palm into it and looked around for something to tie it off with, but there wasn't anything. She grabbed her white, button- up blouse and tore it down the back. Then she made several strips and wrapped the fabric around her thigh. She wrapped a second half around her leg tighter than the first but blood drenched the fabric. She needed medical attention and soon. She opened the glovebox and pulled out a bottle of pain pills. Popping two in her mouth, she took a deep breath and swallowed them dry.

Slowing her heartbeat was first priority. Her blood pumping hard would only make her bleed out faster. She studied her map. She still had a good ten hours to her destination. She hoped she could make it that far.

CHAPTER SIX

William traveled all night, his eyes trained on the blinking red dot that hadn't moved since he'd awoken. At four in the morning, he drove less than twenty minutes from where the GPS told him Evan's car sat. The restlessness that had plagued him over the past eight hours had morphed into full-blown panic.

He needed to check in with Danika, but he couldn't. Not yet. To lose Evan after getting almost completely across the US wasn't an option. He cursed himself for not putting a GPS tracker in the clothes he'd given her as well as the car.

Fifteen minutes later, he slowed his vehicle and rolled to where the beeping red dot remained. He crested a small hill and caught sight of it a mile off, upside down in a ditch. His gut churned and he scanned the area. There were no other cars around and nowhere to obscure his vehicle. He'd have to go in with no cover. If it was a trap, he'd be a fish in a very open glass bowl. But if it wasn't and she was stuck inside…

He lost all sense of reason and hit the gas. Reaching the car in less than a minute he slammed on the brakes and jumped from his SUV, not even bothering to turn off the engine. He ran down the small embankment to the driver's side where Evan hung upside down.

William grabbed the door, wrenched the bashed in piece of metal off its hinges, and tossed it away.

"Evan!" He felt her throat for a pulse. The scent of blood slapped him and made his fangs ache.

He turned her head to face him. Her nose seeped blood and mixed with the caked blood from a gash above her eye.

"Evan! Evan?" She shook like a limp rag doll at his touch. He grabbed the seatbelt and yanked it free. She slid downward and he caught her, dragging her onto the grass.

In the glow of his headlights, her skin held an unusually pale sheen. He spotted her left leg wrapped in the now-red dress shirt he'd given her. He unwrapped it. Blood poured from a large gash.

"Shit." He wrapped it back up, but the damage was done. He hopped to his feet and raced to his SUV, grabbed the medic kit from the back, and then headed to her side.

He pulled it open, and scanned for something to use. His mind raced, recognizing everything in turn, but suddenly unable to remember what any of it was for.

"Think, William." He took a cleansing breath. She needed a sterile bandage, but to take off the shirt again could be catastrophic. Her thready pulse belied the fact that she'd lost too much blood. What the hell had happened to her?

He closed his eyes and swore. Only one thing could save her. The one thing he didn't want to do and the one thing she wouldn't want him to do. His gaze traveled to her pallid face and he cupped her cheek with his palm. She was going to kill him... but as long as she lived, he could take it.

His limbs shook as he pulled her half-naked body onto his lap and rolled up his sleeve. He'd never fed someone before. He tried to remember what Danika had done when she'd fed him.

He bit into his wrist and placed it over Evan's mouth. Blood dripped from the shallow wound onto her face. He pried her mouth open and the blood dribbled in. He pumped his fist several times in an effort to get the blood to flow better, but it continued to trickle.

"Dammit." He bit into his wrist again, this time hitting his mark. Blood flowed freely into her mouth.

She coughed and gagged.

"Swallow, you PITA!"

Her eyelids fluttered but didn't open. She swallowed once and then twice. He pulled his wrist away and licked it shut, unsure of how much would be too much. She sucked in a deep breath and moaned.

"William," she whispered.

He stared at her, unable to move. Had she really said his name? He brushed it off. She only said it because he'd found her. There wasn't time to think on it though. He had to move her somewhere safe... and cleaner.

He picked up the medic kit, threw it in the car, and tossed all his supplies into the trunk, then came back and scooped Evan into his arms. Her warm arms pebbled at the contact with his cool skin. Her breasts heaved up and down, barely covered by the light pink, lacy bra. He laid her on the backseat and covered her with his UV blanket and his coat.

Jumping into the front seat, he closed the door. He glanced in the backseat where she lay motionless, pulled up the GPS, and located the nearest town. There wasn't much, but hopefully he could at least find a clean motel to dress her wounds.

He pulled away from the crash, praying she'd be okay.

. . .

A MOTEL FLASHING A LARGE ARROW WITH A VACANCY SIGN APPEARED AT his right. Probably one of the last small businesses left in an outskirt town.

He stopped the SUV outside the lobby and hopped out. An old vamp greeted him and took the cash without even asking William's name. He simply nodded and handed William a key.

He didn't want to be noticed, but no way would he chance another deserted motel. Even though the motel had only one vamp cashier and two other cars in the parking lot, he was pretty sure anyone looking for an easy mark would go elsewhere.

Hefting his bag over his shoulder, he reached in and grabbed Evan, still wrapped in a blanket. He cradled her against his chest, her temperature cool on his skin. Her head lolled to the side, revealing the fact that her skin color was no closer to normal than it had been on the ground. *Dammit.*

He hurried and unlocked the room and then pulled the key from the door. Stepping inside, he kicked it closed behind him. He lay Evan on the first of the two beds and set his bag on the second bed. Then he rushed into the bathroom, grabbed a towel, and wet it. A second one he ripped into strips. He located the lamp and flipped it on before opening the medic kit and locating the small bottle of peroxide and a tube of antibiotic. It still amazed him how easy those simple things were to procure in Vampire society. A brown bottle and a yellow tube of ointment. The two things that could have saved his mother's life.

He set them on Evan's bed and stared at her for a minute. He had to get the bloody pants off. He stared at the beautiful slender waist and belly button that peeked out from over her waistband. The tips of several tiny silvery scars snaked down below the belt line.

Gently he unwrapped the two pieces of dress shirt from her leg. Though the bleeding had slowed, it hadn't stopped and the wound wasn't healing. It should at least be closed from how much blood he'd given her. At least... he was pretty sure it should. Instead it looked worse. Something wasn't right.

He ripped the leg of her pants apart to get a better look at the wound. The edges of the fabric clung to the gash. He blew out a breath and grabbed the wet towel. Dabbing at the wound, he tried to wiggle the pieces of fabric loose.

Evan moaned and stirred. Her eyes fluttered open, and he continued to wipe at her leg.

"Where am I?" She scanned the room and then locked glassy eyes on him. "Who the hell—" She sucked in a breath. "What are you doing here?"

"Nice to see you as well."

Panic traced her features. "Have you been following me this whole time?"

"You crashed the car."

She looked down at her leg and threw her hands into her hair. "I passed out." She probed her face with her fingers. "Great. I messed up my face. I liked my face."

"Yeah, well, I wouldn't be as concerned with that right now as with this leg. What happened?"

She stared at him for a moment and bit her lip as if trying to decide something. "I got stabbed," she finally said.

"By who?" He tried to keep his temper in check.

"Some stupid vampyr dick. I shot him."

William stopped and looked up at her. "Well I hope you got him good."

"I knew I shouldn't have stopped there for gas."

William blew out a breath. "Okay, look. You need help with this wound. It isn't healing like it should."

"Well it just happened a few hours ago. I heal fast but not that fast."

His gut clenched. "You should though."

"Why?"

Telling her not to freak out wouldn't get him far, so like a bandage, it was best to rip it off and deal with the consequences. "I gave you some of my blood."

She opened and closed her mouth several times. He waited for her fury to rain down on him like venom.

"That won't work on me," she said simply.

Not what he'd expected at all. "Okay, and why is that?"

She licked her lips. "Because I was inoculated against it."

He stared at her, wide-eyed. "I'm sorry?"

"It was a test to see if we could become immune to the bite."

His brain worked in overdrive. "And it worked?"

She shrugged. "For the most part. We can't be bonded as slaves or turned, but the healing bit doesn't work on us either. And we age slower and move faster and are stronger than normal humans."

"How?"

"Like most immunizations, we were injected with dead Vampire cells. They bonded with ours and made us something else."

"Daywalkers. Humans made you what Vampires failed to do with the V2000 virus." So it was possible. Someone had done it.

"No! I am no Vampire, or vampyr or whatever. I'm human. Totally human. But whatever the immunization did, it makes it impossible for your blood to help me."

"Then we need to get you to a doctor."

"No way. If we do that, they'll figure out what was done to me for sure, and I'm not becoming some Vampire doctor's guinea pig."

"But your leg—"

"Do what you have to. I'm not going to a doctor."

He blew out a heavy breath. "What about your people? The enclave you were going to. I can take you to them."

She searched his face. "You think I'm gonna take you there?" Her eyes narrowed. "Wait a minute. How did you know where I was going?"

"We knew you'd try to escape."

She crossed her arms over her chest. "You set me up."

He nodded.

"Man, you're a dick."

"And you're a pain in the ass that doesn't listen. Are we even now? Unless you want this thing to get infected, we need to scrub it out."

"Fine."

"Take your pants off," he ordered.

"Excuse me?"

"Your pants. They need to come off so I can get to the wound more easily."

"Do you have a knife?"

He searched his pack and handed her a knife. She slit the pant leg in the back and ripped it off, revealing her entire silky leg.

"You already get to see my boobs. I'm not letting you catch a peek at the rest of me as well." She flicked the knife closed and shoved it in her waistband.

"Really? You still don't trust me?"

She gave him a winning smile. "Nope."

He shook his head. "You have issues."

"You have no idea."

FOR THE NEXT THIRTY MINUTES, HE PICKED THE PIECES OF FABRIC FROM the wound, making the bleeding begin afresh. She held back cries of pain, but the way her fingers dug into the bedspread showed her agony.

"It's down to the bone," he said. "You really need some stitches. I don't know how to do that. Please let me take you somewhere."

"Just tape me up and I'll heal."

"Evan—"

Her gaze iced over. "Tape. Me. Up."

William sighed and shook his head. He poured the peroxide on her leg, though the warning label cautioned against it, and waited for the bubbles to settle before dabbing the wound with the wet towel once more. Then he put the antibiotic gel on a sterile pad and taped it to her leg, before covering it with the dry towel strips.

Anxiety shook his body. He didn't know what else to do for her. If he took her to a hospital, they'd possibly find out about her blood anomaly, and she'd definitely be tested on. If that happened, they'd never find her enclave—and he might never get her back.

When he finished taping her up, he rinsed out the towel and came back. Her head still needed to be checked out.

He sat next to her and she scooted away. "Let me clean your face," he offered.

"No thanks."

He glared at her. "Stop being such a PITA and just let me."

She rolled her eyes. "This doesn't mean I forgive you."

"I didn't expect you would."

She scowled. "Really? JA?"

"JA?"

"Figure it out."

He leaned in, his arm brushing her breasts as he dabbed her bloodied nose. Her eyes stayed fixed on his face, and he tried to concentrate on the task at hand instead of her perfect, half-naked body and the peachy swells of her breasts begging to be kissed.

Confusion clashed inside Evan like a tidal wave. Her anger at being set up jabbed her pride. But she had to admit that if William hadn't come along, she'd probably be dead.

He pressed the cloth lightly onto her forehead, sending pain coursing through her temple. His gaze flicked to hers, but for the most part, he concentrated on his job.

His handsome face and bright blue eyes made her stomach quiver. If he'd been a human, she probably would have kissed him as a thank you. She wrapped her arms around herself tight, to keep her quivering stomach in check. She wasn't falling for a vampyr. No matter how sexy his smile or how gentle his manners.

Dirt and blood smeared his blue dress shirt. She wondered what it would feel like to slide the rumpled cotton off his hard body and run her fingers over his chest. She closed her eyes and sucked in a sharp breath. She had to pull it together.

"Did I hurt you?"

She opened her eyes and he dropped his hand. It had been

almost two years since she'd been with anyone. Why in his presence had it suddenly become an issue?

"I think I'm done for now," she said.

He nodded and pulled open the first aid kit. He grabbed a small bottle and poured two pills into his palm. He handed her the pills and then a bottle of water.

"Take those. They'll help with the pain."

"I'm fine without them."

His eyes grew serious and she reluctantly put the pills in her mouth and chugged them down with the entire bottle.

He scanned her face. "I'm going to need to rest, but if you're gonna run, I'll stay awake."

"What are you going to do with me?" Fear crept into her voice. She crushed the water bottle in her hand, cursing herself for her weakness.

"I need to get to the humans. I told you before that we need their help. Or at least their weapons."

"And I told you that I'm not taking you to them."

"Then we have a problem." He stood and unbuttoned his shirt.

"What are you doing?" Her heart thundered like a herd of elephants.

He looked down. "Changing my shirt."

He removed the shirt, and she had to keep from moaning at the sight of his strong, lean muscles cut with precision down to his perfectly tailored suit pants. The lines of his sinewy muscles begged for her to touch them, while the dips between each defined ab called for her to run her tongue up and down him. Visions of him underneath her as she licked his salty skin filled her head. His hands tangled in her hair, calling her name-

She coughed and their eyes locked until her cheeks heated and she glanced away. He walked to his bag and pulled out a T-shirt and plaid pajama bottoms. She took the opportunity to survey his tight backside. Her fingers twitched with the desire to squeeze it.

Damn. She had to get her crap together before she did something she'd regret. Again.

She turned away before he could notice her staring and the sudden movement made her head feel like it'd been stuffed with cotton.

"I'm going to shower. Are you going to run?"

She should run. She should take off and get back to her people the moment he stepped into the bathroom. But her leg pulsed and throbbed and who knew how well it would hold. She had hours of driving to do to reach California and the only car available would most likely his. Which he would track. Plus, whatever pain pills he'd give her were probably good enough to end her in another ditch if she tried to drive.

"No. Not yet anyway."

He grabbed the car keys off the dresser and headed for the bathroom.

She hunkered down in the bed and rolled on her side. "What? You don't trust me now?"

She yawned as a wave of fatigue engulfed her.

He smiled at her. "Never have."

CHAPTER SEVEN

William exited the shower thirty minutes later, clean but pent up.

He scrubbed his hair with a towel. "Are you hungry?"

Her eyelids fluttered open revealing eyes like brilliant, blue glass.

Good, the drugs were knocking her out. She needed to rest. To heal.

"I could go for a burger, fries, and soda."

He walked to his duffel bag and unzipped it. Rummaging inside, he grabbed a protein bar and a bottle of water. He walked over, opened the water, and ripped off the wrapper of the bar for her.

"Wow, for me? Really?" Her words held sarcasm but none of her earlier venom.

"I don't have time to go out. The sun will be up any minute. This will have to do for the time being. I have more than a dozen bars in my bag. I'll get you some real food later."

She took the bar and bit into it. "So, what am I supposed to do all day?"

William pulled the covers down on his bed and lay on the scratchy sheets. He stretched out and then relaxed onto the saggy mattress. Man, he missed his bed... he really had gone soft. He couldn't even imagine going back to an enclave to live.

"I suggest you get some rest. You need to heal." He closed his eyes and tried to let his mind wander. He thought about his bed at the coven house. His gut twisted and he worried about Neeman.

She yawned loudly. "I'm bored."

He sighed. "Then go to sleep."

She blew out a breath and tossed her wrapper unsuccessfully at the trashcan. "You're a vampyr."

"Guilty."

"So were you human once?"

"Also guilty."

"When were you turned?"

Really? Now she wanted to get to know him? When he could barely keep conscious and had given her enough pain meds that she should be in dreamland.

"I'm pretty sure you've heard the story from all the other humans."

"I want to hear it from you."

He turned to face her. Her eyes held nothing but sincerity. He stared up at the ceiling again feeling his body sink deeper into the bed, willing him to go to sleep. He shouldn't talk to her. He should shut up, roll over, and leave her to her boredom. He needed to rest because getting her to agree to guide him to her enclave would take all the energy he possessed when he woke up.

"I lived in an enclave in the mountains for years. Over a

year ago, I went on a supply run with Mason and a group from our encampment. We hit a house we shouldn't have. A group of slavers followed us. They attacked when we met up with others from our enclave. Several of us ran into the mountains in an effort to wait them out till dawn, but they caught up with us."

"Is that the guy you stuck a knife into?"

"Yeah."

"So what happened? You ended up in a slave auction?"

"We were there about a week when Lord Danika showed up. She bought me and Mason, and Ike for Lance and Sinya. I became her assistant and we formed a friendship. One night she was overseeing appeals and Neeman brought in a rogue vamp. The girl was out of her mind with bloodlust and she grabbed a gun. She pointed it at Danika. I jumped in the way and got shot."

"Why would you do that?"

He looked over at her. "What?"

"Why would you save Danika? You were a slave. Were you in love with her or something?"

His gut clenched and he licked his lips. "Danika was the first person since my mom who treated me like I had potential. In the encampment, I was nobody. Danika may have paid money for me, but she did it because she saw what I could become. Did I love her? Yes, I did and I do. But not the way you think."

"So you were injured and she gave you her blood?"

"We'd not started the bonding process up to that point, so I'd never had her blood before, and she didn't know how much to give me."

"You hadn't bonded?" The surprised that laced her voice made his gut clenched and a savage protectiveness ripped through him.

"You really do need to give her some credit. She's not like other Vampires. She didn't want to bond with me till *I* was ready."

Her brows furrowed.

"What about you? How did you get into the slave market?"

She stared at him for a minute before yawning. "You know, I am getting tired."

She rolled away from him. He stared at the soft curve of her body under the sheet. He wanted to run his fingers down the length of her and bathe in her scent. It surprised him that she hadn't yet asked for a shirt to cover up with.

He took in the soft roundness of her shoulder and slender dip of her waist. The indent of her spine just begged to be licked. He took in every inch of her and wondered what had happened to her before she'd shown up at the coven house.

EVAN STOOD IN THE MIDDLE OF A BEAUTIFULLY DECORATED ROOM. Cream carpet tickled her toes as the faint sound of classical music poured through the wall of the adjoining room. A beautiful, jade green, silk bed took up most of the space while expensive, dark furniture lined the rest.

She stared at the white door, her heart racing so fast she waited for it to explode. Footsteps moved closer down the hallway. She wiped her sweaty palms on the white sundress she'd been given and tensed as the knob turned.

A dark-haired, tall Vampire with handsome, sharp features and an expensive suit smiled at her.

"Hello, Evan."

She wanted to speak but her voice wouldn't work. She tried to swallow but couldn't conjure any saliva.

The Vampire closed the door and strode closer to her. His hungry eyes devoured every inch of her before he offered his hand.

"I'm Travis."

Her limbs shook as she grasped his cool palm. He caressed the back of her hand with his fingers and she pulled away.

He chuckled. "I'm not going to hurt you. You know why you were bought, right?"

"Yes," she croaked.

He moved closer and brushed her cheek with his knuckles. "You are beautiful."

Every fiber of her wanted to scream, to run, but she'd never make it. Travis pressed his body into hers, then leaned in close and sniffed her.

"Please." An unexpected tear slipped from her eye. He kissed her throat lightly, making her skin pebble. She clenched her fists tight.

"Don't worry, Evan. I won't do anything until we know each other better."

Evan screamed and shot straight up in bed. Sweat covered her body and soaked through the sheet.

A hand fell lightly on her shoulder. "Are you okay?"

She struck out and connected with someone. He grunted and the other bed creaked. She scanned the room remembering where she was.

She turned on the light and rubbed her eyes. "Sorry."

William touched his nose where she'd punched him. "You had a nightmare."

She dropped her head into her hands and sucked in several deep breaths.

"Do you want to talk about it?" His tone remained gentle. Caring even.

She didn't want him to sound like that. Didn't want him to

be nice to her. She could deal with him being mean, cruel even, but she couldn't handle nice.

She'd never told anyone about what had happened to her. About the burning shame that scorched her daily with the flames of guilt. She tried to hide it deep inside. Locking it away with the memory of many other things she didn't want to deal with.

"You can talk to me. I'm not as bad as you think."

Her head whipped up. "Can you stop being so damn nice all the time?"

"I'm sorry?"

"Nice. You're nice all the time. Why? Why are you nice to me? I've been nothing but a total wench and yet you continue to be nice to me."

He stared at her and blinked several times. "I... I'm nice to you because I know the persona you show isn't who you really are."

"How do you know who I am? I could just be this way." Fire burned in her belly. Anger for the things that had been done to her. For the things she'd allowed to be done.

He sat for a minute and didn't speak. "I'm a man bought by a good and decent woman. She treated me with kindness and respect. But I'm not an idiot. I know that I was one of the few lucky ones. Human women have it much worse. You don't have to tell me your story. I see the bite mark scars on your neck. That combined with the fact that you're beautiful can only mean one of two things. You were a blood slave, or a breeding slave."

"Breeding slave," she said. "Though I'm not sure I wasn't a blood slave as well." She swallowed and stared the other direction.

"I'm sorry," he said.

Memories bombarding her like an emotional air strike avalanching down on her till she thought she'd suffocate. She refused to cry and instead stuffed everything back down until only the ever-present empty hole.

"Yeah. Me too."

WILLIAM WANTED TO COMFORT HER. HE COULDN'T IMAGINE THE horrors she'd endured. If he'd been bought by anyone else the likelihood that he'd be a lowly slave scraping to survive did not escape him.

"Do you have any family?" he asked.

She looked over at him. "An uncle and a couple of cousins. My parents and little sister died soon into the outbreak. My uncle took me in. He and my cousins were real doomsday nuts." She chuckled. "Who knew they'd been right all along. Of course, they thought the zombies would get us, not Vampires."

William laughed. "I thought it would be zombies too. Man, when people were turning into vamps and they started attacking, I was sure they were zombies."

"How old were you?"

"About seven. You?"

"I was seventeen."

That couldn't be right. "How's that possible? That would make you—"

"Twenty-eight."

His mouth opened and closed. She appeared to be no more than twenty-one.

"It's the inoculation I received. I age slower."

"Where'd you get that inoculation?"

"In the encampment my uncle took us too. They have scientists there working on stuff. When they needed volunteers, my uncle wanted me and my cousins to be the first in line. He swore never to allow what happened to my aunt and others we knew to happen to us."

"So your aunt..."

"Became a vamp."

"Did she stay with your uncle?"

Evan looked down at her hands. "No."

He swallowed, remembering the night his mom pulled him out the window.

"My dad died trying to protect us during the Awakening. A vampyr broke into our apartment. My mom barely got me out in time."

Sadness crossed her features. "I'm sorry."

"We're not as different as you think, Evan. We've both lost people."

"But you're not human anymore."

"No, but from the sounds of it you aren't exactly human either."

"I am human. More human than you."

He shrugged. "Only in biology. I still think the way I used to. Still love the way a human would. Still laugh and cry and desire."

"And kill."

His spine stiffened. "I've only ever killed in self-defense. Are you telling me you've never killed anyone?"

"Not a person." Her words were pointed and cryptic.

Anger flared within him. "So I'm not a person."

Silence fell between them thick as a storm cloud.

She bit the inside of her cheek. "I didn't say that."

"You didn't have to." As much as William wanted her words

not to stab him, they did. A twisting between the shoulder blades, digging deeper and deeper with every syllable she uttered. It didn't matter what he did, she saw him as a monster.

He glanced at the clock. "We should try to get a few more hours of sleep before I find you food and figure out what we're going to do."

"I'm still not taking you to California." She closed her eyes and pressed her lips together, shaking her head. "Damn."

"Well, then I guess we're staying here." He turned out the light and rolled over. He tried to show no reaction to her words. But inwardly he jumped up and down in a flurry of hallelujahs. Finally, he had an inkling of where they were headed. California was a huge place to search for an enclave. But it was a start.

WILLIAM AWOKE SEVERAL HOURS LATER AND WENT IN SEARCH OF FOOD. Evan still slept when he left, but by the time got back from the store, she had showered and now wore one of his shirts tied off at the bottom and a pair of his sweat pants pulled as tight as possible around the waist. He groaned at the site of her skin all covered up, but it was for the best. She wasn't for him.

He set the groceries on the table. "How's the leg?"

"Almost healed."

He pulled a salad, fruit, bread, and cheese from the bag. "I didn't know what you'd want."

She shrugged. "It doesn't matter. I've had to eat just about everything at least once in my life."

He had to tread carefully to get her on his side. "So, the enclave where you lived, was it well supplied? We lived in the mountains and never had enough."

"The enclave is self-sufficient."

That meant it had to be big and in a real building. Possibly one with kitchen access. There would only be a handful of buildings like that. Schools, hospitals, corporations with cafeterias or hotels. And they wouldn't be in populated areas. Too many Vampires still lived in Los Angeles, San Francisco and San Diego. That eliminated the coast. They'd have to be in the east somewhere, or maybe the redwoods. Possibly the desert.

"Here." He handed her the salad and a bottle of Gatorade. "You need to keep up your electrolytes."

She snorted. "Are you a doctor?"

He stiffened. "Or you can not eat."

Her smile fell. "Sorry. I'm afraid my snarkiness has become who I am now."

He pulled a Savor from his bag, popped the lid and took several gulps. Her face held no revulsion, only curiosity.

"What does that taste like?" She pulled the plastic lid off the salad and mixed it with her fork.

He shrugged. "I don't know exactly. Like blood but without any of the organic nuances. There's no aftertaste. No lingering flavors from the food eaten or chemicals people come in contact with. It's hard to explain."

She ripped open the dressing with her teeth and squeezed it on the lettuce. "Tell me about the demons."

William stared at her, the bottle of Savor poised at his lips. Did she believe him, or was she just probing? "What do you want to know?"

"They're real?"

"Yeah. And they aren't as warm and cuddly as Mason either."

"Cuddly isn't a term I would use to describe him." She licked her fingers, making his desire stir.

He cleared his throat and tried to focus. "You would if you saw the others."

She shrugged. "So tell me."

What could he tell her that wouldn't scare the crap out of her? Maybe he should scare her. Maybe scaring her was the only way to get her to really pay attention.

"I—" His phone rang on the dresser. He put the lid back on the Savor and grabbed his phone.

"Hello?" Probably better to not scare the crap out of her. He needed to be more strategic in what he told her. He looked to Evan and then headed out the door, closing it behind himself.

"William, you didn't check in." Danika's voice held an urgent, strained edge.

"I'm sorry. There's been a bit of a problem."

"What kind of problem?"

William thought it best if he tried to sound as casual as possible. "Evan was injured and crashed the car. I got her out and she'll be fine, but she won't tell me where the enclave is."

"You need to get her to tell you." Panic laced her voice.

"I know. I know. She did say that the enclave was self-sustaining though and that she headed to California. Maybe check for buildings like that that might be used for an enclave?"

"In California? That would take years of searching."

He blew out a breath. "How are things there? How's Neeman?"

"Neeman will survive. As for the rest of us... that is becoming unclear. The waves of attacks are getting worse. It's only a matter of time until Mason's father comes through. Honestly at this point, I don't know what he's waiting for. We spotted Melton this morning."

"He's in Chicago?"

"Outside the office building."

"What was he doing there?"

"I am assuming he had something to do with the top three floors being blown up today."

William ran his hand through his hair and grabbed it by the roots pulling on it. His gut twisted like a coil and he had to force himself to ask. "Is everyone okay?"

A long pause drew out and William bit his lip.

Danika's voice cracked and she sniffled. "Lance is dead. Ike too."

William's heart sank and he slid down the cement wall of the motel. Oh no. "Poor Sinya. I'm so sorry, Danika."

Silence stretched out as William tried to hold it together. First Neeman injured, now Lance and Ike... The toll grew heavier and heavier and the real fight hadn't even begun yet.

The sounds of Danika's anguish from the other end of the line made him want to get in his car and head back to Chicago. How many more would die before the end?

He held back tears and coughed, trying to clear his throat. "I'll find the enclave and talk to them. I promise."

"I trust you, but things have changed. Now we need any and all nuclear weapons they might have. We need an advantage in this damn war. We can't lose any more family. *I* can't lose any more."

He nodded at the words she didn't say. "I understand. I'll call you later."

"Six hours. You call me in exactly six hours."

"Six hours." He hung up the phone and leaned his head back against the wall. His stomach flopped at Danika's words. Demons were murdering their family.

It was all on his shoulders to keep the demons from destroying everything he cared about. How in the world did he persuade Evan to tell him anything?

CHAPTER EIGHT

E van spent the next twenty-four hours trying to figure out a way to get to California without William. He'd been unusually sullen since his first conversation on the phone and every other time he'd left to make a phone call he'd come back looking a fraction worse. She hadn't wanted to pry, but her curiosity had gotten the better of her. An attack in Chicago had killed a vampyr and human William knew. The news made Evan more anxious than ever to get back to her enclave and away from the Vampire infighting for dominance. The next night when William got up, her skin prickled and she couldn't seem to get comfortable.

"You don't look good," he said.

"How kind of you to say." She groaned and tried to roll on her side but the pain that radiated from her thigh refused to be ignored. "I don't feel good."

He stepped toward her but she jerked away. "I just want to feel your head. To see if you have a fever."

"Trust me, I have a fever."

"What about your leg? You said it was healing."

"It's healed."

He looked at her. "You should check."

"I said—"

"I know what you said, but you should check anyway. I'll even leave so you can do it without me." He walked into the bathroom.

She moved her leg and pain shot up through her hip and down to her knee like a lightning bolt. She stood on her good leg and slid down the sweats revealing a bright red, swollen thigh. She removed the bandage and discovered the wound had re-opened. Hot to the touch it reminded her of an oozy, over-ripe tomato.

"Shit. William!"

He ran out of the bathroom in a flash. Kneeling by her leg he inspected it while fear trickled through her like a ghost.

"This is not healed." His face held concern.

"It *was* healed. Now it's not."

He shook his head and sat on his mattress still looking at her leg. "You have an infection. Maybe something lodged inside the wound, or it could have gotten dirty... There's any number of things that could have happened. We need to get you to a doctor."

She broke out in a sweat and her head grew dizzy. She sat shakily on her bed. "I told you, no doctors."

"I get where you're coming from, but you have three choices right now. We go back to Chicago and I take you to Doc to fix you up. If we do that though, you're right back where you started. I can find a hospital and take you there or... I take you where you want to go."

Evan closed her eyes and swore. None of those three things were what she wanted. But dying from sepsis wasn't what she wanted either. At the enclave they had more than enough resources to take care of her... at least they did three years ago. She could only assume they'd gotten even better in the last years since she'd not once heard of a large enclave being found and had never seen another human she knew.

What was the worst that could happen if William took her to the enclave? He'd know where it was and they'd possibly make him stay. A far as vampyr went he was as human as any she'd met... maybe they'd even accept him after a time. Maybe she would...

"All right. You can take me to my enclave. And in return I'll get you a meeting with our head guy. But you have to let me do it my own way. No barging in, unless you want to get yourself shot on sight." If Norman, the leader of their enclave, hadn't changed, he wouldn't be easy to convince.

"Fine but you have to take one of my phones. Keep it on you the whole time and call me when you've convinced him to speak to me. I won't leave until I've spoken to him."

What a nightmare. She was putting the enclave in jeopardy. William would know where they were. And if he knew where they were, the likelihood that they would let him leave if they didn't believe him was beyond miniscule. Even so, a piece of her trusted him. Trusted that he didn't want to hurt or enslave the humans.

"You promise not to call in backup and try to overrun the place?"

"Even if I did call for backup, there is none. They need every body they can get to hold back the onslaught."

"So you came all the way out here, alone, in the hopes of finding an enclave, knowing that you wouldn't get help if there was trouble?"

His face grew serious. "When we left they said they'd come

if there were problems, but I knew from the beginning this might be a one-way trip. But if I can save every person in my family, it's worth it."

Could he possibly care about other people that much? It had been a long time since she'd met anyone who wasn't out for themselves in the end. And especially not someone of the vampiric persuasion.

"Palm Springs." She blurted the words out before she could change her mind. "There's a resort there."

He gave her a tight smile and nodded. "Then we go to Palm Springs."

PALM SPRINGS LAY EIGHT HOURS FROM GALLUP, NEW MEXICO. THEY left at eight PM and stopped to get gas and food along the way. William couldn't help the nervous tickle that started at the base of his spine when they crossed into California and how it grew worse the closer they got.

Danika wanted him to go to Palm Springs for the weapons, but his concern was for Evan. So when Danika had called, he'd lied and told her he was still trying to find out where the enclave was. He'd never lied to Danika before. It made him squirm.

Evan's skin had taken on a waxy, pale sheen, and she'd fallen asleep about an hour into the trip and only stirred when he woke her and made her drink or eat something. Every once in a while he would feel her skin, but to his ever-cool temperature she resembled an oven.

As the moon dipped low on the horizon, William's body began to feel the strain of not having slept well or in his own bed for close to a week. He'd have to suck it up though. Who knew how long it would take before he'd be sleeping in his own bed? If ever.

Ten miles outside of Palm Springs dawn remained less than an hour away.

"Evan. Evan?" He shook her shoulder and she opened her bleary eyes. "Which exit?"

She glanced around. "Exit?"

He pointed at the sign. "Palm Springs. Where do I go?"

"Palm Springs. Country Club Drive."

At the next exit, William pulled off the highway and stopped at the corner of Country Club Drive. The fast food restaurants showed no sign of life. For the first time since becoming a vampyr fear raced over him at the prospect of going into a town. It wasn't his town and his people lived thousands of miles away. Hell, the nearest Vampire city was a three hour drive. Memories of being handcuffed and pushed into an SUV with Mason and the others from his group swirled in his mind. He was once again going somewhere that he wouldn't be able to control what happened to him. To be at the mercy of others... only this time those others were humans.

He drove past subdivision after subdivision scanning the wide boulevard for signs of life. Within a couple miles light shone from up on the left. A large resort came into view. He slowed his vehicle, turned off the headlights, and pulled to the side of the road.

He needed to get the lay of the area before going further. It was one thing to try to help; it was another to end up dead because he went in the wrong way and scared someone.

He looked over to Evan, who had fallen asleep again. He slid from the driver's seat, raced across the boulevard to the other side, and crept down the street until the resort lay before him.

A giant dark lake surrounded it, and inside the lake stood a barbed wire fence at least ten feet high. Only one road that led into the facility as far as he could see. A handful of guards and dogs walked the perimeter. He watched them for close to thirty minutes memorizing the pattern they took as they swept the area near the fence.

It amazed him no one had found the place before. But Los Angeles was the closest big city, and the likelihood that they'd travel several hours out into the desert, driving from exit to exit on the chance that perhaps somewhere there might be some humans wasn't very likely. Especially now that finding slaves had started going out of fashion in the best parts of society. Palm Springs wasn't near any major cities, and unless he'd known to come down this exact exit he would have continued on past, believing that Country Club Drive remained as desolate as every other exit he'd passed in the last five hours.

It amazed him how well put together Evan's enclave was. The resort seemed to have sustained no damage from the wars. The large cream and peach stucco building surrounded by lush green grass had been maintained better than he could have imagined. To do so had to be a feat. The palm trees appeared healthy and trimmed. The large fountain in the front roundabout trickled water out of the mouth of a large fish. Even the flowers bloomed purple, pink, and white. He wondered if the resort ran on its own well water and solar. It had to. The Vampires monitored every electric and water company across the US for anomalies in smaller and more rural sectors. Surely they would have noticed a huge wattage and water usage out in Palm Springs.

William pushed the questions from his mind and focused on the problem at hand. How would he get Evan inside the compound without getting them both killed? The fence surrounded the property a good hundred yards away from the front door. And large street lights ran the length of the road. Besides the palm trees at the edge of the property there wasn't anywhere to hide once they got close to the fence. They'd be out in the open for everyone to see.

Getting Evan inside wasn't going to be easy. He could possibly take her halfway to the fence, and she could walk the rest of the way on her own... but what if she couldn't? He blew out a harsh breath. They didn't have many options. It just had to work.

He jogged back to the car and opened her door. A bead of sweat trickled down her temple. Even in the minimal light from the resort he could see the deep blush that had invaded her cheeks. He touched her head to find her fever like an inferno. She didn't have much time. If she didn't get help in the next few hours he wasn't sure that she'd make it. The thought twisted in his gut like a carving knife. He couldn't bear to have come so far only to lose her. He took off her seat belt.

"Evan. You need to get up now. We're here."

She moaned and opened her eyes.

"There's only one way in though. I'm going to take you halfway to the fence, but you'll have to go the rest of the way on your own." He pulled a cellphone from the glovebox. "Here's the extra phone. My number is programmed into it. Call me when you're ready for me to meet you."

She nodded and he tucked the phone into her hoodie pocket.

"Okay." William lifted her out and cradled her against his chest. The heat of her body burned like he imagined it would feel to hug Mason in full Maelstrom form. He closed his eyes as she clung to him and he kissed the top of her head. "Come on, PITA."

He headed for the corner of the resort. Though he knew no cars were in the vicinity he looked both ways before crossing the road anyway. Evan's arms curled around his neck like a woolen scarf. Please let them help her. Please let her be okay.

He stopped behind a large palm and sucked in a deep breath. He looked around the tree and spotted the guards on duty. One headed down close to the entrance of the resort. Another moved right up to the gate on the road, turned and headed the other way. A third moved away from them down the center toward the fountain. This was it. If he was spotted, who knew what would happen.

"William." Evan's eyes fluttered open and closed. "Are we there?"

"Yeah. Just a few more feet." He wanted to say more. To kiss her and tell her that he cared about her. That he hoped they could fix her because he didn't know if he could live with himself if anything happened to her. Instead, he stepped out from behind the palm tree and walked down the sidewalk, the resort floodlight coming closer and closer to exposing him. His body tensed like being zapped by a live wire. Being back on the mountainside chased by slavers again, flashed through his mind. He finally reached the road leading into the compound and headed toward the gate.

"Stop," she croaked. "I can go from here."

He set her on her feet and she wobbled. Her glassy, blue gaze met his and she smiled at him. She reached up on her toes and kissed his cheek. She lingered for a minute, hugging him tight.

"Thank you, William."

Words failed him and he nodded. "I'm not leaving here till I talk to your leader."

"I'll call. You should go before the sun comes up." She

hobbled off down the entrance drive, her pace labored. She dragged her left leg like an anchor. She stumbled and he forced himself not to run and help her. As if knowing his thoughts she turned to look at him and shook her head.

She stopped a few feet further along and bent over to catch her breath.

"Come on, PITA. You can do it."

She continued on after a moment and then about thirty yards from the gate her leg buckled and she dropped. In her dark hoodie and pants, she blended into the asphalt almost completely. William lurched forward and then stopped himself.

"Get up," he whispered.

She lay on her side, motionless.

"Get up," he said louder.

Still she didn't move. The minutes dragged on. What if she'd gone unconscious? The guards at the gate were far enough from where she'd stumbled that it could be hours before they finally found her. William continued to wait until he could no longer take it. He had no choice; he'd brought her this far.

Quick as light William raced to her side and lifted her. "Sorry, babe, things aren't turning out like we hoped."

She didn't stir. He ran for the fence and shook her lightly. "Evan... Evan..." Still she didn't move. *Dammit!* He needed to do this to save everyone, her included. Spotting the nearest guard he yelled, "Hey! This girl's hurt!"

The guard turned and raised his gun while rushing forward. "Don't move!"

"She's hurt. She needs help." William advanced.

"I said don't move!"

"She's hurt, dammit! Her name is Evan. She needs help."

The guard shot at William. He spun out of the way and the bullet whizzed past his shoulder.

"Stop shooting, I'm only trying to help!" Another bullet whizzed by. Suddenly the sound of dogs and other guards came from all directions. If he stayed both he and Evan would end up dead. He laid her on the drive as the guards ran out from behind the gate. He kissed her forehead, his heart breaking for having to leave her there. *Please let the humans help her in time.* William moved a hair from her face and then stood and raced away from the resort. Gunfire rang out, and he prayed that they weren't shooting at Evan. He'd made it out to the main boulevard when the sounds of vehicles roaring to life and horns honking cut through the air behind him. He glanced back to see two military vehicles speeding up the drive.

He dashed across the street to his car and hopped in as the military vehicles rolled onto the road. William started the engine and threw the car in drive as the two assault vehicles barreled his direction. He turned on his lights and flipped his car around before gunning it. The back windshield shattered as bullets pelted the car. He sped toward the on ramp, the gas pedal pressed to the floorboard. The humans behind him continued to fire, and he had to duck in his seat to keep from being hit.

One of them gained ground and pulled alongside him. He was less than a half mile from the freeway. They smashed into his vehicle, sending him sailing sideways. He corrected and gunned the vehicle faster. If he could get to the highway they would turn back at some point. They slammed him again and his car swerved but he kept control. Bullets riddled the passenger side and the right side windows exploded in a shower of glass.

The sign for the freeway onramp flew past. He headed up

the overpass and banked left for the on ramp. He'd almost made it. He turned the wheel and hit the gas as the other car smashed into the rear of him sending him careening sideways. He crashed into a guardrail and the car teetered on it for a moment. William grabbed the handle of the door, preparing to jump. He got his door open just in time to see the second vehicle pound into his driver's side. The guardrail gave way and his car pitched sideways down the embankment to the ravine below. He tumbled over and over, his face smashing into the window and then the steering wheel.

He flew into the passenger seat and then tumbled into the dashboard before his head hit windshield with a crack and glass showered his face.

CHAPTER NINE

E van's eyes fluttered open and closed as someone ran with her down a long expansive hallway that smelled of soap and furniture polish. She jostled against strong arms, her leg screaming in pain.

"Bring her in here. Lay her on the table," called a man.

"William?" she croaked.

"Hang on, baby girl, I gotcha." *Not William.* "Uncle Lou?"

"You hang tight, girl." The running stopped and she was laid on a padded surface that crinkled when she moved.

"Check her for bite marks," her uncle said.

"Hey, sis, can you hear me?"

Evan turned her head and tried to focus on the tall blond that picked up her hand and squeezed it.

"Tommy?"

"I'm right here." He pushed the hair from her face. "What's wrong with her?"

"I don't know yet." A man in a lab coat approached her and pushed a stethoscope beneath her shirt. "Her heartbeat's too fast." He scanned her head with a thermometer. "And she's burning up."

"My leg," she said.

The men looked at each other and her eyelids fell shut. "Get her pants off."

Before she could protest, her sweats were yanked off and the tape on her leg peeled back.

"Knife wound," said the doctor. "Possible staph infection. I'm gonna need to clean it. Get a round of antibiotics. We should knock her out."

"No," she managed. Every part of her pressed down like the padding beneath her was quicksand sucking her down.

"Don't worry, baby girl. We're gonna fix you right up." Her Uncle Lou's lips brushed her forehead, and then the sting of a needle jabbed her arm and she lost hold of consciousness.

"Will..."

THE SCENT OF EGGS PULLED EVAN AWAKE. SHE LOOKED AROUND TO find herself in a nicely decorated hotel room. Her heart did a mixture of thundering and dropping at the same time. A stereo stood in the corner surrounded by several stacks of CDs. A black jewelry box sat slightly ajar on the metal desk next to a wardrobe where several scarves hung off the door. A television peeked out from inside it. The brown wood nightstand next to her held a bulbous white lamp, black alarm clock, and a small stack of worn books. Her room. The room she'd left over three years ago. Nothing had changed.

"Hey."

She turned to find her cousins Peter and Tommy sitting at the small table, eating. Peter's blond hair had been cut shorter, but Tommy's dark golden waves were almost down to his shoulders. They both sported their dad's deep brown eyes that punched her in the gut. The same eyes her dad used to have.

She sat up and propped herself against her pillows. "Hey yourselves."

Tommy smiled and both cousins came over. The familiar scent of hotel soap and shampoo wafted off them. She honestly had never thought she'd see them again. She held back tears as they pulled her close and wrapped her in their strong arms. After a minute they let go, all three sniffling but refusing to cry in front of the others.

"We thought you were dead, sis," said Peter.

"Or worse," said Tommy. "What happened?"

She swallowed hard and contemplated lying, but why bother? "The worst."

Peter got to his feet and ran his hands through his hair. He moved to the window and looked out. The older of her two cousins, he'd always considered himself her protector and big brother. Tommy had always been a younger and gentler soul. They'd called her sis since the first year they'd taken her in.

"I'm fine," she said. "I was never beaten or starved or treated too terribly—"

"But you were bitten." Peter turned back to her.

She couldn't deny it. They'd obviously seen the bite marks on her neck.

"Good thing Pop got us those inoculations. Don't know what I'd do if you came back like one of them." Peter's voice held the same kind of venom that she herself had spewed a million times over. But for some reason hearing it from someone else struck an eerie chord with her.

She tried to remember how she'd gotten to the enclave. "How long have I been here?"

"About two days," said Tommy. "You've been super sick

from that infected stab wound. But Dr. Nicholas fixed you up right good."

She threw the covers off to find her leg wrapped in fresh bandages. She ran her tongue over her teeth. She needed a shower and her teeth brushed as well as her hair. She stared at the shirt and remembered the feel of William carrying her toward the gate.

"Hey, did you guys see me show up?"

Peter and Tommy exchanged a look.

"Sorry," said Peter. "We were inside. Do you remember how you got here?"

A trickle of fear traced up her spine. She wasn't sure what they knew or what to say. "I don't. I'd been driving and was attacked and then..."

"So, you don't remember anything or anyone?"

"I remember walking up toward the gate and falling."

"Do you remember anyone helping you? Or hurting you?"

"I was stabbed by a vampyr."

"He stabbed you?" A dark expression came over Tommy's face.

"You know we should let you clean up," said Peter. "Then you can eat and we'll take you to talk to Pop. He's been such a mess since you disappeared. He's real happy you're back." He took her hand. "We're all happy you're back."

Her ribcage squeezed at the thought of her uncle, who'd been both father and mother to her over the last decade, being so worried about her.

"Your old clothes are still in the closet," said Tommy. "We didn't let 'em touch nothin'."

She gave a tight smile. "Thanks, guys." Peter picked up his and Tommy's plates and then nudged his brother for them to leave.

Tommy turned back at the door. "I'm really glad you're okay."

She pushed her hair behind her ear. "Me too."

"We'll see you in a bit," said Peter.

She nodded. The heavy metal door slammed shut and she blew out a breath. A strange uneasiness settled over her. Something about what Tommy had said scratched at her mind.

"He stabbed you?"

She'd never said the vampyr was a "he." A pit grew in her stomach but she shook it off. Of course they'd think the vampyr was a he, she'd told them she'd been attacked.

She threw the covers all the way off and stood slowly, testing her weight. Her leg held but shot pain down to her ankle. She looked around, a feeling of nostalgia washing over her. Though she'd dreamed about getting back to her room a million times, but she'd never actually believed it would happen. Now seeing all of her things still sitting in the same spots, waiting for her return, it all seemed unimportant.

She limped to her metal desk and ran her fingers over the objects. William's dark hoodie and sweats lay crumpled in a ball on the chair. She trailed her finger over them and lifted the hoodie, bringing it to her nose. Surprisingly his scent still clung to it. The sweet scent of his rich cologne mixed with his shampoo. The sadness the scent evoked troubled her. She looked out the window into the sunlight and wondered where he hid and if he was all right. Reaching inside the deep pocket, she found the phone he'd given her. She checked it but there were no messages. She should probably tell William she was all right. Knowing him, he'd worry— especially if it'd been two days. He might even think she was dead. The thought made her pause. If she didn't call, and he thought she had died, maybe he would go back to Chicago and forget about her and trying to get to talk to the boss.

But did she really want him to forget about her? After all he'd done for her it would be cruel to not help him as she'd promised. She went to the call log and dialed the last number on it. The phone rang a half dozen times and then went to voicemail.

"It's me. I just wanted you to know that I'm okay. I'll call later and see if you're awake... okay... bye." She stared at the phone and anxiety draped over her like a wool coat. In the entire time they'd been together for the trip she'd not seen William miss a phone call. Not once.

She shook her head. Why was she so concerned about William? It wasn't like they were friends or lovers or anything. He was her babysitter, that was all. Besides, he was most likely asleep at the early hour, nothing more.

She tossed his sweatshirt to the floor and returned to inspecting her desk. Locating a small black box which held a dozen different cords to various electronics, she found one that fit the phone and plugged it in, then set it on the desk and covered it with several magazines so no one would see it.

She stared at the magazines for a minute and then rearranged them and threw a scarf on top for good measure. She spotted a butterfly knife inlayed with mother of pearl and smiled despite herself. She lifted it and flicked it open. She twirled the blade around her hand and then around her fingers. Man, she'd missed her knife. She lifted various items on her desk until she located what she'd been searching for. She pulled the leather rolled case from under a pair of underwear and undid the leather strap. Inside lay six throwing knives that Tommy had given her for her eighteenth birthday. She pulled out one of them and turned. On the back of her door her target still hung. She aimed at the target and threw the knife. It zipped through the air and impaled the bullseye. Evan chuckled. She still had it.

She wanted to show William, but a gnawing grew in her stomach and she chewed her lip. Maybe she should try calling him again... Instead she hobbled to her closet and pulled out a blue T-shirt, a pair of jeans, and new underwear, then made her way into the bathroom. The clean, working, private shower made her sigh. Man she had missed having a bathroom all to herself.

EVAN SHUFFLED DOWN THE QUIET HALLWAY AND MADE HER WAY TO THE elevators. Nervousness coursed through her dulling the ache in her leg. It'd been years since she'd been back, and she wasn't sure what to expect.

The elevator opened and she hopped in. She hit the lobby button and ran her hand over her thigh and leaned back against the wall. Already she wanted to sit down and rest it. The doors inched closed when a hand shot between them making her jump.

They bounced back open and a tall, handsome guy in a tight green T-shirt and jeans stepped in and smiled.

"Hey."

Evan swallowed and nodded in his direction. He stared straight ahead, but Evan couldn't help but glance over. He wore a couple days' worth of stubble, and his jet black long hair had been slicked back like a surfer cut. His golden-tan skin made his bulky muscles appear even bigger beneath his shirt.

The elevator pulled them down toward the lobby.

"Are you new here?" he asked. "I've never seen you before."

"My name's Evan."

His eyes widened. "Tommy and Peter's sister?"

She gave him a tight-lipped smile. "Guilty. Cousin actually, but yeah, we were raised together."

"Wow!" He stuck out his hand. "I'm Joe."

She took his calloused, firm grip in her own. His rough palm scratched her softer one and shot a tingle through her belly. His touch felt different from William's. She jerked her hand away at the thought.

The doors opened and she stepped out. Why the hell had William come into her mind just because she'd shaken hands with Joe?

She glanced around the enormous lobby, and her stomach growled at the smell of food.

"I'm going to get something to eat. You want to come with?" Joe asked.

"Uh... Thanks," she said. "But I should probably go find my uncle first."

He nodded. "Lou should be in the executive offices down in the basement."

Evan stared at him for a minute. "The executive offices?"

Joe nodded. "Yeah, do you need me to show you where they are?"

"No. I remember." Her mind reeled with questions. "So, my uncle..."

"He's the leader now."

The news made her head swim. "What happened to Norman?"

"Went out on a raid, never came back. Like you." He gave her a sad smile.

Lou was in charge. The idea sent her gut plummeting to her toes. She loved her uncle; her adoptive father, but he wasn't an easy man, and his rules weren't meant to be broken. And his number one rule was no associating with the enemy. Which meant William.

"You know what? I think maybe I will eat first."

Joe smiled. "Well, let's go."

Evan walked with Joe as he pointed new things out to her. In the lobby, where before there had been huge planters of various ornamental plants, there were gardens. The skylights above let in ample light and the scent of vegetation permeated everything in the lobby. People tended to the garden as well as cleaned floors, or talked, or sat and read as if they didn't have a care in the world.

In the center of it all, the check-in desk had been turned into a security command. Three guards sat at the counter talking and lounging while behind them over a dozen computer screens showed every inch of the property. She wondered if they had seen her when she'd approached the gate.

"How long have the gardens been inside?" she asked.

"About two years. It gets so hot in the summer that they decided to try growing stuff inside as well as outside. All the tennis courts were turned into green houses and housing for the animals."

"Animals?"

They walked toward the hotel restaurant. People looked up at her as they passed. Some waved, others smiled, but even more of them just stared. She didn't recognize a single one of them.

"We have a couple hundred chickens. So eggs are good. We have about a dozen pigs, a herd of goats and sheep. We currently have a decent grape production growing in one of the greenhouses. Citrus trees are producing. There are still all the orchards down in the old Orange County region south of Los

Angeles. We go down there and raid everything we can carry a couple times a year. There are some apple orchards up north near Bakersfield, so we go there as well. Everything is brought back and eaten, canned, or dried. All together they keep us fed, but we have to be careful. Everyone is given chips for the week."

"Chips?"

He pulled out a chain necklace from under his shirt. On the chain hung what looked like a dozen small coins.

"Ration chips. Three per day. And you can only turn in three per day. But if you have up to three chips left at the end of the week you can turn them into the commissary for canned goods or anything that's in there."

"Things sure are different." She looked over her shoulder at the guards near the entrance. All three of them stared at her and whispered to each other. She turned back quickly, avoiding their stares. She'd been one of the first groups to help settle the enclave and yet she felt more like an outsider than ever.

He nodded. "It works better now that we have close to a thousand people. Your uncle has really helped streamline and keep the problems to a minimum."

"A thousand people?" When she'd left they'd had a little over a hundred. "Where are they all?"

They entered the restaurant and headed to the long, buffet-style counter. Joe grabbed a tray for her and one for himself as well.

"Most are out working the farm. We all have a job and take shifts. Weeding, planting, feeding the animals, collecting, you name it. We have about sixty who clean and then about a hundred guards and a hundred out on raids at any given time."

"Wow." She shook her head.

He chuckled. "You keep saying that."

"Yeah, well when I left we had hardly any of this." She laid her tray down on the buffet counter. From a basket of apples and oranges she grabbed an apple. She took two hard boiled eggs along with a couple pieces of bread, and a bowl of what looked like oatmeal. Lastly, she grabbed a packet of sugar and a glass of water. Joe grabbed about everything she did and then they slid their trays to the end of the row where a cashier sat reading a book. He glanced over their food.

"You can only have one egg and two bread or two eggs and one bread." He pointed to her tray.

"Come on," said Joe. "She just got here."

The guy shrugged. "Sorry. You know the rules, Joe."

"Fine." Joe pulled a chain off his neck and unhooked it. "Here, take three chips for today then."

"No," said Evan. "You won't get anything more to eat till tomorrow."

He winked. "Trust me, I've had it worse."

The cashier stared at them. "Fine with me."

Joe went to hand him the three chips.

"No." Evan slapped his hand away and glared at the cashier. "He's not spending a whole chip for one egg. I've been here three days and this is my first meal, as far as I'm concerned, I'm paid up." She grabbed her tray and started to walk around the cashier.

He jumped from his seat and blocked her way. He stood a couple inches taller but not too heavy. Evan could take him easy.

"No chip. No food," he said.

"You better get out of my way."

He reached for her and memories of the vampyr attack flooded her. She tossed her tray onto the buffet, grabbed his arm in a flash, and twisted it behind him, moving so fast that even Joe backed up. She slammed the cashier's face into his chair.

"Don't. Touch. Me."

"Hey! Evan!" Tommy ran over and stood behind her. "Hey. What's going on?"

"He tried to put his hands on me." She wrenched the guy's arm higher on his back, and he groaned into his plastic seat.

"She took an extra egg," the guy mumbled.

"Okay. Okay. Easy. Evan, let Chuck go." Evan towered over Chuck for a minute more and then released him. The guy sucked in a deep breath, and Evan stepped away from him.

Chuck got to his feet, his face beet red and fire flying from his eyes. "She assaulted me. I want to file a complaint."

"That won't be necessary." Tommy's voice came out calm and diplomatic. "Evan's new and doesn't know all the rules."

She glared at Tommy. "Where is the rule that he can try to accost me for taking an egg?"

"Okay. Let's all calm down." Tommy, ever the peacemaker.

"I want to file a complaint," said Chuck. "She almost broke my arm."

"Trust me, if I'd wanted to break your arm I would have."

Tommy blew out a heavy breath and shrugged. "If you want to file a complaint, you can go to my dad and tell him what my sister did. I won't stop you."

Chuck's anger flew away from him faster than a bird from a cat. "Your sister?"

Tommy threw his arm over Evan's shoulders and kissed her hair. "She was captured by slavers a few years ago. She just got back."

Chuck blanched and his shoulders slumped. "Man... I'm sorry."

Evan picked up her tray and put everything back on it. Joe gave her a weak, embarrassed smile.

"Here." Tommy put a chip on the counter. "That's for her food." Chuck nodded but didn't say anything.

Evan headed to the far end of the restaurant and sat at a corner booth overlooking the entrance of the hotel. She dropped her tray to the table and took several deep breaths. What was wrong with her?

"Uh... I got you a spoon." Joe held a spoon and napkin out to her.

She took them and sat them on her tray. "Thanks."

Tommy walked up peeling an orange. "Scoot."

She moved over and both he and Joe sat down. She stirred the sugar into her soupy grain mix, realizing it wasn't in fact oatmeal.

"What is this stuff?" she asked, lifting some and letting it drop back into the bowl.

"I think that's quinoa," said Joe.

"What the heck is quinoa?"

"A grain," said Tommy. "We went up to Utah and found a ton of old warehouses outside of Salt Lake full of bags and bags of wheat, oats, and other grains. We learned how to sprout and grow some stuff out on the golf course."

She chuckled. "You're serious?"

"Yup."

She shook her head. She couldn't imagine Tommy out in the fields tilling the ground and stuff.

"So what are you up to today?" Tommy asked Joe.

"I'm helping maintain the moat for a few hours and then I'm on guard tonight till midnight." He peeled his egg and then popped it in his mouth.

Evan ate her grain cereal and wished she'd added more sugar.

"Pop wants to see you," Tommy said.

Evan nodded. He'd want to debrief her as soon as possible most likely. But she wasn't looking forward to it. Not now knowing that he had been put in charge of the enclave.

"What will my job be around here?" she asked. "I'm sure Pop has something in mind already."

"He wants you to take it easy for a couple days, and then I think he has something special planned."

She snorted. "The last time Lou said he had something 'special' for us, we ended up taking military training classes, shooting practice, and tae kwon-do."

Tommy snorted. "Hopefully be easier. But no promises."

She looked over at her cousin and her heart warmed. She and Tommy had always been close. With him being only a few months older than herself they'd been more like twins than cousins. People had even mistaken them for twins growing up.

Until that moment she hadn't realized just how much she'd missed him. Her chest tightened and she rested her head on his shoulder for a minute.

"It's good to have you home," said Tommy.

Home... she wasn't quite sure that word applied to the enclave anymore. Only time would tell.

CHAPTER TEN

E van said goodbye to Joe and followed Tommy down to the basement of the hotel where the offices as well as tons of storage areas were housed. The smell of water and cleaning products permeated the cement hallway. They passed a large room that appeared to be a type of root cellar full of jars of vegetables and fruits as well as other food items. A woman wearing a housekeeping uniform pushed a cart out of the next room full of paper goods and cleaning supplies. She couldn't imagine how many places they'd raided to obtain that many supplies.

The housekeeper smiled at them. Evan nodded and they continued past. They turned a corner into a nicer carpeted hallway. Tommy stopped at a large wooden door and knocked before opening it.

Lou sat behind a modest wooden desk in a nice leather chair. The moderately sized office had been decorated with functional items only. Lou never had been one for frills or excess.

"Evan." He stood from his chair, his heavy frame dwarfing his desk, and moved toward her. He took her in his beefy arms and pulled her against his chest in a bear hug. He held her for several minutes, and she was transported back to right after her parents' deaths when he'd shown up at her house, whisked her into his truck with her cousins and taken off. She'd never been so happy to see someone in her life up to that point.

Finally, he let go, sniffled twice and swiped at his eyes. "It's good to see you, baby girl."

Evan swallowed the lump in her throat. "You too, Pop."

He motioned for her to sit. She picked one of the tan upholstered chairs and sat on it, careful of her leg. She rubbed her thigh gently, massaging the muscles.

They stared at each other for a minute across the desk piled high with forms, papers and photos. The old computer in the corner beeped and chirped. Three monitors behind him rotated various views of security cameras around the hotel.

"How long have you been in charge?" she asked.

"About a year and a half. Norman disappeared on a raiding trip to New Mexico."

"Why did he go?"

Lou shook his head. "We'd lost a lot of people up to that point. Supplies ran low. He insisted on going himself. You know how he was."

She nodded.

"You want to tell me what happened?" asked Lou.

Evan looked down at her hands. "Did anyone from my raid group make it back?"

"No."

She swallowed hard. "That means four are dead."

"That many?" Her uncle's face held anger.

"We'd gone out toward Vegas. Rick wanted to get as close as possible to raid. He decided on Henderson."

"He wasn't supposed to go out there," said Tommy.

"We argued about that, but he wouldn't listen. We got there and headed into a subdivision. It seemed deserted but it wasn't. We cut it too close to sundown. The Vampires descended before we could get away. Rick and Fiona went down first. Drained dry. Josh, Sarah, John, Gordon, and I were cornered. The Vampires argued about whether to call the slavers or drain us. Josh and Sarah made a break for it. They got to the truck. I thought they got away. Apparently not. The rest of us were tied up and sold at the slave auctions."

"And you ended up as a slave?" asked Lou.

Goosebumps piled up on her skin and memories bombarded her. *A large wooden bed, the scent of spicy aftershave, the sound of her name on his lips.*

"Evan?"

Her head snapped up. "What?"

Lou's face softened. "Nothing. It doesn't matter. You're home now. Can you tell me how you got here though?"

Damn. What did she say? Closest to the truth would be best, she assumed.

"I bounced around from house to house in the Chicago area trying to fulfill the mission Pop gave us, in case we ever got captured- get the other slaves to rise up or run. I escaped a week ago when they went to transfer me again. I drove till I got almost here, and then I was attacked and stabbed by some slavers. After that it gets a bit fuzzy." Leaving William out of the equation was best for now, she decided. At least until she got a hold of him.

"So, you don't remember arriving here?"

"Vaguely. I remember walking toward the gate. And you carrying me... And a doctor."

"What about the guy that brought you in?" asked Tommy.

She swallowed hard. So, they had seen William. A trickle of fear skated down her spine and the desire to run back to her room and call him again almost had her lurch from her chair. "Just... tallish and maybe... dark hair?"

Her uncle studied her. "You didn't know him?"

She really wished she'd thought things through better and even talked to William about what to say. But the state she'd been in when he'd dropped her off hadn't lent itself to much conversation. She remembered the look in his eyes as he'd carried her to the gate and set her on her feet. The desire that flooded his features when she'd kissed his cheek. How in that fleeting moment she'd almost told him she didn't want him to go. She'd almost asked him to stay with her. To tell him she was scared.

She massaged her temple, pushing away the memories of being in his strong cool arms. "I don't really remember, sorry. Was he a member of the enclave?"

"No." Lou studied her and she fought the urge to fidget while holding his gaze.

She needed to change the subject. "Tommy said you had something special for me to do."

"You should wait a couple days. Get readjusted," said Lou.

"I don't know that I could sit around not doing anything." Though going back to bed was exactly what she wanted, if she didn't act normal they'd know something was amiss.

Lou chewed the inside of his cheek. "I heard there was a problem in the restaurant."

"Nothing I couldn't handle," she said. "Look, there's no need to readjust me. I'm fine. I want to get to work. If you need me to go out there and get supplies or try to find more humans—"

Lou held up his hand. "That's not really what we're trying to do here anymore."

"It isn't?"

He looked between her and Tommy and then smiled. "I think maybe I should show you. You of all people will understand, I'm sure."

"Pop, maybe we should wait. She's been through a lot," Tommy offered.

Lou gave him a hard stare and Tommy shut his mouth. "Your sister is tougher than you'll ever be."

Evan had to bite the inside of her cheek to keep from coming to Tommy's defense. It would only shame him further.

Lou turned his gaze to her. "Come see what we've been up to."

LOU AND EVAN WALKED DOWN THE HALLWAY AND TURNED A CORNER to the adjoining corridor. Tommy walked behind them, hands in his pockets, eyes on the floor.

A barred door stood in the middle of the hallway, new and out of place. On either side of it waited an armed guard.

"What is this?" she asked.

"You'll see." Lou motioned her forward.

The guard nodded to them.

"This is my daughter, Evan," said Lou. "She is to be given access to every part of this facility."

The guard stepped aside and held out his hand to her as she passed.

"Nice to meet you. I'm Seth."

Evan shook his hand but said nothing. He wasn't much

taller than she was, but almost twice as wide with muscles bulging in every direction. Seth unlocked the door and they stepped into hallway exactly the same as the one before. Cream walls, beige carpet, twenty or so doors.

Lou led her past several rooms and then stopped. "This is where we keep the prisoners."

"Prisoners? Like, enclave members who don't follow the rules?" They'd never had prisoners before.

"No." Lou unlocked the door and pushed it open. The smell of urine and blood tickled Evan's nose. Inside the carpeting had been ripped out revealing bare cement. On the far side, a small window with bars shed light on the dark space. The faded paint on the walls peeled, revealing more dulling gray cement, and a single dead light bulb hung from the ceiling. In the corner, shackled to the wall, a man curled into a ball. His clothes and beard denoted that he'd been there for months. Possibly longer.

He turned his head, revealing bright blue eyes and pale skin. *A vampyr.*

Her skin crawled as if a million ants danced on her arms. "I don't understand." She backed out of the room.

"We've been working on something for a while now. A vaccine." Lou closed the door and then continued down the hallway.

"Like the one I was given?"

"No. This one is different. It's a vaccine for the vamps."

"The vamps?" She didn't understand.

Her uncle turned and his eyes held sadness. "If we can cure the vamps, they'll be human again."

Like Lou's wife, her aunt Candice. If the vamps became human again, they'd be able to outnumber the Vampires. It made sense. Why try to free several thousand slaves when you could free millions?

"What do you need from me?" she asked.

"I need you to get information." Lou continued down the hall to the last door on the left.

"What kind of information?"

He unlocked the door and opened it. "I want you to find out who this one really is and what he's doing here. Peter has been questioning him, but I don't believe why he said he's here."

Evan stepped into a room exact the same as the other. In the corner lay a man coiled into a ball away from the sunlight.

The hairs on her neck stood on end.

The man wore a dirty and ripped blue dress shirt and black slacks. Her heart sank to her toes. *William.*

"What did he say?" Her voice barely came out above a whisper.

"He said he was trying to save your life."

Her throat dried like the Palm Springs sands. And she fought every reflex in her body that screamed for her to run in and check on him.

"I FIGURED IF ANYONE COULD GET INFORMATION OUT OF HIM, IT'D BE you. Since you're the one he carried to the gate before he ran," said the man in the doorway.

William stared at the wall and breathed in as deep as his broken ribs would allow. Evan's scent floated over to him, and he resisted the urge to look at her though every fiber of him wanted too. For the last days, he'd only wanted to know that she'd lived.

"Well, why don't you give me a few minutes to see what I can find out?" she said.

"Tommy will stand outside the room. I have some things to attend to. Knock when you're done. And here. Take this in case he gets any stupid ideas," said the man.

"Will do." Her voice came out choked with strain.

There was some shuffling, and then the door closed. He waited, staring at the wall. After several seconds, footsteps rushed closer.

"William?" Her hand fell on his shoulder, and he turned over. She blanched looking at him. "Dammit. What are you doing here? I need to get you out of here." Her words came out so fast he was barely able to track them.

He sat up and leaned against the wall. Parts of him hurt that he'd never known could. "They ran me off the road. Some of the injuries came from the car rolling down the ravine and me not having on a seatbelt."

She licked her lips and reached toward him, turning his head to the side. Her soft fingertips brushed the hair from his eyes. "That's a pretty bad gash."

"It was down to the bone yesterday. It's getting better."

"I thought you'd be healed by now," she said.

"Not without blood." He searched her face. "You look a ton better."

"Thanks to you. I owe you my life."

He shrugged, sending a pain through his neck.

She cupped his cheek with her palm. "I'm going to figure out how to get you out of here. This isn't right."

She stood to go, but he grabbed her hand. "You can't."

"Why not?" Anger burned in her gaze.

"I've learned a few things since I've been in here. One, they are working on something big."

"A vaccine for vamps. It's not our problem. Right now, my biggest problem is you getting beaten for saving my life. I'm gonna kill my cousin."

"Stop." He pulled her back down to the floor. "You know there's another reason I came with you. If they have nukes... We may need them to use against the demons."

She sucked in a deep breath. "You came for weapons that you say are for use against demons but in actuality you could try to use against us."

"Us? You, them, me. We're all us now. With demons attacking, we need to band together. How can you not see that?"

She sat silent.

"I tried to tell the guy who came in with you. I tried to explain about the demons, but he didn't want to hear it."

"My uncle Lou."

"Your uncle?"

"He raised me after my parents died. He's in charge now."

William chuckled. "Well that explains why he wouldn't listen to me. He's like you."

She gave him a sarcastic smile. "Ha-ha. Very funny."

"I don't want to be beaten and chained up in here, but I came to do a job and you pushing me out just as I got here defeats the purpose. If there are big weapons being kept here, we need them."

"Man, you're a masochist."

"Not normally."

She hung her head in her hands for a minute before shaking it and looking at him again. "Don't Vampires have their own bombs?"

"Not that I know of. We have some weapons but nothing big enough to blow up an entire continent."

She looked over him for a moment. She touched his cheek

and her eyes softened in a way he'd never seen before. She looked at him, not with pity, but with genuine affection. She ran her fingers through his hair, pushing it from his face and in that moment he wanted to kiss her more than he'd ever wanted anything before.

"What do you want me to do?" she finally asked.

"I came with a vial. Mason gave it to me. It contains his blood. They took it. If they experiment on it, they'll see that it isn't Vampire or human or anything else. Then they'll have to believe me."

"I'll see what I can find out." She searched his face. His eyes were sunken in, and purple bags painted his lower lids. "Have they fed you at all?"

He shook his head. "I'm okay right now. But in a few days..."

"What'll happen?"

"I've been hungry before, starving even, but not as a vampyr. I don't know what will happen."

"I'll see if I can find you something."

She looked at him for another minute and then stood. "They want me to get information out of you."

He nodded. "They've been doing that for days. I've told them everything I can."

She chewed her lip. This wasn't right. How could they profess to be better than the Vampires if they treated Vampires worse than the Vampires treated humans?

"I won't hurt you," she whispered.

"I'll understand if you do."

She blew out a harsh breath. "Why are you like that? So understanding? You should be snarling and yelling and telling me how horrible we are. Hell, you should be trying to kill me."

He shrugged. "It's not who I am. It's not who most of us are. I can assume I'm not the only one of my kind here. Ask your uncle how many have been killed here, beaten and tortured. And then ask him how many fought back, tried to kill anyone or actually acted like the monsters you think we are. I'm not saying there aren't those out there that are monsters. I'm simply saying humans aren't all that much better than Vampires. Trust me. I know firsthand."

She'd never really thought of William as anything but a vampyr before, but he'd been human for decades and only a vampyr for less than a year. She wondered what he'd been like before. A dozen questions popped into her mind. She wanted to comfort him. To take him to her room and clean him up and get him into some fresh clothes. To do for him what he'd done for her; to save his life.

A rap sounded on the door.

"I'll see if I can find you some food," she said. "And I'll try to get a handle on what's going on here. It wasn't like this when I left, but then, my uncle wasn't in charge back then either."

William nodded and then leaned back against the cement wall. "I'll be here."

She turned; the urge to hug and thank him almost overwhelmed her.

This wasn't right. It wasn't who they were. She had to find out what the hell was going on.

WILLIAM WAITED TILL EVAN LEFT BEFORE SHIFTING HIS WEIGHT. THE broken ribs hadn't healed yet, neither had the broken collarbone. He held his breath and moved to lie down. A moan escaped his throat, and he tried to reach some level of minor comfort on his left side. He hadn't wanted her to see him in pain. Hadn't wanted her to see his weakness. But if things continued the way they had for the last two days, it wouldn't matter what he wanted her to see, she'd witness all of his humiliation.

The car wreck had left him dazed and with the gash to his head, the rest had been done upon his arrival. Dragged, kicked, punched, chained, and left in the cell, William had spent two days trying to formulate a plan on how to convince the humans that he needed their help. Now with Evan on the mend and her uncle being the one in charge, hope lit inside him at a decent outcome. He just had to last that long.

His thirst wasn't killing him, but agitation had taken up residence inside him like a swarm of bees buzzing in his head. Like an itch he couldn't scratch that became more persistent the longer it went on. Only the itch wasn't in one small part of him. It crawled up his throat that tightened with each passing hour. His fangs that throbbed. His tongue that clung to his dry cheek like Velcro. His limbs that fell weakly at his side, and his legs that had a slight tremor when he tried to stand. He remembered what Danika had looked like the first time he'd seen her in the slave market. Eyes deep with shadows and sunken in. Skin so pale it was almost translucent. The heavy way in which she'd moved as if every step cost her. He wondered if that was what it would be like for him if he starved too long. Or if it would be different since he was only a vampyr. Would he turn into a raving lunatic that only craved blood, like the rogues?

All he could only hope. Hope that Danika would realize something was wrong since he hadn't called her in days. Hope that Evan would be able to talk some sense into her uncle. Hope that it wasn't already too late and that the demons hadn't come through the portal and ripped Chicago to pieces.

The world had ended once already. He wasn't willing to see it happen again. He had to hang on. Had to stay strong. Had to succeed.

CHAPTER ELEVEN

"How did it go?" asked Tommy.

Evan glanced around. She couldn't see Lou and the guards were out of earshot.

She grabbed Tommy by the arm and started moving down the hall with him. "What the hell is going on? Why do we have Vampires locked up and being starved in cells like animals?" She tried to keep her disgust in check, but it wasn't easy.

"Because they are animals. They eat humans. Prey on the weak and innocent." His face held confusion.

"And what is this?" she asked. "What do you consider us doing this to them?"

He stopped and stared at her as if he didn't know her. "How can you of all people not understand? After what you've been through. What they did to you."

"I know exactly what I've been through. I've lived it. But for all of it they never once tied me up, beat me, and starved me."

Emotions stormed over his face leaving him peering at her in a state of confusion.

"I need to talk to Lou." Tommy wouldn't be able to do anything. Lou was in charge.

He nodded. "I think you should. He wanted me to take you up to the lab anyway."

Tommy was a good guy deep down, always had been. Growing up they'd been best of friends. But Tommy never had once defied his dad. He wasn't a leader, a thinker, he was a follower. Which was why she'd always been able to get him into trouble when they were kids.

They passed Seth with a nod. Evan's conscience tore at her like being mauled from the inside out. How could Lou do these things? The man she'd grown up with had been hard, not cruel. She wasn't an idiot. She hadn't been blind to the fact that William had barely moved. He hadn't gotten to his feet, or gestured with his hands or anything. When he'd grabbed her hand to stop her, she'd felt the shake of his touch. She knew pain, and he was in pain. Broken arm maybe, or ribs, maybe both.

They reached the elevator without a word and stepped inside. Tommy produced a card key from his pocket and slipped it into the slot that gave them access to the top floor. The doors shut and she was grateful there wasn't any fake soothing music. She wanted to say something to Tommy to smooth things over with him, but she needed him to think about her words. Think about what they were doing.

The doors opened and she blinked several times as she stepped out of the elevator. She caught her jaw before it fell open. The entire floor had been remodeled. The doors and most of the walls had been removed. Instead of thirty partitioned hotel rooms, there appeared to be only a dozen smaller ones.

All with glass walls separating them. The floor had been stripped of carpet revealing the cement. Inside the glass front rooms sat several people. They stopped and stared at her as she stepped off the elevator. Seven men and five women. Each had their own room except for the last which held two women almost identical in appearance except that the taller of the two wore her white hair shaved on the sides and long on the top, while the smaller of the two allowed her hair to grow down past her shoulders.

Tommy looked over at the enclosures. For a moment his eyes locked with the smaller twin and she gave him a small smile. He smiled back and then looked around quickly and finally to Evan.

"Who are they?" she asked. "I don't remember them."

"They are the Hybrids."

"Hybrids?"

Tommy continued further into the lab. Evan looked over her shoulder at the Hybrids and then continued on.

Lab equipment covered every surface. Computers and machines, exam tables and test tubes. The buzz of electricity pulsed in her ears. How in the world had they gotten all this stuff? Where had it come from? A half dozen people in white lab coats moved around the enormous space.

"There he is." Tommy pointed to a corner office and headed for it.

Evan followed close behind. They reached the office and Evan found a dark-haired, pale-skinned man sitting behind an immaculate desk speaking to Lou. She swallowed hard as the man's dark ebony eyes connected with hers. *A Vampire.*

Lou turned and waved them in. Both men stood as Tommy pushed into the office.

"Ah, good. Any progress?" Lou looked between them.

"I think we should talk about that later, Pop," said Tommy.

Lou's gaze flickered to Evan and then nodded. "Evan, I want you to meet Nicholas. He's the one who's been working on a cure for the vamps."

Nicholas moved around the desk gracefully and held out his hand. Evan shook it, and he gave her a welcoming smile that struck her as somewhat familiar.

"It's a pleasure to meet you, my dear. I've heard much about you."

She nodded and then shoved her hands in her pockets. "Are you the one who fixed up my leg?"

"Unfortunately, I'm not much of a doctor, so you'll probably have a nasty scar. Sorry about that."

"No need to apologize," said Lou. "If it wasn't for you, she'd be dead."

"Is this where you're trying to find a cure for the vamps?" she asked, trying to keep her voice even.

"Let me show you around," Nicholas offered.

The group walked out of the office to the lab. Evan's leg twinged and she rubbed at it with her palm.

"The vamps' DNA was mutated by a virus," Nicholas explained. "A virus meant for Vampires. We believe that if we can adjust the virus it will be able to bring vamps back from a mutated state."

"But how can you do that?" she asked. "Do you know anything about the original virus?"

Nicholas' gaze flicked to her uncle for a moment and then he cleared his throat and stepped up to a computer and tapped on the keyboard.

A chill ran through Evan and she got the distinct impression that Nicholas was intimately familiar with the original virus. Maybe he'd even been the one to create it.

An image popped up on the large monitor in front of her.

"This is vamp blood." He pointed to the screen. "See how there are these black cells and then there are also the red blood cells?"

Even looked on with interest. "Yup."

"The black are the vamp cells, the red are the human cells." He tapped on the keyboard again. A picture appeared of blood cells, only all of them were white. "This is Vampire blood. All white. No black, mutated cells at all. Now if we can get a new virus, a stronger virus, into a vamp's body, we are hoping to turn vamp cells on themselves." A video appeared.

A rush of grayish cells merged in with the black and red cells. The gray cells attached to the black cells and the black cells in turn began attacking each other. Soon all of the black cells turned gray and then shrunk.

"So the new cells make the black cells kill each other off, but then what?" she asked. "The cells are still in there."

"Then we have a full blood transfusion and hopefully wash all the dead cells out," said Lou.

"Have you tried it yet?" she asked.

"Oh yes," said Nicholas. "Dozens of times."

"Has it worked?"

"Not yet. But we're almost there," said Lou.

"And what do the vampyr in the basement have to do with this?" she asked.

"We need their blood, and we need to try different serums on them as well," said Lou.

"But the cure is for vamps, not vampyr."

"True, but we take what we can get for now. Right now, we have three Vampires and two vampyr here. Sometimes we have ten or more vamps. It depends on what we are able to get. But since the vamps were mutated by a virus meant for Vampires technically the cure should work on vampyr as well. They used to be human as well at one time."

Her stomach churned. They were going to use William as a guinea pig. She stared at the doctor. "You're a Vampire. How can you do that to your own kind?"

He shrugged. "You're a human. Humans have created wars, genocide, starvation, homelessness. How did you do that to your own kind? The V2000 virus wiped all that out, and my people are the ones who have kept it at bay. We all have our faults. The one thing I've learned in my considerable number of years on Earth is that none of us is better than the other."

"Exactly. If we're equals then Vampires and vampyr aren't just animals and they don't deserve to be tested on like lab rats."

"Evan, do you even grasp what we are trying to do here? We're trying to right the wrong that's been done," said Lou.

"But at what cost? What level do we have to stoop to?"

"Evan—"

"Have you looked around? This enclave is lucky to have what we have, but most don't. Most still live in squalor. Do you know how many humans are still out there in the woods, scraping to survive? We should be looking for them, bringing them here, helping them as well as doing this."

"Don't lecture me on what's going on in the world. I know all too well what the humans are suffering."

Evan swallowed, remembering William's words. "You have no clue what's going on out there. There are things, new things and they're coming. It's already started in Chicago and if we don't help the Vampires every last one of us is dead."

Lou's expression hardened. "You know, I think this is too much too soon. You should go lie down. Some rest will do you good. We wouldn't want you to have any lasting damage to that leg."

Evan clenched her jaw at the look Lou shot her that told her there would be no more discussion. She looked to Tommy for support but he wouldn't meet her eye. Nicholas gave her a gentle smile and then turned back to his lab equipment.

Evan spun on her heal and headed for the exit. She couldn't get out fast enough. Experimenting on vampyr. She may have no love for them, but one thing she did know, they weren't all bad and they didn't deserve to be treated lower than common house pets. And Lou...

She didn't even know him anymore. There would be no convincing him to help. She'd just have to figure out how to do it herself. She glanced once more at the glass rooms as she pushed the button for the elevator. The girl with the shaved hair stared at her through the glass. A strange sensation rushed over Evan and suddenly a voice sounded in her head.

"Help us."

WILLIAM COUGHED AND GRABBED HIS SIDE. THE MOON HUNG HIGH IN the sky allowing him the opportunity to get up and move around without worry of being burned, as well as use the pot in the corner.

He stretched his painful muscles and shook out his legs, wishing for the backseat of his SUV to lie down on.

The door to the cell opened and in walked the tall blond he recognized as a bystander from his previous beatings. The blond closed the door and leaned on it heavily, spending several minutes watching William.

"Was there something you wanted to know?" William finally asked. "Or did you come to beat me like the other one?"

"My brother, Peter, has always been one to use his fists first."

William looked the younger guy up and down. His posture remained relaxed and not hostile.

"Aren't you afraid of me?"

"Should I be? You're chained and in a heavily armed prison area."

"Plus, I've not fought back once."

"That too."

The conversation waned but William caught a glimmer of hope in the fact that the man wanted nothing from him. Maybe... maybe this was where he started. If he could make this one understand...

"I'm William. And you are..."

"Tommy. Peter and Evan's brother."

"Evan's brother?"

A strange expression crossed Peter's face. "Do you know her?"

Damn. William swallowed a barren lump in his throat. "I met her yesterday."

"Uh—huh." Tommy stared at him again. "You seemed surprised when I said she was my sister."

He needed to change the subject. He couldn't afford to get Evan in trouble.

"So, if you aren't here to beat me, is there something I can do for you?"

"I've just been wondering why you helped my sister? Why you risked yourself to bring her here? You had to know there was a large chance you'd be caught."

William tried to find an answer that would stop Tommy's line of questions. "She was hurt and in trouble."

Tommy shrugged. "But you could have taken her to a Vampire hospital."

"She asked me not to."

Tommy's brow furrowed. "Really?"

William backpedaled quickly. "When I found her, she was delirious. I was headed this direction anyway, and figured it would be better if I brought her where she asked to go. If I took her to a Vampire hospital, I'd feel responsible for her. I'd have to explain where I found her and where she came from, and I figured if she were out on her own like that, she was probably running from someone and for good reason."

"You don't believe in human slaves then?"

"The area I'm from no longer allows human slaves. They've been freed."

"Really?"

The door had been opened. This may be the opportunity William had waited for. "This facility is rather large and advanced."

"One of the biggest."

"So, there are others?"

"Dozens that we've found."

"And they are all as big and well-armed as this one?"

Tommy straightened suddenly and reached for the door. "I've said too much."

"Wait." William reached out but then his hand fell into his lap.

Tommy stopped.

"Do you think I could get something to drink?"

Tommy shook his head. "Sorry. I'm not allowed."

William nodded and it was suddenly as if his entire body

had lost all moisture. His sight locked on to Tommy's neck. Tommy had to be at least six foot one and two hundred pounds of muscle. Plenty of blood pumping through his veins. Surely, he wouldn't miss a pint or two.

William turned his head away and ground his teeth together until his fangs dug craters into his lower lip. Tommy's heartbeat sounded in his ears like hoofbeats against his brain. His throat burned and his stomach growled.

No. He couldn't do that. Evan's face floated into his mind. To hurt Tommy would be to hurt Evan.

William lay back on the floor and rolled toward the wall. "Thank you anyway."

"Hey." Tommy stood outside Evan's room.

They stared at each other for a minute before she opened the door wider and let him in. She stomped back to her bed and threw herself down on it, picking at the edge of a pillow, her anger still swirling inside like a vortex. It'd been almost twenty four hours since Tommy had shown her to the lab and neither Lou nor Tommy nor even Peter had come to see her in that time. Her meals had been brought up by guards and that had been it.

"I'm sorry coming back is upsetting," he said finally.

She exploded. "How can he do this? How can this possibly be okay? What the hell happened here?" she asked. "When Norman was in charge we were missioned with finding other survivors and bringing them to safety. Helping them. Now we're what? On a mission to destroy Vampires?"

Tommy blew out a breath and sat heavily on her bed.

"Things have changed, sis. Lots of things." He looked up at her with his big doe eyes and the faithful soldier façade cracked.

The anger whooshed out of her and she sat next to him. "What happened?"

Tommy shook his head and shrugged. "It was chaos after Norman left. He'd heard there was a small enclave that needed help. He left Pop in charge. But days turned into weeks and people started to panic. We'd had an influx of new people months before and most of them only knew Norman as a leader. Pop had a hard time controlling them. That's when the rules started getting stricter. The patrols started and everyone got assigned a job. Things got tighter. Food rations, work hours, all kinds of stuff. Most of it good, some of it not so good."

"Like what?" She didn't want to ask, but she needed to know.

"There were a couple of accidental deaths. Several not accidental. And a group of people exiled."

"Exiled?"

"They refused to follow the rules. So, they were driven down to Los Angeles and let go."

"What? How could you just leave them there in a Vampire city? That was as good as walking them into a slave auction."

"Pop said it was for the good of the enclave. We had to think of the whole not the individual."

"But wasn't that risky? If they're captured they could tell where this place is."

"Pop said it was a chance we had to take."

Her gut twisted. Pop. Pop. Pop. It all came back to Lou. And Lou may have changed but she knew one thing for sure. He wasn't one to leave things to chance. He'd never have let those people get close to Los Angeles.

She stared at Tommy and wondered if he really believed the lie that those people had been exiled to Los Angeles or if he'd already figured out the truth. Those people were in a shallow grave somewhere in the desert.

A question churned in her mind, something she needed to know, but wasn't quite sure how to broach the subject without seeming strange.

"Where did all the guns come from?" she asked. "We never had all these weapons before."

"We went up to Idaho. There was a base up there in Mountain Home, about forty minutes from Boise. We took everything we could find."

"So, if we were attacked, guns are all we have?"

He gazed at her for a minute and then shook his head. "A group has been searching other military bases for a couple years now. They've been coming back with some bigger weapons."

"Bombs?"

"I don't know. But I wouldn't be surprised. They're stored in a bunker even I'm not given access too."

"Have you heard Lou say anything about using weapons and going on the offensive?" She held her breath.

"Why so curious?"

"There's a lot of people out there. Humans and vamps. Innocent people. I'd hate to see them hurt, is all."

He patted her knee. "It's good to have you back, sis. I missed you more than you can know. But be careful. This isn't the place you left. Objectives have changed. It's not about helping others anymore. It's about our own survival."

"Sounds like it isn't even about that. It's about retaking the world."

"Is that a problem?"

They had a right to live in the world as free people, but if it was at the cost of millions of lives...

"How can you have doubts?" he asked. "After what you've been through, I'd have thought you of all people would be the first one to pick up a weapon and lead the charge."

"Don't get me wrong. I want to live without walls and bars, but I don't want my freedom at the cost of other people."

"They aren't people anymore. Some never even were."

"How can you say that? Your mom—"

"Is gone."

She shook her head. "You sound like Lou."

"How else do you expect me to be? I thought you were gone, and it almost killed me. I can't think of her being out there. Living as one of those things—"

"They aren't things. They're people. They live, eat, breathe, sleep, work. They're different but they aren't things." When had she starting standing up for vamps?

"What happened to you out there? You're different."

"Nothing." She shrugged. "I just think the way we're treating them here is the same thing we fought against them for doing. How can we be on the side of good if we act like them?"

"We're not on the side of good. We're on the side of humanity."

"And is this? What's happening down there. Is it humane?"

He clamped his lips shut tight. She didn't expect him to go against his dad. She wanted him to see that things weren't black and white. Being out there in the new world had taught her that much, even if she didn't want to admit it.

"I'm gonna let you rest." He stood and headed for the exit.

"Tommy?"

He turned.

"If they aren't people anymore and some never were, why is Lou working on a cure?"

His brow furrowed so deep his eyes almost closed. His mouth opened and then closed. He threw the door wide and stormed out to the hall.

Evan laid herself back on her bed and tossed her arms overhead. The movement pulled on her leg muscles, and she lowered her arms and rubbed her thigh.

Her thoughts turned to William and the hard, dark cell he lay shackled in. She needed to find him some food. But getting it wouldn't be easy.

WILLIAM AWOKE SOME TIME LATER TO A SCORCHING PAIN IN HIS HAND. The sunlight had crept across the floor. He pulled his hand to his chest and tried to sit up. His ribs ached but not as much as they had. The sound of the door unlocking had him completely alert within seconds.

He tried to straighten his dirty clothes, hoping it would be Evan.

The door pushed inward and in stepped Tommy and Peter. William's stomach flopped.

"You awake in here, bloodsucker?" asked Peter.

William refused to answer. The games had become tiresome within the first hour of his capture. He'd been nothing but forthcoming. And Peter had been nothing but malicious.

Peter crouched down in front of William and stared at him. "I have a question for you. If you answer right, I'll leave. If you answer wrong, I won't."

"I've told you everything you've asked," said William. "Why would now be any different?"

"Do you know my sister, Evan?"

William swallowed and his eyes flicked to Tommy. That was not what he'd been expecting.

"No."

Peter's fist came out of nowhere and connected with William's jaw.

His head rocked back and hit the cement wall, dazing him.

"Wrong answer," said Peter. "Try again. I'll even help you. She's the girl you carried to our gate. She came in here yesterday. You two chatted."

William turned his head slowly and locked eyes with Peter. His jaw pounded with pain, but he refused to let them see it. He spat blood on the ground, splattering his own pants.

"I found her wandering. It seemed the best thing I could do considering her delirium."

"Hmm…" Peter scratched his chin. "You found her wandering down the road and just happened to know where to bring her home. You sure that's the answer you want to go with?"

"I'd found a crashed car a few miles back. She was in bad shape. I only wanted to help. She told me where she'd been trying to get to."

"A few miles back, huh? Where exactly did you find that crashed car?"

"Evan wouldn't do that," Tommy interjected. "She wouldn't give up our location."

William shifted his weight. He'd screwed up. If they went to check, there'd be no car crash to prove his words. He looked up at the earnest face of the younger brother. "We aren't all the monsters you think we are. She needed help."

126

"And what were you doing all the way out here in the middle of nowhere?" asked Peter.

William tried to remember what he'd told them previously. "I was on my way to Los Angeles as an emissary from Chicago."

"So you're not alone?" said Peter. "There are more of you. If you didn't fly, there had to be more of you. Is that the trick? You get in here and find out what our defenses are like so the rest of your group can attack?" The anger in Peter's voice rose with each word.

"I have no group. I came alone."

"Then why not fly?" asked Tommy.

"Because I like the drive. I miss it."

"Miss it?" Peter snorted.

He couldn't miss the opportunity to try and show them that he wasn't any different than them.

"I've been a vampyr less than a year. Before that I lived in an enclave in Colorado, but we got picked up by slavers in Nebraska."

"Colorado? We have a guy here from Colorado. His name's Chuck, remember him?" asked Peter. "Or is that a lie too?"

"There were lots of people in our enclave. I'd have to see him to know for sure." William looked between the brothers. "I'm not here to start an invasion. I'm not here to do anything other than what I said before. The world is in trouble. We need help. *Your* help. The demons—"

"Right." Peter chuckled. "The demons. I forgot that's why you were on your way out here. Demons killing your friends. Sounds like a reason for us to celebrate, not jump to your aid."

"You don't get it," said William. "After the demons are done with Vampires and vamps, who do you think are next? You think they're going to leave you be?"

"Why not? We didn't piss them off."

"They came pissed off. They're demons. Pissed off for having been shoved back into their world hundreds of years ago, and now they want to take this world for themselves once and for all."

"Do you know how delusional you sound?"

William's anger spiked so fast, he couldn't control his tongue. "The delusional ones are you. Thinking you can stay here and be safe."

Peter's fist connected with William's gut. "You have no idea what's going on here. We're stronger than you can imagine. You just wait, bud, we have something fun planned for you tomorrow."

Peter patted his cheek before punching William in the face again. The pain blinded William for a minute.

"Peter, that's enough," said Tommy.

"You goin' soft, Tommy boy?" Peter stood as William laid his pounding head against the wall and tried to blink back the throbbing.

"No. I just think enough is enough. Pop doesn't even know we're in here. Let the guy alone."

"Guy?" Peter stepped up to Tommy so quick that Tommy took a step back. "Did you call that thing a guy?"

"You know what I meant."

"No, Tommy, I don't think I do. It's because of *guys* like him that mom is a vamp and Evan was sold as a slave. It's because of *guys* like him that we live in a freaking hotel and have food rations and water rations and an electric barbed wire fence surrounding us twenty-four seven."

"I get it, okay. I get it. My point is, he wasn't the one who did all that. He was like us till months ago."

Peter's body coiled like a rubberband ready to snap. "Get out of here, Tommy. Get out before I throw you out."

Tommy's chest puffed up, and he stood his ground. "I'll leave when you leave."

They were two rams about to lock horns. Neither wanted to back down. William hated seeing that kind of animosity between family members.

"May I have a drink of water?" William asked.

Nothing happened for a minute and then Tommy's gaze flicked to William and then back to his brother. Peter stood rigid for a moment longer before relaxing a fraction.

"No," Peter said. "Let's go." He left without looking back.

Tommy stared at William for a minute and chewed his lip. Tommy had stood up for him. It might have been a small thing to Tommy but it was huge to William. It told him that something he had said or that Evan had said had made an impact and that's what they needed. To start making an impact.

"Tommy!" Peter shouted from the hall.

Tommy turned and walked out without a word.

William had gotten through to Tommy. Problem was, at the rate things were moving everyone in Chicago would be dead before he could get enough people on his side to actually take any action.

Either that, or he would be dead.

CHAPTER TWELVE

"It's a girl," said Travis.

Elation and exhaustion battled Evan's shaken body. Sweat poured from her brow, and she tried to keep her eyes open to see the baby.

"Look what we made." He rubbed down the pink infant with a soft towel and then set her in Evan's awaiting arms.

The small bundle wriggled and squalled. A tiny fist balled up in her palm.

"Hey there." A tear leaked from her eye. A girl. She had a baby girl. Strong arms surrounded her as a long, muscular body spooned up behind her.

"What should we name her?" he asked.

Evan shook her head, unable to form coherent sentences. Emotions raced through her so fast she didn't even know how to register them.

"You should feed her." A pair of lips touched her hair.

"I... don't know how," she whispered.

"I'll show you." A nurse stepped forward and helped Evan latch the infant onto her breast.

The connection between her and the baby suddenly completed. In the small suckling sensation, Evan's entire being awoke with a protective instinct she'd never possessed before. The tiny being was her life now.

Her everything.

"Chéri," Evan whispered. "Her name is Chéri."

"Like Mon Chéri?" Travis mused. "It's perfect."

Evan kissed her baby's soft, dark curls and then opened the blanket to look at all of her. She was perfect. Round and rosy with a pert, tiny nose and ten pudgy little fingers and toes. Everything about her baby, everything she'd hoped and wished for, had come true.

"A family," she said. "A real family."

"I've spent many years praying for this moment."

She looked up into his dark eyes and smiled. "Me too."

He tilted her chin and pressed his lips to hers. "Thank you."

Evan awoke and sat up suddenly. "Travis!"

She blinked several times and tried to focus on her surroundings as dim sunlight filtered in through the window. She scanned for the baby bassinet, and then reality hit her like a cold slap of ice water.

"Mon Chéri," she whispered, holding the tears at bay.

Her heart ached as memories bombarded her. Clear as a sunlit day, the agony torn her afresh as if it had just happened. Travis was gone. Chéri was gone. And all she had was herself.

Evan stood and walked into the bathroom. She threw water on her face and then brushed her hair. Staring at her reflection in the mirror, she told herself that she couldn't afford a meltdown. Not now. Her thoughts drifted to William. The sun would set soon.

Most of the people in the enclave would head off to bed. She could sneak down and see him. Maybe bring him something to eat and some water. Not that Lou would allow her to. But he had told the guards down there to give her access. So what Lou didn't know…

"Dammit, Evan. What the hell are you doing?" She stared at herself long and hard. Why did she keep putting herself on the line for him? How could she let him get into her head? After everything that had happened, was she really that weak? That stupid? Helping William might very well get her killed.

"Evan?" Tommy's voice sounded from the doorway.

She wiped her face with a towel and then walked into the room.

"How'd you get in here?"

He held up a card key. "I wasn't sure you'd open the door if I knocked. I seem to be pissing off everyone this week."

"Does that open every door?"

"Yup. It's a master key."

"What's up?" she asked.

"I came by to see if you maybe wanted to go eat." He held out a chain with food chips on it.

Her stomach growled loudly. She snatched the chain and slung it around her neck. "Why not?"

"Cool." Tommy gave her a wide, lopsided smile.

She shoved her feet into a pair of boots and followed him into the hallway. After their previous conversation, if Tommy had come to her for company things must not be going well with Lou. "Where's Peter?"

"Uh… He and I aren't talkin' right now." He glanced away sheepishly.

"What happened?" She sighed. The brothers were always at it about something.

"Doesn't matter. But we can eat with his family anyway."

She drew her brows together. "His family?"

They reached the elevator. "Yeah, you remember, Alexa. Short, curvy, mouth like a sailor?"

"Sure," replied Evan.

"They got together about six months after you disappeared and had a kid."

"Seriously?"

Tommy chuckled and nodded.

"I never saw that comin'."

"No one did," said Tommy.

They exited the elevator and walked into the lobby full of people talking or reading. Kids running around and playing games. Guards joked and spoke with each other. Everywhere she looked, there were people.

"Hey, Evan," Joe caught up with them. "How are you adjusting?"

"Great. Thanks for asking." She pushed her hair behind her ear.

"I'm about to head to work. Maybe after we can play cards or something."

The words to decline his offer hung on her tongue. Her thoughts turned to William and for a fraction of a moment, guilt struck her. How could she play cards when he was stuck in a cell?

"Maybe. I'll see how my leg feels."

"Cool." He beamed as he walked away. "Tommy, you're invited too. I still owe you a whooping from the last time we played."

Tommy chuckled and raised his hand to wave.

Joe jogged away and her gut clenched. The feeling of betraying William overpowered her. *Stop that. It's not like we're married or anything.*

A toddler zoomed in front of her on a tricycle almost knocking into a potted plant. "Dang, it's crowded in here," she mused.

"It gets this way at dinner time. Most other times people are working or sleeping. Kids are at school or helping do chores. Dinner is the one time that everyone gets together. Then it's lights out by ten."

"Sounds like a prison."

"It's keeping the peace. Without rules, this place would be chaos."

Dinner consisted of ham and potatoes. There were a variety of vegetables and for dessert was something she hadn't seen in years. Pudding.

"Slaves aren't allowed to eat pudding," she said.

"Why?" asked Tommy.

"They're put on strict diets for health reasons." She turned in her food chip and headed for a table with Tommy.

"I wonder if that will change though," she said. "The restrictions on diets, I mean."

"Why would it?"

"We're being set free."

Tommy stopped and his eyebrows smashed together. "What do you mean, set free?"

"I was in Chicago and the Coven Lord there set all her slaves free. She uncovered a giant warehouse of humans that had been used in an underground blood market. She gave them a choice. Go free, or stay and be allowed to choose who they wanted to work with."

A strange expression crossed his face. "You're serious?"

"I was given the choice myself a dozen times, but they always sent me back."

He chuckled. "I can't imagine why."

She slugged him in the shoulder. "All I did was talk to the other slaves. Tried to get them to stand up for themselves. Tell them there were places they could go for refuge. Like here. Apparently, that wasn't something the Vampires liked."

He laughed again and then his smile fell.

"What?" she asked.

"You were in Chicago?"

"Yeah, why?"

He swallowed. "Nothin'."

A tingle raced up Evan's spine as Tommy refused to meet her eye.

He pointed to a booth in the corner where Alexa sat with a baby in a high chair. She waved them over and they slid into a booth.

"Hi," said Alexa. "I can't believe you're sitting here. I've been listening to the boys bemoan your disappearance for so long it's just so weird that you're back."

Evan swallowed, unsure of what to say. "Uh... thanks?"

"This is Petie."

Evan looked over at the baby and every muscle in her body tensed at the dark hair and large, round, blue eyes. Just like Chéri.

"How old is he?" She cleared her throat in an effort to keep her barely contained emotions at bay a bit longer.

"He'll be a year next month." Alexa spooned mashed up food into his mouth.

Petie smiled at Evan and gave her raspberries, spitting baby food all over his face.

Alexa laughed. "He loves to do that. I swear he gets more on his face and clothes than he does in his stomach."

Evan couldn't tear her eyes away. The chubby, happy baby

face filled her with a bone-deep sense of longing that she hadn't realized was possible.

"May I?" Evan asked.

Alexa handed over Petie's plate and spoon. "Be my guest. Do you mind watching him while I go grab a shower? I have work in thirty minutes."

Evan smiled. "Not at all."

"Great. Thanks so much." Alexa picked up her own empty tray of food and stood.

"You want me to take him to the nursery?" asked Tommy.

"Would you?"

"Sure, Evan can come with us."

Alexa squeezed Evan's shoulder. "I think I'm gonna love having you back."

Evan nodded and looked to Petie. She scooped up some food and held it to his lips. Petie opened and gummed the orange mash before spitting it onto his tray.

AFTER EVAN AND TOMMY DROPPED OFF PETIE AND PLAYED WITH HIM for a while, Peter came to Evan's room to get them for a meeting. Evan had a hard time containing her anger at Peter for what he'd been doing to William, but having played with his son for over an hour made her keep her mouth shut. For the time being at least.

The trio made their way to the lab area of the compound and were met by Lou and Nicholas.

"Feeling better?" Lou asked.

"Yup." She rubbed her leg and tried not to fidget. Lou would notice if she fidgeted.

"Good. We have something we need from you."

Nicholas held up a small vial. "This is the blood we got off the vampyr downstairs. I've analyzed it. It's nothing I've seen before."

"He's telling the truth then?" asked Tommy. "There are demons here?"

Nicholas shook his head. "I don't know. It's possible. But the question is, if the demons are attacking like he said, why would he have a vial of their blood?"

"Maybe he collected it," Evan offered.

"But why?" Peter's tone held an animosity that she'd rarely had directed toward her before.

"Why are your panties in a wad?" she asked. "I didn't do anything to you."

Peter scowled.

"What do you think?" Lou asked Nicholas.

"I think it very well could be Demon blood. And if it is, and he's telling the truth, we're in bigger trouble than we originally thought. Demons aren't beings you can reason with. They'd rather obliterate the Earth than negotiate our existence."

"Can you do anything with it?" asked Lou. "Like you're trying to do with the vamp cure?"

"It's possible I can try to make a virus, only deadly to Demon DNA, but that would take time. On another note, I have what I think maybe finally be a cure for the vamps."

"Can we test it?" asked Lou.

"If we have a subject to test on."

Evan's fists clenched and she wrapped her arms around herself. "Do we have any vamps here?"

"Not at the moment," replied Tommy.

She blew out a slow breath as relief rolled down her body.

"That's easily taken care of," said Lou. "We'll get a party together tomorrow to go down to Los Angeles and round up a few."

Evan turned on her uncle. "What?"

Her uncle's gaze leveled on her. "I understand that you've not had to live this life for a while, baby girl, but you need to see things for how they are here. We are trying to help those things. To bring them back to their humanity. Humanity that Vampires robbed from them."

"No, Lou. Not by all the Vampires, but a few Vampires. Not all of them are like that. But even so, how can you round up vamps like cattle and use them like this?"

Lou stepped closer to Evan and laid his hands on her shoulders. "I'm doing this for you. For Peter and Tommy. So you kids can have a future. A future that doesn't include hiding and scrounging. A life where you don't ever have to worry about being kidnapped and sold again. To ensure that future, I have to kill a few people. I won't lie about it, and I won't apologize for it. And whether or not you agree with how I do it, I'm not going to stop."

She had no words. Her uncle was right. She didn't agree with his methods, but it did no good to argue. All she could do was go along until she could get herself and William to safety.

"Okay." He patted her shoulder. "Tomorrow, Peter, you and a group of raiders will go down to Los Angeles. We only have room for three more vamps right now so that's what you'll pick up."

Peter nodded.

"Let's everyone get some sleep and we'll start again with the vampyr in the morning. Evan, I want you to get him to tell us everything he knows about the demons," said Lou.

Evan swallowed and nodded. She needed to see William before then.

She needed a game plan.

THE DOOR TO WILLIAM'S ROOM OPENED, AND HE SMELLED EVAN before she'd even entered his space. His swollen left eye obscured his view of her, but he could still make out her form. She flipped the light switch and a small bulb popped to life in the corner. She closed the door behind herself and turned to him. Shock registered on her face and she stormed over.

"What the hell?"

"I'm fine." He tried to get to his feet but was unable.

She rushed to his aid and helped him up. "Who did this?"

"It doesn't matter. It'll heal soon anyway."

She searched his face. "Tell me who did this."

He stared at her. She looked as beautiful and radiant as ever. Her peachy skin and blue eyes stood as a testament to her all-American appearance.

He gave her a tight smile, and her posture softened.

Her gaze held his intently. She lifted her hand and brushed the hair from his face. "Why did you help me get here? I know you say it's because you needed to find out about the weapons, but you could have called Danika and told her where the enclave was and they could have flown Roth and the Tracking Squad out in a couple hours. But you didn't. You carried me to the gate."

"It was the right thing to do."

She shook her head. "You could have driven off. Not waited to see if they'd gotten me. You risked yourself. Why?"

She stepped closer to him and laid her palm in the middle of his chest.

His mind reeled. It couldn't be real. She couldn't be standing there talking to him like that. She hated him.

"I told you. It's my job to be here. To try and get the humans to help us fight or to find out if they have weapons." He swallowed hard.

She stared at him for a minute and ran her thumb over his cracked bottom lip. Then she spun around and headed for the exit. "I'll be right back."

She banged on the door and a guard let her out. William drooped against the wall and blew out a heavy breath. He tried to run his hands through his hair but couldn't because it was so tangled. His teeth felt like he'd wrapped them in woolen sweaters and he needed a shower worse than when he'd lived in the mountains. His dried and cracked scabs itched and his broken bones still ached though they no longer throbbed. He tucked in his shirt to the best of his ability and wiped his face on his sleeve.

Ten minutes later shouting floated through the door, and then it burst inward. Evan carried several items, followed closely by the guard.

"Those aren't allowed," said the guard.

"Then why don't you run tell on me?" She slammed the door on the guy and headed for where William stood.

She looked him over and then held out a thermos. "It's water," she said.

He ran his leathery tongue over his cracked lip and took the thermos. He drank greedily though the water went down with a burn.

"Here." She set down the extra things on the floor and pulled a sweatshirt from the pile. "It isn't as fashionable as you're used to, but it's clean."

He took the gray hoodie from her. "Thank you, but I'm afraid I can't."

"Of course you can," she said.

He held up his shackled hands.

She nodded once. "Right."

She marched to the door and banged on it. The guard glared at her.

"Take off his handcuffs," she ordered.

"Not on your life," the guard replied.

In a flash, Evan grabbed the guard by the shirt and pushed him down in the hallway. She grappled with him and flipped him on his stomach with strength she shouldn't possess.

"Get off me," he yelled.

More yelling ensued and there were several sets of heavy steps. Evan hopped to her feet, a key ring in her hand. She moved to William and undid both wrists as two guards raced into the room.

They raised their guns and pointed them at William. His eyes connected with Evan's, and she gave a slight nod.

The shackles fell away, and he turned his wrists and rubbed at the chafed skin. Evan threw the keys at the guards' feet.

"Get out," she said. "I can handle it from here. Oh!" She walked to the pot in the corner and sat it at their feet. "You can clean this while you're at it."

The men exchanged a look. "It's your funeral," said one of them.

They gathered up the keys and pot and backed out.

"That wasn't smart," said William.

She turned her icy gaze on him. "I don't care anymore."

"They'll tell and things will get bad for you. Bad for me as well."

"You let me deal with my uncle."

"It's not your uncle I'm worried about," he replied.

She searched his face. "Peter?"

"Forget it."

She could be so stubborn, and if he told her about her cousins, who knew what she'd do. She shook her head and then let it drop. She picked up a washcloth and poured some water from the thermos onto it. He tracked her movements as she lifted the washcloth to his face and hesitated. Their eyes connected, and she licked her lower lip. The movement, though subtle, made his desire stir and his pants grew too tight.

She patted his eye with the cloth, moving in so close that her breasts smashed into his chest. His arousal spiked higher, and he cleared his throat and tried to move his hips backward in an effort not to have his erection show.

"Don't pull away," she said. "I can't reach your eye if you do." She moved her hips so they came in contact with his and leaned in to dab his eye again but stopped.

Her hand hovered in the air near his face. Embarrassment scoured his skin. He wanted to say something to release the tension between them. To apologize for his body's reaction to her nearness, but his voice wouldn't work.

After a minute, he realized she didn't move away. He slowly lifted his right hand and set it on her hip. She still didn't pull away. He should stop. He should leave her be. She had enough on her plate without his desires running all over her. But he couldn't. Just the feel of her skin under his fingertips had his body quaking with need. He strained to keep from grabbing her. To keep from kissing her and taking her hard right against the wall.

He ran his left hand up her arm and around her back. Every fiber told him they shouldn't. They were both in enough trouble. If her cousin found out, he'd kill William for sure—and yet he couldn't stop his limbs from moving.

"We shouldn't," he said.

"Of course we shouldn't. You're everything I've hated for the past ten years. But somehow when I look at you I don't see a Vampire. And the way you look at me... No one has ever looked at me that way before. At least no one who meant it."

He didn't want to say the words. If he said them it would change everything. They'd just begun to get along, one slip and he could lose her. But maybe that's what needed to happen. Maybe he needed to give her an ultimatum to get her to stay away from him. To keep her safe.

"I mean it," he whispered.

She leaned in and stopped an inch from his lips. He didn't move a muscle as he waited to see what she'd do. Her breath hit his face and he breathed her in. Her fingers combed through the hair at the base of his neck, sending shivers over his body. She moved closer and her lips brushed his, warm and inviting. His grip tightened on her waist and then she pressed her lips to his, and pulled him closer. William stiffened at the contact but then he laced his fingers in her hair and drew her mouth to his. She tasted like mint toothpaste and her supple lips felt like soft plums. She swirled her tongue against his mouth and moaned, making his head spin. He'd waited months to feel her touch, to kiss her and hold her, and now that he had her, this wasn't how he wanted it. Not in a cell.

He broke the kiss and rested his forehead on hers. "We can't do this. Not here."

She breathed hard and fast. After a minute, she nodded. "You're right."

Every muscle in his body screamed at him of his stupidity.

He'd waited for this woman, and now that he had her, he was pushing her away.

EVAN WASN'T SURE WHAT HAD COME OVER HER. SEEING WILLIAM beaten had caused a surge of protective energy inside her that she hadn't felt since holding her baby. In that moment, a piece of her armor had chipped away, and she'd given in to the budding feelings he caused in her. In that moment she'd wanted to feel him. To have him in her arms. To know if what she risked for him was real or just infatuation. But even as he'd broken the kiss all she wanted was more of him—no matter the consequences.

"Let's get you cleaned up." She wiped his face and then brushed his matted hair. He still couldn't get his arms over his head, so she slid his shirt off and helped him with the hoodie. As her fingers traced over the bruised muscles, she tried to keep her mind on the task at hand. It'd been a long time since she'd been with a man. And though that had never bothered her before, she suddenly craved the release of feeling a man inside her.

Not just any man— William.

"Will you sit with me a while?" he asked.

"I need to talk to you anyway," she said. "They believe you finally. About the demons." She sat on the floor, and he sat opposite her. "Problem is your story conflicts."

"How?"

"You have Mason's blood. Now they think you're in league with the demons."

He snorted and shook his head. "What do you want me to say?"

"Tell them the truth," she said. "Tell them about Mason and Danika and what's happened with the Three Kings and everything. They're coming to question you tomorrow."

"I'd be happy to, but do you think it will make a difference?"

"It might."

He searched her face.

"I don't know," she said. "I really don't. But seeing what you look like right now, not telling them is going to be worse for you."

"Tell me something about you."

"What?" Something about her? Where did that come from?

"I just want to know about you. Anything you want to tell me."

Tell him something. Anything. She could tell him about her favorite movie. The kind of music she liked. Where she lived before the Outbreak. Her dream floated back to her along with the memory of holding, feeding, and playing with Petie.

"I have a daughter." She'd never told anyone.

His brow furrowed. "A daughter? Is she here?"

"No." Her voice came out barely a whisper. "She was taken from me."

His hand gripped hers and she looked down at it. Dirty yet pale, he rubbed his thumb over the pad between her thumb and forefinger.

"Was it the Awakening?"

She shook her head. "Nothing like that." She took a deep breath.

"I was bought from the slave auctions by a Vampire named Travis. At first I was a blood slave for him and his wife. I was terrified, but they were nice enough. I was taken care of and treated like a member of the family."

The memory of Travis' aftershave filled her senses, and she had to gulp in air trying to clear her thoughts.

"After about six months Travis and I started spending more time together. His wife became almost non-existent. He confided in me that they'd been trying to have children for years and had been unable. It had caused a rift in their relationship. The more time we spent together, the more I fell for him. Soon we ended up in bed. When I got pregnant, he was elated. He told me that he was going to leave his wife and we would be together."

A tear slid down her cheek as the pain of loss tidal waved upon her, threatening to consume her.

"His wife left about a month before the baby was due. I birthed at his home, and we spent several days together after. Then one day I woke up, and I remember feeling the warmth of the sun on my face and for a split second feeling utter peace. Then I looked over at the bassinet. Chéri wasn't in it. I raced from the room and found only the butler. He said that Travis and his wife had taken an extended vacation with their daughter and that they wouldn't be returning for some time. I fled that very day."

"Evan—"

"I tried to search for them, but I'm human so it was mere days before I was picked up again. That's how I made it to Chicago and into the blood club."

He opened his mouth to speak again but instead she leaned in and kissed him. She didn't want him to talk. Didn't want to hear him say he was sorry. Didn't want him to show her pity. She didn't need it. If he said one kind thing to her, she might break into a million pieces. He cupped her face, and their kiss deepened. Her thighs tingled, and she wanted to feel his weight on hers.

She broke away and stared at him.

"You should probably go," he said.

"I probably should." She reached over and gathered up the things she'd brought in. "Oh. I forgot. It's not blood but I thought maybe you could use a little something to eat anyway." She handed him a piece of ham on a roll. "It's not much but I'll be able to bring you more tomorrow. I had to snag this without anyone seeing."

"It's great. Thank you." He gave her a genuine smile.

"I'll come back in the morning. Is there anything I can get you?"

"Just stay safe."

She touched his eye. "Are you going to tell me who did this to you?"

"No. But they were asking if I knew you. You need to be careful."

"I'll make sure I'm here when you're questioned again. Depending on how it goes, we may need to figure out another way to get help with the demons."

He pushed her hair behind her ear. "What do you mean we'll need to find another way?"

"I have a feeling that we aren't going to get the help we want."

"If we don't get help here, where do we go then? This is the biggest enclave I've ever heard of," said William.

"They certainly have more weapons than I've ever seen. And that doctor is doing more work on vaccines than I knew were possible. He's trying to make a virus right now from Mason's blood. One to kill demons."

William's eyes widened. "Well that's frightening and ambitious."

"If it works though, it could give you the edge you need."

"I doubt he'd give it to us."

She gave him a tight smile. "Then we'll just have to take it."

CHAPTER THIRTEEN

Evan hurried to see William the next morning after breakfast. She'd held back an egg, a piece of toast, and some juice for him. She'd had a mostly sleepless night trying to figure out what the hell to do next. Her best chance of getting Lou to listen was to get Tommy on her side and Peter out of the way. With Peter leaving to pick up vamps, she'd decided that was when she'd make her move.

She headed down the hallway to the prison area and stepped up to where Seth stood watch. He moved in front of the door, barring her entrance.

"Get out of the way," she said.

"Sorry. Not this morning." His voice held the anger of a man beaten.

The thought of apologizing to him for laying him out and taking his keys crossed her mind, but she'd actually rather do it again than apologize.

"Lou said I was to be given access to this area."

"And I was given orders that this area is on lockdown for

everyone but Lou and Peter until further notice." The smirk on his face told her everything she needed to know. Lou had found out about her late-night visit.

"Listen, ass——"

"Evan!"

Tommy jogged down the hallway toward her.

"What the hell is going on?" she asked. "This bozo won't let me in."

Tommy's gaze flicked to Seth and then back to her. "Let's take a walk."

A pit grew in her stomach and goosebumps pebbled her skin. "I don't want to walk. I want to be let in."

Tommy leaned in close and his gaze traveled to the ceiling. "Not here."

She glanced up and noticed the newly installed security camera, then nodded.

Tommy smiled and waved to Seth, and the two headed back toward the row of storage rooms. They turned a corner, and he pulled her into a side room and shut the door.

"What's going on?" she demanded.

"Seth told Pop about what happened with you and the vampyr last night."

"So? I was nice to him because he saved my life, big deal." She shrugged.

Tommy leveled his gaze at her. "You and I both know that's not all there is to that story."

She swallowed hard. "I don't know what you mean."

"I may be a nice guy, but I'm not dumb. Yesterday you said at dinner that you ended up in Chicago. That vampyr said he was from Chicago."

Damn! Evan blew out a harsh breath and dropped her gaze

to her toes. "Okay. I know him. I was in the coven house where he lives. His name is William."

"Do you love him?"

"What? No..." she sputtered. "No. I don't love him, but he is a good person. And he's telling the truth about everything."

"What about the demons? Is he in league with them?"

"No. Not really. There's a Demon in Chicago. He's married to the Coven Lord Danika, but Mason and his sister are the only things that have kept the rest of the demons at bay."

"So you're friends with demons too?" His voice held tinges of doubt and fear.

"I'm not exactly friends with any of them. I know who they are and they know me. William and Mason are friends. Mason lived in an enclave with William and others until he got caught and sold to Danika. He gave William a vial of his blood for protection."

"What kind of protection?"

She shook her head. "I don't know. To drink probably if there was a problem. Mason's huge. I mean seriously huge. I can only imagine what his blood would do to a Vampire if they drank it."

Tommy backed against the wall and hung his head in his hands. She let him have a moment to process before he looked up at her again.

"What am I supposed to do here, sis? You're different. Pop's different. Peter's different. And each of you want me to do something that goes against the other. I feel like an over-stretched slinky."

Evan set down her bundle of food and walked to Tommy. "I don't want you to do anything but follow your heart."

"Is that what you're doing?"

"I'm trying to do what's right."

"Right for who? For us or for them?"

"See, that's the problem right there," she said. "There can't be an 'us' and 'them' anymore. Not with what's coming. There can only be a 'we', meaning all of us together, if we want to survive."

She sucked in a breath, surprised by the fact that she'd spouted William's own words.

The silence hung between them thick as clam chowder.

"Pop won't change his mind," he finally said.

"Then I'll have to make him change it."

Tommy sighed.

"What's going on in the prison area? Why am I not being let in?" she asked.

"Peter's in there."

Fear scratched up her spine. "With William?"

Tommy nodded.

The wheels spun in her head. "Peter's been beating William, hasn't he?"

Tommy stayed silent.

"Hasn't he?" she yelled. "Have you been in on it too?"

He licked his lips and looked away.

She had to get in there. Tommy stepped in the way.

"You can't. Not this time. Pop was livid after he found out what you did last night. If you burst in there now, Peter will kill William for sure."

"What's his problem with William?"

"Peter's been different ever since you left. It's like it's been his own private mission to kill all Vampires or at least make them suffer. Every one we've had in here he'd ask them if they knew where you were. When we go out on raids, he goes out of his way to kill anyone he comes across. He blames them for everything."

"And yet Nicholas is in the attic doing his mad scientist experiments."

"Trust me, that's not been a pill easy for Peter to swallow. But when it comes to Nicholas, no one interferes or they have to deal with Pop."

"Who is that guy anyway?"

"Norman found him and was going to kill him, but Nicholas begged for his life and told Norman he could cure the vamps. He was kept down here working on the cure without any of us knowing. It wasn't till Pop took over that he was given the big lab up top and all the resources he needs."

"Is Pop doing this for your mom?"

"I don't know. Maybe. I don't even think he knows why he's doing it anymore."

"Peter could be in there right now killing William."

Tommy licked his lips. "He won't kill William. He's not allowed."

"But this is?" she demanded.

"I didn't say it was right."

"I have to get William out of here. He came here to ask for help. He doesn't deserve this."

Tommy stared at her for a minute.

"What?"

He chuckled and shook his head. "You say you don't love him, but the only people I've ever seen you fight this hard for are Pop and me."

She didn't want to admit she had any feelings for William, but she knew the truth. She did care for him. More than she wanted to.

WILLIAM SPIT BLOOD ONTO THE FLOOR. EVERY CELL IN HIS BODY wanted to fight back. The thirst that now pounded in his chest and burned his throat like icy flames had him on the verge of ripping Peter's throat out. Never before had he been so tested. Rage flowed freely through him clouding his thoughts and teasing him into madness.

Peter kicked him again in the ribs, and William crumpled to the ground.

"You aren't even chained, you worthless bloodsucker. Fight back already," Peter taunted.

If Peter hadn't been Evan's cousin, he would have fought back. He would have drained the man, gotten back his strength, grabbed Evan, and run.

Peter hadn't even asked any questions. He'd just come in and started whaling without provocation. William could only assume it was because of what had happened the night before with Evan and the guards. But who knew. Men like Lou and Peter tended to think more with their fists than their heads.

Peter pulled something from his pocket and tossed it at William. The metal object clattered to a stop under William's nose.

"Which of the numbers on that phone will get you through to your Demon buddies?" asked Peter. "I'm assuming it's the one that has called every two hours for the last three days."

"That would probably be Lord Danika actually," William said.

"And what are you to her? Minion? Lover?"

"Family."

Peter chuckled and crouched beside William. "To have a family you have to be human."

"You think so?" William looked up at Peter. "The people in this enclave, are they your family?"

"You better believe it. I'd die protecting all of them."

"But you aren't even related to most of them."

"Blood doesn't make a family," Peter replied.

"Exactly," said William. "I bleed, you can see that. Only my blood is different than yours now. Doesn't make me any less of a being. I love, I laugh, I cry. I do everything you do. So do my family. So why is it that my family is insignificant, and yours is not? Can you tell me the names of every person in this enclave? These people who are your family, can you tell me the names of a hundred of them? I know the names of every single person in my coven family. Every human, every vampyr, every Vampire. I know them by name. I know them by scent. I know them by sight. So tell me. How is it that I can't have a family?"

Peter stared at William for a long minute before snatching the phone away, and walking to the door. He sniffed and banged on the door. It opened and Peter looked back.

"I want you to think about all those family members. Because our first attack will be on them."

Peter walked out with a slam of the door and William crumpled into a heap. He didn't know how much longer he'd be able to take the abuse without lashing out.

He'd been wrong to come. Humans remained just as cruel as before. Danika had been right. The Vampires had been right. Nothing had changed. Humans really weren't anything more than animals.

EVAN WALKED THROUGH THE LOBBY OF THE HOTEL IN AN EFFORT TO keep her mind off her problem at hand. She flipped her butterfly knife open and closed as she walked. It'd been over an hour since she'd talked to Tommy, and he'd promised to let her know when she could go in and see William.

She traveled past the security desk to the hallway opposite the restaurant. The first ballroom held rows of tables with children sitting and writing. A woman stood at the front of the room speaking. Evan continued to the nursery and found a group of small children and babies, playing with toys and running around. She spotted Petie being held by a worker.

The worker waved her in but Evan shook her head. Playing with Petie had been a beautiful but painful experience the day before. If she got any closer to her nephew, she doubted that all the beatings in the world could make her take William and leave. It broke her heart to have to choose someone over family, but what had her family become?

She turned reluctantly from the nursery and stopped at the next room. Inside, small bookshelves full of books lined the walls. A library. Evan shoved her knife in her pocket and stepped inside. The smell of old paper and mildew made her wrinkle her nose.

"Hello." An older woman wearing oversized glasses and a gray cardigan smiled at her.

"Hi," Evan replied.

"Can I help you find something?"

"Just browsing."

"Well, if you want to check anything out, you have to see me, and I'll write it down for you."

"I'll do that." Evan headed to the first stack of books and ran her fingers over them. It had been almost a decade since she'd seen that many books.

"Where did all these come from?" she asked.

"A while ago we asked that when the raiders went out that they please bring back any books they found."

"It's amazing."

The books had been sectioned off by fiction and non-fiction and alphabetized. If she'd been more of a reader she knew where she'd be spending her time.

"Evan, there you are." Tommy jogged over. "It's shift break. Seth is off to get something to eat. Peter is getting ready to leave with the raiding crew. We have about thirty minutes that I can get you in there and cover for you if needed."

She nodded and followed him swiftly out of the library.

"Let me do the talking," Tommy said.

She had to admit that Tommy was better with people than she was. His laid-back air and friendly smile put people at ease in a way that she'd never been able to.

He took the lead and walked toward the guard she didn't recognize.

"Hey, Johnny," said Tommy.

"Howdy."

"Lou sent us down to check on the prisoners. This is my sister, Evan. She's been put in charge of questioning the new vampyr."

Johnny looked between them. "I should call Lou and make sure."

"Sure," said Tommy. "He's out loading the trucks so the raiding team can get on the road. I'm sure he won't mind."

Evan held her breath. If he called Lou, they'd both be dead.

Johnny licked his lips. "Nah. It's cool." He chuckled and opened the door.

Evan's nerves raced like a jackrabbit as she walked to William's room with Tommy.

"I'll wait here."

She nodded and stepped into the dim room. The sunlight crept in through the small window, and William lay on the floor across from it.

"Hey," she called.

He didn't move.

"William?" Chills ran up her spine. "William?" She raced to his side, panic etching her voice.

She rolled him over and he groaned. His face swole worse than before.

"Peter! I'm going to kill him." She jumped to her feet.

He grabbed her ankle. "Stay," he croaked.

She pushed the hair from his face. "What can I do?"

"I need blood."

Her mind raced. "I don't think there is any here. I can see if maybe there's some in the lab. Or..."

"Blood."

She licked her lips. It'd been a long time since she'd let someone drink from her. And that hadn't been by choice. Never once. Not even after she and Travis had started sleeping together had she willingly given him blood, not that he'd ever asked her permission.

She lifted his sweatshirt with a shaky hand revealing every battered and bruised inch of his torso. It had been at least two weeks since he'd had real blood. He wouldn't heal without blood. Human blood. Not animal. Not synthetic.

A cold sweat bloomed on her skin and her palms grew clammy.

She tried to swallow but her throat clenched so tight she thought she'd choke herself.

"Okay," she finally said. "Where do you want me?"

"Evan–"

She shook her head. "Don't even try to talk me out of this."

She pushed up her sleeve and held her arm out to his mouth. He couldn't even lift his head and his weak grip on her skin made her have to help him bring her wrist to his lips.

He hesitated and his eyes connected with hers. Her gut clenched, but she nodded.

His eyelids closed and he bit into her wrist. She let out a shuddered breath as the pull on her vein shot horrible memories through her. A moment of panic crawled up her spine, torturing her. She wanted to pull away. To scream and slap him.

His fingers caressed her forearm, and she looked down to find his eyes on her again. The cooling pull on her vein conflicted with the warmth that spread through her body. He gulped over and over. Minutes passed and his drinking slowed until he finally licked her wound shut and pulled her down on top of him in one fell swoop. His lips attacked hers. His tongue plunging into her mouth, probing and searching every surface.

His hand traveled up her spine and tangled in her hair. The cement floor dug into her elbows as she tried to prop herself up. He broke the kiss, and his lips glided down her throat.

"Evan," he murmured against her skin.

"Evangeline," she whispered. "My name is Evangeline."

He crooned her name again sending a chill over her.

"I want you," he said.

It'd been so long... She didn't want to give in, to tell him the truth. To tell him how she felt about him would open a door that she wouldn't be able to shut again. If she let him in, she was opening herself to the pleasure as well as the pain that came with caring for someone.

"I want you too," she said.

His hands pushed under her shirt.

"Wait," she said. "We can't do this now."

"Why?" He kissed her again.

"Because..." She pulled away. "You haven't had a bath in a week."

A wide grin broke across his face. "It's been longer actually."

"Even more reason."

His smile fell a fraction and he pushed her hair behind her ear. "I want to make love to you. I've wanted to make love to you since I first saw you. In a soft bed with lots of pillows. Feeling your weight on my body, your nails on my skin—"

"You've had a long time to think about this."

He kissed her. "A very a long time."

The door to the cell flew open.

"Evan!" Peter rushed into the room and pulled her to her feet. "Are you all right?"

William jumped up. "Get off her."

Peter's fiery gaze stabbed him. "You disgusting son of a bitch."

William took a step closer to Peter and Evan. "I said, get your hands off her."

"William, I'm fine." Evan wasn't sure what to do that wouldn't make things worse.

Peter looked between her and William. "What the hell is going on here?"

"I can explain," she replied.

"Are you screwing this bloodsucker?" Peter's fingers pressed into her arms.

Anger coursed through Evan and she tried to wiggle out of his grasp. "You're hurting me."

"I'm not going to tell you again to get your hands off her," said William.

"Tell me!" Peter shook her.

Before Evan could speak, William grabbed Peter and threw him across the room. Peter scrambled to his feet, but William crossed and slammed him into the wall before kneeing him in the ribs. Despite Peter having a good forty pounds on William, William's vampiric nature gave him the upper hand.

"Don't you know you never put your hands on a woman?" William punched Peter in the face.

"William, stop." Evan crossed to him and grabbed his arm.

William turned to her, and in that moment, Peter punched him in the jaw. William stumbled, and Evan took his place and slammed Peter into the wall.

"You've done enough."

"How could you?" Peter yelled. "He's a bloodsucker."

"What the hell is wrong with you? You're not this person Peter, I know you aren't. You have to stop this now before you can't go back. Think of Petie. He needs someone to look up to."

"What do you think I'm doing this for? So my son learns the difference between us and them. So he doesn't have to grow up afraid. I'm going to show him we're just as strong and twice as good as these vermin."

"He's a person. His name is William. And he saved my life."

"What the hell is going on?" Lou walked in with the other guard.

"She's screwing this bloodsucker," Peter said.

"I haven't slept with William," she protested. "Lou, I won't deny that he is someone I care for."

"Evan!"

"He's a good person. He saved my life. And what he told you is true. There are demons in Chicago, and they are trying to take over."

"You've seen them?"

"I've seen two. Two that are trying to help us."

"I can't believe you've done this, Evan. I knew you weren't ready to deal with what we're working on here, but I had no idea you were this far gone."

"I'm not gone. I see more clearly than ever. Vampires are no longer our enemy. There are those out there who need our help."

"You've been brainwashed. That's the only reason you would lie to me about knowing this bloodsucker." Lou turned to Tommy. "And you. Did you know about this?"

"No." Evan wasn't about to let Tommy get a tongue lashing for what she'd done. "I dragged Tommy down here. Told him I was going to question William. He had nothing to do with any of this."

Tension lingered in the air.

"Everyone out. Evan, you are forbidden from coming to this area again," said Lou.

"You can't do that," she said.

Lou stepped forward. "This is my house, and I can do whatever the hell I want."

"Well the only way you're gonna keep me away from William is by either chaining me up or kicking me out. You've been letting Peter come down here and beat the crap out of William and William hasn't fought back. Not at all till now.

Because of me. Because I was in danger. Something I never thought I'd ever have to worry about from my own family."

"Are you questioning my methods?" Lou demanded.

"How many have you let Peter and the others work out their anger on?"

"That's enough!" Lou yelled. "I will not be questioned by you. You've been compromised. We'll have to deal with it accordingly." He motioned to the guard from the hall.

The guard moved toward Evan. William stepped between them.

"Leave her alone. I did it. I enticed her. It isn't her fault."

"William, I'm capable of taking care of myself." She tried to step around him.

The guard lunged for her as did Peter. William growled and pounced on the guard, kicking Peter out of the way at the same time. The guard threw a punch at William but William caught it and pushed him back. Lou advanced, producing a stun gun from his pocket. He aimed it at William, but Evan shielded him with her body.

The charge hit her like lightning to the chest. Every muscle clenched tight as a coil and then sprang back into place. Over and over her muscles contracted and released. Screaming and yelling filled her ears from all directions, but she couldn't concentrate to figure out what was happening.

Lights flickered on and off before her eyes, and her teeth chattered together so hard she thought they would splinter. Finally, the shockwave stopped, and she dropped to the ground like a pile of dirty laundry. The yelling became nothing more than a buzz in her ears as aftershocks left her twitchy and discombobulated. Bodies moved all around her. A pair of strong arms grabbed her around her waist and pulled her out of the fray.

WILLIAM FLEW AT LOU, TACKLING HIM TO THE GROUND AND PUNCHING him over and over. Peter jumped on his back, and William continued to swing at the older man as Peter attempted to cut off his airway.

Lou put up his hands to protect his face, and Peter squeezed tighter, dragging William away. The guard snatched up the Taser from the floor and headed for William but William kicked out and connected with the guard, pushing him back. He flipped Peter over his shoulders and Peter hit the cement with a crack and a scream. William bared his fangs and dove for Peter's throat.

"Stop!" Tommy yelled. "Please. Stop."

William's head whipped up and his gaze connected with Tommy. The large man held Evan in his arms. She twitched but her eyes remained fixed on him.

"Please," Tommy begged.

William looked down at Peter and then over at the guard and Lou. All three lay winded and battered.

William had tried not to lose his temper. He hadn't meant to, hadn't wanted to. But threatening Evan and then Tasing her... He couldn't just stand by and let that happen.

"William." She held out her hand to him.

He crawled away from Peter to her side and stroked her cheek. "I'm sorry," he said. "I shouldn't have lost my temper."

"No," said Lou getting to his feet. "You shouldn't have."

A shot rang out, and a sting struck William in the arm. A dart protruded from his torn sweatshirt. He pulled it out and everything went fuzzy.

His gaze connected with Evan's.

"William?"

He dropped to the cement, his head hitting it with a crack like thumping on a watermelon.

She crawled closer but the sound of his name on her lips disappeared. Then, everything else did as well.

CHAPTER FOURTEEN

"*W*ake up. Wake up!*"*

William awoke, his eyelids like lead. Bright lights shone from every angle, searing his eyes. A faint beeping sound and the smell of antiseptic permeated the air. He glanced around and found himself surrounded by medical equipment. He tried to sit up but couldn't. Only in his underwear, he lay strapped to a hospital bed. Panic gnawed at his gut. His arms, feet, and chest were restrained with leather straps. It surprised him to find that he'd been washed. An IV dangled from his left arm and a clear solution dripped into his veins. To his right hung a clear curtain separating him from the rest of the facility. In an office at the other end of the room sat three men William couldn't quite make out.

Along one wall several glass enclosures housed a dozen or so people. A girl with bright white mohawk type hair stared at him from behind one of the glass walls.

"You need to get up. You need to get out of here."

William heard the voice in his head as if someone sat right

next to him and whispered it in his ear. He shook his head and then dropped his heavy head back on the pillow.

He tried to collect his thoughts as memories of the fight in his cell surfaced. He groaned, remembering the pain Evan had endured at the hands of her uncle. Humans and Vampires alike could do horrible things, even to those they cared about, if they thought it was for the greater good.

Four humans in lab coats sat at various metal tables working. The plastic curtain rustled, and William turned. A tall guard with red hair and freckled skin stared at him.

"He's awake!" he yelled.

The men in the office stood and the door opened.

A man in a lab coat and Lou walked to William's bedside. Another person in scrubs came in with a chart, jotting down notes.

"What's going on?" asked William.

"I'm Nicholas," said the man in the white coat. "You're in my lab."

A Vampire was the scientist? "But what am I doing here?"

"I'm sure Evan told you, one of our main goals here is to find a cure for the vamps. With you two being close and all," said Lou.

William stayed silent. He didn't need to get Evan in any more trouble than she already had. The desire to ask if she was okay bubbled in his throat, but he swallowed it down. He prayed that she was fine and already on the run from this horrible place.

"Peter and a group were supposed to go out and round up a couple vamps for us to try our latest serum on. But you broke his leg," said Lou. "Compound fracture."

"My work must progress," said Nicholas. "If what you say is

true about the demons, and I suspect it is, it is more important than ever that we find a cure."

"Unfortunately, we don't have any vamps at the moment. So we're going to use the next best thing."

"But I'm not a vamp." Fear mixed with dread inside him. He was about to become someone's lab rat.

"It shouldn't matter too much," said Nicholas. "Your blood is similar to theirs."

"Similar but not exactly the same," William replied.

"I don't care either way," said Lou. "Be glad this was what the doctor suggested for you, bloodsucker. If it was up to me, you'd get far worse."

Another assistant walked in holding a syringe.

William pulled at his restraints. His skin crawled like a million snakes slithering over him.

Nicholas took the syringe and walked to William's IV.

He didn't want to show fear. He wanted to stay strong. For Evan, for Danika. But all logic left him as the needle plunged into the port at his wrist and a burning sensation raced up his arm.

"What... What's going to happen to me?" he asked.

"To be honest," said Nicholas. "I don't know. But I hope this will make you human again."

"Human? I don't want to be human."

Lou stepped closer. "Well then maybe you'll get the outcome I'm hoping for. That you'll die slow and painful. What you did to my baby girl—" Lou turned and strode out.

The assistants gathered their things to leave, but Nicholas hung back a moment until they were all out of earshot. "They said you're from Chicago," he said.

William couldn't take his eyes off his arm as the veins under the skin turned from white to black to blue. "Yes."

"Did you happen to know a Danika Chekov?"

William's head snapped up. Danika? How did Nicholas know Danika? His mind raced wondering if it would hurt him or help him to divulge their relationship- but the burning from the serum turned to acid in his veins. and every question vanished in one foul breath.

"I'm her fledgling," he managed through gritted teeth.

William dropped his head onto his pillow. His body lurched and convulsed at the serum made its way through him. Every inch of him burned like his skin melted off his bones. His muscles twisted and he writhed in agony, straining against his bonds. His eyes grew hot and waves of nausea coursed through him.

The scientist's lips pressed together in a tight line. He nodded once. "I truly hope this works. For your sake, and Danika's."

The thick plastic curtains swung together, and the scientist's form blurred and disappeared.

"I hope I die," William croaked.

EVAN HAD BEEN CONFINED TO HER ROOM THE ENTIRE FOLLOWING week. By the second day she'd decided that she had to get William out of there. She'd gone to see if the phone he'd given her had any other phone numbers in it but his, but to her torture, the phone had vanished. She'd ripped her entire room apart and even asked the guards if they'd been in her room. They said they hadn't so she assumed Lou had taken the phone. She blamed herself for not hiding it better.

Every morning Joe brought her food, set it on her desk, and

asked if she was okay. And every morning she would ask about William and Tommy. The first day he'd informed her that Peter's leg had been broken in the fight. She wished she'd been the one to break it. And a bunch of his other parts as well. But knowing Peter's healing abilities, he wouldn't be down for more than a couple weeks. And every day Joe would say he didn't know anything about William and Tommy before leaving.

She, however, found her own leg to be less than cooperative. Though the wound had closed and only a jagged crimson scar remained, at odd moments it would ache or spasm, making it unreliable at best.

An hour after Joe would leave, Lou would arrive. He'd show her photographs of her parents, her siblings, his wife, and dozens of other people, telling her the horrible things that Vampires had done to them.

He made her stand, arms outstretched for hours while he played videos of news clips from the Awakening and the Outbreak.

For seven days, he came and tried to bring her around to his way of thinking. And for seven days Evan thought of nothing but William.

By the following week, Evan had begun going stir crazy. She'd spent so many hours practicing with her throwing knives that nothing remained of the target but the hook nailed to the door. She'd wished she had a gun to practice with as well, but Lou knew better than to give her a firearm.

Being locked in her room with guards posted outside was worse than being at the coven house. She'd taken to counting the guards outside her window and writing down their rotation schedule to keep occupied. She calculated the steps to the fence, its height, and what it would take to jump it. Every moment not spent with her uncle was spent planning her escape.

Tuesday, the following week Tommy brought her food. She ran to him and threw her arms around him in joy.

"Oh my gosh. Are you okay?"

He pushed past her and set her food on the desk, refusing to meet her eye. A chill ran up her spine, and she grabbed him by the arm before he left. His head snapped up, and she noticed his black eye and split lip.

"What's going on?" she asked.

His brow furrowed and he shook his head. He stepped closer to the exit and she blocked his path.

"You've been in a fight. Please, Tommy. I've been in here for almost a week and a half. I don't know what's going on with you or William. I didn't even know if you guys were dead or alive or being tortured. I know you're mad at me because of what happened to Peter and I'm sorry about his leg but please... Tell me what the hell is going on. Is it William? Did something happen?" Panic scoured over her.

He opened his mouth, but the door swung inward and one of the guards looked in. "Tommy. Lou asked to see you."

Tommy nodded and pushed past Evan. Tears blurred her vision, and she swiped them away. Her lies had cost her the only friend and family she had left.

She had to get out.

WILLIAM COUGHED VIOLENTLY. BLOOD TRICKLED FROM HIS NOSE AND mouth down onto his bare chest. His head pounded as though it were in a vise grip. Sounds were muffled from the buildup of dried blood caked in his ears.

Nicholas had inclined the bed two days prior, afraid that William would choke on his own blood. From his vantage point, William had a view of the entire lab. For the past week, everyone had gone about their business as if William wasn't even there. Everyone except Nicholas, who spent hours talking to him about the demons and Chicago and his life there. It wasn't a friendly conversation as much as a fact-collecting expedition.

The only other company he had had was the prying eyes of the people in the glass cells and a voice rambling at him in his head. Something told him that the voice belonged to the tall white-haired girl in the glass room, but he didn't know anyone who had a telepathic ability so in the end he blamed the voice on his ever deteriorating mental state.

The thirst had built day after day to the point where his every focus had become blood. He tracked the humans that came into the room with predatory precision. The sound of their veins pumped in his ears like a maddening musical earworm he couldn't get rid of. The scent of their fear if they had to enter his section was a fragrant wine that delighted his senses. Like a starving man in the desert, his every thought consisted of the feed.

Twice so far they'd tried to give him human blood transfusions, but it only made him hungrier. The small, beady-eyed lab tech with the pockmarked face who gave them took special pleasure in sticking William over and over with the needle, claiming to have missed the vein. Holes and scabs zigzagged from his hands to his elbows, itching and stinging the skin that he was unable to scratch.

The bell on the elevator rang, and William's head whipped

that direction. He tried to focus his thoughts as Lou stepped out of the elevator with Evan in tow. His mind jumped between wanting to scream at her to get away and the all-consuming need to drain her dry like the rest of them.

Her beaten expression stretched to the rest of her body as her shoulders slumped and she trudged forward. Lou pushed her toward the clear plastic barrier that separated William's area from the rest of the lab. Evan spotted him and dashed away from Lou. She threw the curtain wide and ran for his bed. Feet from him, she skidded to a stop.

The pulsing of her veins was like a jackhammer in his head.

"William?" Her tentative and fearful expression ripped through him.

"Don't... come... closer..." he croaked. He licked his lips at the sweet fragrance of her body.

Tears welled in her eyes and she stepped closer. His muscles twitched at the thought of draining her. She reached for him, and he bared his teeth and pulled on his restraints to get at her. The restraints creaked and groaned but held tight.

Lou tugged her away.

"See," said Lou. "He's like all the others. He wants nothing more than to drain you dry."

She yanked from Lou's grasp. "What did you do to him?"

"I did this for you, baby girl. To save him for you. To make him human again so you could be together proper if that's what you wanted, but you can see now that it isn't possible. Vampires are Vampires. They always will be. Nothing but the thirst matters to them. I'm sorry. I truly am."

She looked back at William. "I don't believe you. William isn't like this."

Inside the recesses of his mind, he wanted to tell her that she was right, this wasn't him, but he couldn't get the words out. He had no way to tell her what Lou had done. Every shred of his remaining sanity focused solely on trying not to kill her and everyone else in the room.

"Evan..." He moaned and closed his eyes. When he opened them again, she'd stepped closer. "Go."

Again, he lurched from the bed, unable to take the scent of her any longer. He tugged at the leather cuffs, flexing every muscle in his body, but in his weakened state, he was no better than a human at trying to break them. He growled and snarled and then flew into a coughing fit, spewing blood over the front of her. She gasped and stepped away.

"You! You did this," he yelled at Lou. "I'm going to kill you. When I get off this bed, I'm going to rip your head from your spine. I'm going to tear your throat out and bathe in your blood. Then I'm going to find Peter, and I'm going to remove his arms and beat him to death with them. I'm going to drain every last miserable drop from the humans in this place. I'm going to kill you all. That's what you deserve. All of you. You deserve to die."

His eyes landed on Evan, and she swallowed hard, backing away. He didn't care what she saw; he didn't care what she thought. All he wanted in that moment was her blood.

EVAN USED HER T-SHIRT TO WIPE WILLIAM'S BLOOD FROM HER FACE. Her hands shook so hard she could barely make them do what she wanted them to. She'd never seen a Vampire or vampyr look that bad before. Blood dripping from every orifice, staining his chiseled, pale chest. But the blood hadn't been the worst of it. The worst had been his eyes. Greedy, hungry eyes that wanted to devour her. She'd heard of bloodlust before, but this was different. He was different. Lou had taken a gentle soul and turned him into the monster that they had always been taught that Vampires were. How could he do that to someone? Someone who'd taken all the abuse they'd shelled out and only when she had been threatened had he finally reacted.

She walked to her room in silence. The two guards still stood faithfully outside her room as Lou followed her inside. She headed for her wardrobe and stripped her T-shirt off, then grabbed another and yanked it on.

"I tried to tell you, baby girl. Now you see. They want for nothing except to use us as food."

She turned to face him. For several moments she couldn't speak.

"I'm sorry you had to see that." His face held true remorse.

"No. You aren't." Her voice came out flat and emotionless. "You thought taking me to see him like that would tip me back over to your side, but you don't know me anymore, and I don't know you."

"You need to understand—"

"No." She held up her hand. "You need to understand. What I saw up there, what you did to him, only confirmed to me that you are not the man that raised me. It confirmed to me that we aren't any better than the Vampires."

"How can you say that?"

"You took a kind and selfless man and turned him into a monster!" she shouted. "He risked his life time and time again for me. He has done nothing to you or to Peter but what you deserve. You twisted him and tested on him and have not a single ounce of remorse."

"Why should I? They killed my mother, my father, my brother, and his wife."

She stepped toward Lou, her fists balled. She wanted nothing more than to punch him in the jaw. "But not him! He didn't do that. He used to be human too. And this is the thanks he gets for having something happen to him that he had no control over."

"No matter how it happened, he isn't one of us anymore. He's one of them."

She nodded. "That's what I thought too until I met him. You took the one person who came here with goodwill, asking for help, and you murdered him. The one person that could have made a difference. And now... When his family finds out what you did... God help us all."

"Are you threatening me? Are they a threat? We are more than capable of taking care of those kind of things here." He took several steps closer to her.

She shook her head. "You have no idea what's out there. You live here, safe in this bubble, and you rule this world but you have no clue what it's like. I've seen the horrible and ugly things that happen, but no worse than the horrible and ugly things that happened when humans ran things. And then I come here. The one place that I dreamed every night of coming back to when I was out there, and I find the horrors even that much more unfathomable. And you. The man I once called dad. You're the worst of them all."

"Well then. If it's so bad here, and I'm so horrible, maybe you should go back to where you came from."

The offer hit her like a sledgehammer to the ribcage. If she left this time, there would be no returning. She'd live the rest of her life out there, on her own, on the run. Even if she went back to Chicago, without William, who knew what would happen to her. But if she could get William back to Chicago...

She blew out a heavy breath and looked at her feet. Finally, she wrapped her arms around herself and looked up at her uncle. "You're right," she said. "Maybe I should."

The door opened and Tommy carried in a tray of food. He looked between them, and then Lou swore and stormed out. Tommy jumped out of his way, almost spilling the contents of the tray on himself.

The door slammed shut and then the sounds of Lou cursing and punching the wall several times reverberated around the room.

Tommy set down the food.

"You already brought me something to eat," she said.

"I know." He stared at her long and hard before swallowing. "I want to help."

"Help what?" she asked.

He held up his key card. "You and William. I want to help you escape."

CHAPTER FIFTEEN

"Where are we going?" Evan swatted a fly away from her face and followed Tommy as closely as she was able in the dark without holding on to him. The scent of sweet fruit and dewy grass reminded her of home before the Outbreak.

They'd snuck out of the restaurant through a service entrance and ended up in the back area of the property. Impending rain clouds obscured the moon, and she barely could see her feet as they trudged through the orchard that had once been a golf course. To the left the sounds of chickens and pigs resounded from the converted tennis courts. She wondered if the swimming pool still remained or if they'd repurposed that as well.

"It's not much farther," Tommy whispered.

The sound of laughter stopped them in their tracks. Her heart pounded so loud she was sure Tommy heard it. Footsteps crunched on sticks and twigs and the sound of voices drew closer. Tommy pushed her behind himself and flattened them into the trunk of a giant apple tree. They held their breath as two guards passed by them a row over.

After several minutes, Tommy stepped away from her, and started again in the direction the guards had come from.

"There shouldn't be any more for at least fifteen minutes," he said.

"We'll have to hurry and get in and out."

His steps picked up and soon she ran to keep up with him.

They headed toward the far end and stopped at the edge of the orchard. He pointed into the darkness.

"There."

A large metal building with a faint light over the entrance gleamed in the night.

"What is it?" she asked.

"Used to be the maintenance shed. Now it's the weapons depot."

Tommy looked both ways across the fifty yards of open space that surrounded the building.

"Aren't there security cameras or something?"

"Nah. Who's going to steal the weapons? People here are wanting peace, not conflict. And no one outside of us know that it's here."

She nodded and again she wondered if Tommy truly thought Lou had just let those exiled people go.

"Ready?" he asked.

She sprinted into the open without asking permission. Tommy hissed her name but the two raced flat out across the expanse. Because of the inoculation, they crossed the area in under five seconds and hit the side of the building laughing.

"Beat ya again," she said.

"Because you got a head start," he countered.

"Because you're going soft from all this easy living, and I've had to keep on my toes out there." She smiled and he chuckled.

Evan tried the door handle. It was locked.

"You got the key?"

Tommy gave her a sheepish grin.

"Seriously, how do you expect us to get in? You lot never thought it prudent to teach me to pick locks." She tried to keep the irritation out of her voice.

He gestured with his head and rounded the building. Halfway down the side he pointed to a small window toward the top of the building. Beneath it hung a small ledge.

"You're joking, right?" she asked.

"You get a running start, I'll boost you up, and you make a grab for the ledge."

"That's got to be twelve feet up."

He grinned. "No higher than your bedroom window when we used to sneak out. Chicken?"

She grumbled. Tommy knew that word that could get her to do about anything. He and Peter had used it on her frequently growing up to get her to prove herself.

"Okay... but how do I know it's unlocked? And even if it is, there's no guarantee I'll fit through that thing."

"Well I'm not going to fit, that's for damn sure. It's our only option. We need weapons. This is the only way."

Evan stared at the window and ledge. It was high. Higher than she'd ever tried to jump before. No matter what Tommy said. With him boosting her up she might make it... maybe. And if she did make it...

She backed up twenty feet from the building.

"A little more." He motioned her back further.

She took another three steps and breathed deep. Tommy

laced his fingers together and braced himself by squatting down.

"Ready?" she whispered.

She neither saw nor heard his reply. Running, she headed straight for Tommy and leapt. Her foot connected with his hands, and she pushed off as he boosted her up. She leapt into the air and reached for the platform. The fingers on her right hand grabbed the ledge but her left hand slipped, and she dropped down to the ground with a thud. A jolt coursed through her leg. She cried out and grabbed her thigh.

"Dammit." So running she could do but falling upwards of twelve feet to the ground, not so much.

"Are you all right?" Tommy rushed to her side.

The pain zigzagged up to her hip and down to her knee. She rolled on the ground cradling her leg.

"Damn that hurt." She breathed through the pain until it subsided.

"Maybe this is a bad idea."

"No." She got to her feet and tested her weight. The leg ached and shook but held. "I can do it. I just need to try again."

"I don't know. That looked worse than I had imagined when I thought this out."

She put her hand on his shoulder. "We have to do this. It's fine. I'm fine. I'll make it this time." She had to make it this time. She refused to let the attack from a stupid slaver cripple her for life. But she knew her leg wouldn't give her a third chance at the jump.

"Again." She hobbled back to her starting position. Her leg shot a pain like every nerve had been flayed open and attached to a live wire. She had to do this. William lay in the lab strapped to a table and dying because of her.

She nodded, reassuring herself more than trying to reassure

Tommy. She sucked in a breath and raced at Tommy again. Her leg screamed, but she just gritted her teeth and ran harder, pushing off as he boosted her up. She reached as far as she could and grabbed the ledge with both hands.

"Yes!" She grinned like an idiot.

Dangling high above the ground, she pulled herself up to her elbows. The bumpy corrugated metal of the platform gave her traction but the rusty plates dug into her armpits. She threw her foot up on the ledge, hoisting herself up.

She rolled onto the metal the bumps of it pressing into her shoulder blades. She sucked in air and waited for her pounding heart to die down. Soon the adrenaline would wear off and she'd get shaky.

Above her, the small window waited to be opened.

"Are you okay?" Tommy called softly.

"Yeah." She got to her feet and inspected the aluminum-framed sliding window. Getting through would be a trick as it was no bigger than a vent window above a shower.

She pressed her fingers into the edge and tried to pry it open, but it wouldn't budge.

"I'm gonna have to break the glass," she called.

"Be careful."

"Be careful," she muttered. "Now he wants me to be careful?"

She glanced around for something to break the glass but there was nothing so she slid off her boot and shoved her hand inside it. Pulling her arm back, she tested the length and then punched the glass. It cracked and spiderwebbed but didn't break. She took a deep breath and, envisioned that the window to be Peter's face, she let her fist fly. The glass cracked and fell inward. It clattered to the ground a story below, and the noise reverberated around the building.

"Way to go, sis!" Tommy whispered.

She cleaned out as much glass as she was able and then slid the boot back on her foot and looked inside. A walkway hung inside the building about four feet down from the window.

She pulled herself into the ledge and tiny shards of glass on the top of the frame dug into her skin. She slid her legs inside and twisted so she rested on her stomach. When she got to her hips, she couldn't get through. Darn those extra eggs and toast.

Evan wiggled and twisted to take advantage of the diagonal space. Her shirt crept up and her side pressed down on the glass and then stopped.

"Are you okay? We have to hurry," said Tommy.

The air squeezed tight in her chest. She pressed and wiggled in the window frame trying to get free.

"I'm stuck!"

Tommy cursed.

If she stayed stuck in the window not only was she dead meat, but Tommy would be as well. She pushed with her arms and wiggled her torso. The glass shards dug into her sides, cutting her skin. She grimaced and muttered a string of profanity as blood trickled down her hips. She slipped a little, then took a breath and shook her head. This plan really sucked.

Leaning into the glass shards, she forced them to cut deeper into her skin. She shimmied again and slipped through the window, landing hard on the walkway.

Blood slicked her sides and stained her pants.

"Damn." Her body stung from her hips to her breasts. She wiped her torso with her T-shirt and pulled several slivers of glass from her stomach.

The floor of the building contained several large military trucks, tables full of guns, and ammunition and crates stacked high all along two walls.

Lou hadn't been lying when he'd said they were prepared for any attack. She jogged down the walkway but where there should have been stairs they'd been ripped off. *Great.*

She headed back to where she'd started and hopped over the railing. Lowering herself as far as possible, she dropped to the top of the truck. The vehicle shook beneath her and she slipped as she landed. She slid down the windshield, then bumped over the hood and landed hard on the dirt ground.

Her body ached from the jump, the fall, the cuts, the stab wound to her leg. She lay winded on the cement dreaming of sipping a margarita next to a pool instead of breaking into a weapons building. Not that she'd ever had a margarita. But she remembered seeing a movie when she was a kid. A woman on a tropical island sipped a margarita while a cabana boy fanned her. Evan had always thought that would be the height of luxury. Too bad everything had happened before she'd gotten old enough to drink.

She got to her feet, located the door, and limped to it. She opened it and peeked out.

"Tommy," she whispered.

There was no answer.

"Tommy—"

A large hand clamped over her mouth and shoved her inside. She kicked out and tore at the hand as the door shut and locked.

"Shhh... Evan, it's me." Tommy removed his hand from her mouth.

She smacked him in the chest. "Dammit, Tommy, what did you do that for?"

"Shhh..." He held his fingers to her lips. His eyes stayed focused on the entrance.

Someone outside tried the handle and then two people continued a conversation and moved on.

"Sorry," he said. "I saw them coming right as you opened the door."

The longer she stood the more her energy waned. She headed for the tables of guns and ammo. "Let's move."

"You're limping."

"Yeah, well, running, jumping, falling, falling again, and then falling again. All while having been stabbed in the leg only a week ago, tends to leave me a bit sore." She scanned the dark table and found a revolver with the appropriate ammo. She shoved the gun into her waistband and the ammo into her pocket. Then she grabbed two hunting knives and put one in each boot.

"The big ones will be harder to hide," said Tommy.

"Then we have to stay small." She scanned over the remaining guns and picked out two more. Lifting her shirt, she pushed them into her waistband.

"What the hell?" Tommy stepped up to her and lifted her shirt.

"I couldn't fit through the window." She lowered the black shirt back over the deep gouges. She looked like she'd been in a wrestling match with a lion. The cuts had stopped dripping but they still oozed.

"You'll need to tend to that," he said. "After this I'll go to the hospital wing. I'll get as many bags of blood as I can conceal and some first aid supplies as well."

She headed to another table and looked at the items laid out. She picked up several flash grenades as well as three regular grenades and put them in her waistband.

"William had bags of supplies. Do you know what happened to them?"

"The vehicle was trashed, but if there were bags inside it, I'm sure the supplies were scavenged."

"Look for black duffel bags. There should be three or four. It'll save us time if you can just grab those and not have to find all the supplies individually."

Tommy nodded.

She stared at her cousin and her chest squeezed. Doing this for her meant he'd be turning his back on his own family.

"You don't have to do this, Tommy. I can knock you out, and you can tell them I forced you to help me when they find you."

His brows furrowed. "Do you not want me to come with you?"

"No, that's not it at all," she said. "I just... I don't want to be the reason you turn your back on Pop and Peter."

Tommy licked his lips. "You aren't the reason. William is. I saw what they did to him."

"But they've done it to others before."

"Yeah, but I never really saw it until now. I never realized how far we'd fallen and how bad it had gotten. Not till I saw you with him. I tried to deny that Pop had changed. Telling myself that as soon as all this was over we'd be like we used to be. But we won't, will we?"

"Who knows if it will ever be over. And if it is... None of us can go back to who we were before."

He nodded. "Then I'd rather go with you. At least I know you're still trying to do what's right."

Evan hugged Tommy tight and kissed his cheek.

"Thank you, bro."

"Hey now. Be careful." He pushed her to arm's length. "You have explosives all over your body."

She chuckled. "We better get back."

She turned in a circle and spotted a stack of black cases neatly tucked next to the tables. She crossed to them and flipped the latches of the one on top.

She couldn't keep the smiled and chuckle that emerged. "Well, hello there."

GETTING BACK INTO THE RESORT TOOK MUCH LONGER THAN IT HAD TO get out. But when they got inside they didn't return to their rooms. Instead, they took the black weapon cases down to the parking garage. Tommy located one of a hundred SUV's that would be easy to maneuver out of the garage and they slid the cases into the trunk.

"Now we just need to get the first aid stuff, and get out of here."

Tommy looked at his watch. "It's two-thirty. If we can get out in the next sixty minutes, we have a better chance of people not noticing we're missing until at least seven or eight. Possibly later."

"I'll go to my room and wait."

"Pack light but take what you want. We won't be coming back and even if we did, I doubt anything we leave behind will be there."

Evan pulled him into a light hug. "Be careful."

He closed the trunk. "See ya soon."

EVAN PEERED DOWN THE HALLWAY TO HER ROOM; THERE WASN'T another soul in sight. Thus far, she and Tommy had been able to keep out of the view of the cameras. The ones in the larger areas rotated and by timing them, they'd been able to move freely. But the one in her hallway stayed stationary. The only way to avoid detection was to act as though she belonged. Not drawing attention was the best form of camouflage.

She took a breath and walked into the view of the camera. Face passive, gait slow but steady, she headed for her room. To her surprise, the absence of the two guards hadn't caught anyone's attention yet. She had to consciously keep herself from glancing at the camera as she pulled her key card from her pocket and slid it into the lock. The light turned green.

The door swung inward and the now conscious guards lay hog tied and gagged on her floor.

She closed the door behind her, the two men shooting daggers her direction. She stopped and glared at them.

"Don't give me the stink eye. We could have killed you but we didn't." She walked to the bed, being careful to step over the smaller of the two guards, lifted her shirt, and set all of the grenades as well as the guns and ammo on the bed.

She walked to her wardrobe and pulled it open. There wasn't a suitcase but there was a backpack. She tugged it out. Her mom had gotten it for her on her thirteenth birthday. A black and pink plaid backpack for school. She let out a hiccuped sigh and walked to her CD collection.

She pulled out her five favorite CDs. Then she grabbed her favorite scarf, a couple pairs of underwear, T-shirts, and a new pair of pants as well as some sweats. William would need clothes too, but he'd have to wear something of Tommy's.

Lastly, she went to her small jewelry box and put it inside the backpack along with the leather case of knives. She looked around her room at everything left.

She valued nothing else. All of it could be replaced in the future, if she lived that long. Nervous energy settled in her bones, and she sat on the bed to wait. She refused to let "what if" scenarios infect her and take over her thoughts. Instead, she went over the plan. She ran it through her mind over and over until there was nothing but the plan. The plan and William's handsome face.

CHAPTER SIXTEEN

William's eyes burned as he tracked the one remaining human walking around the lab. The one who liked to stab him with needles. He had no concept of how much time had passed since Evan had come to see him. The thirst stormed his brain like a dense fog, sweeping over every thought and tainting the air a grayish blue.

The man moved from his station at a microscope to a machine that looked like an oversized microwave. His scent and the pounding of the blood in his veins assaulted William. The man walked back to the microscope and their eyes connected.

"Stop staring at me, leech," the man spat.

William ground his teeth. "When I get free, I'm going to kill you first."

The man snorted and pushed his glasses up his nose. "When you get free, it'll be to put your rotten corpse in the furnace."

William growled low in his chest. Dried blood caked the front of him, making his chest and face itch. The bleeding hadn't stopped, and it surprised William that he wasn't dead already.

He slammed his head back on his pillow and howled in rage, pulling on the restraints again and again.

"Quiet down over there!" the tech shouted. "Some of us are actually trying to undo the crapstorm your kind unleashed on the world."

The tech turned up a stereo on his table.

William stared at the white lab coat, picturing it on the floor splattered in blood, and wanted nothing more than to make that happen.

The elevator rang and William's gaze whipped to it. The doors opened and Tommy stepped out. He growled at the sight of Tommy. William would kill Lou and Peter for what they'd done to him and if it would hurt them, he'd even kill Tommy. The pain he'd envisioned inflicting on the two men over the past week burned in his mind he'd been having trouble figuring out whether or not he'd already killed them.

Tommy's face registered shock at seeing William. Good. Let him be afraid. Let them all be afraid.

Evan stepped out from behind Tommy and in a snap his heart and mind collided in an avalanche of emotion and conscious.

She peeked around Tommy's shoulder. He bared his teeth, but she held her finger to her lips and then pointed to the lab tech. He tried to concentrate on her miming but the lust in his gut only made him think now there were three. Three people he could drain instead of one.

No! He shook his head. Trying to hold the thirst at bay was like trying to stop a broken levee with a cardboard box.

Evan. He concentrated on her face. Her beautiful blue eyes and the stubborn yet soft way they commanded his attention. He'd never drain her. Never.

She whispered something to Tommy, who nodded. The lab tech still had his back to them, his music drowning everything out. Tommy headed with quick, cautious steps toward the tech as Evan made her way toward William.

She parted the clear curtains and her scent slapped him in the face, making his stomach growl and his fangs ache to taste her, to bleed her, to drain her dry.

No! William threw his head back and squeezed his eyes shut tight. *No. Not Evan.* He wouldn't do that to her. But the other two...

A warm hand fell on his cheek and his eyes whipped open. The distinct odor of fear trickled up his nostrils.

"We're getting out of here," she whispered.

William tried to nod his head, but his eyes latched onto her jugular and the pulling rhythm entranced him.

Tommy snuck up on the lab tech. Evan's breath caught as Tommy wrapped his arm around the tech's throat cutting off his airway. The tech flailed and kicked. His foot connected with the stool he'd been sitting on, and he knocked it over with a clatter. Every person in the glass rooms got up on their feet at the sound. The white haired twins looked at each other and then stared at William.

Evan unbound his wrist and headed for his ankles. "We don't have much time."

William unbuckled his chest restraint. Every nerve awoke ready to feed. He waited till she finished with his ankles, and then he sprang from the bed.

"William!"

He dashed past her and pushed Tommy out of the way.

Before anyone could stop him, he climbed on top of the unconscious lab tech and sank his fangs into the man's soft flesh. The first gulp of blood gushed into his mouth and coated his tongue. He moaned and sucked harder.

"William! Stop!" Evan cried.

A pair of strong hands gripped William's shoulders and tried to tear him away. William wrapped his arms around the tech's torso and continued to drink. Strength rushed through his limbs, and he hung on tighter.

Euphoria burst through like an electric blanket and the thirst dissipated slightly. Tommy tried to pick William up and shake him off, but William hung on.

The blood flow slowed. Just a few more swallows and he'd be finished. He should stop. Let the man go and get the hell out of there. But he didn't. William gulped down the blood. He deserved every last drop the bastard had to give him.

A blow to the kidneys made him howl in pain and release the tech.

He whipped around and spotted Tommy. He bared his teeth and lunged.

Evan stepped between them and raised her forearm as a shield. William grabbed it and bit into her wrist. She cried out as he took his first gulp.

"Get off her!" Tommy lunged, but Evan pushed him back.

"It's okay," she said.

William sucked greedily from her vein. Her eyes connected with his and softened.

"It's okay."

He sucked hard from her weak wrist veins trying to pull out more blood. Evan lifted her other hand and stroked his cheek.

"I know you're in there," she said. "I know you can hear me, William."

He stared at her and continued to drink.

She stumbled slightly but held Tommy back.

"He's going to kill you," Tommy said.

"No." She kept her eyes on William. "He won't. I know he won't. I know William. He's hungry but he'll stop."

Stop. Stop. Stop. He blinked several times and stared at Evan. *Shit.* What was he doing? The thirst clicked off and William scrambled to remember what was happening. He licked her wound shut and gathered her in his arms.

"Evan. I'm so sorry. The thirst... the hunger..."

She gripped him fiercely. "It's okay. It's all right. But we need to go. We have to get out of here."

He looked around the lab. Go. Leave. Yes, they needed to get out.

"I have no clothes."

"Here." Evan crossed to the dead lab tech. "Help me." She stripped off the tech's shoes and socks and then undid his belt.

"We don't have time." Tommy watched William warily.

William stared down at the dead man. He'd done that. He'd killed a man. He'd almost killed Evan.

"Go," he whispered. Guilt ran through him like a stampede of horses.

Evan glanced up as she tried to tug off the man's jeans. "Yes, we have to go."

"No." He pulled her to her feet. "You have to go. I have to stay."

Confusion played over her features. "You can't stay. If you stay you'll die."

The thirst scratched up his throat again.

"If I go with you who knows how many people will die."

"But you've fed. You'll be fine until we get you to Chicago." She searched his face.

He turned to Tommy. "Take her and leave. You aren't safe with me. Neither of you. Even now the thirst is building again. I won't risk killing the two of you. I'm as good as dead anyway."

Her palm came out of nowhere and smacked him hard across the cheek. William growled and whipped to face her.

Her icy stare was one he'd seen too many times before. "Now you listen. You aren't going to kill me or Tommy and you are coming with us back to Chicago. So help me get the clothes off this man and put them on, or I'll give you a fight you won't easily win."

The anger in her voice both frightened and turned him on. Visions of bending her over the lab table and taking her right there flashed through his mind.

He nodded once, trying to keep from attacking her, for blood, for sex. Right then, his body didn't care. She threw the jeans at him and he yanked them on. Then he helped her get the T-shirt off the dead man. He slid his feet into the crowded shoes and tried not to be grossed out by the fact that he wore someone else's sneakers without socks.

"We've wasted enough time."

Evan took William's hand. "Stay with me."

He squeezed her hand tight.

The group headed for the elevator.

"Take us!"

William turned and looked at the twins.

"Take us with you, please."

The taller twin's voice reverberated through his mind.

He pulled Evan to a stop.

"What is it?"

"We need to take them too." His eyes never left the twins.

Tommy looked at the glass enclosure and the smaller twin smiled at him. Without another thought Tommy walked to the room, punched in a code on the door and pushed it open. The minute the twins stepped out of their room the other people went crazy. Banging on their windows and yelling to be let out.

"We can't take them all," said Evan. "Those two are all we can fit in the car."

Tommy looked at the others and then jogged back to Evan. They started again for the elevator but then the bell rang and they froze.

"There's a stairwell this way." Tommy led them the other direction.

They ran for the stairs and darted through as someone stepped out of the elevator.

Four of them leapt from stairwell to stairwell down the six flights of stairs. But the taller of the white-haired twins jumped down the entire staircase and landed in the middle on the bottom floor before anyone else had gotten half way down.

"Holy shit! What else can you do?" asked Tommy when they hit the ground level.

She shrugged. "What can't I do?"

William stared at her and she turned to look at him. Hybrids. That's what he'd heard the techs call the people in the cells. But hybrids of what?

An alarm blared through the hotel.

"We have to get to the garage," Tommy yelled over the noise.

"How?" Evan asked.

"Stay out of the way and act natural."

Evan turned to William. "Stay behind me and keep your head down."

Act natural. The only *natural* way William wanted to act at the moment was to *naturally* drink every human in the hotel dry.

Tommy opened the door and looked out. The group headed into the hallway and turned left. A chaotic mess of guards with weapons ran in every direction.

Across the lobby, William spotted Lou and Peter, using a pair of crutches. He lunged that direction but Evan's grip on his hand tightened.

"No," she said.

He looked between her and Lou. His muscles twitched with wanting to rip the man's face off.

She stepped in his line of sight, breaking his focus.

"No," she said softly.

His arousal stirred again and like a puppy on a leash, he followed her in the opposite direction.

They headed down the hallway and toward a side exit. The door opened and Joe ran in, a rifle in his hands. He stopped in his tracks when he spotted them. His gaze traveled between the group and landed on William.

Everyone froze.

"What's going on here isn't right, Joe," said Evan. "If you let us go, I won't tell and we won't ever come back."

"Please," said Tommy. "We've been friends a long time. I'm begging you."

Joe's gaze didn't move from William and neither did his rifle.

The taller twin stepped up to Joe. "Go and forget you saw us."

Joe's eyes glazed over and he jogged past them without a word.

"Is he going to be okay?" Evan asked. "What did you do to him?"

Jealousy spiked in William at Evan's concern and his fist clenched tight.

"He'll be fine," said the smaller twin.

"Now or never," said Tommy.

Evan grabbed William by the wrist and propelled him forward. They raced down a set of cement stairs and then into the underground parking garage. They skirted around car after packed-in car until they reached one near the front.

"Get in." Evan pointed to the back seat. She hopped in the front with Tommy and William slid in the back seat with the twins.

He found several of his black duffel bags in the back. Tommy started the engine and pulled out as William ripped open a bag and grabbed two bottles of Savor. He drained the first one before they'd even left the garage. Then he opened the second one.

"Hey." Evan's hand fell lightly on his knee. "Save them. You're gonna need 'em." Her finger traced a soft pattern on his leg. He swallowed back the burn of the thirst and closed the bottle.

Not good.

"What are your names?" Evan asked.

"I'm Grace and this is my sister Ryann," said the smaller twin.

"Are you human?" William asked.

The two exchanged a look.

"We don't know," Grace finally said.

They rolled out to the hotel drive and several guards ran by, weapons in hand. Tommy drove up the long, isolated stretch of road that was the only way in or out of the hotel compound. As they neared the exit gate William's tension ratcheted higher. He rubbed his palms on his jeans. He needed to get out of the car. He needed to go back inside the hotel and drain them all dry.

"Get him to lie down." Tommy's cautious gaze stared at William in the rearview mirror, angering him.

His throat burned to drain Tommy.

"Lay down," Evan told him. His gaze flicked to hers and he licked his lips. "Lay down or you'll get us caught. All of you."

William slid onto the floor behind her seat and stretched out. Grace climbed into the trunk and Ryann lay on the back seat and pulled a coat over herself. Tommy slowed the car and rolled down his window. "Pop said for us to patrol the outside neighborhood to make sure no one got out."

"I didn't get that order," said a man. "Hey! Did you get directions from Lou to let Tommy out?"

"No," a man farther away called.

"Sorry. We haven't heard anything. I'll call it in."

"We don't have time," Tommy called. "Pop said they could be out there already. Just let us out. You know who I am."

"Rules, man. I'd rather your father be pissed at me for not letting you, than for letting you go."

"Your funeral." Tommy laughed.

Footsteps crunched away from the SUV.

Every second they sat the had William close to snapping as the vehicle surrounded and enveloped him. His body wanted to burst from the car and run free. Being strapped to a table and not even allowed to piss by himself for over a week had him ready to tear apart anyone who stood in his way.

"You want me to take care of it?" asked William. "I don't mind."

"No!" Evan and Tommy said together.

"I could do it," offered Ryann.

Evan looked into the backseat at both of them and then unzipped something.

"We could use the flash grenades," offered Evan.

"I don't want to hurt them," said Tommy.

"These won't hurt. You know what's gonna hurt? Those bullets in their guns when they rip through this car and kill everyone in it."

"Do it," Tommy said.

William shut his eyes as Evan rolled down her window.

Shouting sounded from far away and William recognized the voice. The jacket pulled off Ryann's face and she looked directly at him. Her eyes transformed from blue to silver.

"Lou."

There was a ping sound and then Evan grunted. A second later metal hit metal and Evan slid back in the car.

"What the hell?" someone said before a small explosion and a huge flash of light. Men shouted outside and Lou's voice grew louder.

"Go. Go," Evan yelled.

The SUV lurched forward.

"Hang on," said Tommy. The vehicle impacted the gate, and William's head slammed into the bottom of Evan's seat and then the back seat. Gunfire rang out and William covered his head.

Evan looked over her seat. "Lou's comin'."

Tommy backed the vehicle up and then put it in drive. "I hear him."

The tires squealed and spun as they rammed the gate a second time.

William bumped around like unbagged groceries as they slammed into the gate again.

"Thomas! Evangeline!" Lou's voice raged from somewhere outside the car.

William's whole body tensed at the thought of jumping out and sucking every drop from the man who'd turned him into a monster. He could hear Lou's pounding footsteps growing closer to them along with several others.

Tommy floored the vehicle again, and William braced for the impact.

The sound of grinding metal reverberated through the car as they burst through the gate and gunfire peppered the vehicle and William jumped up and pushed Evan down in her seat, covering her with his body.

They bumped over the gate and then the vehicle skidded out onto the road.

William looked out the back window. "They're going to follow us."

"Pop doesn't give up easily. Which way are we going?"

"East," William replied.

East, toward home.

CHAPTER SEVENTEEN

P op followed them for almost an hour, but they'd pulled off an exit and lost him in a subdivision maze of tract housing.

They took a different route back to Chicago then the way she'd come. She couldn't remember exactly which way she'd told Lou she'd driven but she knew she hadn't gone down through Arizona so they headed that direction and would then head north.

Evan tried to shake off the itch that scratched up her spine by having William seated behind her. She tried not to think about the look on his face when he'd bitten her. The barely-there thread of humanity that kept him from attacking Tommy. The animalistic predator gaze he tracked her with. He was not her William. Not that William was hers, but this William, the injured and starving William, was... she had no idea what he was anymore.

She'd never seen a being so starved. Even in all of her time on the run with Lou and the boys. She'd seen and experienced hunger, thirst, and fatigue, but she'd never seen anything so primal in all her life.

When he'd sucked the life out of the tech on the floor, she'd not been able to believe it. Her William would never hurt anyone. Yet he had. Right there in front of her, in front of Tommy. And he hadn't even tried to hold back. Hadn't even tried to stop himself.

She tried to keep her eyes trained on the endless blacktop in front of her, but she couldn't. She swiveled her head and glanced in the back seat. William sat stark still staring at her. Like a pale, blood-soaked statue, he neither blinked, nor smiled... nothing.

"Are you doing okay?"

He nodded but said nothing. Ryann looked at him sideways but then turned and looked out her window.

Evan turned back around and faced her side window. Tears formed behind her eyelids and rolled down her cheeks. She prayed that Danika would be able to help him.

SIX HOURS LATER, THEY PULLED INTO AN ABANDONED GAS STATION JUST outside Flagstaff, Arizona.

The bright sun blared through the front window, blinding her. Tommy cut the engine off, and they both stared at the boarded-up convenience store.

"Hope the pumps still work," he said.

"Me too."

He stepped out of the car and crossed to the building. Evan's stomach rumbled and she opened her door.

She glanced through the headrest at William, who lay on the floor in the shadow of the seats. Covered in a UV-proof blanket, he stared up at her. He hadn't spoken a word since they'd left.

"You want anything from inside?" she asked.

"Can I drink another Savor now?" His flat monotone voice sent a chill up her spine.

Her chin quivered and she cleared her throat. "Sure."

He ripped into the bottle he'd been holding the entire time and drank it down in three large gulps.

There was a crash from the store as Tommy ripped a board from the door and threw it aside.

"I'm gonna go get something to eat and I'll be right back. You stay here." It wasn't a request. She grabbed her backpack and slung it over her shoulder.

"We need to stretch," said Grace.

Evan nodded and the two women climbed out of the back-seat while William completely covered himself in the UV blanket.

Her boots crunched on glass as she pushed the doors to the convenience store open. Tommy flipped on the switch for the pump behind the cash register.

"What do you want?" she asked.

He shrugged. "Not much left after looting. Whatever you can get, I guess."

She nodded and turned.

"Sis."

The heavy tone of Tommy's voice held all the things she didn't want to hear him say.

She glanced out the window at the twins who talked animatedly off to the side of the car, glancing over their shoulders at it every few seconds.

"He'll be fine. We'll get him back to Chicago and he'll be fine," Evan said.

"You don't know that." Tommy's eyes held compassion. "If he can't make it that far... If he attacks you or me or—"

"Then I'll do it myself," she said. The thought of killing William shot through her like an icy bullet to her heart. "If he attacks you or the twins, I'll kill him myself." She turned and headed down the aisle. She didn't want to even think about that happening.

Evan drove for the next eight hours while Tommy slept. She stopped at the Texas Oklahoma border about six in the evening. The sun had begun to set and her eyelids grew droopy. She'd driven close to one hundred the whole way and had been able to gain some time. Tommy snorted awake and stretched.

"What's going on? Where are we?" He yawned.

"Just got in to Oklahoma," she said.

"Damn, is that all?"

"Afraid so.

"How much farther?" he asked.

"About fifteen hours." She reached behind herself and rubbed her shoulder.

"Fifteen's not bad," he said. "I can take the next stretch and then we shouldn't have too much left." Tommy got out and headed to the convenience store to turn on the pumps.

She opened her door.

"I have to get out," said William.

The sound of his voice startled her.

"You can't. It isn't dark yet," she said.

"We need to stop for the night."

Evan swallowed hard. She didn't want to stop. She wanted to keep driving. To get to Chicago. To fix William. The twins exchanged a look.

"If we don't stop and you don't let me out of this car, I'm going to drain your cousin dry."

William's words sent a chill up her spine and anger stormed her brain. She spun around in her seat.

"Now you listen to me. We saved your ass even after you drained that tech. If it wasn't for Tommy you'd still be strapped to that bed. So don't you even think about laying a fang on my cousin."

His icy blue eyes narrowed. "You should have let me die. It would have been better than to live a few more days like this."

Her heartbeat pounded against her ribcage.

"I hear your heartbeat, Evan. You're terrified of me."

"No, actually, I'm not. I'm pissed off at you, you stupid jackass. I know you're thirsty—"

"You don't know anything."

"Stop talking to me like that!"

"I can't," he yelled. "Don't you get it? You think I'm thirsty but you have no idea what thirst is. This thirst inside me. It's not like a mild, I haven't had water in two days thirst. It's a bone-parched, muscles rubbing against your skin like sandpaper thirst. An everything-I-see-is-blood thirst. A drain-the-only-woman-you've-ever-loved-to-sate-it thirst. That is the thirst I fight, and every minute in the car with you and Tommy and the twins is as agonizing as if you'd impaled me on a bed of nails."

"Did you just say you loved me?" she asked.

The twins slid out of the vehicle silently and walked into the convenience store.

Evan crawled between the two seats and he sat up, his back to the side door. She straddled his hips and pushed the hair from his face.

Bloodstains smeared his cheeks, chin and throat. But he

needed to know that it didn't matter to her. The only way he could beat this was to know she still believed in him.

"I trust you," she whispered.

She bent her head and pressed her lips to his. He stiffened but she coaxed his lips apart with her tongue. She touched the tips of his fangs, sharp and ready to tear her to shreds, and a thrill of desire washed over her.

He tangled his fingers in her hair and plunged his tongue deep into her mouth. Powerful and strong, he kissed her hard, tugging her closer. He growled like a thunderstorm and her body pulsed with need.

The car chimed as Tommy opened the door. "Pumps aren't working," he said.

She broke the kiss and sat up. Tommy's cheeks reddened when he spotted her.

"Uh... yeah... okay," she said. "Then I guess we'll have to find another station. We have about fifty miles left in the tank."

He swallowed hard and nodded. "We could go into town a bit, see if we can find another one."

"Or another vehicle," she said.

"That would take time."

"I know, but we're gonna need to stop for the night anyway."

His brows furrowed. "I thought we were going to drive all the way through."

"About that. William is still covered in blood and needs to get out of the car and stretch. I think it would be good for him to get some air. He went from being cooped up in that cell to the lab..." She gave him a pointed look she hoped he understood.

"Sure. I'll see if maybe I can find a motel and drop you guys off while I search for gas or a new car."

She gave him a tight smile. "Great."

Tommy hopped into the driver's seat and started the engine. She pushed off William and sat on the back seat. His grip remained tight on her ankle.

The twins opened the side door.

"Grace why don't you take the front seat," Evan offered. "You've been stuck in the back this whole time."

"Thanks." Grace gave her a tight smile and then both sisters rounded the car and got in on the other side.

Evan hefted her backpack over her shoulder. She glanced at the open motel door where she'd helped William rush in minutes before.

"Are you sure you'll be okay?"

"I'll be fine." She gave Tommy a tight smile.

"If he hurts you..."

She stepped up to the car and kissed Tommy on the cheek. "He won't hurt me."

She walked to the motel room and waved at Tommy.

"We'll be back within the hour," he called.

"Don't get lost!"

He chuckled and shook his head before jumping back into the vehicle with the twins and pulling off.

They'd driven further off the freeway and found a small motel on a side street. If they were still being followed, Lou would be looking only at places easily accessible from the freeway, not places further in. There was no way they could search every exit as well.

She dropped her bag onto one of the beds next to William's duffel bag. He sat waiting for her, an empty bottle of Savor in his hand.

"How many bottles are left?" she asked.

"Four."

She hoped it was enough. "We should get you cleaned up." She headed for the bathroom and turned the water on in the white-tiled shower. For being crummy on the outside, the inside of the motel was pleasantly remodeled, as if the owners hadn't gotten around to upgrading the outside before they went under.

The water didn't warm, but she supposed with William's body temperature it didn't really matter. She walked back out to where he sat and then kicked off her boots and pants. He pulled her close and traced his hands up her bare thighs to her buttocks.

She tugged him to his feet and ran her hands under his shirt. He moaned and she tried to keep her arousal at bay as she lifted his arms and tugged off his shirt. He bent in close and rested his lips at the base of her throat as she undid the button on his jeans and then pushed the clothes over his hips and dropped them to the floor. He pressed his arousal against her, long and hard.

"You should shower." Her voice came out in a harsh whisper and his eyes met hers. He dropped his underwear to the floor and followed her command; stopping at one of the black bags, he pulled out a toothbrush and toothpaste before heading into the bathroom.

The sight of his tight, firm rear almost had her overlooking the fact that blood caked him. When she heard the sound of him brushing his teeth she tossed herself back on the bed and threw her hands over her face. Her body ached to feel him. As much as she wanted to distance herself, to shut down, to be objective, she couldn't. William had seeped inside her and brought her stone heart back from the brink. No matter what happened now, she wouldn't leave him.

The water in the shower turned off and after a few seconds, William re-emerged with a small white towel wrapped around his hips, water dripping from his lean, muscular frame.

He walked to her and pulled her to her feet. His cool body made her skin pebble. His hungry gaze stayed fixed on her face as his hands snaked under her shirt. She winced as his fingers ran over her cuts.

His gaze lowered and he pulled her shirt higher.

"What happened?" He removed her shirt and then dropped to his knees in front of her, inspecting the bandages that covered her sides.

"I had a little trouble getting into the ammunition building. I've always been too curvy."

"Never. Your curves are one of those things I love most about your body."

Her abs quivered as he ran his fingers gently over her skin. He peeled the tape off the blood-soaked bandages and gently removed them. He sniffed her belly and unwrapped her entire stomach. He let out a shuddered breath as he finally reached her skin.

"Your curves. Your little scars. Your warm peachy skin." Licking across her wounds, he swirled his tongue in the dried blood.

She twisted her fingers into his hair as he moved from her hip up her side to the outside of her bra. He kissed across the peaks of her breasts and up over her collarbone finally to her mouth.

Nothing about him was gentle as he yanked her closer by the hair and claimed her mouth with his. His hands roamed her body, and he fumbled with the front clasp on her bra. He growled in frustration and she unlocked her lips from his.

"Easy," she said. "It's the last good bra I have."

"Get it off."

Usually she didn't like being commanded, but the fire in his eyes made her skin flush with heat. She undid her bra and flung it to the floor. His mouth covered her left breast as his fingers pinched and kneaded the right one. She ran her fingers down his spine, and when his fangs grazed her nipple, her knees almost buckled.

"William," she moaned.

He released her breast from his mouth and licked up the side of her neck. Picking her up, he backed her into the nearest wall. Sliding his fingers inside her panties, he rubbed at her most sensitive nub.

She clawed at his back and panted as he brought her spiraling closer to release. She'd needed the feel of a man for so long that her body almost exploded at the slightest show of interest.

"Say my name," he demanded.

"William."

He rubbed her harder and faster. "Who do you belong to?"

"No one." She tried to keep her wits about her.

He kissed her hard and pushed her panties down between her knees. He used his foot to get them down to her ankles and then she stepped out of them.

She pulled off his towel, and he spread her thighs with his and hefted her off the ground.

He held her hands high above her head as he pressed against her.

Arms stretched tight, he found her breasts again, teasing them with his mouth.

"William, I want you," she crooned.

He looked up at her, his eyes icy fire. "Who do you belong to?" he asked again.

Her brain told her to say nothing. She'd belonged to a Vampire once before and it had ended with unimaginable heartbreak.

She kissed him hard and bit down on his lower lip. He growled and pressed closer to her. She wiggled her arms and got one hand free. She gripped him tight in her fist and stroked him once.

He dropped her arm and grabbed onto her waist.

"You tell me," she said, barely able to contain herself. "Who do you belong to?"

"You," he said. "I belong to Evangeline."

She stroked him hard and then he pushed her hands away and thrust into her, filling her completely. She cried out as her back slammed into the wall and he lifted her hips to meet his. She wrapped her arms around his neck as he thrust again, his rhythm hard and fast. Their bodies slammed together in a painfully pleasurable joining that had her crying out. He covered her mouth with his as the waves of ecstasy overtook her and she broke apart.

He continued to thrust as her muscles clenched tight around him. She reveled in the pain and pleasure of it. His eyes met hers as a bead of sweat licked down the side of her neck.

He carried her to the bed. She lay limp as a rag, allowing him to do whatever he wanted as he kissed his way from her neck to her toes. He rolled her on her stomach, climbed back on the bed, and parted her thighs.

She started to lift up on her elbows but his body covered hers and he flattened her. He grabbed a pillow and put it under her hips, raising her up before entering her again.

He shuddered and ran his hands down her spine. Going slow, he bent over her and hooked an arm underneath her for leverage. His mouth found her right shoulder. She grabbed onto the bed, trying to hang on. He reached between her legs from the front and found her nub again. His breathing became quick and short and his thrusts harder and faster as he pumped. The spiral of ecstasy wound tight within her once more.

"William," she moaned as tingles traced up her spine.

"Who do you belong to," he asked again, his voice tight with need.

The first shockwaves hit her like a tornado. "William," she cried. "I belong to William."

His mouth fell onto her shoulder and as she climaxed for the second time, he bit down and moaned. He kept going, driving into her and sucking from her vein at the same time. She pressed her hips back to meet his thrusts till he tensed and cried out her name. When she grew light-headed and melted into the bed he removed his fangs and fell on top of her.

Her muscles shook and every part of her burned from the workout. She smiled into the pillow as he licked her wound shut and then withdrew from her and got to his feet. She rolled on her side, completely sated.

Before she could say a word, he walked into the bathroom and this time closed the door.

Anger mixed with fear as she tried to process what had happened. They'd made love and he'd just gotten up and left her like a used blow up doll. Tears threatened to spill and she covered her face with her hands.

She'd let him in and he'd already turned on her. The anger overtook her.

Not this time. She wasn't going to be played for a fool again.

WILLIAM CURLED INTO A BALL ON THE SHOWER FLOOR AND POUNDED on his head. He couldn't focus. Evan surrounded him. Her smell, her taste, her voice. All of it clouded his judgment and made him unable to deal with the changes happening to him. He'd wanted to drain her and instead he'd screwed her and made her confess that she was his like a common slave. He pounded on his temples trying to hold the hunger at bay.

Shame rocked him to the core. He'd taken her like a whore instead of making love to her the way he should have. Soft and slow and beautiful. With candles and foreplay and... everything he could no longer give her. She'd been hurt before; she deserved so much better. Danika had warned him that this would happen as a fledgling, but it hadn't for him somehow until that day. And now that it had... she wasn't there to help him figure it out. He'd not been prepared for the feelings and thirsts and inability to control himself. All he'd wanted to do was screw Evan until he died. She didn't deserve that. She didn't deserve to be treated like that.

Even as he sat on the floor having once again drunk from Evan, he should feel healthy, alive, sated. But the thirst burned his gut and pounded in his mind until he couldn't see straight.

The bathroom door burst inward.

"How dare you?"

William's head whipped up. Evan's beautiful, naked body stood before him taut and angry.

"How dare you toy with me? After everything I told you.

You think you can use me and throw me away like trash? You can have your way with me and then send me back to the barracks when you're done? I will not be a slave, William, so if you think I'm just going to stand by and take that? I have news for you, jackass, you better think again."

"I'm sorry." His voice came out flat as ever as he tried to see her through the haze of bloodlust.

"You're sorry? You bet you're sorry. And to think I actually believed you might love me."

"I do." The veins in her throat beckoned to him like a siren's song.

"Like I'm supposed to believe that."

He closed his eyes and clenched his fists causing his nails to bite into his palms. Then pressed them in harder trying to do anything to take his mind from the bloodlust.

"It's true, Evan. I swear it is."

"Don't think for one second that—"

He was on his feet so fast it made his head spin. He grabbed her around the waist and pulled her to him, clamping his hand over her mouth.

"Shut up. Please." He kissed her forehead and her eyelids and her nose and then laid his cheek on hers. His body shook with the strain of trying to keep from biting her again. "Please," he pleaded. "Please."

She stood stiff for a minute and then relaxed into him. He tried to calm the lust enough to speak.

"I can't... I can't control it."

She peeled his fingers from her mouth.

"Control what?" she whispered.

"The thirst. This virus inside me. It's eating me from the inside out. Melting away every shred of who I am until there is nothing left. All I can think about is the blood. Your blood.

Tommy's blood. The bottles of Savor. I can't control it. And the more I drink, the worse it gets." He rubbed her throat with the pad of his thumb. "I can't see you anymore. All I see is the blood and sex."

"We'll get back to Chicago and they can fix it."

He pushed her away. "No they can't!" he yelled. "Don't you see? I'm dying. The only reason I didn't die already was because I killed a man! I killed him. I drained him dry and stole his clothes and—"

She stepped up to him and took his face firmly in her palms, forcing him to look at her. "We'll fix it. Do you understand? I'm not going to let you die. I'm not." She searched his face and then held him tight again.

He clung to her, fighting the shakes, fighting the thirst, fighting the drive to take her again.

"Think of something," she said. "A memory. What is your best memory?"

"I can't." He shook his head. "The thirst—"

"See past the thirst. The thirst isn't you. See through it and beyond it. Remember a time when you were happy. The Peter Pan pixie dust memory. The best one there is. Find it and tell it to me."

He held her close and kissed her neck. He tried to see past the thirst, past the pain. A memory surfaced.

"The day I was adopted."

"Good. What was that day like?"

He'd never told anyone he'd been adopted. "I was five. I wore a blue plaid shirt with a green alligator bow tie. Sister Margaret held my hand. I remember sitting on the hard pew in the hallway outside her office and thinking that I'd never be alone again. The door opened and a couple walked in. A bald man with glasses and a lady graying at the temples. She clutched her purse handles so tight I thought she was going to break them. I couldn't bear to look her in the eyes. I was afraid that if I did, I'd see her disappointment in me and they'd walk away. She wore a blue flower dress with tiny red polka dots. She got down on her knees in front of me and lifted my chin. With tears in her eyes, she told me she'd waited her whole adult life for her son to arrive. That was the best day."

She held him tight as he clung to the memory. "Remember what she wore. Remember what she smelled like. Remember what you heard. Cement that memory. That's the memory you want to hold on to. The one you look for when you want to see past the thirst."

William closed his eyes and hung on to Evan, afraid if he opened them he'd wake up back in the cell, and she'd be gone. He remembered every detail of that day. Of his mother. His father. His new bedroom. The new pajamas with trains on them that he wore that night.

"Promise you won't leave me," he begged.

"If you promise not to keep things from me from now on."

He kissed her head and fought off the building bloodlust. "I promise."

CHAPTER EIGHTEEN

E van slept in William's arms. Tommy and the twins got
their own rooms. When Evan emerged in the early
hours of the morning she knocked on Tommy's door
and the twins' door. Tommy came out looking a bit tired but
clean at least.

"Morning," she said.

He nodded. "Morning."

She knocked on the twins' door again. "Grace, Ryann we
need to get on the road."

Tommy hefted his bag and walked to their vehicle. "They
aren't in there."

Evan turned to him. "What?"

Tommy opened the trunk and threw his bag inside.
"They're gone. I helped them find a working vehicle when we
got gas."

Evan tried to wrap her mind around it. "But... they wanted
us to help them."

"Yeah. Help them get out. They weren't sure whether they

would stick with us from the get go, but after spending time in the car with...” His gaze drifted to her hotel room door. “Anyway, they said they felt more comfortable going it alone.”

“But they’re human. Where do they think they can go?”

Tommy chewed the inside of his cheek and finally shrugged. “I don’t know.”

William exited his room and looked between them. “What’s wrong?”

Evan shook her head.

“The twins wanted to go it alone,” said Tommy. “They left a couple hours ago.”

“But Danika could have helped them.”

“After being held prisoner and experimented on I think they didn’t want to take the chance of being caged again.”

Evan appreciated Tommy trying to deflect the truth of why they’d left. No matter who a person was, he cared about them and tried to protect them as best he could. Even William.

William seemed to accept the answer. He walked to the car and put both of their bags inside. Then the trio got into the car and Evan helped William settle in the back on the floor. Before the crack of dawn they were on the road again.

“We’re gonna try to drive straight through,” she said. “At dark we can get out and stretch but I think it’s best that we keep moving.”

William nodded and his gaze flicked around as if searching for something.

She pulled his face to hers. “Focus. I’m here.”

He nodded again.

She kissed him, trying to calm herself as much as him. The drive ahead wasn’t going to be fun for any of them.

WILLIAM SLEPT FOR SIX HOURS STRAIGHT. ABOUT ELEVEN, HE AWOKE with the burn of the thirst clouding his senses once more. He swiped at his face to find blood dripping from his eyes and nose.

"Dammit!" He sat up quickly and rubbed at his face.

"You okay?" Tommy asked.

Evan turned in her seat and then reached for one of the duffel bags.

"Here." She shoved a pack of wet wipes at him.

William snatched them from her and tore into them. His chest tightened and a violent coughing fit over took him. Blood sprayed the back of Tommy's seat.

Evan twisted out of her seatbelt and grabbed a bottle of Savor. She ripped off the cap and tried to hand it to him.

"Drink this."

William continued coughing.

"William, please," she pleaded.

"I don't want it!" He shoved the bottle away, splashing the front of Evan's shirt.

"Knock it off!" Tommy bellowed.

The coughing subsided and William's gaze narrowed on Tommy's in the rearview mirror. Tommy slammed on the brakes and William fell forward between the seats. Sunlight filtered through the windshield, burning his hands and his face. William scrambled back into his seat.

Evan wiped at the spilled Savor with a towel and Tommy turned in his seat. The veins in his forehead and neck bulged so large that it took all of William's willpower not to leap on him and tear out his throat.

"Look," Tommy said. "I get it that you're in pain. And I get it that things are in the crapper for you right now, but you have no right to be rude to Evan. If it wasn't for her you'd be dead already. Now I'm not saying what my Pop did to you was fair, but we're trying to make it right."

Hunger gnawed at William's gut. His fangs burned with the need to feed. He stared at the pulsing, throbbing vein in Tommy's neck, every thought clouded in a haze of red. Tommy didn't move, but soon his pulse slowed and the veins smoothed out under the surface of his skin. William swallowed hard and wiped a trickle of blood that dribbled from his ear down the side of his neck. His hands shook and his body sank into the seat as if it swallowed him whole.

"Here." Evan held the bottle of Savor out to him once more.

He took it with shaky fingers but couldn't seem to grip it tight enough and it dropped. Tommy caught it before it hit the floor.

Evan's eyes held fear and pain. "You're getting weaker."

William nodded and then closed his eyes. He laid his head back on the seat and pictured his mother's blue dress with faded flowers. The overly large fake pearl earrings that dangled from her ears and the smell of lavender and mint that always permeated her.

I'll see you soon, Mom.

Tommy handed her the bottle of Savor and she put it in the cup holder and then laid her hand on William's knee. He gripped her fingers but didn't open his eyes.

"I don't know that we're gonna make it in time," Tommy whispered.

"We'll make it." Her words rang hollow. William's skin had gone from pale to ashen in the last eight hours. The blood that dripped from him had turned a thin, watery red consistency. Even his grip on her hand seemed faint.

Evan hadn't been much of one for God since she'd lost her family, but at that moment she prayed. Prayed for William. Prayed for Tommy. Prayed for herself. They were almost to Kansas City. Another seven and they'd be back at the coven house.

"We need gas," Tommy said. "We have to stop in the next thirty minutes."

East of St. Louis they spotted several gas stations.

"One of them has to still have gas," said Tommy.

They'd bypassed two previous exits with gas stations because something about the places hadn't seemed right. As they pulled off the highway memories of being attacked and stabbed flooded Evan. She rubbed at her leg absently.

"Keep your eyes peeled," said Evan.

"Something wrong, sis?"

"Bad memories is all."

"We could keep going."

"There won't be anything for the next while. Better to stop here where we have options."

They pulled into the first gas station and William stirred in the back seat.

"Where are we?" he croaked.

"Still a ways to go. Just getting gas." Tommy put his gun in his waistband and stepped out of the car.

Evan looked at William, blood drenched his shirt. "I should go inside and see if I can find you something clean to wear."

"Why bother?" He chuckled. "I'm going to ruin that one too."

Irritation poked at her and she swallowed hard to keep it at bay. "Because I'm sure you don't want to see Lord Danika looking like a mess."

Something sparked inside him and his eyes lit up. For a flash of a moment, she saw the old William. Dignified and kind.

"No," he said. "I don't."

She squeezed his hand. "I'll be back in a minute." She had to get out of the vehicle. The smell of blood and the cold, dead look in William's eyes ate at her soul.

He held onto her hand, preventing her from leaving.

She looked back. "One minute," she said. "Tommy's right there. You'll be fine."

She could see the fear and anguish racing through his mind. It was daylight; he was trapped in a car and not in charge.

His hand slipped away and she got out. She rounded the hood of the car sucking in the dry, warm air. The fresh air invigorated her and made her smile.

Tommy pumped gas without having to turn the pumps on. He glanced over his shoulder at her.

"How's he doing?" he asked in a low voice.

She shook her head. "Not good."

"You really think they'll be able to cure him?"

She wanted to say yes. To tell him she had no doubt at all that Danika would save William. But the truth was... She had no idea.

"I'm going to see if there are any shirts inside and maybe some paper towels so he can clean up a bit."

"See if they have any Funyuns."

She laughed. "No way, you'll make the entire car smell. I'll see if they have something less pungent."

She'd headed for the store when the sound of a car engine stopped her in her tracks. She whipped around. Tommy already looked the same direction.

She raced back. "Let's go!"

"No time." He pulled the nozzle from the tank.

A large black van rolled down the road toward them.

"Could be slavers," said Tommy.

"Not likely," she countered. "It's the middle of the day. It's either vamps or humans."

She pulled her gun from her waistband and her hand flexed around the grip.

"Let me handle this," Tommy said.

William knocked on the tinted window behind her. She turned to it but couldn't see him. "Stay inside," she said.

The van slowed as it neared the station and then stopped in the middle of the street yards away.

Butterflies whirled in Evan's stomach. They didn't have time for distractions and if anything happened to them, William was dead.

Tommy raised his hand and waved at the van.

"What are you doing?" she hissed.

"They're obviously not slavers or they'd have been on us already. They have to be humans."

The van sat for another minute before rolling forward to the edge of the gas station and stopping. The driver's side door opened and a burly man stepped out. A thin, haggard-looking woman exited the other side.

"Howdy," the man called.

"Afternoon," Tommy replied.

The groups stared at each other until Evan's hands grew slick with sweat and she had to run them on her pants.

"Where you headed?" Tommy asked.

"Not sure," said the man. "Been traveling so long we don't right know where to lay our head anymore. How 'bout ya'll?"

"We're headed east," Tommy said.

The man shook his head. "Not too good goin' east. Vampers everywhere that direction."

"We'll keep our heads down."

"Where you comin' from?"

Tommy stayed silent for a minute too long.

"California," Evan said. "There's an enclave out there in Palm Springs. It's nice. You should check it out."

The man nodded. "Why'd ya leave?"

"Family dispute."

The man chuckled. "Seems silly to even have those nowadays, don't it? Family's just about all any of us have left."

"Very true," said Tommy.

"Well, we best be movin' on. If we make it to California, we'll be sure to try and look up your people. Thanks for the tip."

Tommy waved and Evan held on to her gun as the van backed out onto the road and headed for the highway.

When the van could no longer be seen or heard, she leaned back on the car. The world really was in the crapper. So much so that even just seeing other humans made them jumpy as rabbits and ready to shoot at the drop of a hat. She wondered if things would ever be civilized again.

"Come on," she said. "It's my turn to drive."

"What about the new clothes?" Tommy asked.

"It can wait. I want to get the hell out of here."

225

CHAPTER NINETEEN

As Evan drove the car off the ramp to Chicago, she slowed and stared at the horizon.

"Where are we?" William croaked.

It was nine p.m. and he'd done little on their drive besides sleep and wheeze. His skin no longer even carried the ashy tone. Blood smeared him so thick that he looked like something out of a horror movie. Only his bright blue eyes shone beneath the mess.

"We're coming into Chicago," she said. "Do you remember how to get to the coven house?"

"Northeast of the Navy Pier."

She headed toward the signs pointing to the pier. The closer they got to the city the more anxiety mingled with the hope inside her, causing her to shake.

For the past day and a half, she'd banked on the fact that if they could make it back to Chicago William would be healed. That lone thought kept her going. That thought kept spirits high and focused. But now that they'd made it, she had to face the fact that there was a very real possibility he wouldn't be cured.

She pushed down the gas pedal.

"Wow! I didn't realize there was this much destruction in Chicago." Tommy stared out the windows as they passed the business district.

"There wasn't," said William. "Things must be much worse on the Demon front."

"Great. We run from a secure front right into the fray."

"Not helpful, Tommy." Evan glared at him.

"Sorry." He continued to stare out the window.

She turned north and headed past buildings she recognized and then into a more residential area.

"Turn right at the next street," said William.

Evan followed his instructions. Soon they were in the coven house's neighborhood.

"You live here?" asked Tommy.

"Coven House is ahead on the left," said William.

Evan's gut clenched at the sight of the house and she slowed the car. She'd brought William back to save him, but if he died... Not only would she be right back where she'd started, but Tommy would be in the same barred boat. She hadn't thought of that when she'd let him come along. Now more than ever she wished she'd smashed him over the head and left him behind. Not that living with Pop would have been much better for him.

"What are we waiting for?" Tommy asked.

She blew out a breath. "Nothing."

She drove to the entrance. The black wrought iron gates loomed over her and she remembered every time she'd been brought back to the house after her masters had decided they couldn't take having her at their houses anymore. Every time knowing that she would be snickered at, talked about, pitied by the other house slaves. And the look on William's face every time he saw her again. The mixture of joy and disappointment.

She rolled down her window and pressed the buzzer for the house.

A male voice crackled on the line. "Coven House."

"Hi. It's Evan. I have William with me." She tried to keep the quaver out of her voice.

"We have no time for games. Leave the grounds immediately or we will have to use force," said the voice.

"No games. I have William and he needs help. Please tell Danika we are back from California."

Silence emanated from the other side of the intercom.

"I'll talk to him." William sat up and coughed violently. Blood gushed from his mouth like a faucet.

"William!" Evan turned to face him, but he'd stopped coughing. His eyes bulged out and he gagged.

WILLIAM TRIED IN VAIN TO SUCK AIR INTO HIS LUNGS AS BLOOD bubbled up and stuck in his throat.

"You must leave immediately," said someone over the intercom.

His gaze connected with Evan's and she jumped from the car. He coughed and nothing but blood came up. He tried to swallow but his throat stuck tight.

Dogs barked in the distance, growing steadily louder. Through the windshield, he spotted the house guards running for the gate. He tried to breathe through his nose but got no more than a swallow full of air before coughing again.

Evan yanked his side door open. "William, look at me. Breathe, baby. Come on."

"Evan, they're pointing machine guns at us," said Tommy.

"Leave now. You have thirty seconds," said the voice over the intercom.

"Evan!" shouted Tommy.

William gurgled and spit blood on the floor. He coughed and choked. Pressure built inside his chest and behind his eyes until his head felt like a wrecking ball slammed into it.

Evan smacked him on the back hard between the shoulder blades. His lungs tightened down like an elephant sat on him.

Evan whacked him harder and harder until he threw up all the Savor he'd had in the last two hours. The red liquid spewed across his legs and down to the floor. He coughed again and then sucked in a large breath.

"Ten seconds," said the voice.

"Evan! Come on!"

"I'm okay," William whispered, throat burning, lungs like a volcano.

Evan stared at him for another minute, biting her lower lip. Then she slammed the side door and hopped into the driver's seat. She threw the car in reverse and backed out of the drive. The guards at the gate kept their guns trained on her.

"Do you know anywhere else we can go?" she asked. "Any way to get a message to Danika?"

William shook his head, unable to think straight.

Evan looked at Tommy. "We're all in now. We came here to do a job."

Tommy nodded and put on his seatbelt. "Like Pop always says, if you start a job—"

"You finish it." Evan threw the car in drive and revved the gas. She punched the accelerator and headed for the gate. All three of them ducked as gunfire ripped through the windshield. The car slammed the gate and William flew into the back of Tommy's seat, smashing his face.

He crashed backward and hit his head on the side window, cracking the glass.

In an instant, the doors of the car ripped open and Evan tumbled to the ground along with Tommy.

William's door opened but at the sight of him, the guard backed up.

He stepped out, his head foggy from the lack of oxygen and the hit to the window. His skull pounded worse than ever.

"Get off me!" Evan cried.

William snapped into action. He rounded the car to where three guards pinned her down.

"Don't touch her," he shouted.

William ran at the closest guard and flung him away. The other guards caught one look at him and backed up, raising their weapons.

William pulled Evan to his chest and she clung to him. He leaned against the side of the wrecked car, his legs like lead weights. He breathed hard trying to regain the lost oxygen but it only made his head pound harder and his vision blur further.

"You need to lie down," she said.

"I'm fine." William kept his gaze firmly on the guards. "Where's Danika? Where's Mason?"

"You are in no position to demand to see the Coven Lord and her mate," said a guard William didn't recognize.

"You get on the com and you tell Siad that William is here and I'm looking for Danika and Mason." Fury and agitation had him almost ripping the guard's throat out. Only holding Evan and feeling her warm body pressed against his kept him from shredding every one of them.

The guards exchanged a look. "Siad is dead."

Damn. "Then who's in charge of house security?" he croaked.

"I am." A figure strode down the driveway and the guards parted.

"Roth." William filled with relief.

Roth stared at him for a minute. "William?"

William's legs buckled and he fell.

"William." Evan followed him down and turned to Roth. "Please, he needs help. He's dying."

Roth strode forward and stared at William. "What the hell happened to you?"

William's vision grew fuzzy and his sight clouded. "Humans."

"William!" Evan looked on as his eyes closed and his head slumped forward.

"Get him inside." Roth motioned to several of the guards.

They came to pick him up but Evan clung to him, conflicted.

"Where are you taking him?" she asked.

Roth ignored her. "Get him inside. Call Doc."

"Wait." She grabbed Roth's sleeve.

He turned his steely gaze upon her. "Bring the girl and the guy. Get this car off the drive and shore up the gate," Roth barked.

A guard grabbed Evan by the arm and dragged her forward. She met Tommy at the hood of the car.

"Don't struggle," she said.

The guards marched into action, carrying out the orders set forth.

Evan walked up the long drive. She looked behind at the screeching car being reversed out of the drive and onto the street. The gate bent inward but still functioned.

She stumbled when they hit the steps to the front of the house. She caught herself on one of the white pillars when a scream rang out. Evan's head whipped forward. Inside on the floor Danika bent over William with Mason standing close beside. The old physician Doc trudged across the entryway and knelt down beside William and Danika.

Evan stepped through the front door and waited.

"What's wrong with him?" Danika shrieked.

Doc laid a hand on Danika's shoulder. "I don't know yet." His voice remained ever calm and soothing.

"Come on." Mason lifted Danika to her feet, and she clung to him as Doc pulled open his case and started to examine William. Danika pressed her face into Mason's shoulder and then turned and spotted her.

Her eyes blazed like fire as she crossed to Evan. "What happened? What's wrong with him?"

The slightly shorter Vampire Lord made Evan feel like a toddler in time out.

"He…"

"He was tortured." Tommy stepped up next to her. "And then given a vaccine."

"A vaccine?" Danika rounded on him. "What kind of vaccine?"

Mason walked over to stand behind Danika.

Tommy's gaze connected with Evan's.

"A vaccine to cure vamps," said Evan.

Danika's gaze whipped back to hers. "Dammit. I knew that

Xenock wasn't the end of that insane crusade. But he isn't a vamp."

"It's my fault," said Evan. "My uncle and my cousin... They saw us together... My cousin attacked and William tried to protect me. They were angry—"

Danika's eyes narrowed. "You. You did this to William."

"No. I promise. I didn't. I tried to save him. We tried to save him. That's why we brought him here." The words came out weak and childish, but Mason's imposing aura made her skin crawl.

There was a huge gasp and William lurched off the floor, a tube sticking out of his throat.

"Got him breathing again," said Doc.

William's gaze shot around the room. His eyes landed on Evan and his body relaxed.

"William." Danika raced to his side and flung her arms around him.

Mason joined her and they ended up in a group hug.

Tears rolled down Danika's cheeks. "I was so worried. You didn't call, and I was going to send someone to find you but your phone signal went dead. I just..." She hugged him again, sobbing.

William smiled but didn't talk.

"I'm glad you're back," said Mason. "I was ready to fly out there looking for you."

William nodded.

"Okay, okay," said Doc. "Let the boy go. We need to get him to his room so I can examine him."

"Yes, of course." Danika stood and backed away with Mason. She pointed to the guards holding Evan and Tommy. "You, take William upstairs to his room. And get Sue. He needs to feed."

"No," William whispered.

Danika turned to him. "You don't want Sue? You want someone else?"

William pointed at Evan. Danika followed his finger and her eye twitched.

"Let her go," Danika ordered.

Evan yanked her arms away and walked to where William lay on the floor. He held his hand out to her and Danika backed up.

Evan brushed the hair from his face, and he kissed her.

She lingered for a moment but then broke the kiss. "Okay, lover, I'm not going anywhere. Don't worry."

The guards surrounded William and lifted him. He grabbed her hand but she gently removed it.

"I'm right behind you."

The guards carried William to the staircase and halfway up he growled and thrashed. They tried to keep their grip on him but William lunged at the nearest one, trying to bite into him. The guards dropped him and backed up.

"William!" Danika chastised.

Evan rushed up the stairs. "It's all right. I'll take him."

The guards eyed her suspiciously.

She turned to Tommy. "Help me."

Tommy glanced at Danika and Mason for a minute and then scooted around them and up the stairs. The guards headed back down and Evan and Tommy pulled William to his feet, draping his arms around their necks.

"Lord Danika," said Evan.

"Yes?"

"William is going to need Sue. And anyone else willing to donate as well."

"One donor—"

"Trust me," said Evan. "He's going to need more than one. And he's going to need to feed every few hours until he can be cured."

Danika opened and closed her mouth several times before she nodded.

"Come on," Evan said. "Let's get you washed up so you don't scare your dinner to death."

CHAPTER TWENTY

E van and Tommy carried William to his room where he proceeded to yank the aggravating straw from his throat.

"You can't do that," Evan said.

He shook his head. "I don't need it." His voice gurgled and barely came out a whisper. He coughed and touched the hole in his throat. Just what he needed more holes, more scars.

He hobbled to his closet and an audible sigh escaped him at the sight of his own clothes. He grabbed a crisp navy polo shirt and a pair of clean khakis, held them to his nose and took in the wonderful, freshly laundered aroma. He'd never missed a smell so much in his life.

Evan scoffed and took them from him. "Uh, yeah right. I don't think so."

She hung them back up and grabbed a T-shirt instead. Closing the closet, she then walked to his dresser and grabbed a pair of boxers and sweats.

"There's no way you're going to be lying around in those business clothes."

"I want to look presentable," he countered.

"You're sick. You've earned the right to be casual." She shoved the clothes into his chest and turned him toward the bathroom.

"I'm not sick. I'm dying. I don't want people to remember me in my sweats."

"Stop that!" She rounded to face him, her eyes filled with tears. "Don't say that. You're going to be fine. We're going to fix you up."

Her tears were as good as a punch to the solar plexus. "Evan—"

"Stop!"

He softened his voice as much as he was able. "Evangeline."

She shook her head and a tear leaked from her eye. "Let's get you cleaned up and fed. Then the doctor can come check you out." She turned to Tommy. "Can you wait?"

"I'll wait in the hall." He stepped quickly from the room.

Evan pulled William into the bathroom and turned on the shower. His gaze traveled up the slender curve of her hip to the rounding of her shoulder and over the patch of creamy skin that covered the throbbing vein in her neck. His stomach growled like a lion and he clutched tight to his clothes to keep from grabbing her and biting into her.

Not Evan. Not Evan. Not Evan. He closed his eyes and took a deep breath.

"It better be a quick shower." He opened his eyes. "I need blood."

She nodded and stripped his clothes off. He stepped under the spray and let the shower wash over him. The water dripped down his body dousing everything pink. He tried to keep his breathing even and his thoughts focused on the task at hand instead of the pounding behind his eyes and the carnal needs rising inside him. Evan washed his body and hair. Her thin, strong fingers plunged into his hair line and scrubbed soft, spine-tingling circles over his scalp. He tried to relax and let the scent of his favorite shampoo soothe him. But when he closed his eyes, he only saw blood.

Blood on the front of the lab tech he'd killed. Blood dripping down Evan's arm as he bit into her. Blood splattering the car as he coughed. He'd be a fool not to admit that it scared him that he'd passed out on the driveway. Waking up on the foyer floor had been not only painful but disorienting. Even now it took all of his strength to keep on his feet. He'd been pulled back from the brink. He didn't know that he'd make it back if he collapsed again.

"I know I'm not as strong and fast as a lot of vampyr, but this is just embarrassing." He turned off the water.

"Why?" Evan wrapped a towel around him. "You don't like having a woman take care of you?"

His desire spiked and he pulled her into him. "You can take care of me right now."

She snorted. "Let's get you some blood first. Then when you can keep more than just one body part at a time standing up, we'll talk about going a couple of rounds."

He kissed her head. "Fair enough."

She dressed him as he sat on the toilet lid and then helped him into bed. If he'd felt even a fraction of a percent better than he did at that moment, he'd have been mortified to have her helping him like a baby. But after all she'd seen of him in the last weeks, he had neither the energy nor the pride to care.

She grabbed a stack of towels from under his sink and set them on the nightstand. She looked at him for a moment and then picked up a towel and wiped his face, staining the towel red.

He leaned his head on the headboard. "Will it ever stop?"

"We'll find a cure."

"Or I'll die."

She gave him a hard look.

He wasn't trying to be flippant. Over the past week he'd come to terms with the fact that he was as good as dead. He actually begun to welcome the idea.

"Sorry. I'm sorry." He caressed her cheek. "But to be honest, the pain, the thirst, the utter lack of control... I wish it would end."

Her eyes softened and he thought she might tear up again, but she didn't. Instead she set down the towel and stood.

"I'll see if Sue is ready."

He grabbed her hand. "You know it's not her I want."

She gave him a tight smile. "I know, but you've had too much from me already. I need a couple days to replenish."

Of course, she needed time to replace all he'd taken from her. But with Evan at least he had been able to stop himself.

"I'm afraid," he said. "Afraid I'll kill them all the way I killed that tech."

"I won't let you."

Evan opened the bedroom door and outside stood Danika, Mason, Sue, Matthew, and half a dozen others that he could smell.

Evan motioned Danika and Mason in; Sue followed close behind. They stopped at the foot of the bed but Sue stared at him tentatively from across the room. For a moment no one spoke.

"Sue," said Evan. "If you could please sit on the bed."

Sue looked at Evan and then back at him. She walked

around the side of the bed and sat near him, her brown hair tucked behind one ear. The vein in her neck pulsed with life. He gripped the sheets tightly in an effort to keep from ripping her throat out.

"Hi," she said.

"Hi." Was the most he could manage. Everyone stared at him, making his skin itch and his gut twist. He'd never had an audience before. And of all the times to have a room full of people watching him feed, this wasn't the time.

Sue laid her hand on his leg. "I'm glad you're okay. I missed you."

The thirst skittered through his veins and he dug his fingers deeper into the sheets. His gaze darted to Evan, pleading with her to help him.

She stepped forward but Danika stopped her.

"I think he's fine."

"I can feed you," Sue offered.

She raised her wrist to him and her arm trembled. The scent of fear wafted off her like expensive perfume. For the first time the scent aroused him. He liked that he scared her. Liked the way her eyes darted to him and then away. Liked the way her pulse fluttered faster and faster the longer she sat there. Pumping blood harder through her veins, making it flow all that much more easily when he would bite her.

He looked from Sue to Evan.

"It's okay," Evan said. "You can do it."

Sue's vein pulsed with the throb in his head. His gaze transfixed on her neck.

"Bite her, William," said Danika.

"Feed," said Mason.

William's restraint broke and in a flash, he grabbed Sue by the shoulders and yanked her to him, tearing into her throat.

Sue screamed and Danika rushed to the side of the bed. William gulped down the blood.

"William, that's not how we feed," said Danika.

"He can't hear you." Evan climbed up on the bed, and Sue's terrified eyes locked on hers. She squeezed Sue's hand and then turned to William. "William, slow down." Evan eased closer to him and put her hand on his shoulder.

He growled in reply and bit harder, making Sue cry out and tears stream down her cheeks.

"William, stop that," demanded Danika.

"He won't hear you," said Evan. "The thirst is too great." She leaned over his shoulder and whispered in his ear. "Your mother clutched her purse. You sat in the hall on the hard bench, remember. The day you met them. The first day. The best day."

Nothing happened.

"Help me," Sue whispered.

"William, let go of Sue," Evan commanded. "Let her go."

William reared back and slammed into the headboard, dripping blood down the front of his shirt. Evan pressed a towel down on Sue's neck to staunch the bleeding. Mason swooped her up and carried her to the door.

He opened it and handed Sue to a guard. "Take her to Doc."

William's icy gaze stayed solidly on Evan's face. She wiped the blood from his chin and the drips from his ears.

"Another," he panted.

Evan looked to the visibly shaken Danika. "He needs more."

Danika's eyes glazed as if she neither saw nor heard Evan.

"I'll get Matthew." Mason called in the next donor.

B<small>Y THE END OF THE HOUR,</small> W<small>ILLIAM HAD DRUNK FROM SIX DONORS,</small> terrifying one after the next. When the last donor left, he breathed a contented sigh and nodded. The bleeding had stopped for the most part, aside from the occasional nose drip. It was no longer pink runny liquid but had gone back to its original viscosity.

Danika stood nervously with Mason who seemed unfazed by what he'd witnessed.

"I'm sorry you had to see that," William said in a voice almost his own.

He held tight to Evan's hand.

"What... what's happened to you?" Danika asked. "Even when you were newborn you weren't like that."

"We don't know," answered Evan. "The vamp vaccine is killing him."

"Then why did you come here?" asked Mason. "We don't know how to cure him."

"I didn't know what else to do," said Evan. "If he stayed there he'd be dead for sure. You have a company that makes synthetic blood. Surely you have scientists that can help."

Danika shook her head. "My building is gone. Demolished. My company is in ruins. The last Demon attack took such a heavy toll that even Selene and Neeman took off."

"Took off?" asked William.

"They've been gone for three days," said Mason. "Disappeared right after the message arrived."

"What message?"

Mason and Danika exchanged a look. "My father is coming. For Selene and for me."

"He sent you a message to tell you that?" asked Evan.

"But why would he tell you?" asked William.

"To frighten us," said Danika.

"But Mason's not scared of anything," said William.

"Not us," replied Mason.

"Us. *Vampires*," said Danika. "To divide us and weaken us."

"Has it worked?"

Mason's gaze landed on her. "My sister ran. So yes, I'd say it's working."

"I brought something that might help," said Evan.

"What's that?" asked Danika.

"Weapons."

EVAN SETTLED WILLIAM IN BED AND THEN TOOK A SHOWER HERSELF. The week's events caught up with her and she sat in the tub and wept. She'd been reunited with her family and then betrayed them. She'd fallen for a man only to now sit by and watch him die. It wasn't fair. But then things hadn't been fair in the world for decades.

Finally, she stepped out of the tub and wrapped a towel around herself, realizing she had nothing to wear. She opened the bathroom door to find the doctor taking blood samples from William.

"Sorry." She started to close the door and the doctor looked up.

"Don't worry about it. I'm done here anyway." He gathered his things. "We've never formally met. I'm Doc."

"Evan. Nice to meet you."

He nodded. "Would you mind terribly if I took your blood? William tells me that you were given a vaccine as well some years back."

Evan nodded. "Sure." She glanced around and found a table and chair. She sat as Doc set his bag on the table and opened it.

"Not sure what good my blood will do," she said.

"Never know," said Doc. "Could be the miracle we're all looking for."

She nodded, not understanding his meaning.

He spit on his fingers after removing the needle and rubbed it on her arm. The bleeding stopped immediately.

"William, you stay in bed till I get some answers as to what the hell they put in you." Doc toddled to the door.

"Will do." William wiped a drip of blood from his nose and smiled at her as the door closed. "Alone at last."

She returned his smile. "Doc did say you had to stay in bed."

"But he didn't say I had to stay alone." He gave her a charming, bright smile and her heart leapt at the sight. Despite the pale bluish skin tone and the deep purple circles, he looked like William. *Her* William.

For a fraction of a second she became self-conscious about him seeing her naked. It was silly; he'd seen her that way several times. She hesitated but then stood and dropped her towel to the floor. William's ice blue eyes sparkled. She crawled across the bed and sat on his lap. His hands found their way to her rear and he gripped her skin as she threaded her arms around his neck and kissed him. She wondered what he thought of her body. Her scars and tiny stretch marks. Her wider hips and curvy shape. His hand trailed up her spine and pressed her closer.

His arousal hardened beneath her and told her everything she needed to know. She lifted his T-shirt and tossed it aside. His pale, taut muscles quivered under her touch.

"Evan, I want you to know, in case something happens to me, I'm going to talk to Danika to make sure you're provided for."

She kissed his chest and licked over his nipple. "I don't want your money."

"I know, but if I go—"

She shut him up with another kiss. Her heart couldn't take losing anyone else. Especially him. His lips grew from soft to needy in seconds. She lay down beside him and he stripped off his sweats and underwear.

He poised above her and kissed down the side of her neck. "I've loved you since you first arrived," he said. "Every moment of every day since you came here, all I've wanted was you."

She wrapped her arms around him and nipped at his shoulder.

"I want you too."

He slid inside her, making her claw at his back. She couldn't deny the feeling that they were meant to be together. He kissed her hard and his rhythm increased. His thrusts grew more forceful and she tried to hang on.

"Hey," she pulled his face so he looked her in the eyes. "Slow this time." She wanted him all to herself. As much as she didn't want to admit that he might not be around much longer, she knew that there was a chance they'd not have many rounds left.

She kissed him slow, letting her tongue glide across his lips and entangle with his. His muscles shook as he started again, the pace slow, every movement rubbing against her, the friction sending her higher into orbit.

He kissed down her neck, licking her collarbone and then nibbling on her breasts. The sensation sent her into overdrive. She tried to focus but drew closer to the edge of oblivion.

"William," she moaned. Her body quivering with the anticipated release. "I love you."

He swooped down and smothered her mouth with his. She grabbed his rear and pulled him inside her. Lights shot behind her eyes as her back arched and her muscles pulled tight. She cried his name and her breath caught in her throat as wave after wave of ecstasy overtook her. She just started to come down when William gasped and her name burst from his lips.

She rocked him through his climax until he fell on her, completely spent. Her body hummed from the love-making. Terror and happiness mingled inside her. She'd opened herself up again. Made herself vulnerable to pain and heartbreak. And to a vampyr no less. The one species she'd vowed to hate forever. To destroy. But that had been before she'd met him. Never before had she met a Vampire or vampyr like him. William had shown her kindness she didn't deserve and loved her despite her faults.

He gathered her in his arms and she kissed his chest, pushing away all thoughts of what might come.

"What do we do now?" she asked.

He snuggled her closer. "I like what we just did. I wouldn't mind doing that another hundred times."

She laughed and then her stomach growled.

"But maybe we should get you something to eat first," he said.

"There's no 'we' in that statement," she replied. "You have to stay put."

"I'll order room service."

His jovial mood struck an eerie chord with her. She knew

that his back to normal nature would only last as long as the blood did.

"I'm sorry about being a monster," he said.

She looked up into his eyes that held nothing but sincerity. "You aren't the monster."

He brushed the hair from her shoulder and ran a finger down her arm.

"I suppose this is how the vamp rogues feel. Their all-consuming lust for blood that drives them insane."

Her gut clenched at the thought. "But you're fighting it. Trying to be better. To not give in."

"Because of you." His gaze met hers. "If you weren't here I'd have killed Sue and Matthew and all the others. I'd have drained them dry without a care and then tried to move on to Danika and possibly Mason."

"But you didn't."

"Only because of you."

"I don't believe that. Yes, I'm here and yes, I reminded you of who you were but deep down, you're still you. You don't want to kill people. If you did, you'd have killed them no matter what I said. You'd have killed me and Tommy on the way here."

She could see in his eyes that he wanted to believe her.

She kissed him and rolled out of his arms. "I need to check on Tommy and get some food. I'll be back soon."

He watched her as she dressed in one of his shirts and a pair of pants.

"Why do I find it sexy that you're wearing my ill-fitting clothes?"

She leaned over him and kissed his forehead. "Because you're thinking about taking them off me."

"Would it be sexy if I wore your clothes?"

She envisioned him in her T-shirt and camo pants and then wrinkled her nose.

He chuckled. "Yeah, I didn't think so either."

"Try to get some rest while I'm gone."

"Will I need it for when you return?" He arched an eyebrow.

She smiled and walked to the door. "Try to rest."

He nodded and leaned back into his pillows.

She turned and her smile fell. A hollow ache settled in her chest. As she closed his bedroom door she once again prayed for a miracle.

CHAPTER TWENTY ONE

Vampires swarmed the entrance hall. Evan recognized some of them, but most, she didn't. Danika and Mason stood at the entrance, welcoming people and pointing to the large atrium used for parties.

Danika spotted her and she whispered to Mason before heading for the stairs where Evan met her at the bottom.

"You shouldn't be down here," she said. "You should be with William."

"I need something to eat and I want to check on my brother."

Dark shadows puffed under Danika's eyes. And her usually impeccable appearance seemed strained, like she'd been washed and ironed too many times. Her unusually pale skin showed several bruises on her forehead camouflaged by makeup and her nails polish had chipped and several nails were broken- something that she'd never seen before.

"Why is everyone here?" Evan scanned the crowd.

"We've had this many and more arriving daily since

Mason's father announced his impending arrival . They've come to fight. Two of my Underlords are bringing their entire areas to fight."

Evan fought the urge to laugh. The Vampires that walked through the foyer weren't fighters; they were businessmen and women. Spoiled, rich people who'd probably never scrapped for anything in their lives.

"Your brother went with Sue to the barracks. You know the way," said Danika. "But be sure to keep to the left barracks. Don't go near the right one."

"Why?"

Danika didn't answer for a minute, she stared at Evan as if sizing her up.

"Because it's full of newborn vampyr."

"Excuse me?"

"We gave every human here a choice. They could stay as they were, or they could become vampyr. We've taken heavy casualties these last weeks. We need all the bodies we can get."

"What about the vamps?"

Danika shook her head. "At this point we aren't telling them. We don't want to incite panic."

"But if what you try doesn't work, they're in danger as well."

"I'm aware of that." Danika held her head high.

"William was attacked by vamps who'd been selling Vampire blood. They said vamps were turning into vampyr. If you want to increase your army, that's where you should go, not to humans. There's so few of us left as is."

"Danika," Mason called. "Sherman is here."

Danika looked over her shoulder and then back at Evan. "You and I will need to speak. Until then though you may check on your brother and then you are to go back upstairs and take care of William."

The hairs on Evan's neck stood up. "I'm not your slave."

"No, but you're in my house."

Evan bit her tongue. It would do William no good if she got in a fight with Danika and ended locked up in the barracks.

Danika turned and strode across the hall to where a tall, white-haired Vampire waited.

Evan swallowed and headed into the kitchen. She pulled out two plates and opened the fridge. Inside she grabbed food without thinking and tried to keep calm as she headed out to the backyard toward the barracks.

Through the front window, she spotted Tommy sitting on the couch near the television, surrounded by a small group of humans.

She pulled open the door and walked in. Everyone turned. Tommy hopped from his spot and took one of the plates.

"Hey, sis. How's William?"

She glanced at the slaves listening from the couch. "Better."

He nodded and turned to the group. "I'm sure you all remember my sister, Evan."

Some of the group nodded or gave a weak wave.

"How's Sue?" she asked.

He shook his head. "I don't know. Doc went up and tended to her and the others but it wasn't good. I think she was in shock. She just kept sayin' she didn't understand."

Evan nodded. "She and William used to be... close. I have an old room upstairs. You can have it if you want. Or I can try to see if I can find you something in the house..."

"Nah. I'll hang out here."

"I'll come check on you. If you need me, you know where I'll be."

He pulled her into a one-armed hug. "You did the right thing, sis. No matter what happens, you did the right thing."

"Do you think Pop will come looking for us?"

"Part of me hopes so, but part of me prays he doesn't."

She knew that feeling all too well.

Tommy released her, and she backed out the door and headed for the main house. The entourage had convened in the atrium and she tiptoed up the stairs when Mason ducked into the foyer. For a moment, they stared at each other, and then he crossed to her.

"How is he?" Mason asked.

"Better." Somehow knowing Mason's true nature made her want to run.

Mason nodded and looked at the upstairs landing. "He saved my life once."

"He told me."

"I'll do the same for him if I can."

She wasn't sure what Mason could do for William. She wasn't sure what any of them could do for him.

"Is it true that Selene and Neeman left?" she asked. "They didn't seem the type to run from a fight."

Mason's amber eyes met hers. "After Neeman got injured, my sister freaked out. She'd do anything not to lose him."

"But where would they go? If the demons take over, no one will be safe."

"I'll make sure that doesn't happen." His eyes held such solid conviction that she believed him.

"You'd go back with your father. To save us all."

"You turned your back on your family to save William. Would you go back to them if it would save him too?"

"In a heartbeat."

"Then you understand my position. If leaving Danika is the

only way to save her, I'll do it." He glanced at the atrium. "I should get back. I only came out to grab something for Sherman. If you'll excuse me." He jogged around her, took the steps three at a time, and then bounded down the hall.

Would she go back to Pop and Peter if it would save William? Be subjected to their brainwashing and torture of people... She already knew the answer. She'd do whatever it took to make William well again. Even that.

WILLIAM COUGHED AND A SPATTER OF BLOOD SPLASHED HIS PALM. THE fullness in his stomach quenched the ever-present bloodlust enough to see and think straight. But not much else. It took everything he had just to do those two things. His time with Evan had been more than he could ever hope for. He wished he could do more for her, but even with the blood coursing through him, he limbs trembled weak as a newborn babe.

The door opened and Evan entered with a plate of food.

"Did you sleep at all?"

"Nope."

She shook her head, moved to the other side of the bed, and sat. "You want to watch some television?"

"I'd rather talk."

"Okay." She picked a piece of beef off the plate and bit into it.

"What's going on downstairs?"

"I don't know. There's a ton of Vampires down there in some kind of meeting."

"Members of the house?"

"More. Maybe a hundred. Most I've never seen here."

He nodded. "I'm sure they'll be pouring in from all over the US and maybe abroad to find out what's going on. Did you see Tommy?"

"Yeah. He's concerned for Sue."

"Good. She deserves someone who cares for her."

"I don't think it's like that. Tommy cares about everyone." She cocked her head to the side. "It wouldn't make you even a little bit jealous? If he liked her?"

"She was never the one I wanted. I've told you that."

Their eyes connected and he stared at her for a long while. The beautiful way her lips curved. Her cheekbones high and proud that framed her thin pixie nose. The way her fingers delicately picked at the items on her plate. Yet he'd seen them be strong and forceful as well. In a different world, she could have been a model or an actress or a beauty queen.

"If you'd met me when I was human you wouldn't have given me the time of day," he said.

Her eyebrows drew together. "That's not true."

"It's not an accusation, just an observation. Because of what I am now, I was able to meet and love you. If nothing else, that alone was worth it."

"I don't love you because of what you are. I love you because of who you are."

He took a deep breath. Just those simple words. Her telling him she loved him made everything that much more bearable.

"What would you say if I asked you to marry me?" he asked.

Her brow furrowed. "What?"

"What would you say?"

"William, I don't really think this is the time."

"Why? Who knows how much time we have left. How much time I have left."

She smiled. "Oh, so this is one of those take pity on a dying man proposals?"

He shrugged. "If that works."

She shoved a piece of meat in her mouth and shook her head. "You're insane."

"With what I've done lately I'd have to agree with you on that, but I'm asking you this now while I'm as sane as I can be."

She licked her fingers. "Okay. I'll play along. Say we did get married. How do you see our life together?"

"Well, we'd live here."

"Next to Danika and Mason? I don't think so."

"We could find our own room somewhere else in the house. Maybe a room down by Lance and…" Lance was gone. "Sinya." His heart ached for Sinya and what she must be going through.

"Maybe a room not next to a baby. I get cranky when I don't get my beauty sleep."

"You don't want kids?"

Sadness clouded her features. "Maybe. I don't know."

"I'm sorry." He grabbed her hand. Anger at what she'd been through coursed through him. "As soon as all of this is over, I'm going to find that bastard and we're going to get your little girl back."

She shook her head. "She doesn't know me. It's been years. It's not fair to disrupt her life. I would like to know that she's okay though. Loved and taken care of."

"I wasn't adopted till I was over twice her age. You deserve to see your child."

"Slaves don't have rights."

He'd never thought about it before. All those women who'd given birth as breeding slaves to vampyr babies. What happened to them?

"Then we'll change it. Make sure that never happens

again." So many things about the society he lived in needed changing.

"I never knew you were an idealist."

"I'm not. I'm a... fairest."

"A fairest? I'm not even sure what that means."

There was a knock on the door.

William pulled on his sweats and T-shirt before calling for them to come in.

Danika and Mason walked into the room followed by Sherman and Roth. William tried to straighten the covers, and Evan put her plate on the nightstand.

"I think this is yours." Roth held Evan's backpack out to her.

"My clothes." She took her bag and set it on the floor by the bed.

Danika sat next to William, her eyes filled with concern. "How are you feeling?"

"Better." He tried to give her a reassuring smile but he felt a drip on his neck and her eyes traveled to it. He reached for a tissue and blotted the blood from his ear.

"Can you tell me what happened?"

"I followed Evan like we'd agreed. She was stabbed by vampyr slavers. Infection set in, and I took her the rest of the way to her enclave. I was captured and tortured for information. I gave them everything they wanted to know, but it still wasn't enough. In the end they used me as a guinea pig for a new vaccine they are trying out to cure vamps."

"Cure vamps?" asked Sherman.

"They want to turn them human again."

Danika's gaze shifted to Evan. "Have they had success?"

"Not yet," she replied. "They think they're close but who knows."

"And how do they have the equipment to do these kinds of tests?" asked Sherman. "Who's doing them?"

"A Vampire named Nicholas. He had something to do with the original virus, I think," said Evan. "They have an entire lab set up on the top floor. It's pretty advanced. Equipment of all kinds. They've gotten it from hospitals and medical labs and military facilities."

Danika's face grew paler than William thought possible.

"Are you okay?" he asked.

Sherman moved around the bed to face her. She looked up at him and shook her head. "It's not possible. He's dead."

"The body wasn't recovered," replied Sherman.

"What's going on?" William asked. "Who's not dead?"

"Nicholas," she replied. "My father."

Her father? That would explain all the questions.

"I knew it," said Evan.

The group looked at her.

"When I saw him the first time, I knew he reminded me of someone. It was you. You look like him, except for the red hair. His is black."

"Then it is him," said Sherman. "But why would he be helping humans?"

"I don't think he is," said William. "I think he wants to undo what was done and the humans just happen to want the same thing."

"But he could have come to me," said Danika. "Why wouldn't he come to me?"

"Chase has only just died," said Mason. "Maybe your father feared for his safety and yours. As far as he knows Chase is still alive."

The anguish on Danika's face broke William's heart.

"But why would he experiment on you?" she asked.

"He didn't, sort of," said Evan. "Lou, my uncle who raised me, wanted to kill William. Nicholas offered this as a different option. He believed it would work so Lou went along with it."

Danika shook her head and covered her face before looking up at William again. "Then the mission failed."

"Not exactly," said William. "We now know how big that enclave is and what their firepower is like. It's true I've never seen one that big or that organized before but they are out there. And not just this one either."

"They have weapons," said Evan. "I've seen them, but not nuclear weapons. Lou and my cousin Peter are mad at the way things have gone for humans, but I don't think most people in the enclave feel like they do. I think most humans want what we've always wanted. Freedom."

"Are they a threat?" asked Sherman.

Evan looked around the group and then her gaze landed on William. "I think if they're left alone, they'll leave us alone. All of them."

"All of them?"

"I was told there are dozens of compounds around the country like ours."

"Thousands of humans?" asked Danika.

"Tens of thousands."

"But they won't help us?" asked Mason.

Evan shook her head. "No. And I won't tell you where they are."

Danika waved her hand. "We have no interest in finding them. However, I would like to have words with your uncle for what he did to William."

"What happened downstairs?" asked William. "Do we have enough on our side?"

Danika pressed her fingers into her temple and Mason rubbed her shoulders as they slumped.

"We don't have enough to keep the demons at bay. But we have enough to put up a fight. I've been in contact with Vampires from all over the world in the last two weeks. The entire second barrack is full of fledglings. All the houses in the neighborhood are occupied by Vampires and vampyr ready to fight."

"But most of them look like they've never seen a fight in their lives," said Evan.

Danika nodded. "And therein lies the problem. We have all the trackers that we could find, but we've lost heavy casualties in our fight so far. Without a miracle, there's nothing that will stop the demons from taking over. And with Selene gone..."

"There's no one to teach them how to fight demons," William finished.

"I can teach them," said Mason. "But unlike my beautiful sister, when they see me, they're simply reminded of what's coming."

"I don't want to talk about it right now," said Danika. "I want to hear what Doc has found out and figure out a way to cure William."

She gave him a tight smile and with all she had going on, he didn't have the heart to tell her his wishes for when he died.

"I'll get him." Roth turned to leave.

"What do you think?" William called.

Roth stopped and turned back, his expression guarded. "I think I'll go down fighting to keep this world and everyone in it safe. As will every one of my men."

The unspoken words hit like a slap to the face. Even if they cured William, it wouldn't matter. They were all going to die.

CHAPTER TWENTY TWO

Over the next forty-eight hours things got worse for William and more crowded at the coven house, leaving Evan feeling more out of place than ever. William had begun to feed almost every two hours and they were running out of donors. The mental toll on Evan had become a strain. She found herself needing to get out of the room and go for a walk more and more frequently. William's inability to control the lust wasn't something she knew how to handle. The greedy, hungry look in his eyes never left anymore and Doc had yet to find anything to help. He'd told her he'd never seen anything like the virus before. Though neither she nor William spoke of it, the thread of hope grew thinner and thinner.

Tommy had taken to watching William for her when she went out to get air. She'd protested at first; she couldn't deal with coming back to find Tommy dead on the floor. But William had promised to keep himself in check while she was gone, and she had to trust his word.

Danika and Mason had been doing little more than answering the now ever-opening front door. Vampires and vampyr from all over poured into Chicago by the dozens. But for every one that came, excuses followed as to why another half dozen couldn't.

Evan stood in the garden aiming her knives at a large oak tree next to the pond, her thoughts on the nights sleeping in the bed of her uncle's truck before they'd arrived at the enclave in Palm Springs. Every night had been fraught with fear of death as well as finding a new home. After all the years in between, tonight was no different. She threw a knife at the makeshift target on the tree and hit it just right of center.

"Can I join you?" Mason walked toward her.

Evan shrugged and walked to retrieve her knives from the tree. "It's your house."

He sat on the rock wall and looked up at the stars. "Beautiful night."

She pulled the blades from the wood and unease settled in her bones. "Yup."

"I used to sit and stare at the stars back before I was captured. They always seem closer and more brilliant in the mountains."

"That they do." She walked back to where he sat and flipped one of the knives around her hand before shoving it in her boot.

He stared up into the sky for several minutes before he dropped his gaze to his hands. "Doc said there's nothing he can do for William."

"When? Is he up there?" She tossed her knives down on the leather case and wrapped it up.

"Danika is with him now. Give them some time. They're close. She feels responsible for what's happened to William."

"Why?"

"He saved her life."

"And she saved his."

Mason shook his head. "She doesn't see it that way."

"What did Doc say?"

"The virus has spread too far. The blood he drinks is like putting a bandage over a gushing wound. All it does is replace what he's losing hourly."

"So, if he keeps drinking he can live?"

"Is he really living? Lying in bed. Drinking from people. Bleeding from everywhere."

Her heart squeezed at the truth. She plopped down next to Mason. "Then there's nothing to be done." The very words threatened to have her crying again.

"I didn't say that."

They stared at each other for a long time.

"What then? Tell me and I'll do it," she whispered.

Mason looked at his hands again. "I may be able to cure the virus."

She jumped to her feet. "Then what are we waiting for? If you have a cure, if you can fix him—"

"I didn't say I could fix him. I said I could stop the virus that's killing him. But there will be consequences. Side effects."

"What kind of consequences?" Her heart beat so wildly that she could barely keep it in her chest.

"I'm mostly Demon. I have blood and I have magic. Together I can stop the virus, but it will change William. Into what, I do not know."

Evan processed Mason's words, trying to get them to make sense. "A Demon."

"It's possible. There are those in my home world that are demi-demons. Almost like vamps are here. They're a lower class of Demon made up of those who used to be human, Vampire, vampyr, and Fae. They aren't as strong or powerful as demons but they're pretty close. The problem is that it's unpredictable what kind of demi-Demon will be produced. He could be as he is now, or he could be something terrible. It all depends on his soul."

"William has a good soul. He's a decent person."

"That may have been true before. But not now. You can't tell me you haven't seen it. The bloodlust in his eyes."

"So... he could end up being that person permanently."

"Yes."

She blew out a harsh breath. All she'd prayed for over the last several days was a miracle. She'd pleaded with God. Begged. Anything. She would do anything just to keep him alive... but having him turn into a Demon... she didn't even know if she understood what that meant. But in the end... it wasn't her life. He needed to make the decision for himself.

"Have you asked him what he wants?"

"I've talked to both him and Danika. But William wanted me to talk to you as well."

She licked her lips. "What does he want?"

"You. Or at the very least more time with you."

She shook her head. "I don't want him doing that for me."

"He wouldn't do it for you. I think he just wants you to tell him it's okay to do it."

"We've only been together for a couple of weeks. I can't have that on my shoulders."

"I think he wants to do it. He just wants all of us to tell him it's okay to make that choice. That we'll still be there for him if it goes badly."

"I've been cleaning him up for the past week. I wouldn't do it if I didn't care."

Mason nodded and his eyes softened. "I'm sure that's true, but I saw you with him when he fed. It's very well possible that this is a life-long commitment. He responds to you the way my inner Demon responds to Danika. And Selene responds to Neeman."

Her stomach knotted and a wave of nausea had her putting her head between her knees and breathing deeply. A life-long commitment. Her life span was unpredictable. She could easily live to a hundred, two hundred maybe. Two hundred years was a long time to clean up blood.

"Well, how long is that really going to be if we get overrun by demons next week?" she asked.

"If you're in this for the long haul, you need to tell him."

The nausea subsided and she lifted her head. "When would you do it?"

"The sooner the better. We don't know when exactly my father will be showing up, but it'll be in the next few days. We need to deal with everything that will take away from that focus now."

"Well, let's get to it then." She breathed deep and her head spun.

Mason reached out to steady her. "Are you okay?"

"Yeah. I just haven't eaten."

"Danika made a bunch of paninis earlier if you want one."

"What the heck is a panini?"

"I think it's just a fancy word for a grilled sandwich."

They both chuckled and then she looked up at the sky. It hadn't changed. Everything on earth had, but the sky remained ever the same. How was that even possible?

"If you don't think you can do this—"

"I can do this." She tried to make herself sound more confident than she felt. Then she turned and strode into the coven house.

WILLIAM'S EYES BURNED IN HIS SKULL. DANIKA HELD HIS HAND, TEARS in her eyes, but all he wanted to do was shrink away from her icy touch. He tried not to think about what Doc had told him and instead focused on Mason's solution. Danika was against it, but he would die if something wasn't done. To him it was worth the risk. If it gave him more time with Evan. More time on Earth. More time to live... it would be worth it.

"Promise me," said William. "If I become worse, promise you'll kill me. I don't want you and Evan having to deal with me like that. You both deserve more than to have to take care of me for the rest of my immortal life."

"I can't do that," said Danika. "I would rather clean up after you than keep that promise."

"I'll keep it," said Tommy.

William had forgotten Tommy stood in the corner.

"I'll do it," said Tommy. "Not because I don't like you or anything, but because I don't want Evan to have to do it and I don't want to see her suffer."

William nodded. The part of him that still clung to sanity was glad he hadn't killed Tommy. He wanted Tommy's blood, but he needed Tommy's strength. And Evan would need him as well after William passed on.

He'd witnessed her fragility beneath the tough exterior. Losing her daughter had eaten a hole inside her. A hole she'd built a thick cement wall around. A wall that he'd inadvertently begun to tear down. And with each block that crumbled, she opened up to her heart to being impaled forever.

There was a knock on the door and Mason and Evan stepped into the room. She walked to him, her face a mask of non-emotion.

"Could you give us a minute?" he asked Danika.

She nodded and she, Mason, and Tommy exited.

"Is this what you really want?" Evan asked.

"What I want is to live. Live without seeing everyone as food. Live without almost killing everyone I drink from. Live without the thirst being like a red stain in my eyesight that everything else is tainted by. But most of all, I don't want to die."

"I don't want you to die."

"Does that mean you're saying yes to marrying me?"

She smiled. "Let's try and get through this first, okay?"

He brushed his knuckles across her cheek. "I want you to know something, and I don't want you to get mad."

"That doesn't sound good."

"If I do this and I come out... worse, I made Tommy promise to kill me."

Her eyes hardened and she pursed her lips. "How could you do that? How could he do that?"

He cupped her face. "He said he'd do it so you wouldn't have to. I don't want you to remember me as more of a monster than I am now. If I turn worse, I would rather go than hurt you."

Her eyes held emotion that she tried to hide. "You won't. I know you won't. Your soul is good. No matter what happens or who you become."

He wanted to believe her words, but the things he'd done lately... He wasn't sure.

266

"I love you, PITA." He pressed his lips to hers and breathed her in. It was the one memory he wanted to take with him if everything went wrong. His new Peter Pan memory.

"Okay." He broke the kiss. "Let's get this over with before I start spewing blood again. I can't imagine what the laundry load looks like right now."

He kissed her again, and she rubbed his cheek with her palm. It was all he'd dreamed of for months. Having her look at him like that and kiss him the way she did told him everything he needed to know.

She loved him.

Evan's emotions flew all over the map. She wanted William to live, but what happened if they didn't work out? They hadn't even liked each other that long. Her stomach roiled with nervous energy, making her feel like she might puke.

"So how do we do this?" asked William.

Mason licked his lips. "It won't be pretty. I'll need to drain you, and then you'll need to drink from me, much like how you became a vampyr. While you drink from me I'll perform a ritual."

"Sounds easy enough," said William.

Mason's gaze flicked to Danika. "The problem is I can't do all that in this form."

William's eyes widened. "Maelstrom."

Mason nodded once.

"Maelstrom?" asked Evan.

William squeezed her hand. "He has to take his Demon form."

"This is Demon magic, not Fae magic. Only in my true form can I do what needs to be done. Only as the son of my father can I create demi-demons."

She glanced around the group, Tommy paled, and the rest looked worried.

"So what's the problem?" asked Evan.

William gave her a tight smile. "Maelstrom is..."

"Unpredictable," said Mason. "He'll listen to Danika but the biggest problem will be once he and William are in the same room, I don't know what will happen."

"But he's you," said Evan. "And you've done this before, right?"

"He is me... but the worst part of me. Think of Jekyll and Hyde. He's Hyde on steroids," Mason said. "And no, I haven't done this before, but I've seen it done hundreds of times."

"Great." Fear gripped her so tight that a trickle of sweat snaked down her spine. So William wasn't the worst thing to worry about, and Mason had only ever seen this thing done, not actually done it.

"Should we go outside for this?" asked William. "More space and all."

"It's better if we're in a more familiar space for both of you," said Danika.

"Okay." William blew out a deep breath. "Let's do it."

Mason stood and scanned the room. He rubbed his face with his hands till Danika pulled them away and squeezed them. His agitation did nothing to squelch Evan's fears. She'd never seen him nervous. And the fact that someone as large and powerful as Mason could be nervous about something only served to make her rethink the whole idea. Maybe they should wait. Maybe they could still find a cure. She could go back to the enclave...

"I'm right here," said Danika.

Mason nodded.

Tommy cleared his throat. "Maybe I should go into the hall."

"I might need your help," said Evan. "But if you can't, I understand."

Tommy's cheeks flushed pink. "Way to put my manhood on the line there, sis, thanks a lot."

Everyone laughed and the tension in the room eased somewhat.

Tommy walked to Evan's side of the bed and pulled up a chair. She took his hand and gave him a tight smile. He'd always been there for her. No matter what.

Mason stripped off his expensive, button-down shirt and handed it to Danika. He blew out a deep breath and then took her in his arms. She smiled up at him and whispered something Evan couldn't hear. The laugh that rumbled from Mason's chest wasn't human. He looked at her hard for a second and then kissed her hard, crushing her into his chest.

A growl shook the room. Evan's heart raced as Mason's skin darkened and he grew taller. Danika stepped away and Mason's form widened and shifted as huge leathery wings spread from his back and spanned almost from wall to wall. His suit pants stretched and groaned as his thighs thickened and elongated. Every inch of him almost quadrupled in size and it took everything inside Evan to keep from screaming and running in terror.

Tommy jumped to his feet. "Holy—"

"Stay where you are," Danika held her hand up and Tommy sat slowly.

She connected gazes with Mason again and laid her hand on his chest.

Mason raised a large hand and caressed her cheek with his enormous talon tipped fingers. "Danika."

"Maelstrom. I need you."

"Yes."

She looked to William. "We need you to help William. He's dying. I need you to turn him."

Maelstrom turned his fiery gaze on William. "Why?"

"Because I care for him," said Danika.

Maelstrom growled.

"No." Danika turned Maelstrom to face her. "Family. William is like my son."

Maelstrom nodded and stomped to the bed. His footsteps shook the lamps and the floor. Evan stood to move away, but William clung tightly to her hand and she sat again.

"You want to be like me," Maelstrom asked.

"Yes." William's voice came out strong and clear.

Maelstrom chuckled and pulled William to him. "I can arrange that."

Maelstrom's chin-length fangs lengthened and in a flash he bit into William's throat. William grunted and Evan's mouth opened in a silent scream. He crushed her fingers in his grip. Her eyes met Danika's and they offered each other silent support. Danika hugged Mason's shirt tight. Tommy whispered into Evan's ear but she didn't hear a word as she watched the color wash out of William like someone hosing down a water-color picture.

Minutes passed and Evan's anxiety grew to an almost choking terror as William's grip slacked on her fingers. His glassy gaze connected with hers.

"I'm right here," she croaked trying to hold back tears. "I'm not going anywhere."

William gurgled a reply and his eyes fluttered open and closed.

"He's slipping away." Evan tried to keep panic out of her voice.

Danika took a step forward and placed her hand on Maelstrom's shoulder. He shrugged her off and growled. Her eyes flashed and her fangs lengthened as she stepped close, whispering in his ear. Evan tensed as nothing happened for a second and then Maelstrom suddenly threw William down on the bed and pulled Danika onto his lap, kissing her hard. She returned his kiss but her hands pushed against his chest.

Evan crawled over William, his body grew deathly cold, and his eyes barely held the spark of life.

"Danika," she said. "Danika! Do something!"

Maelstrom continued to kiss Danika.

Evan turned back to William. "Stay with me. Don't go. Stay."

He didn't move.

Forbidden tears slid from her eyes. She bent close to his ear and whispered to him. "Stay and I'll marry you. I'll stay with you all my life and take care of you if I have to. I'll bring you every human I can find to feed you, just don't go. Don't leave me. Please."

"Evan?" Danika's voice pulled Evan from her thoughts.

She looked up and Maelstrom had already begun to chant.

"He's gone," said Evan. "He's already gone."

"Not yet," Maelstrom replied.

He lifted William from the bed and bit into his own wrist. Maelstrom pressed it to William's mouth and continued chanting in a language Evan had never heard before. A minute passed and then a second. William's eyes fluttered and he coughed. He grabbed Maelstrom's wrist tight and latched on.

His arms and legs shook but his teeth and his eyes stayed fixed on the huge Demon. His skin took on a humanlike tone and Evan backed away. Her heartbeat pounded and her mind tried to process the scene. He lived, that much she could see, but how he would be when it was over remained a mystery. Maelstrom finished chanting.

William lurched off the bed, sucked in a huge breath, and then cried out.

"Hold him," said Maelstrom.

Danika shoved Mason's shirt onto a chair as Maelstrom's wings folded into his back and he shrunk.

William ripped at his chest with his nails, shredding his T-shirt and scoring the skin beneath. Blood oozed from the cuts welling on his skin like a strand of red pearls. "Kill me!"

Evan grabbed one arm and Danika grabbed the other. Tommy hopped from his seat and took hold of William's feet. Together the three of them tried to keep him down.

William started by swearing at them, cursing them, all manner of vulgarity that Evan had never heard him say. When he turned his eyes on her, she almost lost her nerve. Terror and pain etched on every crevasse of his handsome face as he begged her to kill him.

"Your gun is in your backpack. Please, Evan. End this."

She hated herself for being weak. For needing him so damn much, but she couldn't let him go. No matter what it meant.

"No," she whispered.

She watched on in horror as William's skin turned black and then back to a dark tan color. His muscles bunched and refined further. His abs tightened and all fat melted away revealing taut, stacked muscles that cut down to his sweats in a shapely V. The sound of ripping fiber filled her ears and he screamed as his legs lengthened and his sweats pulled tight around his expanding thighs. Evan's body responded to his bulkier, sexier physique. He'd been handsome before, but the changes now had likened him closer to a Norse god. His mouth opened in a silent scream and his fangs ripped through his gums, pushing his other teeth out of the way and extended down to his chin. His entire body went slack and he fell silent on the bed, sweat slicking his newly tanned skin.

Motionless, his breathing slowed and then evened out. Minutes passed and they all exchanged frantic glances. Was it over? Had it worked? No one dared move for fear of what might come next.

"It's almost finished." Mason threw his shirt over his torso. "You can let go of him. That was the worst of it."

Evan scanned his new physique trying to acclimate to his new form. Every inch of him had been cut into a muscle. His jaw more angular. His hair a lighter mix of golden and wheat. She grabbed his hand once more, but he didn't even stir at her touch.

"William?"

He didn't respond.

She looked from Tommy to Danika and finally to Mason. "What do we do now?"

Mason sat heavily on the floor and stretched out. "We wait."

CHAPTER TWENTY THREE

Every one of them refused to leave the room as the minutes stretched into hours and the night continued on. Neither Danika nor Mason left to welcome guests that night. Instead they sent Roth to handle the task.

Evan spent the hours brushing William's hair or tending to the cuts on his torso. She propped him up on pillows and stroked his cheek, but no amount of coaxing got him to wake up.

Fear spider webbed in her mind, taking over every thought and leaving her on the edge of a panic attack.

"Should it be taking this long?" Danika asked.

"It takes longer to corrupt a good soul than an evil soul," Mason replied. "It's a good sign."

"But he will make it, right?" Evan stroked his cheek.

Mason didn't answer.

Near two a.m. William sucked in a shuddered breath.

"William?" Evan's voice came out barely above a hoarse whisper.

His eyes flew open and he looked over at her, drinking her in. Bright red eyes replaced his icy blue ones and bore into her, sending chills up her spine.

A sex-wrapped smile planted on his face, making her belly quiver.

"Well hello, beautiful, fancy a tumble? I'd give anything to sink my fangs into your soft flesh as I—"

"William," Danika snapped.

William's head whipped to Danika. "I know you." He looked at her for a moment as if trying to place her. "You made me this. You think that I'll continue to stay your little puppy now?"

"That's enough." Mason's voice reverberated around the room. "You are William and we are your family."

The laugh that erupted from William was not his own. Deep and resonating as if it emerged from the depths of hell, it chilled Evan to the bone.

"I am Seksi."

Mason looked William from head to toe and a slight smile crossed his lips.

"What?" asked Danika. "What's so funny?"

Mason rang his fingers through his hair and shook his head. "He's a Begær Demon."

"A what?" asked Evan.

Mason licked his lips. "A lust Demon. His deepest desire was to be wanted and admired before his change. That's what he now embodies. It's why he looks the way he does. Taller, more muscular, more alluring."

William flashed Evan a smile that left her almost powerless to resist. His gaze locked on hers, beckoning to her.

"Let me take you." His voice held such seductive, raw sexuality she found herself wanting to strip naked for him in front of everyone.

William grabbed her by the back of the head and plunged his tongue deep into her mouth, probing and claiming her.

"Stop," Mason commanded.

William huffed but let go of Evan with a small nip to her bottom lip. She sat back, head spinning. What the hell was going on? The flip flop from the William just hours before to the William now had her ready to shout for joy and burst into tears at the same time.

Mason moved to the side of the bed. "You aren't to use your power on anyone."

William smiled. "But why? There are so many women waiting for me to show them the pleasure they are capable of experiencing. And this one is incredibly beautiful."

"You will not use your powers here. Do you understand?"

William pouted. Actually pouted.

She didn't like this side of him. It was false, manipulative. Two things she'd never known William to be.

"Fine. But can I use them outside this room?" asked William.

"No," said Evan.

"Why?"

"Because you're mine," Evan said.

William's head whipped back to meet her gaze. "I belong to no one."

Evan glanced around the room and swallowed hard. "What's my name?"

William flashed her a toothy smile. "Does it matter?"

"Yes." Evan's voice hardened as anger flushed her skin. "It does."

"Is it... Jane?" he teased.

"No."

"Prudence?"

Evan glared at him and he chuckled.

"Okay, not Prudence. How about Candy? Or Cindy? Mary-Ann? Trisha?"

"Shut up!" Her entire body shook. He didn't remember her. She'd been prepared for anything. For him to be a monster. Hideous. Blood thirsty. A razor wielding death machine. Anything... anything but that.

"I'm sorry," said Mason. "I didn't realize he'd forget his former life. The memories are in there. I'm sure they are. He just has to find them."

"Give him some time," Danika said gently. "He's only just become... Just give him some time."

Evan nodded but said nothing. The walls of her newly built world seemed to be crumbling down around her, toppling her and crushing her from the inside out.

"Come on," said Mason. "This is between them."

"No way," said Tommy. "I won't let him hurt her."

Evan looked to her cousin. "He won't hurt me."

William took a fake nip at her arm and smiled. "I might. I like biting. And tying up and being tied up and—"

Mason rolled his eyes and wrapped his arm around Danika's waist.

Tommy looked to Evan and she nodded.

"I'll wait in the hall."

"It's okay. Why don't you go check on Sue?"

"Sue?" said William. "Is she the tasty little brunette?"

Tommy's expression darkened and he left without a word.

William remembered Sue but not her? She sat next to him but was unable to look at him. His body temperature now rivaled her own.

William brushed her hair from her shoulder. "I feel like I know you but I can't quite place you. Are we lovers?"

The sentence sounded strange. He looked like William, sort of, yet he wasn't William.

Determination set inside her. She would have to take the initiative. Make him remember. She straddled his hips and he purred in delight.

"You remember what you asked me last night?"

His brows furrowed and he gave her a gleaming smile. "To engage in a night full of endless pleasure?"

"You asked me to marry you."

He laughed. "Such a simple concept. Marriage. Two people committing to each other and none else for the entirety of their lives. But there are too many females in this world worth having to settle with just one."

"Oh really?" Evan tried to keep her cool.

"One female could never satisfy my needs. And I can be so much to so many. There are endless pleasures and desires and fantasies to fulfill." His hands roamed her body but she refused to give in to his touch. "Mason says I'm not allowed to compel you with my talents, but I don't think I'll need them."

She smacked his hands away and he chuckled.

"Oooohhh. I like you, feisty."

"Feisty is not the word you should be using to describe me right now," she countered.

"I've offended you." He thought for a moment and an adorable set of wrinkles creased between his eyebrows. "Because I said I don't want to marry you?"

"No." She hopped off him and he groaned.

"Don't be like that."

He reached for her but she slapped his hand away and moved nose to nose with him in a flash.

"Until you are ready to commit to me and no one else, you do not get to talk to me."

He smiled seductively. "I can smell the way you want me. You can't resist me. No woman can."

"Watch me." Rage heated Evan so deeply it surprised her hair hadn't caught fire.

"Evan," he called as she strode from the room. "Your name is Evan!"

She slammed the door and stood in the hall, head in her hands.

"Are you okay?" asked Danika.

Evan's head whipped up, and she wrapped her arms around herself. "Not really."

Danika walked toward her slowly. "It's not what I expected either. I should have though. As soon as Mason said his deepest desire would define him, I should have known what would happen. All William has ever wanted was to belong and have people like him. This was a natural progression."

"He doesn't want me anymore," said Evan.

"Not true," Danika replied.

"He wants everyone now."

Danika nodded. "Part of him might want everyone. But even someone who wants everyone still wants a special someone to come home to. When Maelstrom first woke up he almost killed me. He didn't remember me either. But eventually he did."

"So, you think I should indulge him. Share him with other women?"

"Hell no." Danika and Evan laughed. "What I mean is what happens in his thoughts and his pants are not something you are going to be able to control. What you do to keep him in your bedroom is up to you."

"You think I need to satisfy him to keep him? That he doesn't need to do anything to keep me?"

"I never said that. You need to show him who's in charge. You need to lead. Remind him of who you are and make him remember you." Danika looked Evan up and down and then put her arm around Evan's shoulder. "And that part I can help you with."

CHAPTER TWENTY FOUR

William had been stuck in this room for the last three days with only Danika or Mason as company. The craze of being locked in the room set him on edge. He craved the company of someone else. Preferably a willing female. His brain and crotch had both almost exploded with thoughts and desires over his time of imprisonment. There were so many things he wanted to try. So many pleasures he wanted to experience. So many women he wanted to test out.

He lay on his bed staring at the ceiling listening to the sounds of the house. Every heartbeat of a human, every sigh of a Vampire made him want to go explore and entice. But something about Evan conflicted with the need inside to tease and flirt and conquer every woman within a hundred miles. Vampire, vampyr, human, it didn't matter.

Her face lingered just below the surface as a memory he could not seem to grasp or shake off.

He wished Evan would come to see him. He was sure if he

could talk to her, she'd fall in bed with him willingly. Any female would.

Flashes of a woman in a blue flower dress pulling him through the dark woods interrupted his thoughts. Her stern yet loving face filled his mind.

"Selfishness is an ugly trait, William Scott." Sadness and dread washed over him. He couldn't place the woman but her words stung him to the core. He shook his head and took a deep breath.

Like flashes from an incomplete film, memories had plagued him over the past days- but none as much as the memories of making love to Evan.

The feel of her soft skin on his, the sweet scent of her sweat slicked body. William groaned and threw his hands over his face. He needed to screw someone. Or a whole room full of someones.

A knock on the door pulled him from his thoughts.

"You need to get up," said Mason. "Dinner is being served downstairs for everyone to mingle. We won't have many opportunities left, and Danika wants everyone to enjoy themselves."

"Wonderful. Are there women down there?"

"You are to keep your hands and your mouth to yourself."

William smiled. "I can do many things without using either."

Mason sighed. "Look, bro. I know that all of this is new for you. Being a demi-Demon can't be easy. Having a full-fledged Demon side is hard, but having your entire personality change and memory wipe overnight has got to be even harder. Even so, there are rules here. We don't live with our own kind. We live with others who are susceptible to our influence. But using it takes their ability to choose, away. In the end it will do you more harm than good. You need to try and look at people, especially us your family, as people. Not love machines."

"So you are telling me to not bring everyone the immense pleasure I was made to bring."

"You weren't made solely to bring pleasure. You are more than that. You are a friend, a confidant, a helper, a brother, a fixer, a supporter, a son. You are a being. You are more than just a penis. So start thinking with more than just that one part of your body."

"So… if I think about talking to someone and then think about having sex with them, and then do have sex with them, is that okay?"

Mason pointed at him. "Your junk stays in your pants until Danika or Evan say otherwise."

William sighed. "What a bore. I might as well stay here."

Mason shrugged. "Suit yourself. But you aren't allowed to entice anyone as long as you live under this roof."

"I can leave and find someone?"

Mason ground his teeth together. "After my father comes and things are decided, you can go where you please."

William found the connection to Mason strange. As if some part of him was bound to obey Mason's commands. Almost like an oppressive aura, William felt that Mason was superior to himself. Someone he couldn't help but respect and listen to. He could not resist Mason's commands, even though he wanted to.

"You don't like me," William said.

"I like who you used to be."

"But you made me this. I can't help who I am now."

"I did make you this. To save your life. The life of a brother who was kind and generous and selfless. But you are wrong about one thing," said Mason. "You have a choice like all of us.

Like you did when you were a vampyr. You can choose to give in to your baser instincts or you can choose to be more. You can be the man we all know and love. The man that I myself aspired to be one day."

Why be more when being himself could be so pleasurable?

"I'll dress and be down in a minute," William finally said.

Mason nodded. "Know that the only reason I'm letting you out of this room is because Danika requested it. If it was up to me, you'd stay locked in here until you learn how to treat ladies. Being a new demi-Demon can be hard on this plane, but it doesn't give you the right to treat those who care about you like just pieces of meat."

Mason left without another word. The thought stabbed William somewhere he couldn't place. He and Mason had been friends, but now...

William frowned. He didn't like the feeling that Mason no longer cared for him. The rejection hit him harder than he wanted to admit.

"You look beautiful," said Danika.

Evan didn't feel beautiful; she felt naked, queasy, and alone. It'd been three agonizing days since she'd seen William. Part of her wanted to force him to remember her. But another part couldn't bear the pain of seeing those vacant red eyes that didn't remember her.

Instead, she'd spent her time trying to recuperate from her ordeal. It surprised her how much the last weeks had fatigued her both mentally and physically. Her leg had healed completely, but every once in a while it would still ache. She found that even though she once again had all the food she could want, nothing sounded appetizing.

"Do I really have to do this?" she asked.

Danika turned from her jewelry box while putting on her earrings.

"You don't have to do anything you don't want to. But I'm telling you, William has been asking for you every time I see him. He's remembering, and seeing you like this may very well be the thing he needs to knock those memories loose and bring him back to us."

Evan nodded and fought the urge to wrap her arms around herself. She wasn't just doing this for herself, she was doing it for all of them. More than anything in the last three days, she'd seen the pain that William's change had brought to so many people. Danika and Mason especially. She looked at herself in the mirror and swallowed hard. She just hoped Danika's plan worked.

WILLIAM DESCENDED THE STAIRCASE, FEASTING ON THE SPECTACLE before him. Swarms of people mingled in the foyer. Vampires, vampyr, and humans alike. The sights and sounds and smells had him turned on and ready to party. So many women to pleasure and be pleasured by. So many men to have groveling at his feet.

A banquet for the senses.

He scanned the crowd trying to find familiar faces. His gaze landed on a tall blond vampyr holding a baby. The sadness that radiated from her slammed into him from all the way across the room. *Sinya.*

She greeted the well-wishers and those consoling her with a pasted-on smile that didn't reach her eyes. A memory surfaced of Lance and Sinya standing by him as they stood up for Danika and Mason against the Three Kings. He swallowed hard against the sadness that her pain awakened in him.

A tinkle of familiar laughter piqued his interest. As he looked to his left, his gut clenched, and every nerve in his body lit on fire. Evan stood in the corner of the foyer, near the atrium. She wore a tight black dress with a neckline that plunged almost to her belly button. Her wheat-colored hair had been swept up in an elegant chignon exposing her long, slender throat. She laughed again and laid her hand on the arm of one of the Vampires she spoke to.

Her bright blue eyes flicked his direction and his arousal grew, making his already tight suit pants even tighter. She spotted him and turned pointedly away, sipping her champagne and exposing her entire back down to the hollow of her spine. He gripped the railing of the stairs so tight it groaned under his fingers. It took all of his control to keep from rushing to her and kneeling behind her while running his tongue over that southern-most indent of her spine.

He envisioned sliding his hands up her perfectly shaped calves, and silken, exposed thighs before grasping and molding her perfectly round rear being pushed up by the crimson red heels she wore. A memory triggered of her in black cargo pants and T-shirt. He liked the dress much more.

"William."

His gaze whipped to see Danika walking toward him.

"How are you feeling?"

He turned back to watch Evan. "Hungry."

"Wonderful." Danika linked her arm with his. "Come. I've arranged companionship for you tonight."

He looked to Danika. "I want Evan."

"She's off limits." Danika pulled him in the other direction, and he craned his neck but could no longer see Evan.

"Why?" he asked.

"As I've told you for the last three days, she isn't much for sharing. And as you have expressed the desire to be with more than one female, she's decided to find herself another bene-factor tonight."

"What?" William pulled his arm from Danika and stopped. "She couldn't— She wouldn't do that. She said she wants to marry me."

Danika nodded as if talking to a small child. "She did want to marry you, before."

"Before? But I'm better now. Look at me."

"You are better to look at, somewhat. But looks aren't everything. More than anything she wants a family of her own. You should know that."

"Oh." His talents and passions were to take pleasure and give pleasure to everyone. It was what he was created for. Yet those he'd met didn't seem to want that. They were all happy being with just one person.

Danika walked him to the conference room. She opened the door and inside stood two vampyr and two humans. The vampyr drank from the humans and the very sight sent William into a tailspin of desire.

"Ooohhh, he's finally arrived," said an Asian human.

"He's big," said the other human, who had black hair cut into a bob. The two vampyr stopped drinking and looked over to William.

"You're amazing." The brunette slid across the conference table.

"I'll leave you to it." Danika patted him on the chest and closed the door behind him.

William swallowed hard and smiled. A smorgasbord of pleasure awaited him. The brunette crawled toward him, followed by the redhead.

They backed him into the wall, each running their hands over his body in different directions. William closed his eyes and purred as the redhead unzipped his pants and knelt in front of him.

The brunette turned his head, so he looked at her.

"I've been told I'm delicious." She pulled her hair away from her neck and leaned into him.

He snaked his hand around the slim waist that was slightly smaller than Evan's. He ran his hand down her rear, cupping her too flat bottom. Evan had been blessed with a nice round and curvy rear. The thought both annoyed and surprised him.

The redhead slid her hand inside his pants, and he strained to keep his wits about him. He bit into the brunette and took a long draw from her. She tasted sweet and salty, but not quite right. Her blood was like wine for his senses. Not at all something needed but a delicate pleasure nonetheless.

The redhead's hand on his shaft was soft but too small. His frowned at the thought. He should be enjoying himself, but somehow the moment seemed off. Wrong even. All of it. The blood, the women. Evan's face passed through his mind. The picture of her resting her hand on that Vampire's arm made his anger spike.

He retracted his fangs from the brunette's neck.

"What's the matter, lover?"

"I'm sorry." William reached down and zipped his pants. "I apologize, ladies, but I'm afraid this isn't what I need."

The redhead giggled. "How's that possible? We're every man's fantasy."

He nodded. "Unfortunately, I'm not a man anymore. If you'll excuse me."

"But—"

William opened the door quickly and then shut it behind himself. He took a deep breath and blew it out again. He looked around the family room and kitchen area. Everywhere he looked humans, Vampires, and vampyr mingled together. Taunting him, teasing him. But he didn't want them. He only wanted one person. Why? Why her?

He strode out to the foyer but couldn't find Evan. Anxiety gnawed at his gut. Why did he need her? A room full of willing females, and all he wanted was the blonde that no longer wanted him.

"Done already?" Danika walked to him quickly.

"I couldn't... I didn't..." He ran his fingers through his hair. "Where's Evan? I need Evan."

Danika smiled. "I told you. Evan's with someone else."

Anger surged inside him. "Where is she?" he hissed.

Danika's expression grew hard.

"I'm sorry. I just... I need her."

"So, you remember then?"

"Yes. No. It's... I have flashes of my time with her, but I don't know why I want her so badly."

"I won't allow you to toy with her. She's not a pet. She's a person. If you want to have sex for fun, you need to find someone else. Not her."

"Why not her? She's beautiful, and from the little I remember we were very compatible."

"Because what Evan wants is the William who loved her.

Not the one who thinks he's the world's new pleasure package."

"But I'm the good one. The desirable one. I'm made for—"

"Bringing pleasure, yes, you've informed me. But pleasure comes in many forms, not only sex, and if you don't learn that you're going to have a very hard time living in this world."

"Then maybe I'll go somewhere else."

Danika's gaze grew frosty. "If you cannot behave then I think you should go to your room for the evening."

William clenched and unclenched his jaw several times. The sights and smells of so many people made him want to take Evan up to his bed and screw her until she couldn't walk straight. He scanned the room for her once more, and then headed for his room.

Slamming his door, he flung his tie to the floor and ripped the shirt from his body. He pounded on the wall and threw the chair across the room, breaking the legs. Anger coursed through him and pain pulsed behind his eyes. He pulled the sheets from the bed and threw them at the door just as it opened. The linens hit Evan in the face.

"Excuse you!" she said.

His muscles relaxed. "Evangeline."

"Don't call me that." She balled up the sheets and dropped them to the floor. "I didn't think you'd be in here."

He crossed to her in a single stride and took her face in his hands.

He kissed her hard on the mouth, tasting her. The lingering sparkle of champagne stayed on her tongue. She tasted right, felt right. He reached down and cupped her rear. Round and tight.

"Okay." She pushed on his chest. "Okay, that's enough."

"Evan. I want you." He kissed down her throat.

"Yeah, yeah. Stop, William, stop now."

He pulled back. "What's wrong? I thought you wanted this."

"I'm only here to grab my pack." She pointed to her backpack in the corner.

He looked over and spotted the handbag. "Your bag?"

"I'm going out with a few people, and I need it."

"Out?"

She shook her head and walked past him.

"Evan, wait."

She grabbed her bag and searched inside and pulled out a leather case and a black box and then put them back inside.

"This is the last thing I think I left in here. I'm staying in my old room in the barracks. That way you can have this one to yourself and whomever else you want to share it with."

She didn't meet his eye as she headed for the door. He slammed his hand against the smooth wood so she couldn't leave.

"Evan, listen to me, please. I need you. I'm sorry. I was wrong. I only want you."

"Really?"

"Yes. You're the one. No one else."

"Huh?" She looked at him quizzically and then wiped his cheek. She showed him her fingers stained with red lipstick. "I can see how much you've changed already."

"That's not what it looks like." He became flustered and unsure. *Why did she have this effect on him?* "Okay, that is what it looks like, but I didn't like it. When I drank from her all I could think of was you. Your rear is rounder. I remembered that."

"My rear? Really? You remembered my rear?" She pressed her body into his and grabbed his crotch making his knees almost buckle. "What about this? Did she do this to you?" She stroked him through his pants. And he closed his eyes. "Did you like it?"

"No, it wasn't her. That was the redhead."

Her hand stopped moving and his eyes flew open. The icy glare she gave to him had him going soft instantly.

"Two?" She raised an eyebrow.

"Like I said, I didn't like it. I only want you."

"You love me? You want to marry me?" Her voice held a sarcastic note that he didn't like.

"No. I don't but—"

She wiped a spot of blood from the corner of his mouth. "I have two someones of my own waiting. Two someones who want no one else but me. Until you're ready to act like the William I fell in love with, I'm not interested."

"Evan, please—"

She stepped out of his room and closed the door. He banged his head on it and roared in anger. Damn Mason for making him promise not to use his powers on people. Evan would be in his arms and in his bed that very minute if he'd been allowed to use his charms. The whole situation had him so pent up he thought he might explode. Ripping off his suit, he headed for a cold shower.

EVAN WALKED DOWN THE HALLWAY, FORCING BACK TEARS. DOING what Danika had prescribed had worked, but for how long? How could she be sure that once William had her again, he wouldn't change his mind?

She knew he was in there. Her William. The one she'd fallen in love with. He may be sexy as hell, not that he hadn't been before, but she wasn't going to just fall for an amazing looking man again. The last time had almost killed her.

She re-entered the foyer where everyone continued to enjoy themselves. Her stomach lurched as she hit the bottom stair and she stumbled.

"Are you okay?" asked Danika.

"I think I had a bit too much champagne. I'm gonna head to my room."

"Are you sure? I know two gentlemen dying to take you out."

Her stomach lurched again and she covered her mouth. "No. I think I really should go lie down."

Danika nodded. "We'll try again tomorrow night."

Evan stumbled again and Danika steadied her. "Maybe I should get someone to escort you."

Evan shook her head. "I'm fine. But you might want to have someone check on William before he destroys his entire room."

Danika frowned. "He better not. That was my birth mother's room."

The thought struck Evan right in the heart. The reverence that Danika had for her birth mother. Evan wondered if Travis even told their daughter about her.

"Good night." Evan hurried for the back door, trying not to stumble again in the heels she wasn't used to.

She rushed outside and took the shoes off. She ran to the barracks and threw the door open. Tommy sat on the couch with Sue.

He looked up when he saw her.

"Whoa, sis! I don't think I approve of that dress."

"I'm headed to bed."

"Evan, are you okay? Evan?" he called.

"I'm fine. 'Night." She raced up the stairs as her stomach

rolled for the third time. She barely made it to the common bathroom before throwing up. Her stomach lurched and she threw up a second time.

Sweat trickled down her brow. The sour taste of fermented champagne and stomach acid made her mouth taste like rotten fruit.

She plopped down hard on the tile floor, leaned back on the bathroom stall, and burped. She'd never had champagne before in her life. Never had more than one beer in her life, either. Her head spun as memories of William's red eyes floated in her mind. Her heart ached for wanting him. Two females. He'd been with two. How far had he gone?

She hung her head. She didn't want to know.

The outer bathroom door opened. "Hello?"

She didn't answer.

Someone knocked on the stall door. "You okay in there?"

"Fine," she croaked.

"Need some help?"

Evan got to her feet shakily and flushed the toilet before opening the door. Matthew looked taken aback at seeing her.

"Oh, it's you." She pushed past him and stumbled to the sink.

He grabbed her around the waist to steady her. "Are you okay?"

"Just peachy." She turned on the water at the first faucet and splashed it on her face. The mascara Danika had put on her ran down her cheeks. She grabbed the bar of soap and scoured her face trying to get the makeup off. Blinded by the water in her eyes, she felt around for a towel.

Matthew pushed one into her hands and she blotted her cheeks.

She opened her eyes and handed it back to him. "Thanks."

"I'm not trying to be rude, but you don't look good. Maybe you should get to bed."

"Great advice. I think I'll do that." She spotted her backpack on the floor, bent to pick it up, and swayed slightly.

"Whoa! That's a good way to get a concussion." Matthew grabbed her around the waist again and helped her up right. The pressure of his fingers on her sides reminded her of her lovemaking with William.

"Don't touch me." She pushed him away and her vision blurred. "If I call for Tommy, he'll kick your ass."

Matthew held up his hands. "I only want to help you to your room." He grabbed her backpack and slung it over his shoulder.

She scoured him with a look. "Why are you suddenly being nice to me? I'm not going to sleep with you."

"Well thanks for clearing that up for me." He sighed. "I'm trying to help you because you're drunk and if you get hurt now I'll be responsible and your brother will definitely kick my ass."

"I'm not drunk."

He nodded. "Okay, well then why is everything you say about two octaves too loud and one second too slow?"

It is?

He held his hand out to her. "I'm really not as big of a jackass as I pretend to be."

Jackass. William was her jackass. She stared at Matthew's hand for a minute before nodding. "Thank you."

"Think nothing of it." Matthew put his arm around her waist and walked her to her room. He opened the door and everything spun.

She staggered forward and landed face first on her comforter.

"Okay then. I'm gonna leave this bag and these shoes here for you."

"Sounds good," she said.

"And I'll turn out the light?"

"Yup."

"Night."

She didn't bother to answer. As soon as the light dimmed, she slipped out of the party dress and dove under the covers in nothing but her underwear.

Her stomach lurched but she swallowed down the bile. She didn't have the energy to crawl back to the bathroom, and there was no way she was puking in bed.

CHAPTER TWENTY FIVE

William tossed and turned the rest of the night and most of the morning. By midday though a thought struck him, and he walked to his heavily curtained window, threw it wide, and gasped. For the first time in hundreds of sunrises and sunsets, he could feel the sun on his skin without it trying to kill him. How had it taken him three days to realize that?

A great pleasure blossomed inside him, and he turned to tell Evan, but she wasn't there.

His heart sank and he growled deep in his chest. He couldn't understand why with all of the beautiful women in the world his heart pined for only one of them. Four women. Four beautiful women had been in that room the night before, ready to fulfill his fantasies, yet... They'd caused him to stir only briefly before he'd remembered Evan.

His memories remained foggy. He'd grasped bits and pieces but nothing coherent. Like he watched all of them as a specta-tor. No feelings attached. Emotionless as watching a television show with the sound off. His heart told him that he loved Evan. His body told him that he loved Evan. But the essential nature of who he was told him he was made for loving everyone. Made for women to worship him, pleasure him, and be pleasured by him.

He huffed and turned from the window, his enjoyment of the sun ruined by his desire for Evan—the one woman off limits to him. Why should he care? Evan had basically chosen someone else by turning from him, what should it matter then who he spent time with? Just the idea that she'd been able to resist him and had chosen someone else made him growl deep in his chest. If he could use his powers on her, she'd not so much as even look at another man again.

William threw his hands into his hair and roared in anger. There were tons of other beautiful women. He could have any of them. Why her?

He stopped and looked out the window again. Mason had said he couldn't use his powers on them. He'd never said he couldn't be himself.

A grin spread across William's face. He stripped naked and walked to the shower. He didn't want to smell like last night's leftovers when he went to woo a woman.

THIRTY MINUTES LATER WILLIAM JOGGED DOWN THE STAIRS IN A PAIR of khakis and a green dress shirt open in the front. House servants milled about cleaning up after the dinner party. They stopped when they saw him as if confused by his presence.

He flashed them a smile and waved them on to their duties. More than one cast backward glances as if afraid he might gobble them up if they weren't looking. The idea made him frown.

He decided to look for the one person he remembered had always been receptive to him. The human named Sue.

He searched the lower level of the house, and when he didn't spot her he headed to the barracks.

After walking into the backyard, he stopped and sucked in the fresh air. The glorious scents of grass and flowers made him smile. Though he'd only been shut in his room for three days his body reacted like it had been locked up for months. Memories of a dark, hard cell floated into view. His muscles shook as someone kicked him in the gut repeatedly.

He panted hard, trying to control his mounting anxiety. His gaze whipped around to make sure no one had seen his moment of terror. He caught a glimpse of a woman moving around in the barracks kitchen. Short brown hair, slender build. *Sue.*

He smiled to himself and washed the horrible memories away before stepping inside the building. He tiptoed up behind her and covered her eyes with his hands.

She gasped and then laughed.

"Very funny, I know it's you." She spun to face him and her expression dropped. "W-William?"

"How are you?" He laced his hands around her waist as apprehension crossed her features. "Don't be scared. I know I'm a bit different, but I'm still me. Only better."

"Oh... I... uh..." She seemed at a loss for words.

He nuzzled her neck and she stiffened. "Don't worry," he said. "I no longer have an appetite for blood, though I do still enjoy it."

She didn't relax.

He kissed her playfully on the throat, and she yipped and jumped away, bumping into the counter. A pot of tea whistled on the stove, and she stepped around him to grab it.

"I was thinking." He ran a finger down her bare arm, noticing how pale it seemed compared to Evan's peachy skin. "Maybe you and I could spend some time together today."

"Oh!" She gave a nervous laugh. "I'd love to, I would, but I uh... can't, I'm afraid."

"You can't? Or you're afraid?" he asked.

Her hand shook as she poured the hot water into a teacup, splashing it all over the counter.

"Sue?" A set of heavy footsteps bounded down the stairs. The blond guy that had been in his room with Evan and Danika and Mason turned the corner and spotted them. "William."

William racked his brain for a name. Evan's cousin. "Tommy."

Tommy crossed to Sue. "You have the tea?"

She nodded vigorously and refused to meet William's eyes. "I was just looking for some crackers but couldn't seem to find some."

Tea... crackers...

"Are you having a tea party?" William joked.

Tommy and Sue exchanged a look.

"Evan has a bit of a hangover," said Tommy. "I'm sure she'll be fine in a couple of hours. She's never really had alcohol before and the champagne had last night seems to have gotten to her."

"Evan's sick?" A protective instinct kicked into overdrive.

Tommy nodded to Sue to take the tea up. She gave William a tight smile and ducked around him.

"Just a hangover," said Tommy again.

He wanted to ask to see her, but Tommy's body language told him the answer would be no. Not that it mattered. Tommy was human and he was so much more than human. Still, concern rooted in his chest and made him uncomfortable. No matter what he did, Evan seemed always in the forefront of his thoughts. He didn't understand what was going on inside. He needed to talk to someone but no one wanted to talk to him.

"You've changed," said Tommy. "And not in a good way, bro."

"It's true I'm different. But I don't see how my changing makes me worse than I was before."

"At least when you were blood crazy you needed and loved my sister. Now the only person you seem to love is yourself." Tommy walked to the stairs and stopped. "My sister's been through enough pain already. She gave up everything to save your life. The least you can do is respect her wishes and leave her alone. She deserves better than you."

The words cut William more than he'd like to admit. Tommy disappeared out of sight as one of the humans from the night before entered. Petite with wide features, she wasn't beautiful but she wasn't plain either. Jet-black hair framed her face in a Cleopatra style that suited her.

A smile spread across her face at the sight of him. "Well hello, lover. You ran off so fast the other night that I didn't get to introduce myself to you. I'm Irena."

Desire spiked in William despite his concern for Evan.

Irena strode forward and stretched out her hand. He took it in his own and shook it. She barely came up to his chest but under her T-shirt and jeans he spied a lovely set of curves.

"William," he replied. "I've never seen you before."

"My master was killed in the last attack. I've only been here a week, with my sister slave Janet."

"Sister slave?"

"Yes. She was with me in the room as well. Asian, petite like me. Not quite as pretty though."

"Says who?" asked an Asian coming down the stairs.

Irena giggled.

The other woman stalked up to William and pressed her body against his. "Do you think she's prettier than I am?" Janet swayed her hips against his and smiled.

"I think he finds me just as attractive as you, sister. Maybe even more so."

Desire consumed him and his fangs elongated.

Irena pressed into him from the other side and slid a finger down a fang, sending shivers over his skin.

"I think he likes us both," she said.

"Well then?" asked Janet. "Why don't we both show him what we can do?"

The niggling feeling in the back of his head that told him he should walk away was silenced by the stroke of Irena's hand over the front of his pants. Evan didn't want him. And Danika had offered these two women to him the night before...

He smiled. "My room awaits."

AFTER THE SUN DROPPED A KNOCK PULLED WILLIAM FROM HIS slumber, tangled in between Janet and Irena. He wrapped the sheet around himself and shuffled to the door. He opened it a crack and yawned.

Danika and Mason stood in the hallway.

"What's up?" He scratched his head. They both stared at him and then Danika flung the door open and pushed past him. The expression on her face when she saw the two humans in his bed went beyond anger.

"How dare you," Danika spat. She shoved him in the chest. "In my house? In my birth mother's room? Who the hell do you think you are?"

She stormed to the bed and flipped the mattress up so the two girls rolled onto the floor.

They screeched and slammed into the wall on top of each other. Danika pounded around the room snatching up articles of clothing and throwing them at the two women.

"Get out!" she screamed. "Get out of this room! If I catch either of you in here again I'll... I'll..." Danika's fangs burst through her gums and her eyes shot scalpels at them. "Get out!"

Wide eyed, the girls grabbed their things and raced for the door.

Danika rounded on William. "And you!"

"What did I do?" he asked. "You're the one who told me you'd gotten them for me. You said—"

"Shut up! Shut. Up! You weren't supposed to sleep with them. I was trying to teach you a lesson. You dare to dishonor my birth mother's room with those harlots?"

He didn't understand.

"Danika, it doesn't work that way with demi-demons," said Mason.

She stomped to the door and William jumped out of the way. Her body shook with rage as she looked up at Mason.

"You better deal with him or so help me..." She threw William one more icy daggered glare and tore off down the hallway to her room. Russian curses flew from her mouth so fast even if he had known the language William doubted he would have caught them all. The door to her room slammed shut behind her.

Mason looked William up and down and shook his head.

"What did I do?" he asked again.

Mason stepped into the room and closed the door. "Sit down."

William straightened his mattress and sat on it heavily. "I don't get it. One minute she wants me to be with other women, the next she doesn't."

"She never wanted you to be with other women, you idiot."

"Well then why did she tell me she did?"

Mason sighed and pulled up a chair. "I get that you don't have much experience with women. Not when you were human and not when you were a vampyr. So let me tell you a couple of things. First of all, they never want you to be with another woman. Even if they say they don't care, they care."

"Well the two I had in here didn't seem to mind."

"That's not the point. I get what you're going through. Your Demon side has just been unleashed and everything seems like a party you want to join in. Sex, alcohol, blood, all of it. But you can't be like that and live in this world."

"Why?"

"Because this world isn't like that anymore. And you live here in the Coven House as the family member of the Coven Lord, Danika. You have responsibilities."

"The old William had responsibilities. But I'm not a vampyr anymore. I'm not her fledgling. I don't have to live by Danika's rules."

"You do if you want to stay here." Mason's voice came with a hard edge. "I know that inside you are William's memories. His thoughts, his feelings. You should search those out and hang onto them. William was a good man, loved by all. He loved Evan and was willing to give his life for her. He loved Danika too and cared about this coven and what happened to it."

The words sank deeper into William's heart than he cared for. "She doesn't want me."

"She doesn't want you as you are now."

"You made me what I am. You know I can't go back to being him."

"No, but you can try to be both. You have a choice. His memories are your memories. It's up to you whether or not you take them on and make them your own or whether you don't."

"But what if I like who I am?"

"Most demons do."

He studied Mason for a minute. "You don't. You hide your Demon side. Selene too."

"Trust me, when you've been around as long as we have you come to realize that finding someone you love, a home, a family, is much more satisfying than all the blood, sex, and destruction in the world."

"But you're tethered to Danika. Never who you truly should be."

"No." Mason shook his head. "I'm free because of her."

"I don't understand."

"I hope someday you will. If we live that long." Mason stood and walked out.

William stared at the spot he'd left for a long time trying to get his old memories to surface. He caught glimpses again of things he'd already seen. *Danika feeding him. Stabbing a Vampire in the neck to save Mason. A human punching and kicking him in a dark room. A woman in a flowered dress crouching down and smiling at him. Evan's face floating above him in a haze of pain and confusion.* But he didn't understand any of it.

He flopped back on the bed and closed his eyes. Maybe he'd be better off if he sided with the demons when they showed up.

Evan dragged herself from the bed and forced herself to shower. Her head pounded, her body ached, her stomach felt as if she were on a rollercoaster, and every ounce of energy had drained from her body. She'd kept down the ginger tea Sue had brought for her, but the two aspirin had done nothing to touch the pain.

The water flooded over her and eased the tension in her back, but every move she took felt as though she did it with a stack of bricks on her shoulders.

"I'll never drink again." She remembered watching movies and television shows when she was young. They'd never showed this part of drinking at parties—the after part. And she hadn't even had that many drinks. She wracked her brain and counted up the glasses. One, two, three, four.

Four? Had she really had four glasses? Those thin little suckers sure packed a punch!

An enormous bang rattled the entire barracks. The lights flickered, and she hurried and turned off the water. Yelling and shouting sounded in the hallway. She quickly toweled herself and pulled on her clothes. She jogged to her room and grabbed her boots, shoving her knives back into them and then jumped the stairs, and burst out the front door as a huge plume of smoke rose into the sky. All the humans gathered on the grass looking up at the smoke.

All fatigue retreated from her as her adrenaline kicked up.

"Everyone back in the barracks!" Roth shouted. The house servants didn't need to be asked twice.

Evan located Tommy and jogged over. "Another attack."

"Probably." Tommy nodded.

She yanked her boots on her feet. "I'm gonna help."

Tommy grabbed her arm. "You should stay here."

"Why?" she asked. "If the demons break through, we're all dead. This is why we came back."

"But you don't know what you're getting yourself into."

"Selene trained the house guard before I left. I listened and I can fight."

Tommy shook his head.

Roth approached them. "Inside."

"I can help," she said.

"We don't need your help."

"You do and you know it. I can fight." She refused to back down.

"No. Inside." He turned his back on her.

Damn. Did she have to prove herself to everyone? She ran at him and jumped on his shoulders. Swinging her body around him, she wrapped her thighs around his neck and pulled him to the ground. He struggled but she flipped him on his stomach and wrenched his arm behind him. He rolled out of the hold and flipped her on her back. He jumped on her just as she grabbed the knife from her boot and held it an inch from his throat.

Roth had a good hundred pounds of muscle on her and probably a foot of height, but in a fight, they'd be closely matched with her enhanced abilities. His stern eyes focused on her as he breathed hard. His strong jaw worked hard as he stared at her, trying to decide.

"I can fight," she said again.

He hopped to his feet and then offered her a hand up. "Vans are out front."

She let him pull her up and then shoved her knife back in her boot as Roth headed into the second barrack.

"Are you okay?" asked Tommy.

"Perfectly. I'll be back soon."

"I'm coming too."

She gave Tommy a sharp nod. Evan took off through the back door as a league of newborn vampyr poured out of the second barrack under Roth's command. She raced through the kitchen into the front hall.

"Evan!"

She turned at the sound of her name. Danika and Mason descended the stairs as Tommy caught up with her.

"Go on," she told Tommy. "Save me a spot."

He nodded and continued out front.

"I don't want you to go," said Danika.

"Why?"

"You're the only person who can possibly keep William in line," said Danika.

Evan snorted. "I think we both know that's not true."

"Please," said Danika. "I know he doesn't remember right now, but he will. And he'll need you."

"And until that time, I need to be helping. I have to get out of this house. I can fight. I'm good."

"I'm sure you are but please, don't do this."

"You need all the bodies you can get." She turned to go but Mason grabbed her by the arm. She tried to pull away, but her head went dizzy and she tipped sideways from the quick movement.

Mason grabbed her around the waist to steady her. His palm splayed on her belly. He stopped and his eyes widened. "Evan—"

"Let's go, everyone!" Roth ran in through the back door followed by his army of newborns.

Evan pulled from Mason's grasp and blended in with the group as they headed out.

"Evan! Evan!" Mason called.

She hopped into the van next to Tommy just as the doors closed and the driver pulled off. Mason barreled onto the drive. Danika came to a stop beside him and they had an animated conversation.

Evan wondered what they talked about but she had no more time to dedicate to it.

The van pulled out on the street and they drove out of sight.

CHAPTER TWENTY SIX

William jogged downstairs to find the commotion headed out the front door. He met Danika on the front steps as she rushed to an awaiting car. Mason's inky dark form flew in the distance.

"What's going on?" William asked. "Is it the entourage you've been waiting on?"

"Possibly." She turned and for a moment looked conflicted.

"Should I come with you?"

"Yes." She jumped in the driver's seat, and he jogged down and joined her in the passenger seat. The gates opened wide, and he'd barely gotten his seatbelt on before Danika tore out of the driveway.

All along the street vehicles rushed out of driveways, all Vampires and vampyr headed the same direction.

"I'm not sure I'm much of a fighter," he said.

Danika threw him a dirty expression. "You really aren't like William at all. Even though he wasn't the strongest in the group, he was the first one to step up when his family or those he cared about were in trouble."

She rounded a corner and he held onto the handle as the tires squealed on the pavement. They wanted him to fight his own kind. Other demons. For them. But he wasn't even sure whose side he was supposed to be on.

Although, Mason had saved him and so in a way he supposed he owed allegiance to Mason.

"If Mason tells me to fight, I will."

She glanced over at him. "Well that's a start I guess."

He looked down. "I sure do hate to ruin an expensive shirt though."

Danika shook her head.

Within minutes they pulled into view of the smoke, Evan and the rest of the riders burst from the van and ran into a park. Smoke plumed from the far side. The smell of charred wood reminded Evan of her time camping in the woods with Lou and her cousins.

"Evan!"

She turned. Soldiers threw guns out of the back of the van to one another. Roth pulled out one of the big black cases she'd brought with her from the enclave and she smiled. Tommy caught two weapons and ran to catch up with her, tossing her an assault rifle. She checked the chamber and turned off the safety.

"Over there," a soldier called.

They rounded a cluster of trees and came to a halt at the scene that lay before them. Mason stood in the forefront, wings spread like storm clouds. Behind him, thousands of Vampires and vampyr waited. Some held weapons, others lumbered from foot to foot. The newborn vampyr passed her and joined the army.

"Come on." Evan and Tommy pushed their way through the crowd to see better. Once in the front Evan froze. Her heart pummeled her ribcage. Suddenly she wanted nothing more than to run back to the shelter of the enclave and hide behind the walls Lou had built.

Across the field from Mason stood a rippling surface like an upright translucent pool the size of a small storefront. In front of it stood a legion of demons. Some tall and thin, others short and wide. Humanoid and non-humanoid alike. They all waited like impatient attack dogs. Snarling, barking, hooting, laughing. Some leather faced, some smooth and sleek, others not even discernible. She'd never seen anything like it. Not in books or movies.

In front of the horde an enormous man, skin black as ink and wings that stretched twice as wide as Mason's, towered over the masses like a god. Dozens of Vampires flanked him, some she recognized from the Coven House but many she didn't. She wondered how they'd known where he would show up and when.

The gigantic man stepped forward suddenly, his arms wide. A smile spread across his angular face revealing a row of teeth like daggers. Sharp, long, and ready to shred anything they touched.

"Maelstrom. Son." He man walked toward Mason.

Mason didn't even flinch at the sight. "Mephisto."

The man stopped and his smile dropped. "No greeting for your father? After a couple thousand years I expected at least a hello."

Mason remained silent.

Mephisto looked around. "But where is my daughter? Where is my Seraphine? I heard that you two had reunited."

"Gone. She wanted nothing to do with you."

Mephisto dropped his arms. "I must say that this isn't the family reunion I had hoped for."

"I tried to warn you, Lord, that this world has changed them." A light- haired, hawkish-looking Vampire stepped from the gathered group.

"Garon." Danika appeared at Mason's side with William in tow. "I'd hoped you'd finally show your traitorous ass."

Mason's arms caught fire and he pointed at the Vampire. "You're mine."

Mephisto laughed heartily. "There's my boy. I knew he was in there. Come to me and together we'll take this plane and rule as I'd always planned."

"I'll never rule with you," said Mason. "This is my family now."

Mephisto's gaze shifted to William. "So, I see. I never took you for a maker."

William stepped forward, but Mason put his hand on William's shoulder and pulled him back.

Evan shook her head. What was he even doing out here? Stupid, vain Demon. Her stomach churned with nervous energy and her palms grew slick. She wanted to knock some sense into William. The jackass was going to get himself killed.

"So where does this leave us?" asked Mephisto. "You over there, me over here, your sister nowhere to be seen."

"You go back where you came from, and we all leave alive," replied Mason. "Except for them. They belong to us." Mason pointed at the Vampires that stood opposite him.

"These rabble?" asked Mephisto. "They're yours. Take

them. Consider them a welcome home present. You come with me and I'll give them to you."

"Now wait a minute." A short and wide Vampire with dark, slicked- back hair and an expensive-looking suit stepped forward.

"You promised us ruling rights if we helped you," said another Vampire.

"All the scum is crawling out of the woodwork," said Mason. "You will burn for what you tried to do to my mate, Melton and Eliander."

Mason threw a fireball, and Mephisto sidestepped as it hurtled toward the Vampires. They ducked for cover and the demons behind them roared and stomped in anger as it hit a dozen of them, setting them on fire.

Mephisto laughed. "On second thought, I'll let you have them for sport. It's been a long time since I've seen a good fight."

"I'll tell you what," said Mason. "I'll do you one better. I'll fight *you*. If I win, you leave forever. If you win, I'll go with you."

"No." Danika grabbed Mason's arm.

He caressed her cheek but said nothing. Then he turned back to Mephisto.

The demon's eyes glittered. "Accepted." The demons roared in excitement and Mephisto laughed. "Well, come on, boy. Show me what you've turned into."

Mason shifted fully as he walked into the open field to meet Mephisto. Danika walked at his side holding his hand. The further they walked the smaller Danika's hand got in his until it finally disappeared in his massive fist. Flames licked up Mason's arms but Danika remained unharmed by them. Evan jogged to keep up with them, as did most of the Tracking Squad. The rest of the army hung back awaiting the outcome.

"You'll be safe." said Mason in the same voice she'd heard him use when turning William. "I win, he leaves. I lose, I seal the rift inside."

"No." Danika shook her head. "I won't let you do this. Maelstrom, we can fight."

He knelt in front of her, his body almost eclipsing her's in size. He kissed her. "I fight. For you. Always for you." He stood and looked to William. "You take care of her."

William nodded and put his hand on Danika's shoulder. Mason spotted Evan and pointed at her. "And her."

Her gaze locked on William's and his eyes widened in surprise.

"Well, are you coming?" Mephisto taunted.

Mason turned to face his father, and Evan jogged up next to Danika.

"He'll be okay," she whispered.

Danika clutched William's arm but said nothing.

Mason and Mephisto circled each other like two Titans getting ready to battle. Their enormous Demon forms took up nearly the entire soccer field.

Mephisto swung in a circle and spread his wings, knocking Mason off balance and sending him crashing into a nearby tree.

"Come on, son, I thought you were going to actually fight."

Mason flew out from between the branches straight at Mephisto. He let two fireballs fly but Mephisto swatted them away and the fireballs soared toward the spectators. Mason took the advantage of the distraction and planted his feet in Mephisto's chest sending him sailing across the expanse. He wasted no time, and landed on top of Mephisto, punching him repeatedly.

Mephisto grabbed Mason by the wing joint and slammed

his fist into it. Mason roared in pain and his wing slacked to the ground.

Danika lurched forward but William held her back. He whispered in her ear but Danika shook him off. Evan moved closer, but William grabbed her by the arm and dragged her back.

"What are you doing here?" he demanded.

"What does it look like?"

"It looks like you're going to get yourself killed." He glanced around. "Come on."

She pulled away. "I'm not going anywhere. I'll fight to the death to protect this world and the people in it. Believe it or not, not all of us are just out for ourselves. What are you doing here? Don't you have some women to seduce or something?"

He growled. "I wish I did, but for some unknown reason I feel the need to be here against my better judgment."

She rolled her eyes. "You really are a jackass."

"And you really are a pain in the ass." His gaze raked over her and he grunted. "Stay close to me."

"Why? You gonna protect me?"

He looked at her in confusion. "Yes. Maelstrom commanded me to."

A howl of pain pulled both her and William's attention. Mason had Mephisto pinned on the ground, his teeth latched on to Mephisto's throat.

Mason's arm bled heavily and Mephisto clawed at Mason's back, opening deep gashes and splashing blood everywhere.

William trembled next to her. All around Vampires and vampyr groaned and stepped forward. Evan backed up as a niggling of fear coursed up her limbs.

"What's going on?" she asked.

Danika scanned the Vampires and vampyr. "Damn. It's

Mason's blood. He's part Fae. The blood is enticing to Vampires."

The crowd moved a fraction closer to the wrestling match.

"Uh... You better get this under control," said Evan. "Or we are going to have a serious problem."

"How?" asked Danika. "There are thousands of them."

A boom shook the ground and everyone grabbed on to each other for support, breaking the spell momentarily.

Mephisto clutched Mason by the throat, slamming him into the ground. Roth and the Tracking Squad raced to Danika's side.

"Set up a perimeter," she yelled. "Don't let anyone near the fight."

"It's getting tough. The fledglings are barely hanging on back there."

Great. They really didn't need everyone turning on each other.

Mephisto punched Mason in the face over and over. Blood splattered the ground.

"Do you yield?" he asked.

Mason's eyes locked on Danika. She nodded her head.

"Yield," said Mason.

Mephisto punched Mason in the face again. "You are not my son," he bellowed. "My son would never yield. He'd rather die than be defeated. You are a failure. I shall kill you now and replace you tomorrow."

Mephisto poised above Mason, talons out ready to strike.

Danika moved fast as a blur. She sprung at Mephisto, grabbing him by the horns, and yanked his head back. Mephisto yowled in frustration and spun in a circle trying to swat her away.

"Dammit." William raced out to help Danika.

"William!" Evan raised her gun but Tommy shoved it down.

"You can't start anything until told to."

Fear coursed through her veins. She waffled between trying to get off a shot and running to help.

"Wait," Tommy urged.

William grabbed Mephisto by the arm and tried to bring him to the ground as Danika bit down on Mephisto's neck.

Mephisto cried out and then threw both Danika and William from his body. "Kill them!" he called. "Kill them all!"

The demons sprang into action. Gunfire rang out as Roth commanded everyone to attack. Chaos ensued. Vampires ran at Vampires. Demons ran at everyone.

Mason staggered to his feet and attacked Mephisto again. Danika and William tried to help Mason, but did little good. Roth and Riley aimed the missiles she'd brought into the back of the Demon horde and fired. They exploded within seconds, spraying bodies in every direction.

"Reload," Roth called.

A thin, slinky looking Demon with eyes like pitch advanced on Evan. She ran down the list of demons that Selene had mentioned. Just as he leapt for her, she dropped her gun and grabbed the knives from her boots.

She slammed them into the demon's eyes and he screeched in pain before he went silent and fell to the ground in a heap. Evan's heart raced as she shoved the knives back in her boots, picked up her gun, and headed into the fray.

"Tommy! With me!"

WILLIAM JUMPED ON MEPHISTO'S BACK IN AN EFFORT TO HELP MASON. He knew he was no match for the Lord of the Demons, but memories of Mason saving his life and the time, days, weeks, and months together in the enclave poured back to him with the first sound of gunfire, inciting him to react.

Between the three of them, they'd barely been able to do more than keep Mephisto from killing Mason.

Mephisto flapped his wings, trying to shake William off his back.

"Don't you know who I am, maggot? You're no match for me." Unable to dislodge William, he took to the sky, heading straight up. William hung on to the thunderous leathery wings by digging his fingernails deep into Mephisto's shoulder blades.

"You think you can take me down, little Begær? You're not made for war. Side with me, and I'll show you what your talents are really used for. I see your loyalty to my son. I can use demons like you in my army."

Going with Mephisto had plagued William's thoughts for the last twenty-four hours. But now that the opportunity presented itself, he couldn't do it.

"Tempting, but, no."

Mephisto grabbed William off his back and held him out by the throat. William's gut clenched as he looked down at the melee below. Even Maelstrom looked like no more than a small car at that altitude. Mephisto pulled him in close, his razor fangs gleaming with spit.

"Too bad."

The vise grip around William's throat slipped away and William clawed at the air as he spiraled downward. His stomach lurched up into his throat as the ground beneath, and the ants that moved around on it, came closer into view.

Thoughts raced through his mind at the thought that he might actually die. What would happen to Evan? And Tommy? What would his mother think of his last, illogically heroic gesture? When he died, would he see her again, or would he just disappear?

A large black flash took drunkenly to the air growing larger as William fell. *Maelstrom.* William reached out, and Maelstrom grasped him by the arms. The weight of William pulled Maelstrom off balance and the two plummeted downward. The wind whipped upward as they spiraled and William's stomach soured like he'd drunk too much.

"Wing broken," Maelstrom said.

William smiled. "I'll live. Probably."

"Get Danika and Evan out."

William snorted. "I don't think they'll listen to me."

Maelstrom tried to right himself but at the last minute, Mephisto grabbed him from behind and pulled on his wings. Maelstrom let go of William, and William dropped twenty feet to the grass below. He hit the ground with a thud as all the air whooshed out of him, and his leg snapped backward.

He cried out in pain, his vision blurred, and everything went hazy. The sounds of fighting pounded in his ears bringing him back from the edge unconsciousness. He looked up at the sky to see Mephisto and Maelstrom battling once more.

A hail of gunfire flew over his head and a Demon hit the ground behind him, its head split wide.

"William!" He turned but his vision remained blurry. Someone rushed toward him and dropped down beside him. She smelled of gun oil and sweat.

"William." She pushed the hair from his face and pulled him into her arms. Her scent filled his nose, soothing him. She kissed him hard, and amidst the turmoil surrounding them, and the pain coursing its way up his leg, his gaze focused on her face and memories bombarded him. *The first time she'd come to the coven house. The night he'd found her in the kitchen talking to Selene. Pulling her from the wrecked car and feeding her his blood. The hotel room where he'd cleaned up her leg. The first time she'd kissed him in the cell at the enclave. Her tending to his wounds and risking her own life for him by jumping in front of the Taser meant for him. Making love to her in the motel. Her feeding him her blood though she'd already done it several times.*

"Evangeline." His mind and heart collided in a battle of emotions and thoughts as everything he'd done, everything he'd been, and everything he'd become smooshed together, all of it trying to sort itself out and fill the same space.

She searched his face and he smiled up at her, still trying to organize his thoughts and memories.

"Hey, PITA," he said.

She smiled. "Jackass."

He pulled her to him and kissed her softly.

"Really?" asked Danika. "I don't think this is the place or time."

Evan broke the kiss and William smiled at Danika. "Hey."

The pain wiped from Danika's bloodied face and tears welled in her eyes. "Seriously? It took this for you to remember me?"

A high-pitched whirling sound approached from the right. Evan hopped to her feet and emptied the rest of her clip into the monster, but it did nothing to deter the creature. Evan ran at the Demon sailing toward them, wings outstretched, his talons and teeth in attack position. She leapt at the beast and climbed on its back, dragging it to the ground. Grabbing her knives, she flipped them in her hands and then sliced the thing's head clean off. Black blood splattered everywhere. Evan kicked the body off and wiped the blades on the ground.

"That's my girl," said William.

"Go help her!" Danika yelled.

William pointed to his leg. "I'd love to but my leg is busted."

Danika looked between him and Evan who had been thrown back into the battle. A knife in each hand she moved with the speed and agility of a trained vampyr.

Danika grabbed William under the arms and dragged him to a pile of mangled bodies and sat him there.

"If you can't help, play dead."

"Wow. Thanks for that."

"I don't have time to stroke your ego, sorry." Danika spotted Maelstrom and raced toward him. "Don't die!" She called over her shoulder.

The smell of gore and death perfumed the air. William tried to push himself up but slipped in the blood soaked ground and landed face first in a dead vampyr's crotch.

"Perfect."

Another two blasts sounded and shrieks and squeals resounded around the park as more demons fell. All around them carnage ensued. Vampires, vamps, and demons strewn the ground in jumbled heaps. The two armies fought in the fiercest combat William had ever witnessed. Even during the wars and the Outbreak he'd never seen beings fight so viciously. He wiped his hands on his pants and pushed off the dead comrade. A half dead Demon slithered across the ground toward him. He looked around for a weapon but couldn't spot on. William sighed and his fangs pierced his gums and scratched past his lip down to his chin. The Demon closed in on him like a python. The beast opened its mouth and screeched at William. William kept still until the Demon struck. Just as his wide shark-like mouth got within an inch of William's shoulder William grabbed the monster by its long, corded neck and tore into it with his teeth. The blood gushed into his mouth and he drank it down. A roar of life spread through him like brushfire. It strengthened his limbs and settled in his leg. He tore out the demon's throat and tossed the body to the ground.

A roar reverberated through the entire park. "Enough!" Mephisto bellowed. He stood with Mason in a chokehold. His wings remained and his skin remained deep in color but Mason had shrunk in size and his fangs and talons had retracted. Blood covered his body, staining him a deep maroon color.

Danika ran forward, but Mason held up his hand to stop her. Evan hurried back to William's side.

"Enough with this child's play. This world is mine. I'll give you one chance to bow down before me and become my servants, or die."

"We will never bow," yelled Danika.

"That suits me just fine." Mephisto's arm tightened around Mason's throat.

Evan helped William to his feet and together they hobbled to Danika. Pain shot up his leg to his hip, making him grit his teeth.

Mephisto dragged Mason to his feet by the throat. "If my son was the best you have left, it will be my pleasure to cleanse this plane of such inferior creatures." He held Mason up. "You are all unworthy to be more than the scorched earth beneath my feet." Mephisto squeezed Mason's throat and Danika screamed.

A tremble raced over the ground, and across the park, the air shimmered and shook. A bright light the size of an apple grew steadily larger to the size of a city bus. William and Evan moved through the masses as dark figures poured through the opening that ripped through the fabric of the Earth plane. One after another, hundreds of tall, thin, flowing haired people marched into the park. The leaders in the front stopped and so did the rest of the army. They removed their hoods.

"Selene. Neeman," Danika whispered.

Selene strode to Danika and hugged her. Neeman gave Danika a one-armed hug as well.

"We thought you'd left us," said Danika.

Selene clucked her tongue. "My brother should know better."

"Why didn't you tell us?"

"Because he would've tried to stop me." Selene gave Danika a tight smile and looked to Evan. "You're back." Then she looked to William. "You're better."

"That's what I keep trying to tell them, but they don't want to hear it," William replied.

Selene chuckled and then turned to Mephisto. "Hello, father." She stepped toward Mephisto with Neeman at her side.

"What am I to do with such disrespectful children? My firstborn won't even acknowledge me, and this one calls me father, yet brings my enemies to my doorstep."

"Let Mason go," said Selene.

"And now you presume to order me about?"

Selene stood her ground. "Let him go and return home and I'll let you live."

Mephisto chuckled. "You think I'm afraid of you and a pack of self-important element users?"

"We'll not let you destroy this world, Mephisto. We didn't last time, and we won't this time." A woman with long, dark hair and a slender yet svelte body that resembled Selene's, stepped forward.

Mephisto's brow creased at the sight of her. "Yelena."

"Husband mine."

Mephisto stared at her. "It's been a long time."

She remained impassive. "Very long."

"Have you come to fight me as well?"

"No." Yelena swept forward within feet of Mephisto. "I've come to go home."

"I won't fall for your tricks again, Fae. You took my children from me once before."

"I did. Along with my sister Pia. Let the boy go and I'll give you another son. A hundred sons and a thousand daughters."

Mephisto dropped Mason to the ground, grabbed Yelena by arm and dragged her forward. He sniffed her hair and ran a long taloned finger from her cheek all the way down between her breasts.

"Why should I believe you?"

Yelena took Mephisto's hand in her own and pressed it to her cheek. "Because I gave all my magic to Selene. I am no more than what you see right now. I couldn't leave if I wanted to once I'm there."

William tried to follow the conversation but didn't quite understand what was happening.

"Your offer is tempting, Yelena, but not as tempting as ruling this world. I'm sorry, my love."

"Take her offer," Selene yelled. "I don't want to have to kill you." Mephisto let go of Yelena.

"Your brother couldn't even defeat me. What makes you think that you can?"

"Because I can do this." Selene swirled her hands together and chanted in an ancient language. A burst of light filled the air and snaked toward Mephisto. It whirled around him like lightning snakes and fastened tight around his middle, clamping his hands down at his sides. He writhed and struggled against the magic bonds.

"Impossible," he cried. "You can't bind me. I'm the Lord of Destruction."

"And I'm the granddaughter of the High Elder. His magic has been passed on to me."

Mephisto raged against his bonds. His body grew impossibly larger and his eyes filled with malice. "Kill her!"

The demons charged again.

Selene turned to the Fae, barking orders, and they sprang into action. Neeman stayed close by her, prepared for anything that might attack. Magic swirled through the air and flew in every direction.

"We need to keep Mephisto out of the fight. If we can keep him incapacitated the Fae will take care of the rest." She looked down at William's leg and knelt at his side. She spoke a word he didn't hear and golden threads shot from her fingers to his leg.

William cried out and almost buckled to the ground. "Damn, that stings."

Evan smiled at him, "Don't be such a baby."

"Mason needs you," Danika urged. Selene nodded and ran toward her brother.

Danika pointed at William and then to Evan. "You take care of her."

She ran off before they could reply.

"Why do they keep telling you to take care of me when you're the one who's hurt?" Evan scowled.

"Because you're the special one." He smiled.

Evan spun in a circle. "Where's Tommy?" Her voice held a panicked edge.

"I don't know." William tested his weight on his leg. It ached but held.

He pulled her by the hand and they headed into the fight. "We'll get him."

All around them Fae and Vampires battled with demons. The Fae fought mercilessly and their magic exploded, froze, vaporized, and disappeared demons at every turn.

William scanned for Tommy but his gaze caught on someone else. Eliander fought a Demon. "You find Tommy, I have something I need to do."

Evan nodded and ran off. William headed for the remaining Russian twin who had betrayed Danika. He jumped on Eliander and knocked him to the ground. A Demon lunged at Eliander, but William growled at him and the Demon backed away.

He flipped Eliander on his back and stomped on his chest.

"Please," Eliander begged. "It was Garon."

William pulled Eliander close. "Don't worry. He's next."

His fangs lengthened, and William ripped Eliander's throat out, gulping down as much blood as he was able before the flow stopped. When Eliander's eyes went blank, William tore his head clean off, laughed, and tossed it. Seeing the head roll in the grass caused him more joy than he thought possible.

He scanned the fight for Garon next but spotted Selene and Danika bent over Mason. A cluster of demons headed straight for them. William sprinted for the demons.

"Danika! Selene!" he yelled.

They turned as the demons reached them. The demons knocked Danika away and she landed at Mephisto's feet. Yelena raced forward and helped Danika up. Mephisto twisted in his chains and howled curses at everyone. The chains shimmered and sparked as the demons attacked Selene and Neeman.

William dove for the closest Demon, punching him in the spine. The Demon spun around, and William kicked him in the face. He fell but flipped back to his feet.

Magic shot in William's direction, and he ducked out of the way. It hit the Demon square in the chest, burning a hole through him and turning him to ash.

A Demon slammed Selene to the ground, his hands around her throat.

Selene grabbed at him and blue electric arcs snaked up his arms, but her magic seemed to have no effect.

Neeman sliced the Demon he fought in half with a long two handled blade, and then ran to the one pinning down Selene and sliced his head off as well.

He pulled her to her feet and kissed her. And in that moment of distraction, the chains that bound Mephisto shattered.

Mephisto stepped forward and grabbed Yelena around the waist. Selene cried out and raised her hands.

"Stop!" Mephisto commanded. "I'll kill her."

Mason moved beside his sister. "Let her go."

"Well, the only thing missing from this family reunion is Pia and some bloodletting. At least the last part I can help with." Mephisto bit into Yelena's neck. She screamed and her eyes went wide as he drank deep for less than a second before dropping her lifeless body to the ground. Selene screeched and ran to her mother. Mason jumped on Mephisto, pummeling him to the ground.

"Mother? Mother!" Selene shook her mother's ragged form, but Yelena didn't respond.

"She's gone." Neeman pulled Selene from the body. Selene grabbed onto him and cried into his chest as her body grew and darkened. A tail split a hole in her pants. She rose from the ground, her eyes glowing like purple embers. Mason continued to punch Mephisto as Selene turned and thrust her hands in front of her, unleashing her wrath.

Mephisto froze as tendrils of rainbow-colored magic gripped him tight in a cocoon.

"You, Mephisto, Lord of Destruction are nothing. You are not a father. Not a husband. Not a Lord. What you are, is dead." Selene clenched her fists tight and Mephisto's body glowed from the inside out. His mouth opened in a silent scream and then Mason slammed his fist through Mephisto's ribcage.

"For our mothers." He yanked Mephisto's beating heart from his chest, and bellowed into the sky.

Mephisto's body spasmed from the onslaught. Selene threw her arms wide and Mephisto burst into a billion particles and disappeared like mist on the ocean wind.

All around, fighting ceased as everyone gathered to witness the triumph.

Mason raised Mephisto's heart in the air, letting out a ground-rattling roar. Then he took the heart and bit into it.

William wrinkled his nose. "Must be tradition or something."

All of the demons grew silent. Mason's eyes glowed brightly as he became engulfed in flames.

"I am Maelstrom, firstborn son of Mephisto, Lord of Destruction, and I now take his place. His kingdom is mine."

CHAPTER TWENTY SEVEN

"That can't be good," said Tommy.

Evan grabbed his hand and pulled him through the crowd and stopped by William.

"There you are." William slipped his arm around Evan.

Mason remained rigid as his body glowed like a giant fire elemental. His horns uncurled from down his cheekbones and instead twisted straight up, growing large as a pair of moose antlers. The flames that engulfed him went from blue to red. His leathery wings knit back together and stretched the length of two school buses. Finally, the runes on Mason's chest brightened and spread with golden light. New runes split his skin up his shoulders and down his arms covering them in vibrant golden symbols attesting to his new position.

"Holy shit," said Tommy.

The chatter of teeth and whines of fear sounded around them. Evan glanced around to see dozens of humanoid demons scatter into the trees and disappear.

Mason threw the remains of Mephisto's heart to the

ground. Danika strode to him and stared into his new form for a long minute before holding out her hand to him. Mason took it and followed Danika, Selene, and Neeman to the huge assemblage.

"Bow," he commanded the group.

The demons grumbled but took a knee.

"I am your Lord. You will do my bidding. Return home and await me there."

The demons looked around and then slowly got to their feet, slipped through the rift, and disappeared. William walked forward but Evan caught him by the arm.

"Where are you going?"

"Mason is my Lord. I must obey his command. I'm sorry."

Panic raced through Evan. "No. Wait!"

"I love you."

Evan tried to hold onto William as he marched closer to the portal. She glanced around frantically.

"Danika!" she screamed. "Danika, stop him!"

Danika looked to where Evan planted her feet and fought to keep William from walking closer to the portal.

"Maelstrom." Danika pointed to William. "Not him."

Mason's gaze fell on William. "Not you."

A wash of relief bathed Evan as she and William toppled backward onto the ground.

"Oh, thank God," said William.

"I wouldn't have let go," said Evan. "No matter what had happened I wouldn't have let you go."

William pushed the hair from her face and kissed her.

"Where is Lord Garon?" Danika called. "Is he dead?"

The Vampires looked at each other and someone from the back called out. "He's here!"

The crowd jostled and rumbled and pushed Lord Garon

forward. He ripped from his traitors' grasps and stood proud at the front of the assemblage.

Danika approached Garon and circled him like he was a slave on an auction block. "This man is a traitor. He consorted with demons and with others to destroy our society. He sold us out in order to save his own skin. For gain, power, and money. In our society such actions are punishable by death."

A murmur of agreement traversed the crowd.

Danika stopped directly in front of Garon. "You killed my family. You tried to kill me. You are poison to our kind. A blight on the history of our world. I thereby sentence you to death."

"You have no authority," said Garon. "Only one of the Kings can sentence me to death."

"And I do." The white-haired older Vampire, leaning on a cane, walked out of the crowd and to Danika's two battered Underlords.

"Sherman," said William. "I didn't know he was here."

"I sentence you to death," said Sherman. "Your name will be blotted out of our society, your lands divided, and your body left for the sun." Sherman nodded. "Let it be so."

"Let it be so," everyone chanted.

Roth stepped forward with two trackers and they grabbed Garon by the arms.

"Lord Danika, he has done you the greatest offense; therefore, you are given his blood," offered Sherman.

Danika stepped forward, her hands shaking. She stared at Garon for several minutes opening and closing her mouth as if to say something. Finally, she spit on Garon and turned to Mason.

"I can't," she said.

Mason pulled her close and whispered in her ear. She clung to him and then sucked in a deep breath and nodded. She didn't move for a moment then in an instant whirled around and slashed Garon's throat with her nails.

The gurgle of blood carried on the wind. Garon clutched his throat. Blood splattered the front of his suit and he dropped to his knees. His eyes never left Danika as he fell to the ground, his blood soaking into the grass and mingling with the blood of all the other dead. Mason picked up Garon and broke the Vampire's neck for everyone to see.

Then Roth and the trackers carried the body to the middle of the park, stripped it, and dropped it to the ground.

Selene stepped forward to the Fae. "Those of you who would like to go back may depart now."

"You must come with us," someone said.

"I'll stay behind and close the rift."

"But the bloodline must continue. Your magic is ancient, and it must be carried on," called another.

"And it still may, but not with the Fae. They wanted to be safe. To live out their lives apart from this world and safe from the Demon realm. I am giving them what they want. Those of you who still want that, may depart in peace. Those who wish to stay, are welcome here with the rest of us." Selene looked to Danika and Mason.

"Those who wish to stay may do so, but you will never be able to return to your plane, and you will be subject to the same laws as everyone else," said Mason.

Dozens upon dozens of Fae walked to stand with Selene. The remainder made their way to the rift and disappeared into the void.

Selene went to the rift and stared at it long and hard.

"Having a change of heart?" asked Neeman.

"Not on your life, lover." She pressed her magic on the sides of the rift and chanted as it grew smaller and smaller and finally disappeared. Mason walked to the Demon portal and Selene joined him.

"There are others who fled into the woods," said Selene.

"Do you think we shouldn't close it?" asked Mason.

"It needs to be closed for this world to heal."

"Then let us close it. We can track down the dissenters another day."

Selene nodded and together, hand in hand, they used their combined magic to close and seal the rift to the Demon world. An oppressive silence fell over the entire park as both rifts drifted away.

Sore, tired, and emotionally spent the remaining survivors leaned on each other for support. They hugged friends and comrades. Cried together over their fallen and lamented those who were injured.

"Are you all right?" asked William. "You aren't hurt?"

"I'm good," Evan replied.

"Are you sure? You didn't get anyone's blood in your mouth? Nothing bit you?"

She chuckled. "I'm good. I'm sure."

William looked her over from hair to ankles and then hugged her tight. "I don't know what I would have done if I'd lost you."

"You know, I'm not hurt either, thank you for asking," said Tommy.

Evan and William chuckled and pulled Tommy into a group hug.

"I'm glad you're still with us too... cousin," said William.

Tommy bear hugged William. "Brother."

Evan fought back tears as the two hugged. She never thought she would see the day when Tommy hugged a... a... vampyr Demon hybrid?

"You will return to your respective residences," called Sherman. "We'll meet tomorrow night after I speak with the Council. We will need a new Lord for Las Vegas and two new Kings as well."

"Don't you think it's time we let everyone have a vote in who we appoint?" called a vampyr.

Sherman stood for a moment and then nodded. "I do. I will bring it up to the Council and find out their feelings on the subject. But for now, rest. Rejuvenate. Celebrate the lives of those who sacrificed everything so we could live on. And be grateful you are still here."

The Vampires and vampyr nodded and then dispersed.

"I'll take the Fae to the building where my old apartment is. There are more than enough empty apartments for them to choose from," said Selene. "We should stay with them until everything is decided."

Sherman nodded.

Selene walked to her mother's body. Neeman lifted Yelena and carried her behind Selene out of the park.

Roth gathered up the remainder of the fledgling vampyr and the Tracking Squad.

"We need to clean up the bodies," said Sherman.

"Put them in a pile and I'll deal with them," replied Mason.

Roth ordered the fledglings around and Evan smacked Tommy in the chest. "Let's help."

"No!" Mason's form shrank and his wings folded into his back.

"We'd like for you to get William back to Doc and have him check out William's leg to make sure he's fine," said Danika.

"I feel perfect," replied William.

"Still. I'd like for you to be checked out." Danika gave him a warm smile.

"You should as well." Mason nodded at Evan.

William turned to her. "You said you weren't injured."

"I'm not."

"We want to make sure you're both all right," said Danika. "You should rest. We'll clean up and be home soon."

William shrugged and wrapped his arm around Evan's waist. "I think they're getting rid of us."

Evan nodded to Tommy and the three walked back to the awaiting vans. Questions swirled in her head about what had happened and what the future held for all of them. The fight with the demons had ended but the Fae had stayed, demons roamed free, and more than anything Selene and Mason were more powerful than ever. She didn't have to be smart to see that the Society was in serious jeopardy of collapsing if Sherman wasn't able to humpty dumpty it back together.

CHAPTER TWENTY EIGHT

E van stared at Doc. "Are you sure?"

"My dear, I've been doing this for a long time. I know a pregnant female when I see one. The heartbeat is strong and you seem to be healthy enough. As vampyr babies grow faster than human babies, I'd say you should be due in about six months."

"Six?" She wanted to wait about six months before telling William. She should have remembered things go faster with vampyr babies, but somehow that knowledge had escaped her thoughts in the fog of all that had happened.

"I take it you know who the father is?"

"Oh, I know whose he is." She tried to process the information. A baby. She was having a baby. The knowledge both elated and terrified her. The last time she'd had a baby... This time she was more afraid of raising the child alone than the baby being stolen.

"Would you like me to inform the father?" Doc asked.

Evan shook her head and jumped from the doctor's table. "I'm good, thanks."

"Are you sure?" His expression remained unconvinced.

"Totally."

"Well, I'd like you to take these vitamins." Doc walked to a cabinet in the corner and pulled out a white bottle. "And you need to come see me every two weeks."

Evan nodded; her mind grew numb yet her body ached from the fight.

"And no drinking or too much activity."

Evan burst out with a laugh. "I guess fighting demons is out of the question?"

Doc's brows furrowed. "Absolutely."

She laughed again and covered her mouth with the back of her hand. "Sorry. Can I go now?"

"Yes."

Evan rushed from the room before her emotions made her do something that would embarrass her.

Tommy waited in the hallway and stood from a chair when she came out. "Are you okay?"

"Peachy." She headed for the elevator at the end of the hall.

He ran to catch up with her. "Sis, what's wrong?"

"Nothing."

He laid his hand on her arm. "Was it the fight? I know killing can be overwhelming. It takes a lot out of a person to do what we did. That was some crazy—"

She shook her head. "It's not that." How could she tell him? She wasn't sure what he'd do when he found out. Would he be happy for her, or would he be like any older brother and want to kill William for getting her pregnant without them being wed?

"What are those?" He pointed to her hand.

She looked down at the bottle and then shoved them in her pocket.

"Vitamins. I'm anemic," she lied. She pressed the button on the elevator.

"Should we wait for William?"

She stepped into the elevator and pressed the up button. "If you want, stay. I'm tired and sore. I'm gonna take a shower and then head to bed."

Confusion etched Tommy's features. "Well, I'll walk with you. I could use a shower too." He jumped in before the doors closed.

Evan refused to look at him. More than anything, she wished she could get in a car and just go for a drive.

WILLIAM EXITED DOC'S OFFICE WITH A CLEAN BILL OF HEALTH. AT least as far as Doc knew. He wasn't completely up on Demon physiology.

He scanned the hallway but neither Evan nor Tommy were anywhere to be seen. He stepped back in Doc's office.

"Did Evan and Tommy leave?"

"She left about ten minutes ago. Is she your slave? I didn't realize."

"No. She's not my slave. We don't have slaves anymore, remember?"

Doc nodded. "Oh yes. I forgot."

"Is she okay?"

Doc stared at him for a minute. "She's perfectly healthy."

"Thanks, Doc."

The old Vampire nodded and William walked up to his

room with butterflies in his stomach. He'd been horrible to Evan the last couple of days. He needed to apologize to her. A pit grew in his gut, and he hoped the two girls from earlier hadn't left anything in his room that Evan would see.

He opened his door and glanced around. "Evan?"

The bed had been remade, the broken chair had been removed, and all of his clothes had been cleaned off the floor.

"Evan?" He looked in the bathroom. His heart sank. She wasn't there.

He didn't understand. She knew that he remembered her. She'd said she would go to the Demon realm just to be with him.

He leaned heavily against the doorjamb of the bathroom. Maybe she'd gone to get a shower and some clothes. He should do the same. Then he'd go see her.

CHAPTER TWENTY NINE

William walked to the barracks where all the remaining humans milled around speaking to anyone they could find. Tommy stood in the midst of them like the day's hero, chatting and smiling. The two girls from earlier sat on the couch. They spotted him and smiled. Memories of their hours together made him smile but then he coughed and turned away. *No. Evan.* He wanted Evan.

He headed to the bottom of the stairs, but Tommy caught him by the arm.

"Hey, William. Uh... Evan is super tired and went to bed."

William looked up the stairs. "Oh. Of course. It's been a long couple of days."

"Yeah. I'll be sure to let her know that you stopped by when she wakes."

"Sure. She knows where I am."

Tommy gave him a genuine smile. "It's good to have you back, man."

William nodded. Every ounce of him wanted to rush up to

Evan and make love to her. The happiness and pheromones floating in the air made him twitchy, and after the fight they'd lived through, he needed some good lovemaking to calm him down.

He glanced up the stairs once more and then headed back to the main house. What he needed didn't matter. He needed to keep his Demon nature as under control as possible. Those things could wait until both he and Evan had healed... and talked.

EVAN WOKE UP AND RAN TO THE BATHROOM. SHE BARELY MADE IT before she retched in the toilet. Damn, she hated that part. She leaned over the toilet bowl, breathing in the bleach fumes and waiting for the nausea to pass.

She'd fallen into bed the night before and cried herself to sleep. There was nothing to do and nowhere to go to think things out and figure out what to do.

If she ran, what would she do with a half-vampyr baby? How would she protect it and take care of it on her own? Not that she wanted to run. She didn't. She wanted William. But would he still want her? He wasn't even vampyr anymore. Would he want a vampyr child? Was he even capable of taking responsibility for a child? He'd only just remembered who he was, but he still struggled with his new Demon nature. She'd witnessed it first hand as they had returned to the Coven House. He'd asked her to go to his room. She knew he'd wanted to make love to her. But she just couldn't. Not until they'd really talked about their future. But this... had not been in the plan.

She dropped onto her butt and hung her head.

The bathroom door opened and she sat silently for a moment, hoping the person would go away.

"Evan?"

She held back a groan. She gripped the door lock and then flushed the toilet and opened the door.

"Hey, bro, what's up?"

His brows furrowed. "You feelin' okay?"

"Yup."

"Don't lie to me."

"I'm fine." She crossed to the sink to wash her hands.

"Were you drinking again?"

"What? No."

"Then what?"

She turned off the water and wiped her hands on a towel. "Don't worry about me."

Silence fell between them for a moment.

"It's good to see William back to normal," he said.

She pushed her hair behind her ear. "Is he?"

"He came to see you last night. I told him you needed to rest. I don't think he was very happy."

She nodded. "Maybe I'll go see him in a bit." She burped and covered her mouth.

Tommy eyed her.

"I'm gonna go lie down some more. I'm still exhausted."

"Okay."

She waved at him and headed back to her room. She shut the door and fell into bed. She couldn't deal with William today. Or Tommy. Or anyone for that matter. Maybe tomorrow.

WHEN WILLIAM AWOKE THAT EVENING EVERY FIBER OF HIM WANTED to go see Evan. Instead he put on a dress shirt and slacks and went to the atrium where he'd been summoned.

Hundreds of people waited for a meeting to start. The energy in the air crackled with anxious anticipation.

He passed cluster after cluster of Vampires and vampyr. Some bowed, some greeted him warmly, most women looked at him as if he were a buffet for the tasting, and though his fantasies involving each of them reached him deep inside, all he could think about was Evan.

He finally spotted Danika, Mason, Selene, and Neeman and headed toward where they stood with Sinya and Sherman.

"William." Mason clapped him on the shoulder. "Thank you for helping me yesterday."

"Thank you for not letting me splat to the Earth."

The group chuckled.

Danika glanced around the room. "Is Evan not with you?"

William's gut clenched and he cleared his throat. "Uh... no. She's sleeping, I think."

Danika and Mason exchanged a look that made the hairs stand up on William's arms.

"You think?" she prodded.

"I haven't seen her since we got back last night. She went to see Doc with me and then went to her room."

Danika's lips pulled into a grim line. "I see."

Did she? The statement frustrated William because he *couldn't* see. He had no idea why Evan had taken off and hadn't come to see him. He'd thought things were going to get better with them. He thought they would talk about what had happened and their future and that they would move past everything that had happened. But maybe she'd changed her mind. Maybe she'd decided that being with a vampyr would have been tolerable, but being with a demi-Demon wasn't something she could handle. All the worries that had plagued him over the last twenty-four hours bubbled to the surface consuming his mind.

"Shall we begin?" asked Sherman.

Danika nodded and stepped onto the small platform holding the three massive Russian chairs that she had told him had been in her family for generations. She stared at them for a moment and then knocked on her flute of blood with a spoon to garner everyone's attention.

"Brothers and sisters of the Society. I and my mate, Mason, welcome you into our home. We thank you all for coming and standing with us in our biggest time of need. As you know, our society has suffered many losses and much shock in the past year. Only our beloved King Sherman is left. I will turn the time over to him to address us. King Sherman."

Sherman stepped on the platform beside Danika as she moved aside to give him space.

"My fellow Vampires and vampyr. I spent the entire night on the phone with the Kings of the other countries as well as the Council trying to come to a decision about what we should do here in America. We have lost two Kings and the Lord of Las Vegas. On top of that we have come to the knowledge that the humans are trying to find a vaccine to cure the vamps."

Whispers and gasps traveled the entire length of the hall.

"It is our desire to fill the positions of the Kings first. Some of you may know Lord Jason Bontel of France. We believe he will bring some much-needed new blood to America. He will take Vinton's place on the West Coast and oversee the reign of the areas there. We also feel that some new blood is needed here in the East. For too long the throne has been occupied by stuffy, old, self-serving Vampires who look to the past instead of the future. A new course and vision is needed to lead our people into a new age. Therefore, we have appointed Danika Chekov the new Queen of the Eastern states."

Danika's mouth fell open and her head whipped to Mason. His brow furrowed but William couldn't help but smile. He clapped and soon the claps and cheers of everyone in the room followed his.

Danika blinked several times and gave a tight smile, the tension and honor of the situation obviously overwhelming her.

Sherman raised his hand and the cheering died down.

"As Queen Danika will be too busy to run this coven, we will need to find a new Coven Lord. There are several names that we are still sorting through but for now Sinya will run the coven. Las Vegas and its Lordship is to be given to Roth Palamese."

Roth stepped forward, stoic as ever, and nodded to Sherman.

"Along with these new positions, it is proposed that we form a worldwide committee. One that will be made up in equal parts of all races that still live here. Vampire, vampyr, vamp, human, and Fae. This committee will counsel together for the betterment of every single person. The idea of slavery is to be abolished here and now in the entirety of the United States. There will be no more slave markets. No more raids. No more capturing of humans. Slaves will be freed and paid."

Again clapping sounded around the room, though not quite as enthusiastically. William figured the freeing of slaves in the

US was bound to take some getting used to. But he loved the change. He only wished that Evan was there to hear it for herself.

"This new Committee of Equality will be made up of representatives elected by the people," Sherman continued. "The only way for us to survive in this new world and make it better for our children and their children, is for us to look to the future. The future means evolving. If we do not evolve, we will all perish."

Danika stepped forward and raised her glass. "Let it be so."

The crowd raised their glasses. "Let it be so."

CHAPTER THIRTY

William stood at his bedroom window staring at
the barracks. It'd been an additional two days, and
he still had yet to seen Evan. She hadn't come to
him as he'd hoped, and every time he'd gone to see her,
Tommy had guarded her door.

The anxiety in William's stomach had morphed into full-
blown panic. He knew he'd been a jerk and it was very well
possible she'd learned about the small indiscretion that still
guilted him like a Jewish mother. If he could only get close
enough to her, he could explain.

The pent-up energy and mounting need inside him had
him ready to explode on everyone. He'd tried to distract himself
with drinking and with helping everyone in the house, but the
more people fawned over him, the worse it became. He'd
locked himself in his room the night before, afraid that if he
didn't he'd drag one of the fawning females into the nearest
room and screw her till he dropped. Possibly several females.

But that wasn't what he wanted. For as much as his new

nature craved acceptance and pleasure, more than that it wanted to love and be loved.

He only wanted that from one woman.

Sue and Tommy walked out of the barracks laughing. Their smiling faces mocked William in his misery. Tommy said something and Sue smacked his shoulder. Another girl followed them out of the barracks and tagged Tommy before taking off around the side of the house toward the front of the property. Tommy and Sue took off after her.

William's heart leapt. Without wasting a moment, he raced into the hall and jumped to the bottom floor, startling several coven members. He rushed through the kitchen and out the back in only a few steps. He ran to the barracks and up the stairs so fast no one had time to stop him. Skidding to a halt outside Evan's room, he took a deep breath and let his hand rest on the knob. Nervousness skittered up his spine as he raised his hand to knock. What if she told him she didn't love him anymore? What if she didn't care? He didn't know if he could take the heartbreak.

He sucked in a deep breath. It didn't matter. The not knowing slowly sucked the life force from his body like a leech. He knocked on the door and then pushed it open. The curtains remained drawn despite it being dark out, and no light illuminated the room.

"Evan?"

Evan's eyes opened and she took a silent breath.

"Evan, are you awake?"

The soft sound of William's voice both soothed and grated on her at the same time.

It had been three days and she still needed more time. Three days of silence. Three days of sleeping and thinking and sleeping some more. And now she lay in her bed feeling more tired than she had when she'd started.

"Evan?"

"I'm awake." She rolled over and faced him. He deserved to know the truth. Even if he rejected her.

He closed the door and moved to the edge of her bed. He sat down heavily, making the box springs creak.

"Are you okay?" he asked. "You've been sleeping a lot. Tommy wouldn't let me bother you."

She pushed herself into a sitting position and tried to flatten her hair and wipe her face before turning on the light.

He searched her eyes in the golden glow from the lamp.

"You've been crying." He scooted closer. "What's wrong? What's happened? Did someone hurt you?"

She shook her head. "No one hurt me."

"Tell me. Please, tell me what's wrong. Did I do something? I know I've been a jackass and I'm sorry. I don't mean to be that way, it's just now that I'm... well... the new me, I guess my dick does a lot of the thinking and I don't—"

"Be quiet." She put her fingers to his lips. "It's not you."

He stared at her and then nodded. "It's okay. You don't have to give me the 'It's not you it's me' spiel. I get it. I've put you through too much. Between the following you across the country to the blood drinking, and me killing that guy to me forgetting you and—"

The words crawled up her throat and burst from her lips.

"I'm pregnant." The weight lifted off her shoulders for

finally having gotten it out, but her gut twisted as she waited for him to say something.

William's mouth hung open. He blinked several times. "Oh," he said quietly.

He looked away and scanned the room.

She held her breath, waiting for him to speak. "That's all you have to say?"

He looked back at her, sadness etched into his features. "I suppose it was someone back at the enclave? A guy you met while you were there? The one in the hallway that let us go that night? It's okay. I understand."

"Wait, what?" She shook her head. "What guy? There was no guy at the enclave, you jackass. The only guy I've been with in the last two years is you."

"Me?" William's eyebrows raised. She watched as his brain finally caught up with her words. "Me? I'm the father? I'm gonna be a father!"

A smile spread across his face, and he grabbed Evan and pulled her into a hug. Then he released her and cupped her face.

He kissed her forehead. "Evan." He kissed her eyelids. "Evan." He kissed her cheeks. "Evan." He kissed her mouth. "Evangeline."

Emotions that had been bottled up inside boiled over and tears spilled from her eyes. William kissed them away tenderly, telling her he loved her with each worshiping stroke.

Finally, she brought her lips to his and kissed him forcefully. He growled deep in his chest and her body tingled all over. She grabbed at his shirt and fumbled with the buttons trying to get it off him. She needed him. Need him all to herself.

He ripped the shirt from his body and threw it to the floor.

She stripped her tank top off and her bra as well. His hard, muscular body covered hers on the bed as he kissed down the side of her throat, his enlarged fangs grazing her skin. He weighed more than he had before and his body covered hers more fully, but it was the heat of his skin she found most enjoyable.

She wrapped her arms around his back, taking stock of his newly broadened frame. His muscled bunched and flexed beneath her touch. He kissed down over her breasts to her stomach. He kissed her reverently and laid his ear on her belly.

"I can hear his heartbeat," he said. "He's strong, like you."

"Oh, you know it's a boy, do you?"

William nodded and then kissed her belly once more before moving back to her mouth. "I love you, Evangeline. I want to marry you, mate you, and make you mine and be yours forever."

She pulled him close and kissed him. She ran her fingers down the flat planes of his packed abs to the sensually cut V that started at his hip and dipped below his waistband. She undid the button of his slacks and went to push them off and found he wore no underwear.

She cocked an eyebrow.

He shrugged. "Makes things easier."

She slid his pants down to his thighs and grabbed his tight rear. "Do you now?" She moved her hand so she could cup him.

His head dipped, and he bit at her neck as she stroked him. Every inch of him was bigger, stronger, more muscular.

"Evangeline," he moaned her name against her throat.

"Say it. Tell me."

His newly crimson eyes looked straight at her. "I'm yours. Now and forever."

She claimed his mouth with hers, and he stripped her of her sweats. She guided his larger size against her, and he pressed inside her slowly, digging his nails into her hipbone. When he was all the way in, his forehead leaned against hers and he panted hard, his muscles trembling with strain.

"I can't hold back," he told her. "Not this time."

She took his face in her hands. "Take me. I'm yours."

William's mouth clamped down on hers, and he thrust inside her roughly.

She moaned.

He rocked his hips, the friction between them making him murmur her name. Evan grabbed his rear and held on. He gripped the back of her neck, and their bodies slapped together in a musical rhythm, her bed slamming into the concrete wall. Within a minute, he called out her name and she looked on as his face turned from a mask of agony to utter bliss within those few passing moments of exquisite torture.

She smiled as he fell on top of her, totally spent. He brushed the hair from her face and ran his fingers down her body.

He wrapped his arm around her and rolled on his side. Caressing her body, he kissed her throat, her breasts, and her shoulders. Every touch a silent promise to worship her forever.

Finally, he looked into her eyes and she kissed him again.

"I love you, William."

A broad smile crossed his face. "I love you too, Evangeline. My mate. My wife."

EPILOGUE

William stepped carefully down the stairs to the front foyer, one hand one Evan's lower back, the other on the railing.

"You do know I've walked down these stairs a million times, right?" she asked.

"Yes, but you've never been this large before," he replied.

She stopped and gave him an icy glare.

"Large and beautiful. Radiant. Bursting with maternal—"

"Shut it." She rolled her eyes and continued downward.

The front door opened and Danika and Mason walked in followed by Selene and Neeman.

"Good evening." Danika strode across the foyer to them and hugged William and then Evan. "Wow, you're ready to burst."

"I wish," Evan replied.

"You have about two more weeks, Doc said," said William. "The baby needs all the time in there he can get."

Evan shook her head. "He's become the biggest nag about everything."

"I don't think that's possible." Sinya walked down the stairs holding her baby girl. "You should have seen Lance when I was pregnant."

"I only want what's best." William kissed her head. He turned to Danika. "Did you speak with Nicholas?"

Danika's gaze flicked to Mason's and he wrapped his arm around her protectively.

"I spoke to my father. He's well."

"Do you think he'll come visit soon?" asked Evan.

Danika shook her head. "I think it will be a while before that happens. I have a lot of feelings to sort out first."

"I know how that is," said Evan.

"This came for you." Neeman walked up to William, handed him a folded piece of paper, and nodded. William fought the urge to tear into the paper and reveal the information he'd spent months tracking down. But he needed to do that somewhere more private. Neeman rubbed at a new bruised on his cheek.

"Rounding up demons again?" William asked.

Neeman nodded. "They're laying pretty low. But we'll find them all."

Evan squeezed his hand and looked at the paper. "What's that?"

William shoved the paper into his pocket. "Later. How did the committee meeting go?" he asked Selene.

"Better. We've been able to convince Evan's uncle and several of the other enclave leaders to meet with us finally. In the place of their choosing of course."

"That's great news," said Evan. "You need Lou on board if we're going to succeed."

William smiled to hear Evan say 'we'. A word he never

thought she would use to encompass not only her, but him and the Coven as well.

"Would you consider being there?"

Evan looked between them. "Me?"

"You know him better than anyone."

The thought made an involuntary rumble escape William's chest. Evan wrapped her arm around his waist and laid her head on his chest.

"I don't want her anywhere near that man." He tried to keep his voice as even as possible, but even he could tell it was a losing battle.

"Ask Tommy," Evan said. "He's better at diplomacy than I am. Besides, I think it would be good for him to see Lou. I know he's missed his Pop a lot."

William relaxed a fraction. "We should go. We have an appointment with Doc and then you need to walk around the property for twenty minutes—"

"And then I need to pee and eat."

The group laughed and William's cheeks heated.

"I stand corrected," said Sinya. "I think William wins. Even Lance didn't have me down to a minute by minute schedule."

William grumbled and Evan reached up on tiptoes and kissed his cheek. He pulled her away from the group and headed toward the basement elevator.

Three human females walked by them, ogling William. He swallowed hard as his arousal peaked, but he kept his eyes straight ahead.

Evan chuckled.

"What?" he asked innocently.

"You're getting better at that."

He pushed the button and feigned ignorance. "At what?"

She pulled him to her and cupped his erection. "Pretending that the attention from others doesn't get you hot."

He closed his eyes as she rubbed him through his pants.

"As long as you stay mine, I don't care how your body responds."

The doors opened and she pulled him inside the elevator.

"You know," he said. "I think maybe we can skip the walk today."

"Really?" A devilish smile came over her face as she rubbed against him again.

His throat dried and he had to clear it before being able to talk. "Yeah. I'm thinking maybe you should rest." He reached between her thighs and rubbed at her as well. "Maybe a massage would be better for you. A nice, relaxing massage." He pressed against her, his lips meeting hers.

The baby squirmed and kicked William in the stomach.

Evan laughed. "I think both junior and I would enjoy a massage." She kissed him again.

William pushed the stop button on the elevator as it bumped to the basement floor.

"What's up?" she asked.

"I wanted to show you this." He licked his lips, unsure of how she would react. He handed her the paper Neeman had given him.

"Ooohhh mysterious. What is it?" She opened the paper and stared at it, her eyes scanning the lines. Her head whipped up and her gaze met his.

"How long have you been looking into this?"

"About four months. It took a while for me to track them down but I found them in Turkey. They'll be returning right away. Danika will see to that."

She shook her head. "William, I don't want that. She won't even know me."

He laid his hand on her belly. "Our son will have a half-sister. They deserve to know each other. And you deserve to know your daughter."

"I..." Anxiety filled her face.

"You don't have to decide now. Just think about it." He stroked her cheek. "Either way they are coming back to the States and they aren't leaving again."

She smiled and kissed him. "Thank you." She caressed his cheek and he turned his face and kissed her palm, his gaze landing on the large diamond ring on her hand.

"You should know by now, my love, I'll do anything to keep my wife happy."

A smile crept across her face. "Then let's hurry with this appointment so I can show you just how happy I am."

THE END

RED THE WERE HUNTER

FAIRELLE BOOK ONE

By Rebekah R. Ganiere

CHAPTER ONE
VOLKZENE, FAIRELLE - 1200 YEARS A.D.
(AFTER DAEMONS)

Another girl had been taken. One moment the small village of Volkzene was silent, with Redlynn drifting off to sleep to the rhythmical sounds of her clock ticking; the next a scream pierced the night.

Redlynn leaped from her bed, grabbed her sword, and tore out to the street. People in their nightclothes, brandishing torches and lanterns, filled the village center.

"Where are they?" she called at the nearest neighbor.

"Cantrel's." The woman ran for the safety of her home.

Anya! Redlynn sprinted toward the south edge of the village. Her best friend was on guard alone at the Cantrel's hut. Breathing hard, the cold night wind whipped her wavy, red hair into her face and raised goose bumps on her skin. The sound of her blood pumping in her ears drowned out the buzz of the village folk.

"Anya," she screamed. "Anya, where are you?"

Redlynn charged through the crowd gathered outside.

"Move," she yelled. Other members of the Sisterhood and villagers backed away at the sight of her.

The smell of blood hit her. She stepped over the threshold, the horror slapping her with force. Her heart faltered, and a cry escaped her lips.

"No!" she screamed. "Anya!"

Anya's mangled body lay sprawled on the floor, her bow still clutched in her pale fingers. Redlynn's mind numbed, unable to process the scene. She spun on the spot. An arrow stuck in the wall next to the door. Bits of wood were strewn about from the smashed kitchen table. Coals tumbled from the fire, and little more than charred cinders remained of the curtains. A pail of water lay discarded nearby. The Cantrels huddled on their bed in the adjoining room, Mrs. Cantrel sobbed into her husband's chest.

"Sasha, my Sasha," Mrs. Cantrel moaned.

Anger and despair ripped through Redlynn's gut. Her sword hit the floor with a clatter and she collapsed to her knees, gathering her best friend's bloody body in her arms. She sucked in large gasps of air, tears streaming down her cheeks. *The very last of my loved ones.*

Anya stared blankly into the night, her eyes transfixed and cloudy. Redlynn stroked her hair and tried in vain to piece the skin together on Anya's neck and torso. At just nineteen, Anya had been through so much in her short life. Too much, and now it was over. Sadness gave way to anger, and bile scorched her throat.

"This is your fault," Mrs. Cantrel screeched, pointing at Redlynn. "Where were you? You were supposed to stand guard with Anya."

Redlynn swallowed the angry words threatening to unleash. "I'll find Sasha," she vowed.

"Find her? Those beasts have probably already torn her to bits. You're the protector, and where were you? Asleep. To let my Sasha be taken, and poor Anya to be murdered. If you can't even do the one thing we've kept you around for, what good are you?"

The words struck Redlynn like a blow to her gut. Her throat dried as she searched for something to say. Something to soothe the mother, to soothe herself. "I'll find her."

"Get out of my house, Cursed!" Mrs. Cantrel screamed.

Redlynn's heart thundered. She wanted to yell at the woman that she was all too aware how the sting of loss felt like a million white hot stabs with a fireplace poker. To scream that at least the woman still had a husband and other children. That Anya was all Redlynn had left. That if the Sisterhood would do its job and go back to hunting werewolves instead of letting them live and breath and breed, that this would never have happened.

But she didn't. Instead, she laid Anya down, grabbed her sword, and pushed out the door, past the crowd of Sisters and villagers. Running flat out, she made for the village gate.

"Red!"

The sound of her name stopped her. Breathing hard, her body surged with adrenaline and her head pounded with the need for vengeance. Her heart ached from the pain of Mrs. Cantrel's words. As much as she pretended that the harsh words and name calling didn't bother her, it was a constant reminder that she did not fit in in Volkzene.

"I hope you aren't thinking of doing anything foolish." Lillith stepped calmly from the shadows, her red stone necklace glowing faintly in the dim light.

Redlynn locked eyes on the head of her Order and ground her teeth.

"You know it's forbidden to go into the woods."

"We need to go out there. Strike them now. Take the fight to them and end this." Redlynn continued toward the gate. "We need to become the hunters we used to be. Not the village guard we are now."

Members of the Sisterhood gathered around.

"Do not defy me on this, Red." Lillith crossed her arms over her chest. "It won't end well for you if you do."

Redlynn closed her eyes and sucked in the chilled night air, trying to get her mind to focus. Anya was dead. Another girl was gone, and they just stood around arguing, like always. It had been the same thing over and over since Lillith had taken over.

Sasha made the second girl this month; twelve altogether. There had been five new girls inducted as full-fledged members of the Sisterhood this year. All of them carried off by Weres. It made no sense. The Weres hadn't attacked the village since before her time. What changed?

A frigid wind hit her skin. Frost from the ground seeped through her stockings, making her shiver in her nightgown. The rage inside dimmed, giving way for a need to understand what had happened.

"Tell me," she demanded, wiping tears from her cheeks. "What happened this time?"

Lillith's voice carried into the night for all to hear. "The Weres came in a pack of three. Snuck in and stole Sasha out of her bed, like all the others."

Redlynn let out a shuddered breath. Anya, a good fighter, would've been no match for three. No one was, but perhaps Redlynn herself. *I shouldn't have left her alone.*

"Who was on watch?" she asked.

The Sisters looked at each other.

"Who saw them come through the gate?" Her eyes raked over the group of women.

"I did." Lillith's back straightened.

"Why was the alarm not sounded?" she yelled, taking a step closer. "How could you let this happen?"

Lillith's gaze flicked to the crowd, then snapped to Redlynn. "Don't take that tone of voice with me, Red. I am the Head of the Order, not you."

"And how many have we lost since you assumed that position?"

Lillith's eyes narrowed. "It isn't I who was made protector of the village. I leave village security issues to you."

Redlynn gripped her sword so tightly that the metal bit into her fingers.

"We need to take care of Anya," one of the Sisters said. "Before the moon passes."

Redlynn took a deep, cleansing breath. She had to keep it together. "I'll do it."

Lillith stepped in Redlynn's path, blocking her. "You don't need to–"

"I will do it." She glared at Lillith before stepping around her.

Lillith glanced away, as everyone did from Redlynn's cursed golden eyes. In times like this she appreciated her strangeness.

"We'll move her to the Hall and prepare, while you clean up."

It was not a request.

The rest of the Sisterhood watched the exchange. Redlynn ground her teeth together so hard her jaw ached. For years they'd all been waiting for the day when she'd challenge Lillith for control as Head of the Order. Their thoughts and silent glances snapped in the air like lightning swirling around her, wondering if today would be the day.

Swallowing her anger and pride, she turned from them and headed home.

She dragged her sword, heavy as an ox's yoke, through the mud to the other end of the village. Her feet were past being numb in the bitter November cold. Fiery pins and needles pricked at her soles with every sloppy step she took.

I deserved this pain. It should have been me. If it had been, Sasha would still be here, Anya would be alive, and we'd have three less Weres in the woods to worry about. The pain in her body and the pain in her soul were the price she paid for allowing Anya to stand guard alone tonight. *I should have stayed with her.*

The wary glances from the villagers made loneliness swell within her. Out of reflex, she grasped the small oval locket hanging loosely beneath her nightgown, and thought of her mother.

She let her feet carry her down the street, past the deserted training ground. Wind whistled through the archery targets and sparring dummies. Clammy air from the small fountain in front of the village hall made Redlynn's gown cling to her legs. She glanced sideways at the village council, who gathered in the doorway of the building that served as school, church and meetinghouse. They said nothing, watching her go.

Why did she stay? She asked herself for the millionth time. Why couldn't she just find a new place? A better place? She knew the answer all too well. She'd promised her mother. Redlynn hiccuped a sob and turned from the council, unwilling to let them witness her shame.

Reaching her wood-and-thatched home, the sounds of the village chatter died away. She walked in the still-open door.

"Dammit!" The fire had gone out. She hurled her sword

across the front room, leaving it stuck into the wall of her bedroom, slamming the door behind her.

Snatching up the fire poker, she stabbed at the crumbling log; sparks swirled up into the flue. Redlynn ignored her quivering chin and concentrated all her efforts into teasing the fire alight. Tears threatened to spill, but she refused to free them. She wouldn't show more weakness. She would swallow it down until the right time, and then she'd get revenge.

The fire caught. Redlynn threw down the poker and grabbed her red cloak from the hook, wrapping it over her shoulders. With trembling fingers, she stripped off her muddy stockings, tossing them into the water basin to soak. Anya's blood-caked Redlynn's hands and gown.

Redlynn tied her long, red hair up in a leather strap, pushed the sticky nightgown down her body to the floor, and plunged her hands into the water bucket. She scrubbed her flesh from under her cloak, with her bloodied gown. She couldn't scrub hard enough; the metallic scent of iron filled her senses.

Biting her cheek, she tried to stop nausea from taking over. Blood never affected her in battle; when every piece of her was fighting for her life, nothing else mattered. But given more mundane circumstances, the scent and the texture of it, the fact that it was Anya's, caused her to almost faint. She grabbed the table where the washbasin sat, trying to steady herself. When the darkness receded from her vision, she threw the gown into the basin.

Shivering, she hurried to her bedroom. She dropped her cloak and pulled on a clean tunic. Looking down, she spotted another of her flaws. A purple birthmark, shaped like a wolf, above her left breast. Tonight the heavy burdens of her life seemed to be piling on top of her.

Redlynn shoved her legs into her breeches and spotted her

mother's bow leaning against the wall.

How many Weres had her mother and grandmother taken down with that bow? Her lineage went all the way back to the first Sister herself. Were hunting was in her blood. Not this pitiful existence she now lived. Her Sisterhood sword, with the wolf's head handle and ruby eyes, hung still lodged in the wall. She stared at the sword. The sword that had belonged to the first Sister. The sword that had slain hundreds of wolves. The sword that she would wield once more. Heat rushed into her chest. She knew what she must do.

She had to kill the beast responsible for ordering the kidnapping of the girls, and the death of Anya. She needed to drench her sword in the blood of the Were King. To feel the sweet satisfaction of vengeance as she ran him through.

REDLYNN GRABBED THE BOW, QUIVER, CLOAK AND HER BAG. FILLING the bag to the brim with herbs, clothes, food and everything else she might need for her trek, she looked around the home that she and her mother had built with their bare hands. All the pieces of her mother's life hung around her. She clutched her locket again as her heart squeezed, remembering the past.

The buckskin satchel her mother had used for her midwife visits. Her mother's teacup set, adorned with giant yellow sungold flowers, passed down for generations. The wicker rocking chair that her mother had sat in to sing, knit, and tell stories.

Come on. Be optimistic. You might not die. Redlynn snorted and reminded herself that she wasn't the optimistic type.

When the Head of the Order had first founded the village decades ago, there'd been over sixty members of the Sisterhood. The Sisters used to hunt the Weres nightly. Now only a handful of active-duty Sisters spent their time as the village guard, trying to fend off the attacks. It had to end. She wouldn't waste away in this hellhole any longer. Redlynn strode to the wall in her bedroom, yanked down her sword, and set it with her pack.

She'd had enough. Her promise to her mother that she'd protect the village wasn't being fulfilled by sitting on her rear, waiting for the Weres to attack. She was sick of girls being taken, never to be heard from again. But Redlynn knew better than to try and fool herself. She wasn't doing this for the villagers; she was doing this for Anya, for her mother. For herself.

Just a few more hours and she'd shed the last of her tears while she cleansed Anya, lock away her sadness deep inside, and allow the anger to take over. Tomorrow she'd become like the Sisters of old. No longer would she wait around for the Weres to attack. She'd raid their caves and drive them out. She'd become Red, The Werewolf Hunter.

"Hey Red," said Yanti, in her cheerful twelve-year-old voice. "I came to see if you were all right."

Redlynn pushed past her, closed the front door, and stepped down onto the frosty dirt road. "Yanti, I don't have time today. I'm sorry."

"Oh."

The sound of Yanti's defeated voice made Redlynn stop in her tracks.

"I brought you this." Yanti held out a small basket. "I figured you wouldn't have time for breakfast."

Way to go, Redlynn. Make the kiddies cry. Redlynn laid her hand on Yanti's shoulder. Yanti continued to look at the basket.

She used her fist to lift the girl's chin and gave Yanti a small smile. "Thank you. If you leave it on my table, I'll eat it when I'm done."

"Sure." Yanti pushed her hair behind her ear.

"Then you run off to school and training. I don't want you wandering about today. Today is a weeping day."

"I'll head straight there, Red, I promise." Yanti smiled again. "I want to be the Head of the Order someday and wear the red stone necklace, like Lillith's." Yanti scrunched up her face. "Red, why aren't you the Head of the Sisterhood, like your grandmother?"

Redlynn's eye twitched. "There's more to being the Head of the Sisterhood than just wearing pretty things and living in a nice home, you know."

"I know, but the necklace is so shiny. And she has a matching mirror, have you seen it?"

A chill raced up Redlynn's spine. "Where did you see it?"

"She was sick a few months back, and my mother had me take her some broth. It was sitting on her nightstand. It must be pretty important to her because when I tried to touch it, she yelled at me and told me to get out. Said it was a present from a special admirer, and no one could touch it but her."

Redlynn swallowed hard. She'd never known Lillith to have any suitors. Ever. "Off to school."

Yanti smiled and headed into Redlynn's house, then ran back out. "Bye, Red!" she called. "I'm gonna be just like you someday!"

Redlynn shivered. Yanti deserved to be a mother, married to a wealthy farmer, passing on her golden curls and green eyes to a brood of chubby children, far from the death and despair of Volkzene. And if Yanti and Redlynn were lucky, she'd be able to do just that. All she needed was for Redlynn to succeed in killing the Were King. Redlynn's chest tightened as Mrs. Cantrel's words from the night before hit her again.

And then, maybe if she succeeded, the villagers would stop using her for protection only, and finally accept her as one of their own, despite her strange eyes.

REDLYNN TREAD WEARILY TO THE TOWN HALL. THE WIND STILL whistled through the main muddy road of the village. She pulled her cloak close and passed the Borwen's pigpen. Quiet stillness emanated through the village at the early hour. A Sister exited her house, stopped short when she saw Redlynn, gave a weak smile, and then hurried toward the village hall. Redlynn sniffed but said nothing. She was used to it. The village wanted her there, only because of who her ancestors were, and her expertise with a bow and sword.

A thatcher loaded up his wagon, not sparing her a moment's glance. A group of young farmers stomped silently through the muddy streets toward their plots of land, south of the village wall.

At the village center, Redlynn pushed open the large doors to the Sisterhood headquarters. The scent of candle wax and incense wafted out. Anya's body lay on the altar, atop a white linen sheet. Tall beeswax candles lined the walls, and robed sisters crushed Volkzene flowers into a paste. She approached Anya without a word, her stomach roiling with acid. Everyone stopped moving. She unfastened her cloak and set it on a wooden bench.

Redlynn's mind flooded with the memory of Anya's last words, and she swallowed hard.

"I can do this alone, Red. Trust me."

Lillith moved forward in her cream ceremonial garb, the

Sisterhood Bible in her hands. Three more Sisters joined her and began the Song of Lament to accompany Lillith's sacred prayer. Redlynn let the words drift away, concentrating only on the task at hand. Picking up the bone needle and white thread, she began at Anya's throat. She blinked rapidly, trying to abate her tears. She couldn't mess this up. Anya deserved the best.

With each piercing of the skin, Redlynn begged for Anya's forgiveness. For each tug of the thread, she swore to avenge her friend's death. She memorized every detail of Anya's wounds. Every bite, every tear. Counting them, until they all blended together in the blur of her tears.

When she finished, Redlynn took the wolfsbane paste and pressed the crushed flowers into Anya's wounds, remembering each laugh, each smile, each moment of friendship they'd shared. The way Anya used to shake her hair out of her face. The determination in her eyes as she aimed her bow. The nights of holding Redlynn as she'd sobbed over the death of her mother.

The drone of Lillith's voice stopped after what seemed like an eternity. Redlynn reached down, kissed Anya one last time.

"Sleep well, my sister. May you find peace on your new journey. My sword will bring thee vengeance, and my heart hold thee always."

Redlynn didn't even see the cloth that she wrapped Anya in through her stream of tears.

Redlynn couldn't cope with the burning of her best friend's body. To smell the flesh and hair as it charred. So instead, with eyes drained of water, like the Daemon Wastelands, she went home and collected her things. Her heart heavy, she looked at her mother's portrait. Redlynn wondered once more why she resembled neither of her dark haired parents. Or anyone else in Volkzene for that matter.

. . .

KEEPING TO THE SHADOWS OF HER NEIGHBORING HOUSES, SHE REACHED
the dirt road and crossed through the wooden perimeter fenc-
ing. No one stood guard, again. So few Sisters remained in the
village. Redlynn remembered a time when the Sisters lived to
be eighty or longer. Now few of the Sisters lived beyond fifty if
they survived childbirth. For a moment she wondered if she
was doing the right thing. If she succeeded, they'd be safe
indefinitely. If she didn't...

She turned, heading across the green toward the woods.
Drawing near the tree line, she heard someone rushing up
behind her.

"Red!"

She'd kept moving, ignoring Lillith's call.

"Redlynn! As Head of the Order, I command you to stop!"

Redlynn halted and turned. Lillith's ample chest heaved up
and down.

"Where do you think you are going?" Lillith tried to catch
her breath.

"Where does it look like?"

"I have forbidden anyone from entering the forest. My rules
are law here."

Redlynn wasn't known for living by Lillith's many rules.
Unlike the other villagers, Redlynn wasn't afraid of Lillith. With
Anya gone now, she had nothing to lose.

"We need you here for protection," Lillith continued.

"You can do it."

"Me? I'm the Head of the Order; who'd lead us if I die?"

Redlynn's head snapped up, and she met Lillith's stare. The
other woman glanced away. Her mother should've been the
Head of the Sisterhood, like her ancestors before her. But due to

Lillith's scheming, her mother had been discredited. Redlynn didn't know all the details. The denouncement had been held in a secret Sisterhood meeting before Redlynn had become a member. But she'd seen firsthand how it'd crushed and ultimately killed her mother.

"Then I guess you better start training the men to protect their daughters," Redlynn bit out.

"Surely you jest? It's been the Sisterhood. Always the Sisterhood. For as long as there have been Weres, there have been Sisters. They go hand in hand, they—" Lillith stopped short.

Redlynn studied Lillith's face, and Lillith glanced away again. That nagging feeling that Lillith was keeping something from the Sisterhood rooted around in Redlynn's mind for the millionth time.

Pulling herself to her full height, Lillith tilted her chin up and glared at Redlynn. "If you leave now, you'll be cast out."

Redlynn didn't bother to conceal her smile. There it was. The final ultimatum. She wondered how long Lillith had dreamed of this moment. The threat meant nothing to Redlynn though. If she killed the King of the Weres, she'd be able to finally leave Volkzene and make a new life for herself. And if she didn't...

"I can live with that." Redlynn walked into the forest.

Lillith huffed behind her. "I mean it, Red! If you go, don't come back."

"Maybe you can find out how the Weres got into the village without the alarm going off while I'm gone," she yelled over her shoulder.

TO READ MORE GO TO YOUR
NEAREST RETAILER!

Dear Reader,

Thank you for taking the time to read *Vengeance of the Demons*. I love writing this series. It's been a lot of fun writing a series about a dystopian world told from the Vampires point of view as well as the humans. Stay tuned for more soon!

If you enjoyed the book, please take a moment to leave a review on your favorite retailer. Your reviews make all the difference to an author and the success of books.

Feel free to take a moment and email me and let me know what you liked about the book or who your favorite character was and why. I love hearing from readers. It makes writing so much more fun when I hear from my readers.

VampWereZombie@Gmail.com

To find out more about me and my Upcoming Releases, Please Join my Street Team for Swag and Freebies.

I also love connecting with readers! Stalk me everywhere!
I look forward to hearing from you!
Rebekah R. Ganiere - BOOKS WITH A BITE

The Society Series

Reign of the Vampires

Rise of the Fae

Vengeance of the Demons

The Otherworlder Series

Kidnapped at Christmas

Vigilante at Valentine

Massacre at Mardi Gras

Hoodwinked at Halloween

Nightmare at New Years (Coming 2023)

Speed Dating with the Denizens of the Underworld

Thor

Loki

Fenrir (2023)

Odin (2023)

Dead Awakenings

Kissed by the Reaper

Dracula's Bride

Rekindling Christmas

Christmas Lodge

Newsletter

To claim your Two FREE Books and find out more about
Rebekah R. Ganiere and her other Upcoming Releases
You can Go Here:
www.RebekahGaniere.com/Newsletter

www.ingramcontent.com/pod-product-compliance
Lightning Source LLC
Chambersburg PA
CBHW020511260626
47156CB00006B/1974